Mary

Medawar

First published by Zohara Publishing in 2019

ISBN 978-0-9956333-0-8

Cover Design by Rosie Palmer
Typeset by James Ward
Printed and bound by CPI Group (UK) Ltd,
Croydon, CR0 4YY

Mary Medawar

Mary Medawar is the author of the epic love story
UNDER THE TRICOLOR, first published by Grafton books;
a division of Collins and GABRIELLA, published by Harper Collins.
Her return to writing is marked by THE SPLIT TREE dedicated to
her late husband Nicholas Medawar Q.C. whose inspiration is infinite.

For my husband
Nick
...wonderful Nick

CHAPTER 1

he priest stepped out from the shadows and took the place of the physician in the lighted alcove. The moment of parting had come. Hermione enfolded the Chevalier's cold hand in hers and tried to convey the rush of emotions she felt. 'Why me? Why did you choose me?' she whispered, realizing she would now never have an answer to the mystery.

'Mademoiselle!'

The priest's tone was urgent. With reluctance, Hermione released the unresponsive hand and leaning forward she touched her lips against André Du Chesne's forehead. 'Adieu. I give my sacred word to cherish Du Chesne; to hold dear your motto *Honorem est silentium*. Honour is silence.

As the priest began to anoint with the sacred oil Hermione sank onto her knees and closed her eyes in prayer. The whispered exchanges between the lawyer and the physician gradually petered out. All listened for the final breath, but it had passed. The Chevalier's life had come to an end, and almost before Hermione had time to rise from her prayers, the lawyer was at her side with not a moment of decency to spare.

'I need you to sign,' he urged, leading her to documents set out on a table. 'You remember I explained the Chevalier's donation to the Hôpital Général takes the greater part of his money, but not to make a donation to charity under current law would make the Will invalid. Oh, and you must not leave Paris till all legalities are complete, mademoiselle. Is it your intention to go to Saintonge?'

'Yes,' whispered Hermione, her emotions still caught up in the profound moment of a life extinguished. 'I don't know where Saintonge is,' she faltered, suddenly grasping the reality of what had until now seemed unreal.

'South of Paris,' he answered, dipping a quill into ink and passing it to her. The physician approached with a weary smile. 'Mademoiselle, forgive my haste, but the hour is late. You have my condolences. The Chevalier's suffering is mercifully come to an end. Can I offer you a ride, monsieur?' he said, turning aside to the notary. 'You mentioned you were without your coach.'

'Indeed, monsieur, I would be glad of the kindness. If you would oblige by witnessing our young lady's mark, I will be ready within the instant.'

Hermione made her cross and handed over the quill to the physician. She could not read or write but was content to be guided by these important, learned men. Shortly, after all was done, the priest joined the men in their departure, and a forlorn peace descended on the chamber. Sinking onto a chair, Hermione looked listlessly before her. All was in darkness save for the candles around the bed in the alcove, and now their wicks were flickering back and forth in a cold rush of air. Hermione breathed deeply, glad of someone's neglecting to shut the outer door, for the herbs scattered on the fire throughout the day had done little to mask the vile smells. There came a sound of water being poured in the kitchen. Of course, the manservant was still here. It was a comfort, for the unsteady candle flames made all seem to move. Shadow and light danced back and forth across the dead man's face until it began to seem as if he might stir. Hermione looked away, and to rid her mind of the horrors that had gone before she sprang up and walked over to a table on which had been left a jar of leeches. The hot embers of the fire sizzled and spat as they took her offering, and a sudden spurt of flames set alight the bloated creatures. At the sound of shuffling footsteps entering the room, Hermione turned. She saw Jean's eyes take in the empty jar.

'God's creatures, mademoiselle,' he said, setting down a bowl of water on the table beside the bed. 'My master needed their help, and so might you one day.' Once again, the stubs of the candles flared and sank as if they might blow out. The air from outside and the servant's words filled Hermione with a desperate need to get away.

'Can I?' she offered with reluctance, for the last thing she wanted was to help lay out the body.

'You are kind, but this is not for you. ' The elderly servant took the napkin draped over his arm and laid it down beside the bowl of water. 'This is the last kindness I can do for my master.'

'Then I'll take my leave.' Hermione slipped her wool cloak about her shoulders and, taking up her lantern, followed the manservant away from the gloom of death.

'In case I am out,' the elderly man said, passing over a key from a table in the hallway. His expression was resentful as he touched his candle's flame to the wick in her lantern. 'I was with the Chevalier some sixteen years,' he said gruffly. 'I hope you won't deny me a few keepsakes, Madame Du Chesne.' Hermione flushed with discomfort at the note of sarcasm.

'Take what you need and what you have an affection for. Only leave me his crucifix. Goodnight, Jean.'

'Goodnight.'

With the aid of her light, Hermione made her way down the crumbling stone steps to the courtyard below and out to the street. Gradually, as she hurried through the Marais, her thoughts turned to how to tell Olivier about what had passed. Her nervous laugh at his likely reaction somehow released the tension of the previous hours, and suddenly Hermione found herself overcome by sobs. She stopped beside a street lantern, unable to walk on till her grief was spent. As calm returned, she wiped her eyes, and feeling better was about to set forth when she realized her outburst had brought her to the notice of a band of men stumbling out of an alleyway.

'Don't cry, wench. We'll soon have you laughing!'

'Come here, *chérie*!'

'Get her!'

Hermione lifted up her skirts and ran. Heavy footsteps pounded behind her, but though she was convulsed with fright she quickly knew she had the advantage; they were drunk. And very soon their coarse laughter and footsteps were left behind.

Guillaume had left the large wooden door into the yard unlocked. Though the hour was late, her guardian Olivier might still be watching over his furnace. Would it be best to go down to the laboratory and tell him now? Exhaustion claimed Hermione. She could face nothing other than to curl up in bed, but when she opened the kitchen door, instead of darkness, there was candlelight and Olivier.

'Where have you been?' he demanded, his tone petulant as she removed her cloak. 'You've been out all day today, yesterday and every day, Lucette says!'

'Didn't she prepare your meals?'

'Yes, but I like you to look after me. How can I think if I know you are not here? Where have you been? Where are you going each day? And last week also, it would seem?'

'I was visiting a sick friend,' replied Hermione, deciding to lead into the matter gently.

'Friend! Is that reason enough to neglect your duties here?'

'My friend was the Chevalier André Du Chesne. He departed this life tonight.'

'I'm sorry,' mumbled Olivier, his angular face expressing a mixture of suspicion and discomfort. Hermione took a deep breath.

'I am his adopted daughter. I am heir to his estate in Saintonge.' For the first time in memory, she had stunned Olivier. It was as if she had hit him on the head.

'Adopted?' he gasped, his eyes bulging from their sockets. '*Mon Dieu*, are you jesting with me?'

Hermione shook her head. 'No, it is true. Let me tell you about it. Perhaps a little cognac, for I am frozen?' Without a reply, Olivier walked over to unlock the cupboard where spirits were secured against Guillaume's weakness. Hermione regarded him with affection; he had no idea about ordinary matters, but he was the cleverest man she knew, and he was all she knew of family. There had been Margot the housekeeper whose rosy plump cheeks she could clearly remember and whose name she never mentioned without feeling a rush of warmth. It seemed odd that Olivier had not hired another servant after her death, and thereafter the running of the house had fallen upon herself.

'I must have been only six or seven years old when Margot died,' she mused, as she accepted the glass of cognac from Olivier. He looked puzzled, and Hermione guessed that he was probably trying to remember who Margot was. 'There must have been some terrible meals, with pans boiling over all the time.' she teased as he took his seat, 'though as your brews still fizz over the crucibles, perhaps I've made more progress than you have.' She turned the chipped rim of the glass around so as not to scratch her lip. So many of Olivier's fine things were spoilt, but money was tight.

'Such a lovely glass, Olivier.' She smiled as he settled back and took up his drink.

'Most things came from my father. After I had served my apprenticeship at the silversmith's I was set to be the finest engraver in Paris. Then a tremor started in my hand ... nothing serious but enough to bring an end to fine work. I came back to live here under my father's roof feeling very sorry for myself. Soon after, when Father died, I closed up the house and went on my travels. Fortune smiled on me, for I found myself with fellow travellers on the road of learning.' His mood, Hermione saw, had softened, and she was glad, for she hated to be on bad terms with him. 'I'm sorry I shouted, but you know how I worry

13

when I find you are not here, and now I see I have cause. I can hardly believe what you have told me. You are legally adopted? How can that be?' He shook his head in utter disbelief.

'I was sworn to secrecy.'

'Who could have the right to ask that of you without my knowledge? Did I not take you in as a baby, and have I not done my best to feed and clothe you for seventeen years? Permitted you to use the name of Lefèvre?'

'All those things, Olivier, but it happened strangely, and I know I must not disturb you when you are doing experiments.'

'Be adopted and not disturb me? Am I a monster?'

'Sometimes,' teased Hermione. Her expression became reflective. 'A manservant came to the house one day and entreated me to go with him to see his sick master, who was anxious that I should come to him.'

'And you went?'

'I felt I should. It seemed urgent.'

'But why? Do you have to attend every stranger and beggar that comes knocking?'

'When I arrived at the house,' Hermione carried on tiring of his interruptions, 'the man greeted me as though he knew me. He spoke only with great effort, for his sickness had made talking difficult. But his eyes smiled when I came close to his bed.'

'And did you know him? What age was this man?'

'His face was haggard … he was old, perhaps in his forties or fifties. There was something familiar about him, but I couldn't quite place him. Then, after my second visit, it came back to me, and I recalled that I had met him here.'

'Here?'

'Yes. It was a day different from others, or I should not perhaps have remembered. The day the noblewoman, the Marquise de Brinvilliers, knelt with the candle and crucifix before Notre Dame for the poisoning of her father and brothers. You were away in Prague. Lucette and

Guillaume had gone to watch the execution on the Place de Grève, but I didn't want to get caught up in the huge crowds. So I was at home in the courtyard when a man came through the gate. His clothes were quite worn. yet he was of noble bearing, and he had arrived by coach, for I glimpsed it waiting outside on the street. He asked if he could consult the seer whose name had been recommended to him. He was embarrassed. And I remember there was something desperate in his eyes, so, though I had not intended to give any readings that day, I led him up to the room. Another thing which made me remember was that he left without paying, though I do not think it was meant, for the moment he entered the room and looked about he became very agitated. And something I saw in the crystal upset him so much he rushed away weeping.'

'Bah!' exclaimed Olivier. 'I knew that superstitious foolery you persist in following would come into it!'

'It helps to pay for things,' replied Hermione quietly. Olivier snorted with impatience, but for once she did not care. She knew that her readings of the crystal paid for a good part of what they ate, and for fuel.

'I have a talent, Olivier, and that is why people come to see me. When I think deeply, I often have a feel of the future and of the past.'

'Think deeply,' sneered Olivier, his voice filled with contempt. Hermione flushed with hurt and anger, but she kept quiet. 'Well go on – go on!'

'He never came back, and I forgot all about him until his servant led me to his house in the Marais. My visits there at first were just once a week. He was stronger then and he would write down his questions: it was easier for him than speaking for one side of his face could not move.'

'But you don't know your letters.'

'No, and nor could his servant read them. So he took to drawing things - flowers and trees - and then I would speak about them. It was like a game, but I think it helped him get to know the things we both liked. One day, when Jean opened the door, I found a lawyer waiting for me. He explained that the Chevalier wished to leave me his estate in the country and to do so he had petitioned the King to allow him to adopt me as his legal daughter.'

'Adopt you! A stranger, and you agreed to it!' Hermione hung her head as her guardian re-awakened the sense of disloyalty which had plagued her.

'I did not mean to hurt you,' she murmured. 'You have always been father and brother to me. But he was in terrible pain and had little time to live. I wanted to make him happy.' Hermione's smile was anguished and her throat contracted at the memory of what she had witnessed.

'But it seems so cold-blooded. Was it for his money? How could you agree to such a charade? It is a pity he is dead, for he would have me to deal with. Will you go to his funeral?'

'Naturally,' she said coldly, cut to the quick by his insult.

'Then I shall come too,' snapped Olivier, his face wearing a possessive expression.

'But you didn't know him.'

'Nor did you, it seems.'

'I knew his soul,' responded Hermione quietly.

'Saw it in your crystal?'

It was too much. The day had been harrowing enough without having to endure cruel taunts. And there was something new, something she had not heard before. Could he be jealous of a dead man? Too weary to think or to listen, Hermione went up to bed. And the moment she was curled underneath the blanket, she was asleep.

On the following day, Olivier did not appear for breakfast, though his footsteps could be heard pacing back and forth overhead.

'The explosion yesterday has put the master in a great state of excitement,' commented the maid, looking upward.

'Perhaps,' said Hermione, inwardly thinking his agitation more likely to have to do with herself. 'Was it a large explosion?'

'Enough to send Guillaume flying out into the yard, though I've known larger.' The girl laughed as she rinsed out three wooden bowls and set Olivier's untouched one on a tray. 'But when the master came back to the house later, he was all smiles until he found you were missing again!' The maid's blue eyes shot a knowing look at Hermione, and she found herself blushing, which was ridiculous. She knew Lucette was implying she had been with her friend Robert. It was tempting to rid her of her silly smirk and watch those sly eyes widen with wonder as she told her she was no longer Hermione Lefèvre, but the adopted daughter of the Chevalier Du Chesne. An inward merriment seized hold.

'Have you ever seen the sea?' she asked innocently.

'The sea?' queried the fair-haired girl in astonishment. 'I can't say I have, but I know about it. It's where the boats bring back salt.' Lucette's expression again became conspiratorial and knowing. 'And is there a certain actor who wants to take you there?' Hermione gave a non-committal shrug, then gestured for Lucette to take up Olivier's porridge.

Outside in the yard, Guillaume's efforts to brush away dust and twigs were being made difficult by a stiff breeze.

'It is not helping you,' Hermione said, stepping out from the kitchen.

'As long as it looks tidy when I look through here,' he grinned, his fingers touching the patch covering his blind eye.

'Things went badly yesterday?'

'Well, they did, and they didn't, Mademoiselle Hermione. For these past weeks the stench would have killed a weaker man, and the strange smoke and fiery explosions put me in a real fright. Master says I'm not to talk about it, but he was so excited. No wonder he took to *le cognac* last night.'

'And I suppose you helped empty the bottle?' she said, catching a whiff of spirits on his breath.

'Found the bottle lying out this morning when I lit the fire,' replied the big man cheerfully. 'There was only a drop left, so no wonder the master is still abed.'

'Stick to wine, Guillaume. It suits your head better.'

'I will do that, Mademoiselle Hermione, but nothing like a little fire in a man's belly first thing in the morning.' With that, he went back to sweeping and burst into one of his raucous songs. Hermione wandered over to the herb patch, which had survived winter and recent frosts. She plucked a few leaves of rosemary and rubbed them 'twixt her fingers. It was one of the herbs André Du Chesne had drawn for her. Towards the end, when the air in his bedchamber had become foul, she had cut masses of it to scatter with the dried lavender they had in store. Her hand touched against the top of her bodice where she had placed the leather pouch containing his ring. With a swift glance to make sure Guillaume was not looking, she withdrew the pouch and slipped the ring onto her finger. As she stared down at the A, D and C of his initials, her eyes brimmed with tears. Her thoughts slid back to her first glimpse of the gold band. On that day it was not Jean who had opened the Chevalier's door, but a black-robed lawyer.

'Mademoiselle Lefèvre, I am honoured to meet you. The Chevalier Du Chesne has requested that I should put to you a proposition which he is most anxious you should accept. I fear there is no hope for Monsieur. His physician says it is a matter of weeks, even days. If you accept the Chevalier's offer, you will have done him a great service and yourself no less. But first, you must make clear the relationship between yourself and Olivier Lefèvre.'

'He is my guardian.'

'You do understand that he is not your legal guardian?'

'Why … I had never thought about it, monsieur.' While she was still wondering how the notary would know such a thing, he had hurried her to the Chevalier Du Chesne's bedchamber. The sick man was propped high against a bolster. About his bony shoulders was draped a green velvet coat; a cap of similar hue decorated with embroidered cream flowers was perched on his grey hair. As they had exchanged smiles, Hermione noted that he was newly shaven, and his gown and bed linen looked freshly laundered. There seemed an air of exuberance about him.

His brown eyes, usually filled with pain and sadness, held a hint of laughter and eagerness.

'Mademoiselle Lefèvre, please be seated,' the notary had begun. 'Out of kindness, you responded to the summons of a sick man. Since then you have visited the Chevalier and he has communicated to me how you have tried to ease his suffering and loneliness. The Chevalier has no family in this world, and before he departs it, he wishes to provide for your future.'

'There is no need … I have done little.' André Du Chesne had then brushed aside her words with an imperious move of his good hand.

'The Chevalier,' resumed the lawyer with great *hauteur*, 'desires to bestow upon you his name – to adopt you as his daughter. For a woman of no rank, it is a singular honour.'

Even now, as she relived the scene, Hermione felt the full shock of those words. They had stunned her then, and even today she could hardly believe that she had agreed to such a thing. Yet who could have been so cruel as to refuse the ring he offered, set within his reach on a kerchief? Any feelings of disloyalty to Olivier had been smothered and overwhelmed by compassion, and by the happy, hopeful expectation in his brown eyes. And so she had stretched out her hand.

'I would be honoured.' She had smiled, as their fingers touched. Then, in his cold voice, the lawyer had rushed on.

'The Chevalier wishes you to inherit his estate. He wishes you to become the châtelaine of Du Chesne. To care for his old home, and to honour his servants Pierre and Marie Paultre when he is no longer in this world. Do you promise to do so?'

Like some piteous creature, André Du Chesne had struggled to push out his words. 'Say yes, *chérie*.' Hardly able to see for tears and not daring to think about what she was agreeing to do, Hermione had whispered her assent.

'I'll be off for the fish now, Mademoiselle Hermione.' Lucette's voice demanded Hermione's attention. 'Those two men who knocked down an old lady will be bound to the pillory again. It was such sport last week throwing rubbish at them. I'll bring back all the gossip.'

'Just so long as you get the fish back while their eyes are still bright,' replied Hermione, for Lucette had a habit of lingering, especially if she met apprentices from the cabinet-makers on the street behind the house. After the gate had shut on Lucette, Hermione took off the ring, which, fortunately, had not been spotted. She would explain matters to Guillaume and Lucette on her return from the funeral. Though as to leaving Paris, could she really bear to do that? What of Olivier, and of Lucette and Guillaume, who likewise had become as family? From overhead, floorboards creaked as Olivier walked towards his door. Hermione snatched up her shawl and purse as his feet sounded on the stairs.

On her way to buy bread, she ran into her friend Agnès, but as there was much to do, she avoided being drawn into conversation.

'I'll call around this afternoon,' she promised with a wave, 'and I would be glad of some sleeping draughts for one of my ladies.' Agnès' busy needle provided for her and her parents, and the buyers of the pretty pouches she made sometimes let her have small samples of the creams, potions, and powders they traded in. These she sold on to Hermione for a few *sous*.

When she returned home, there was no sign of Olivier, who doubtless was in his laboratory. And Guillaume very likely had followed Lucette to join in the sport at the pillory. So after checking the soup, Hermione went up to the room where she gave her readings. All was darkness, but when the kindling in the fireplace flared into life and flames leapt upwards, the silver stars and moons on the black velvet hanging behind her table and chair began to gleam and sparkle. As a child, she had liked stroking her fingers along the pile of the velvet as if it were the fur of a kitten. Sometimes she had spread it out on the floor and pretended she was sitting high up in the night sky close to angels. Where the hanging came from, she did not know. The trunk in which she had found it had served as long as she could remember as a table upon which to put a candlestick. Hermione vaguely recalled fitting a large key into its lock, perhaps some time after the old housekeeper had died. Very clearly she could remember the moment when she had pulled out the magical cloth. Even more exciting had been finding the crystal, which had been in a black silk bag at the bottom of the trunk. Then, some years later, when she was aimlessly loitering on the Pont Neuf, she had watched with curiosity the people coming out of a seer's booth. She did not have the money to go in to see what happened, but one day, after there had been high, violent winds, she had noticed a rent in one side of the worn canvas. Thus had begun her schooling in the art of reading the crystal. Hermione laughed as she thought of the hours she had spent looking into the small globe, hoping to see images. Her first reading! Oh, the embarrassment of it! She had acquired no skill and, seized with desperation had pretended to see within the globe the face of a rich man for the anxious lady. 'I hope by now she has met him.' She laughed as she stooped and threw a log onto the fire, 'La Voisin would have conjured him up for her in seconds!' Hermione shuddered at her boldness to speak out loud the name of the sorceress and felt within a sense of unease and fear. Catherine Montvoisin was sought after by the highest nobles in Paris, even though it was whispered she communicated with the Devil and held the Black Mass. Instinctively, Hermione made the sign of the cross and uttered a rapid prayer under her breath. To distract herself, she glanced around the room to see all was in order for her readings that afternoon. The curtains at the window were pulled to, save for a chink to let in sufficient light to fall upon the crystal. The fire was drawing, and once the room was warmed through, she would ask Lucette to put it out, for once her first client arrived there must be no distractions other than the crystal.

Lucette, to Hermione's surprise, had not dawdled, and by her flushed face and heaving breasts it seemed she had run back from the fish market.

'La Voisin has been arrested!' The words hung in the air. Then, as their impact engulfed her, Hermione turned deathly pale until the smell of soup scorching in the pot liberated her from the thrall of dread which Catherine Montvoisin's name had evoked.

'How did it happen?' she asked, snatching the pot from the fire.

'La Reynie's men took her as she came out of Mass at Notre Dame de Bonne Nouvelle. Her maid Margot has also been taken, her sons as well. I heard they are tracking down anyone who went to her villa. What am I to do?'

Hermione did her best to remain calm so as not to increase Lucette's terror, though she herself was filled with alarm.

'It won't be easy for the police to do that,' she said, thinking it through. 'You told me most callers who went to Villeneuve-sur-Gravois were masked.'

Without warning, Guillaume's shaggy head thrust inward around the kitchen door like a hopeful, hungry hound. Hermione exchanged looks with Lucette, warning her to keep quiet. 'Guillaume,' she said, before he could enter, 'tell Monsieur Olivier we shall be ready to eat within the quarter hour.'

'And he'll be glad of it. We seem to get later every day,' he grumbled, disappearing.

'Oh, Mademoiselle Hermione, what will become of me when they find I worked there?' gasped Lucette. 'I saw things ... heard things! You know I did.' Hermione nodded and tried to find a word of comfort.

'Perhaps it is not as serious as we think.'

'No, no,' wept the fair-haired girl, throwing herself down onto a stool. 'Too many have been taken in for questioning. Remember La Bosse and La Vigoureux were taken off to the Bastille in January.'

Mindful of Olivier and Guillaume's needs, Hermione busied herself gutting the fish, for Lucette was beyond doing anything. 'Have you ever seen anyone from the rue Beauregard since you left?'

'No.'

'And you are sure no one followed you that night?'

'Quite sure. I told you so at the time.'

Hermione nodded. She went across to the fire and placed the fish on the griddle. 'Dry your eyes,' she said gently, glancing over her shoulder. 'For the moment, time is on our side. But once the torturers put the sorceress and others to the Question, they'll know the name of every soul that entered that house.'

The meal was a silent affair, with Olivier seemingly lost in thought. As usual, Guillaume's head was set low over his bowl as he concentrated on every mouthful of his food, while Lucette, unlike her gossipy self, sat silent and withdrawn. Suddenly, the bell in the yard jangled. It was at least an hour before Hermione's first reading. Not daring to look at Lucette, who doubtless like herself was in a desperate state of alarm, Hermione directed Guillaume to go and see who was calling. On his return, she saw with relief that he was carrying a letter.

'The messenger says it is for you, Mademoiselle Hermione.'

'Will you read it, Olivier?'

Roused out of his reverie, her guardian looked at Hermione for the first time that day; his expression was cool and unfriendly. He took the billet from Guillaume and broke its seal. 'Mademoiselle Lefèvre,' he trilled in a high female voice which set Guillaume into a growl of laughter, 'I regret to say that I am indisposed and cannot keep my appointment. Felicitations, Madame P.'

'There goes two *livres*!' grumbled Lucette.

'Remember your place!' flashed Hermione. Both her words and her tone caused the three around the table to look at her with shocked surprise. She flushed, realizing fear was getting the better of her. 'Do you require Guillaume's help this afternoon, Olivier?'

'No, I shall be reading. It will be months before further experiments.'

'Will I disturb you if I come to talk about the matter we discussed last night?'

'Wait till dusk. The ink of the manuscript I'm studying is much faded. It is a strain to read it by candlelight.' With that, Olivier rose

23

from the table and returned to his laboratory. Hermione went to her purse and took out coins to give to Guillaume.

'See what you can find out about La Voisin.'

'Save your money, mademoiselle. The whole of Paris knows her for a foul witch.'

'She has been arrested,' Hermioneed Hermione. 'I need to know if there have been more arrests.'

'And if anyone asks after me,' quipped Lucette, some of her sauciness returning, 'tell 'em I've gone away.'

In the time which now was at her disposal, Hermione went off to collect the sleeping powder she had requested from Agnès. The busy 'ancients', as her friend called her parents, were seated as usual each side of the hearth, their knitting needles clicking back and forth at great speed.

'Are you well?' she called in a loud voice, so as to be heard.

'Very well, mademoiselle,' came back their answer, their heads nodding her way, yet with no pause in their work. 'We're knitting for France … knitting for France!' Hermione smiled as their cackle of laughter filled the room. In a curtained-off corner which served as a small sewing room, Agnès was also hard at work. Some days she would be surrounded by second-hand dresses in need of repair or alteration, which she was permitted to do by the guild of dealers in second-hand clothes. But today she was seated before flounces of green and delicate blue material.

'How pretty,' exclaimed Hermione, picking up a dainty bag with trimmings of ribbons and lace. 'I never tire of seeing your work. My lady cancelled, but I'll still take the sleeping powder she wanted. I can keep it for someone else.'

'You'd best do so,' said Agnès wryly, re-threading a needle, 'for there'll be no more after today.' Hermione's black eyebrows arched with surprise. Her friend's expression became serious. 'Have you not heard La Voisin has been taken in for questioning?'

'I have, but what has it to do with sleeping powders? They are harmless … nothing to do with,' Hermione lowered her voice, '*inheritance* powders.'

'There is certainly no arsenic or vitriol here!' exclaimed Agnès in alarm. 'Remember that, Hermione, if you are arrested.'

'Arrested!' gasped Hermione. 'Why should you think I could be arrested?' Agnès shrugged her brawny shoulders. 'No one is safe. Some are saying a note was found in a confessional box, warning about a plot to poison the King himself! I hear, Hermione, that it will be not only La Trianon and La Dodée and others of La Voisin's coven who will see the inside of the Bastille and Vincennes, but anyone who supplies the ladies of the court with potions … I only pray that nobody has tampered with any of my sachets.'

'Tampered?'

'Treated, you know, with arsenic, as some do with gloves and chemises. This client you were going to give my sleeping draughts to … is she a lady of the court?'

Hermione stared back into the plump, flushed face and slowly shook her head. 'No, I do not think so. Her clothes are good, but not the finest quality. I think she may be someone's maid.'

'That is near as bad! Don't let anyone of consequence or their servants under your roof. They will only bring trouble.'

Leaving her friend to get on with her work, Hermione returned home deep in thought. After Agnès' warning, it was with a sense of relief that she found a second perfumed note had arrived for her. When she took it for Olivier to read, he confirmed it was yet another lady with an 'indisposition'.

'So I lit the fire upstairs for nothing,' she said, glancing down at the manuscript on his desk. The yellowish paper was covered with symbols, some of which were familiar, for, when she was small, Olivier had drawn their shapes in one of the laboratory's sand baths to amuse her. Two wavy lines represented water, while a moon-like shape indicated silver.

'A circle with a dot in the centre means gold doesn't it?' she observed, pointing at the one she was looking at.

'Indeed,' replied Olivier as if humouring a child.

'Why did you stop explaining them to me?' she asked, struck by the thought.

'You were no longer an infant. My work must be kept secret. The tincture which will be the Elixir of Life must not fall into the hands of charlatans who would misuse it to enrich themselves.' His sharp, clever grey eyes shone with a visionary light as he faced her with an expression of delight.

'Imagine, dear Hermione, being able to stop the body ageing. To keep it free from pain and disease. It was what the learned ancients most desired. Paracelsus records how he mixed a Renovating Quintessence with barley and fed it to a very old hen for fifteen days. The hen not only grew new feathers but began to lay eggs again. He repeated the experiment on an old woman who recovered her youth! In my travels, I have met men of learning, but also knaves. I know all their deceitful tricks, but men like the Englishman Robert Boyle, whom I met in Germany, are men of natural philosophy. He works with a young German, Ambrose Hanckwitz, and they are producing Icy Noctiluca. I visited their premises in Maiden Lane in London, and from a mutually absorbing exchange deduced how I might progress. Come, I shall show you something wonderful.'

It was rare to find Olivier in such a mood, and Hermione responded with enthusiasm. 'Where are you taking me?'

'To see the marvel I have produced!'

The small storeroom at one end of the laboratory was forbidden to all, even to Guillaume. On opening its door, her guardian pushed Hermione inward towards the row of shelves, then squeezed in alongside.

'I need light, for the moment,' he murmured. 'But be ready to shut the door.'

'I hope we shan't get stuck fast,' she laughed, for with the two of

26

them there was barely room to move. Turning sideways, Olivier began to fiddle about with things on the lower shelf. There sounded the clink of glass against glass, and it seemed he was undoing something.

'Pass me the tweezers,' he directed, his voice sounding urgent. 'Now shut the door – quickly!'

In the ensuing darkness, Hermione stared towards Olivier as she felt him shift his position towards her. Despite his obvious tension, she could not restrain her laughter, for it was all so mysterious.

'I can't see anything!'

'Keep looking, Hermione.'

At first, there seemed nothing to see, but gradually she became aware of a faint glow, seeming to emanate from a small ghostly mass. The strange shimmering white light was growing stronger. Hermione's shocked intake of breath made Olivier chuckle.

'What is it that glows like moonlight?' she whispered.

'Icy Noctiluca … phosphorus,' responded Olivier, his voice filled with pride.

'May I touch it?'

'*No! Never!*' It is very dangerous!' And it must now go back into its watery balm … give me some light!'

Hermione opened the door and, as light flooded in, she saw there were spirals of smoke lifting off the strange wax-like substance. Then Olivier's tweezers dipped and submerged the phosphorus beneath the water in the glass container.

'What do you think? It took fifty buckets of putrid urine to produce this.'

Hermione wrinkled her nose in remembrance of the foul stench which had for weeks pervaded the yard and the street beyond.

'Its power is immense,' explained Olivier with a smile. 'Put it into a globe lined with a little sand, touch it with a warmed glass rod and then, swoosh fire and strange light.'

'Oh, show me!'

'No, some other time. 'But I'll give you a different glimpse ... not quite as spectacular. Go and take a large piece of paper to my bench and fold it in half.'

Filled with excitement, Hermione sped off and had the paper awaiting Olivier when he emerged from the storeroom.

After setting down the two small vessels he was carrying, one of which contained water, her guardian pulled apart the folded paper and scattered the contents into and along the indentation formed by Hermione's crease. Even though the petal-like shapes had been ground down, Hermione identified flowers of sulphur. Consumed with excitement, she pressed closer to the bench. Olivier, who had just picked up the tweezers, turned on her with a stern look.

'Get back, stand well back! I don't want you burnt! Now, you shall see,' he said in a dramatic voice. As he bent forward, the expression on his scholarly face became intent. 'We take just one grain of Icy Noctiluca,' he murmured, dipping the heads of the tweezers into the water, 'and release it onto the flowers of sulphur.' At speed, he brought the ends of the paper together and, using the blade of a knife, pressed on the contents within the fold. There was a whoosh of flame, and the paper was on fire! The smoke and stinging fumes caught at Hermione's throat and her eyes streamed. Though she was gasping and near choking, as was Olivier, she looked towards her guardian in wonder.

'It is amazing!' she whispered. 'How did you learn how to do it?'

'It was the alchemist Hennig Brand in Hamburg who found the way ten years ago, though there were others earlier who had prepared the path for him. But Boyle in London has really taken the process forward. Not a word to anyone!'

'I promise. But tell me more about London ... you never say anything about your journeys.'

'I will, but not now,' said Olivier, as they walked back to the workbench. 'First, you have to tell me what that silly talk was about last night.' Hermione pursed her lips with vexation. Evidently, he had woken up not believing what she had told him.

'Nothing has changed. Everything you heard was true. Before you condemn me, please believe I had no desire to profit by an old man's death. I went with pity in my heart and in a short time he had become a friend. His sweet nature and brave suffering touched me. I only wanted to make him happy – to give him peace of mind. After his funeral, I must fulfil my promise to care for his home in Saintonge, it was his last wish.'

'To go away – leave Paris?' Olivier's voice was toneless, without displeasure, yet she grasped the impact her words had made. Indeed, having uttered them, she herself could hardly believe what she was proposing.

'I could always sell the estate,' she added, 'but I gave my sacred promise.'

'I do not wish to persuade you,' murmured Olivier, 'but selling would be the most sensible course. After all, you have lived here since you were a child. You know nothing of the country in the south. Besides, my laboratory is here and you are needed by Lucette and Guillaume.' His voice was stern as he spoke of the two servants, and she nodded mutely, feeling the intimacy and enjoyment they had just shared begin to evaporate.

There were but three at the Chevalier's funeral: herself, the priest and the elderly manservant, Jean. The clods of earth around the open grave were wet, for it had been raining hard during the time they had been in church. It was a cheerless day, and the absence of friends and family to mourn the old man's passing made the moment forlorn.

'I'll wish you goodbye, Madame Du Chesne,' said Jean, picking his way towards her with care.

'Do you have another position to go to?' Hermione enquired, wondering if it was her responsibility to offer him a place, though what he might do or what the others would say she could not think.

'I am leaving Paris on Friday to live with my sister in Caen.'

'Will you return with me to the house? There is so much I wish to ask about the Chevalier. It was not possible for us to speak before. Perhaps I might afterwards offer you a hot meal at my home, for it is such a miserable day. You could tell me about the Chevalier when he was young, when he came to Paris.'

With an implacable shake of his balding head, Jean pointed down at the coffin. 'It is finished there. And you, Madame, must make of the rest what you will. It was you that led him to this end.'

'I?' gasped Hermione. 'But how?'

'I took the master to the rue de la Cocotte to consult a seer who he had been told could offer comfort. Instead, he came out weeping like a child. I don't know what you did, or said, but the very next day he had his stroke! It was *me* that nursed him day and night for months. But all he craved when he grew stronger was to bring in lawyers and all I heard was the name Hermione Lefèvre. Then, when some other sickness took hold, he bade me search you out and bring you to him. After all my care, I am left with but a few trinkets and a small pension. So I will not offer you my blessing.'

'God go with you,' whispered Hermione, crushed by his attack. With unhappy eyes, she watched his shuffling retreat along the muddy path taken a moment before by the priest. The gravedigger waiting nearby picked up his spade and advanced to close up the grave. Hermione touched the ring on her finger bearing the Chevalier's motto. '*Adieu*,' she said softly looking down on the coffin, 'I shall keep my promise – *honorem est silentium*!'

CHAPTER 2

acques Maurellet raised the collar of his cape, for the wind coming off the Baltic cut like a razor. In France, green buds would be unfurling, while here an occasional ice floe could still be spotted riding down the Daugava. Tomorrow, God willing, he would say goodbye to the golden cocks on Riga's spires and be on his way home. Since arriving here he had learned never to set forth without carrying on his person his letters of authority, for the Swedes were a suspicious lot. Their wariness of strangers, he granted, was understandable, as it was but some twenty-three years past since Tsar Alexis Mikhailovich's failed assault on the city and two years since a great part of Riga had burnt down. The arsonists were suspected of being Russian.

The strident blast of the trumpeter blowing the hour brought Jacques's attention back to the town square. Now that the livestock had been driven out to pasture, the wagons waiting outside the earthen ramparts had begun to lumber in to take up position beside the huge scales. They would be the first of many which would keep some hundred Latvian factors busy packaging goods for export or directing them on for storage in Riga's many warehouses. Another day of commerce had begun, and it was time for him to make his call upon the agent. On the Daugava side of the square, clerks had begun to register and collect money from the peasants who waited in line to have goods weighed and their quality assessed. Just as his own country produced the best wine, Riga supplied the finest in ship stores. Fir trees from deep within the forests of Russia and Poland arrived at this fortified depot. Hundreds of barges brought flax, hemp, grain, tar, furs and precious beeswax to make the finest candles for cathedrals and palaces. Little wonder the citizens celebrated the thaw and the arrival of the first barge was saluted by the city's cannon.

Jacques left the square, flattening himself against a wall as three overloaded wagons thundered by and continued on past the various merchant houses. As he neared the shipping house he wanted, he glimpsed two men leaving it. He identified the cut of their coats as being English and frowned. Such was his irritation that by the time he entered the building he gave the clerk within no chance to announce him, but strode straight through the anteroom into the contractor's chamber.

'And what is your percentage, Bruyère?' he demanded, his voice heavy with sarcasm.

'Monsieur Maurellet ... please explain yourself. I do not care for your tone! Nor do I comprehend what you imply,' cried the agent, springing up from his chair.

'Nor do I understand, monsieur, how it is possible for you to represent British interests. I suppose you choose to keep them happy?'

'It is not a question of choice. The English Navy is willing to pay whatever the Swedes or Russians ask. What am I to do, tied as I am to a fixed price by France's Marine?'

'Does that explain why there are no sticks at all for our yards?'

'As I explained yesterday, monsieur, the Marine's authority did not arrive until November. I do not need to tell you how far away the forests are. Unless the order reaches me by September, it is too late!'

'So, I must return with unfortunate news!' Jacques glared as the short man spread his small hands in a gesture of distress. Inwardly, he accepted the explanation; the English, damn them, outbid France every time. And with the Russians holding back supplies upstream whenever the fancy took them, there could be no certainty of anything in this unsettled region. Still, it wouldn't harm to keep Bruyère on his toes.

'Remember,' he said, tossing back the proffered vodka, 'firs of over twenty-one palms – anything less is useless. And quality – no knot holes, nothing twisted like the last consignment.'

'The lots are mixed … it is not so easy. As you know, it is not the merchants here who are in charge of grading naval stores, but the Latvians.'

'There are many ways of achieving goals,' replied Jacques cordially. 'Last night, I was an honoured guest at the house of the Blackheads. France sends her wine and salt to Riga and, in return, she imports grain and linseed, a contract of 20,000 thalers! I would not wish to return home and report to Colbert that you have failed his Marine.' Though quietly spoken, Jacques's words had the desired effect. Bruyère sprang to life, making a great show of sharpening his quill. A grim smile touched Jacques's lips, for no rational man would wish to disappoint the Contrôleur Général of France. It was he, after all, who had brought low the powerful Minister of Finance, Fouquet. Next to the King, Jean-Baptiste Colbert was the most powerful man in France. With his son as Minister of Marine, a cousin as Intendant of Marine and other members of his family strategically placed within the church, Colbert's fingers were in every pie. There had never been anything like it: reports, reports, reports, *everything* had to be written down. The roads between the naval arsenals and Versailles must be under a permanent dust cloud; it certainly was an opportune time for dispatch riders. An auspicious time also for young men of respectable birth like his brother, who, amongst others without the high lineage demanded for officer rank, had entered the newly formed corps of cadets at Rochefort.

'So, Monsieur Maurelllet,' said Bruyère with a note of eagerness as he dipped his quill into ink, 'you said yesterday you would give me your personal requirements.'

Jacques's blue eyes became alert. 'Repeat last year's order for deal, also for tar. The usual number of lots for spars and masts, but amongst them must be three firs of at least thirty palms – the finest you can get.'

'This order takes priority over the . . . ?'

'Yes,' said Jacques not letting him put it into words. He detested corrupt practice; strictly speaking, he was here on business for the Marine and should not be looking out for the family shipyard, but the circumstances were special. He was set on building a man o' war for the glory of France. It might still be a dream, but if a contract came his way, he wanted to have the finest timber weathering in the Maurellet yard.

May had arrived, but in Paris its fresh green leaves were obscured by a grimy pall of smoke as the burnings on the Place de Grève increased. La Vigoureux and La Bosse went to the stake, and Nicolas La Reynie's men took away more and more to be questioned and tortured at Vincennes. Paris was gripped by sensational arrests such as those of Madame Poulaillon and Madame Dreux, and there were whisperings about personages so close to the King that everyone trembled. Hermione decided to remove from their lives the greatest danger, Lucette. She would not leave willingly, so Hermione decided she would have to be tricked into it. Only Olivier knew about the house in the Marais, for she had been reluctant to confide in Lucette or Guillaume about that part of her inheritance, lest they spread it around for common gossip.

'I am taking a basket of food to a friend, Lucette,' she said invitingly one morning. 'Would you like to come with me?'

'I'd be glad to,' responded Lucette. 'Do I know her, mademoiselle?'

'I think not,' replied Hermione. Mindful of the possibility of being watched by spies for the police as they made their way towards the Marais, every so often she gave a discreet look over her shoulder.

'That will be La Bosse's son,' commented Lucette, as the jubilant roar of a great crowd went up. 'He is being broken on the wheel.' Hermione shuddered and again looked behind to make sure they were not being followed.

'You're very nervous, Mademoiselle Hermione. Anyone would think you were on the run … have you been doing anything wrong?' Hermione stopped in her tracks as the servant burst into a fit of giggling. Suddenly irritated beyond patience Hermione glared at her.

'Do you not grasp what danger you are in? The danger you are bringing on all of us?'

Lucette's eyes rounded with wonder. 'Me?'

'Yes, you!' snapped Hermione. She paused to fish in her bag for the key to unlock the gate which opened into the small courtyard of the house. After they had hurried through, Hermione faced the girl with a stern look.

'It is as though you've wiped everything about La Voisin from your mind. It is not going to go away! When people are tortured, they will tell everything and make up things. They will say there was a servant working in the kitchen named Lucette. They will say she had a small pointed nose and blue eyes and was a great gossip.' A stony silence fell between them as they moved towards the steps which led to the upper level of the house. Hermione opened up the door, taking no notice of her maid's sulky expression.

'There's candle and flint on that table,' she directed, re-locking the door behind them.

'Is there no one here?' asked Lucette in surprise as they entered the bedchamber. 'It could do with air … it stinks. I'll open the shutters.'

'No, don't,' said Hermione. 'I don't want you to open them, not even for a few minutes. Nor do I want you to answer the door unless you hear my voice.' Lucette's fleshy mouth opened, and she stared at Hermione in bewilderment. 'You are to stay here until it is safe.'

The girl's blue eyes bulged with disbelief. 'Stay!' she gasped.

'It will be only for a week or so.'

'I won't stay an hour, Mademoiselle Hermione. And you won't make me.'

'I should have broken it to you more gently, but it would have come to this in the end.'

'There is no friend!'

Hermione nodded. 'Sit down, I'll explain.'

'Mademoiselle, I am not staying, and if you won't unlock the door, I'll hang my head out of the window and scream for help. Is it that you're trying to protect me?' Lucette added, her tone softening a little. 'Lately you seem frightened of your own shadow. They've got La Voisin, so why would they bother with the likes of me … it's too silly!' Her shrill laugh of dismissal shattered the quiet of the room as she minced towards a mirror. With a pleased look, she twisted around her fingers the long golden skein of hair which had come free from her cap. 'Of course, if your friend comes back, and has a good-looking valet, then … '

Hermione could see there were no words to make the silly girl understand the danger she was in. On the day of La Voisin's arrest she had been terrified, but the fear had soon passed, and once again all she could think about was flirting with the apprentices at the cabinet-makers. After a moment's consideration, Hermione took up the candle and walked purposefully forward. With a darting thrust, she touched the flame against the blonde curl just long enough to make its hairs sizzle. The maid's shocked gape of disbelief gave voice to a loud scream as she sprang away, but Hermione had her tight by the wrist.

'That is what will happen when they tie you to the stake,' she hissed, her black eyebrows drawn back and her eyes dark and intense. 'Do you want to be burned alive?' The fury on Lucette's face transformed to terror. She staggered and collapsed down onto a chair. 'Think how those poor wretches on the Place de Grève must welcome death,' Hermione continued. She drew up a stool and stroked Lucette's shoulder to comfort her as she wept. 'Did you exaggerate a little, the things you told me about La Voisin?'

'No, no, everything happened, and even worse I think than abortions,' answered the girl, her voice muffled within her hands. Presently, she looked up, the whites of her eyes reddened with weeping. 'It was as I told you … voices chanting at midnight, sometimes the scream of a baby … lights in the garden at dead of night and newly dug earth the next day. Once I heard La Voisin laughing because one of the callers was not pregnant, but she still pretended to do the abortion. Do you remember last year when we watched the King go into Notre Dame, how I recognized a face amongst his ladies? It was one whose mask slipped when she fainted.'

'At least you found the courage to run away from the witch's villa.'

Lucette nodded. 'God was guiding me away from wickedness.'

'Well, if you had stayed, you would be suffering agonies in prison now. As it is, you have a chance, so long as you are not found. They would make you talk.'

'I'd tell them gladly about the witch.'

'It might be they want to destroy somebody else as well as her. Agnès says they have ways of making you say things you do not even know.' Hermione paced about the room, realizing she had let the weeks slip by and now there was only one way forward. 'We have to get away, all of us, for if one remains in Paris and is taken, they will track us down. It is not beyond the police to find the link to this place,' she added under her breath. 'Leave? But where would we go if we left Paris?'

'Somewhere far away,' Hermione reassured her. 'Guillaume will come with us, and Monsieur Olivier.'

'Monsieur Olivier will never leave his laboratory, not for anything.' Inwardly, Hermione agreed with her, but somehow she must persuade him.

'He'll see the sense of it,' she said. 'Now let us make up the bed for you.'

'Has your friend gone away without his hat and cane?'

'He has no further use for them.' Hermione turned away to take down the wooden crucifix behind the bed. With a wistful smile, she recalled André Du Chesne sitting beneath it with the green jacket draped around his shoulders and the embroidered cap set at a jaunty angle on his long grey hair. He had been as happy as a bridegroom offering her his ring. The desolate room echoed the sense of loss she felt; there were so many things she would have liked to know about him. The notary knew only that the Chevalier had lived in Paris for many years and that the rent on the house was paid each quarter. If she wished him to renegotiate the arrangement, he would do so; she had declined. She had thought the gloomy house would serve no purpose, but now, in the time left when it was still hers to use, it was somewhere to hide Lucette, and somewhere to store whatever belongings they needed to take with them. On that score, she knew now that Olivier would prove a real problem. Just as the King had men bringing wagons of full-grown trees to the new palace at Versailles, Olivier would want to take every retort and flask, if not his furnace. 'I'll have to drug him,' she declared aloud, laughing.

'Mademoiselle Hermione!' The girl's shocked exclamation delayed Hermione's hand as she was about to pick up a bag in which to put the crucifix. 'Is that what happened here – you sent your friend on his way with inheritance powder?'

'Lucette! How could you think such a wicked thing of me? Rid yourself this instant of such a foul thought! I was thinking of Monsieur Olivier – how it might help to calm him when it is time to leave. The physician who attended here did all he could for my friend, as did the priest. But God's hand was outstretched and neither drug nor man could have kept him on this earth. Do you understand, Lucette?'

'Yes, Mademoiselle Hermione, forgive me. So the food in the basket is for me?'

'Yes, you are not to go out … only to answer to Guillaume or myself. We shall leave Paris in the next few weeks. Is there anything you wish to take?'

'Am I not to go back to the house … not to say goodbye to friends?'

'None of us can make our goodbyes. It is better for friends to know nothing. Later on, when it is safe, you can make contact then.

Just think how exciting it is going to be … a new life,' Hermione said encouragingly, as Lucette burst into angry sobs.

'Will I still be your maid?' the girl asked eventually, a sulky expression on her tear-stained face.

'Yes … that is until you marry a country boy,' Hermione teased, dangling before her the ultimate seduction.

The streets on the return home were crowded but, preoccupied with making plans, Hermione barely noticed. If the Chevalier's coach had not been eaten away by worm, they could use it. Guillaume would need a coachman's livery, and there would have to be travelling clothes for herself. The coat and breeches which Olivier wore when meeting other men of learning would not look at all out of place. Hermione quickened her step, for while demand for her services had practically ceased since the troubles, she did have a booking for a reading of the crystal that afternoon. Indeed, just as she arrived, Guillaume was waving a coach forward into the yard. Not wishing to be seen in her street clothes by her client, she gave a wave to Guillaume and went straight into the house. As she slipped into her long black gown, she found with satisfaction that he had made ready the room. He was a good sort, though his bluff, rough manner was hardly what a lady visiting a seer would expect. Still, it wouldn't matter; in a week or so from now they would be gone. Outside the door the floorboards creaked under a heavy tread and then Guillaume's shaggy head popped around the door. Hermione nodded for him to bring in her client, who like many of her callers offered only an initial instead of her name.

'Greetings, Madame S,' she said, gesturing for the woman to take the seat which faced herself and the black velvet hanging. 'It is not long since we met, I believe. ' In fact, the lady had called but two weeks past. 'Has there been some change in your life?' Hermione's dark eyes dwelt on the woman's hands, which were busy bringing together the edges of her grey cloak. The petticoat beneath was of the vivid green which the guild of dyers had named parrot green after the foreign birds. It was not a colour Hermione cared for: too bright and showy.

'I had to return,' explained Madame S ingratiatingly. 'There is no one else I can speak to about my situation.'

'I cannot talk about what happened last time,' murmured Hermione. 'My concentration during a reading of the crystal is deep; when my thoughts return to my surroundings, all is gone.'

'No, you misunderstand. I do not want a prediction. To be blunt, my husband's infidelity troubles me, and sorely. I can think of nothing else! Last time I was here and mentioned my restlessness, you were kind enough to provide me with a sleeping draught.'

'Did it help?'

'Yes, yes it did. But it has not cured the problem of my husband's passion for a younger woman. You are skilled. I beg you to help me.'

'Let it burn out like a candle,' soothed Hermione. 'Be patient. Would you like another powder to help you sleep when you are troubled?'

'Do you get them from someone round here?'

'No.' Hermione thought it best not to be specific. 'You can get them from any apothecary.'

'It was helpful ... but I need something ... more ... *final*.' Hermione's eyes widened with alarm; was the woman thinking of taking her own life? She was clearly agitated, for though there was only partial light in the room, the puffy face was shining with sweat.

'Nothing can be so bad as to take your own ...'

'Oh, no, it is not for *my* use,' replied her visitor, obviously divining Hermione's alarm. 'A solution, I believe, would be to remove temptation from the path of my poor husband.'

'I don't follow your meaning,' said Hermione stiffly, not liking the way things were going. For response, the woman dipped a hand within her cloak and produced a violet-coloured sachet. With increasing disquiet, Hermione stared at it. Then she noticed the tiny circle of embroidered violets – Agnès' work mark.

'This contained a powder which solved a friend's problem,' explained Madame S, with another ingratiating smile. 'Now her husband only has eyes for her, and her rival ... well, she and her charms fade away every day. If you keep sleeping draughts, surely you must have other powders and tinctures for other things?' Her persistence had become bullying.

'I am a seer, nothing more.' Hermione stood, to bring an immediate end to the conversation.

'Tell me at least who it is who makes such pretty holders. I ... er ... I have lavender in my garden. It would be a pretty task this summer to fill such sachets for my linen press. These are quite distinctive. Could you find out who sewed them?'

Hermione forced a smile. 'I'd like to help, but I really have no idea.' She moved towards the door and opened it. 'There is no charge today, Guillaume. Please show Madame to her coach.' The simpering charm had slipped away from the woman's face and, with obvious irritation, she practically pushed her way past to move to the stairs. For a moment, Hermione regarded her retreating figure, as she pondered on what had been said. Filled with misgivings, she threw off her robe and, after getting her cloak, she ran downstairs. Outside in the yard, Gullaume was pushing back the wooden doors for the coach to leave. Perhaps Lucette was right when she had said she was frightened of everything, but anyone who had seen the magistrate's wife hanging on the place of execution with her right hand cut off would feel nervous. There had been something about Madame S which did not ring true. If she really was genuine, then she was someone who was bent on murder!

'Spare a *sou*,' pleaded a man in rags, stepping forward out of an alley. Hermione refused with a shake of her head and made to hurry on, but the beggar grabbed hold of her and pulled her back towards him. Just beside them, her client's coach had come to a halt, and Hermione glimpsed her profile.

'I've no money,' she hissed at the man, fearing any moment to be spotted. The beggar's fingers dug deeper into her flesh and somehow she managed not to cry out, lest she become the centre of attention on the thoroughfare. With her free hand, she grabbed for the hood of her cloak and pulled it over her head, hoping she had not already been spotted by Madame S. 'Let me go … or I'll shout for the archers … they'll drag you off to the Hôpital Général.' The threat had immediate effect. Uttering an obscene curse, the man roughly shoved Hermione away. The coach now was some way ahead, but by weaving and squeezing her way through the throng of people, Hermione caught up. To her growing dismay, she realized the coachman was heading his horses towards the Châtelet! So the woman was not looking to poison anyone, she was a spy for the police! And indeed, at the entrance to the fortress which guarded the bridge onto the Île de la Cité, the coach paused as Madame S stepped down and hurried in through the gate.

There had been rumours since January. Everyone seemed to know of someone who had been taken away for questioning: apothecaries, midwives, fortune tellers, distillers of perfumes. Until this moment, it had not truly felt real; it was something which was happening to other people. Hermione's heart pounded with fear as she realized she too was caught in the net. The paid eyes of Nicolas La Reynie had called upon her today! Her heart now was racing so fast she could barely think as waves of terror overwhelmed her. How long had she got? Would they send the archers to rue de la Cocotte straight away? What had she told the woman? Think, think clearly. She took a deep breath to calm herself. Time was running out, and the thought of what might come to them all filled her with dread.

There was much to set in motion, but above all else, there was someone she must warn without delay.

Agnès' elderly parents were in their chairs either side of the hearth, absorbed in their knitting.

'How many stockings knitted this week, madame?' enquired Hermione, trying to appear light-hearted.

'More than those poor wretches turn out at the Hôpital Général. If we fall behind here, Agnès gives us no dinner.'

'Oh, Maman!' Agnès' wail of protest came from behind the curtained-off corner as the elderly lady burst into shrill peals of laughter. 'How can you say such things? Don't listen to her naughtiness, Hermione. Come on through.'

'I see your mother has learned to knit with three threads,' commented Hermione, taking up a stool to sit on.

'It's to copy the English stockings that are sent to France from the Channel Isles. Papa can only manage coarse knitting.'

'Well, he looks as fast as any machine.'

Agnès gave a pleased smile. 'We're relieved they've banned worsted being made on the silk machines, not just because of money, but because it passes the hours and keeps them content. What's the use of turning out stockings quickly if poor folk have no way to earn their food? The machines were made to work silk stockings and that's how it should stay.'

Hermione reached down to pick up a snippet of ribbon from the floor as she prepared to tell the grim news. 'This is pretty,' she murmured.

'You can't get it now,' answered her friend, threading her needle. 'The ribbon looms could turn out six of those at a time. But the wardens of the ribbon guild made such a bother a year last February that Nicolas La Reynie had the machines smashed and the ribbons confiscated.'

'Then how ...?'

Agnès gave an arched smile. 'A few scraps came my way. I use such tiny pieces for decoration. Who is to know?' Hermione gave a shrug: receiving banned ribbon was the least of Agnès' worries. 'Your taffeta; where does that come from?'

'I buy leftovers. The best, though – silks from Tours or Lyon. Taffetas come from Nîmes.'

'Have you used violet-coloured taffeta recently?'

Agnès' needle hand paused mid-flight, and she wrinkled her brow as she considered the question.

'Not for a year or so…Why do you ask?'

'I saw a small sachet with a circle of violets embroidered in its centre today.'

'Ah, that could be mine.'

'Do you use the same colour for everyone?' The serious urgency in Hermione's voice brought Agnès' sewing to a complete halt.

'Why are you asking me all these questions? What is it about?'

In an undertone so that only the two of them could hear, Hermione related what had passed earlier. Agnès' earnest face filled with anxiety. 'Think, Agnès, think hard. When did you embroider violets? Had someone given a bunch to you to put them in your thoughts? What colours did you use last year … the year before?'

'Last year, there was parrot green and apple blossom. The year before – that was ten years after my brother died, and Maman, Papa, and I went to the common grave and laid violets there for him and the other poor souls.'

'Now,' said Hermione, her voice steady and intense, 'to whom did you supply violet sachets?' Her plump friend stared back without an answer; then the expression in her eyes altered, and the rosy flush drained out of her round face. Hermione realized the worst. 'You remember,' she whispered. Their gaze held and all that could be heard was the clicking of needles and the old lady humming. Agnès' eyes narrowed as they flooded with tears.

'What will become of my old ones if I am taken?' she whispered. 'I made them for La Vigoureux.'

'And she, thank the Saints, is but ashes now,' said Hermione. 'Perhaps your only danger then is if they want to know the names of other customers.'

'I do not always know. Charles supplies me with materials and tells me how many sachets or bags I must make, and he takes them away and pays me. I never know where they are going. I can only remember

La Vigoureux because he happened to mention it for some reason. And even if I knew where they were going, how am I to know what is put into them? Do you think I am in danger?'

'I hope not. Perhaps it is only me they are interested in.'

'More likely Monsieur Olivier. Alchemists have been taken to the Bastille. A man called Primi Visconti has been taken in for questioning. Maman told me that when they opened the Hôpital Général twenty years ago, thousands of beggars fled to the country so as not to be taken there and locked in. How will I bear it if that happens to her and Papa?'

'Do you have family out of Paris?' asked Hermione. Agnès shook her head.

'They can't travel, and I'll not leave them. They make married couples go into the Hôpital Général if they are poor.'

'Well, at least get rid of this,' Hermione urged, waving the scrap of ribbon in front of her friend's nose. 'And those,' she added, pointing to the assortment of small bags which were decorated with the ribbon. 'If anyone calls asking about the sachets, tell them you never ask where they are going. You sew, and you are paid.'

'And you?'

Hermione gave a cheerful smile. 'We'll be all right. We've committed no crimes.' She hesitated as she suddenly realized she might not see Agnès and her parents again. Their cheerfulness, their industry, had always filled her with admiration. It did not seem they were in great peril, with La Vigoureux executed. However, for them to know that she planned to leave Paris might place them in danger if she or Olivier were on some list, so best not to say anything.

'Dear friend,' she said, kissing Agnès on the cheek as she left. On her way out, she paused to admire the knitting of the elderly couple and touched her lips likewise to their cheeks. 'Take care of yourselves. Keep those needles flying.'

'We have to, dear Hermione, for the man who brings the wool from the Hôpital Général told us every pair of stockings we knit stops English ones coming to France.'

'It is something when a man has to fend off the English with needles instead of a sword,' spat Agnès' father, managing to send spittle into the fire without pause in his knitting. 'Don't get old, mademoiselle … make the most of your youth.'

'I will,' promised Hermione, waving them what might be a last farewell.

Olivier's attention was directed on Hermione in a manner which was normally reserved for his work.

'I do not doubt the gravity of what you fear concerning Lucette, but is it necessary for anyone other than her to leave Paris?'

'Olivier, you never take time for a stroll about the yard, let alone the streets. People are being arrested everywhere, and not just *fortune tellers*,' she quipped. 'No one knows what it is all about, but it has leaked out that there is a secret court at the Arsenal. The wife of an important official of Champagne was brought before it to sit on the *sellette*, and so were the wives of two magistrates.'

'I thought you said it was secret,' scoffed Olivier. 'Ladies of influence are not going to sit on a stool like a common criminal without a fuss,' he added dryly. 'Perhaps Louis should remember the Fronde! If there is a secret court which calls before it members of the nobility, the stakes must be high, and those at the centre of the matter must be near the King. Why else would one remove criminal prosecution from the proper jurisdiction of Parliament?'

'You see the danger?'

'Oh yes. Once blood-letting starts, there is no stopping it, as the Huguenots discovered on the Eve of St Bartholomew. So it is likely men of natural philosophy will be swallowed up along with superstitious knaves.'

'Then you will come away?' Olivier shook his head, then bestowed on her such a fond smile that Hermione's heart contracted with pleasure, yet also with the fear of parting. Olivier was really all she had ever known. 'We can take all your manuscripts and later, when it is safe, we could return for some of your equipment.'

'Dear, sweet girl, how well you have looked after me. You and Lucette shall go tomorrow and Guillaume shall take you. But send him back as quickly as you can, for he is indispensable to me.'

'No, no, you *must* come. Please ... what if they take you? What if they put you to the Question? I cannot bear to think of you being tortured in Vincennes.'

'Greed still perpetuates. The hope of transmuting lead into gold still flourishes, so I do not think they would cast me into the flames before discovering more about my skills. Perhaps I would show them a little fool's gold. No, my dear, it took years to convert the old coach house into a laboratory, and took most of my savings. I cannot leave it, especially now when I am on the verge.'

'Your life is more important.'

'I am on a path to relieve pain and suffering. I cannot halt such work. I promise,' he added more gently as she began to cry, 'that I shall leave at the first hint of danger.'

'Then you will come to Du Chesne, and meantime pay Agnès to bring meals across for you?'

'Enough, enough. I shall not encourage her or anyone else to disturb me. And yes, I shall either be here or with you, but not in Vincennes or the Bastille ... on my word.'

Hermione had no great faith in what he said, for he was quite hopeless in ordinary matters. She made one last attempt.

'You promised always to look after me.'

'I did. Would it make your mind easier if I showed you how I shall evade prison?' She nodded, her eyes brightening with curiosity as he motioned her to follow him towards the storeroom where he kept his precious items.

'In such an emergency, it would be best to shut the door,' he advised in an amused tone, 'but, as you are not some lieutenant-général of police, there is no need for such niceties.' His stained and blistered fingers groped beneath the first shelf, and suddenly there sounded a click and a whirring of mechanism and then the shelves swung away inward into darkness. The narrow gap was just wide enough to pass through. Filled with excited curiosity, Hermione followed Olivier. Once on the other side, he pressed a catch set into the stone wall and the shelves immediately swung back, leaving them in utter darkness.

'I should have brought a light ... what do you think?'

'It is marvellous,' breathed Hermione, experiencing a huge sense of relief. 'At least you have a chance of escape. But where does it lead to?'

'From the angle the passage takes, I believe to the cabinet-makers on the next street. It might once have served Huguenots years ago, during the religious troubles.'

'Then you are not certain you can get out?'

'I found an identical mechanism at the other end but hesitated to operate it because I heard the murmur of voices through the wall.'

'And you never returned?'

'There seemed no need ... it is a filthy passage.'

'But how did you find out about it?' she asked as Olivier led the way back into the laboratory.

'I had dropped spatulas, and as I leaned to pick them up, I felt a current of cold air ... I was curious.'

'It makes me feel much easier on your account.'

'So you will leave the day after tomorrow?'

'Guillaume needs to look at the Chevalier's coach to see if it needs any repair.'

'Make sure to bar your bedchamber door when you stop overnight at a *relais*, and make certain any chest or cupboard does not have a false bottom to let in a thief. In small towns be prepared for hold-ups. Sometimes there are no horses in the morning because they have been taken away to work in the fields, as has happened to me on my travels.'

Hermione nodded, wishing her guardian would always be so interested in her affairs.

'And when will you return?' The question, asked in such a matter-of-fact way, completely stunned Hermione. She realized her departure for him merely represented some tiresome disruption, whereas for her it was becoming more than a temporary withdrawal from danger. She was beginning to think of escaping to Du Chesne as a transition into another life.

'We are a family,' she replied, with no real answer to give, 'and whether here, or in Saintonge, that is what is important.'

'And for me to have the means to continue my experiments,' he added vigorously.

'And for you to be able to do your work,' responded Hermione with warmth.

'I shall go and speak to Guillaume this instant, and before you both depart, I have something that will protect your life.'

Guillaume's reaction to leaving Paris was quite different from that of Lucette: it seemed the offer of adventure. The only thing which put him out was that Olivier's pistol had been entrusted to Hermione. She felt the weight of it now in her skirt pocket as she and the big man hurried towards the Marais after calling in at a dealer in liveries.

'You look the part, Guillaume.' She smiled, giving him a glance of approval.

'As long as I can handle the horses, mademoiselle, you can depend on my sword arm for the rest. If we find ourselves hard-pressed, that pistol may come in handy, though best not to let that feather-brain near it or we'll find both our heads blown off.'

As soon as Lucette had recovered from laughing at Guillaume in his braided coachman's coat and tricorne hat, Hermione broke the news they had to get out of Paris the next day. After a look at the coach, Guillaume seemed satisfied that it was sound, and he set off to arrange for two horses. Not wishing Lucette to go out for fear she would sneak off to make goodbyes, Hermione went to buy food for the journey. Afterwards, she selected an outfit for a maid, and then, thinking of her own appearance, she went on to a dealer in ladies' clothes. By the time she arrived back, Guillaume had managed to hitch two horses to the coach.

'You've done well,' she approved. 'It's a pity there isn't more room for you to practise.'

'I'll soon show them I'm master,' beamed Guillaume, 'or they'll get a flick from this.'

'One flick of that whip will take the legs away from these nags,' shrieked Lucette from the window above. 'I hope, Mademoiselle Hermione, you have brought me something less worn than his; something a maid to a fine lady would wear!'

It was late by the time they got to bed, with Guillaume taking the room which the manservant Jean had occupied and Hermione sharing the Chevalier's bed with Lucette. After a restless night, they rose early and had something to eat, then Guillaume stomped away down to the courtyard, calling over his shoulder as he went: 'I hope that lazy piece will bestir herself, and not leave everything to me.'

'You keep your red nose out of household affairs,' yelled Lucette after him. 'That uniform has gone to your head.'

Hermione raised her eyes heavenward, wondering whether this was a sign of things to come betwixt the two of them. 'Best he should learn his place, mademoiselle,' added Lucette, as she adjusted her maid's bonnet. 'Do you know what he answered when I asked if he knew which way to go? He put his finger on his blind eye and said, "Don't fear getting lost with this to point the way." I'm glad our going is a secret. That old walnut of a coach would have all the apprentices hooting. Even the tanners would be shy of those old nags.'

Hermione half-listened as she put the rest of the second-hand clothes she had bought into an old trunk. Then she motioned Lucette to help her drag it to the top of the steps for Guillaume to load onto the coach. She returned to the room and took up the hat which went with the velvet travelling dress. For a moment, she contemplated the large brown creation with its cream ostrich feathers. Moving across to the mirror, she put it on. Would the Chevalier's servants acknowledge her as their châtelaine? The creamy feathers touched her right shoulder as though marking the boundary of two lives. Below them was the drab wool dress that marked her out as one of humble birth. Above was the sweep and curve of the milliner's art. It made her feel different; altered her expression.

'You need me to curl your hair, Madame Du Chesne!' To Hermione's surprise, Lucette's voice was free of sarcasm, and in some indefinable way, it established a sense of identity which Hermione had automatically felt the moment she had put on the hat. At that moment, seizing her attention, came sound of the bell in the courtyard below. Had Olivier changed his mind, or was it … panic swept over Hermione. She ran to the window and eased it open to hear what might pass below. Guillaume was shouting to whoever it was to be patient. For one awful moment, she anticipated the worst as he pulled back the gate. Then relief flooded over her, for it was not the archers but a solitary messenger. By the muddy state of horse and rider, it seemed they had travelled some great distance.

'I have a letter of introduction for Madame Du Chesne.'

'Madame is busy,' Hermione heard Guillaume respond unhelpfully.

'I only wish to leave my letter so that I might see Madame Du Chesne while I am in Paris. As you see, I am in no fit state to be received, and both my horse and I are in sore need of rest and food.'

'Well, she won't be here tomorrow,' said Guillaume, as he reached up and took the stranger's proffered parchment. 'She is going away and not likely to come back.'

'Then it is imperative you ask her to see me now. It is to Madame's advantage.'

'Wait here. There's water over there for the horse.'

Hermione withdrew from the window, her mind reeling with questions: would it be safe to see this man? Who was he, where could he have come from and why? She gestured to Lucette, who had also been drawn to the window, to help her exchange her woollen dress for the velvet travelling dress. Afterwards, she kicked off her sabots and thrust her feet into the newly acquired leather shoes.

'Tell Guillaume not to say a word about where we are going. Remember we live here, so when you show the man in, act as if visitors are usual.' With a nod, Lucette went away, and moments later she re-entered with the traveller. Both his clothes and his boots were in a fearful state, but evidently he had made an effort to wash the mud from his face. He was of average height, and his features were undistinguished except for marks of the pox.

'Forgive my sorry state, Madame Du Chesne, but it is vital that I should see you before you depart Paris, as your manservant says you are soon to do. I bear a letter from my master, Claude Tilly. He requests me to pass on his condolences to you on the death of the Chevalier Du Chesne. I beg you to read his letter now so that I may return with your answer to Rochefort.' The mention of the town brought an immediate sense of relief, for obviously this man had nothing to do with the police. However, as he withdrew a leather pouch, Hermione was seized with acute embarrassment, for she could not read. Neither could Lucette or Guillaume.

'Thank you,' she said, taking the letter over to the window as if requiring more light. 'Your master lives in Rochefort?' she went on, making a slow thing of breaking the wax seal so as to give herself more time to extract as much information as she could from him, whilst wondering how she might get it over to Olivier to read.

'My master is one of the most important entrepreneurs in Rochefort, as well as in Saintes.'

54

'Did the Chevalier have dealings with him then?' asked Hermione, unfolding the parchment slowly.

'I do not believe so,' rejoined the stranger. 'But his brother-in-law, a lawyer who lives in Saintes, took care of the servants' wages. That is how Monsieur Tilly knew how to contact you.' Hermione stared at the rows of black ink and was encouraged to spot the large D and the large C which the Chevalier had taught her stood for Du Chesne. At least she now knew she was holding the parchment the right way up, not that that really helped. The man shifted his weight from foot to foot with a degree of weary impatience.

'Indeed,' murmured Hermione, as if deep in thought. She bit her lip with vexation and was unable to repress a sigh at the ridiculous situation she found herself in. Inwardly, she vowed to lose no time in learning her letters.

'Do you not think it a fair offer for the property, Madame Du Chesne?'

Ah, now we have the sense of it, thought Hermione with relief.

'I have no real experience in business affairs, monsieur. I will need to consult with my lawyer.'

'No one would offer more money!'

'Do you have authority to speak for your master in this matter?'

'I do, madame. And I have with me, on my person, a pledge that there would be no delay in payment.'

'You have money with you?' repeated Hermione with astonishment, for she had heard the roads were infested with robbers. She looked again at the writing, which apart from the odd letter here and there held no meaning for her.

'So, Monsieur Tilly wishes to buy the château,' she said with slow deliberation, to make absolutely certain she had the gist of things. 'But as you see,' she continued, as the man nodded, 'I am leaving Paris for Du Chesne today.'

'Your journey is to Saintonge!' exclaimed the man. 'You intend to take up residence?' Hermione regarded his shocked expression with mild curiosity. 'Surely, madame, you are dissuaded after reading monsieur's letter! Let me express, even more strongly than he has written, that the château is in a perilous state of disrepair. You are a Parisienne; used to the excitement of the city. At such a young age would you really wish to bury yourself away in a small hamlet? To leave friends for a house that has near fallen down?'

'If that be so, why should your master be so anxious to possess it?' Hermione's question brought immediate silence. The man seemed to have no answer, and as if deciding on some other course, he reached into the pouch and lifted out a heavy bag. Then he walked across to the table and, opening the leather thongs securing the bag, emptied out its contents. The pile of *louis d'or* glinted, and Hermione gasped. It was the largest amount of money she had ever seen in her entire life. It seemed incredible that anyone could be so foolhardy as to travel with so much money.

'Monsieur, I cannot believe you would take such a risk; the robbers along the way!'

Monsieur Tilly's messenger lifted the folds of his cloak and revealed two pistols in his waistband and the heavy hilt of a sword.

'They would have to get past these. This is a measure of Monsieur Tilly's intent. If you agree to his offer, the outstanding amount will be paid within the quarter.'

There was still the need to know exactly what the whole amount was. Even so, with such wealth in front of her, Hermione stared as if hypnotized at the gold cascade. Then she raised her eyes from the precious coins and her gaze went to the alcove before which the curtains were now drawn against the Chevalier's bed. She recalled how happy he had been when she had practised with charcoal to make the letters D and C. It was his wish for her to go to his boyhood home. Deep within, she felt drawn to go there, for something had brought them together that was still unexplained, some deep chord within him that Hermione had revived, so much so that he had wanted her to have Du Chesne. Outside the room, Lucette broke into song, and her voice also reminded Hermione why they were leaving in such haste: their will to survive. She gave a dismissive gesture toward the coins.

'Monsieur Tilly is most generous, but my plans are made.'

'I am authorized to increase the price.'

'It is useless, monsieur,' responded Hermione, picking up the brown gauntlet gloves symbolizing the journey ahead. 'My mind is quite made up. Tell your master, the château of Du Chesne is not for sale!'

CHAPTER 3

ucette's piercing screams added to the terror as the coach began to topple over. Hermione prepared for the worst, but just when it seemed they must crash, somehow the old coach righted itself and settled with a shuddering thump back on its wheels. Hermione dragged herself up from the floor and thrust her head out of the window. They were stuck in some great hole, the muddy waters of which were slopping between the spokes of the wheel and right up to the hub.

'You've driven us into a ditch!' she roared, losing her temper.

''Tis the road!' thundered back Guillaume, breaking off from calming the horses. Hermione glanced back the way they had come – oozing mire as far as the eye could see, but not this duck pond!

'He will kill us before we get there,' shrieked Lucette who, likewise, had been hurled off her seat. Hermione withdrew from the window and flopped back against the torn yellow brocade. She closed her eyes with a resigned expression.

'I need someone to help,' came Guillaume's plaintive cry. For the umpteenth time that day, Hermione pushed back the sodden sleeves of her dress and clambered out of the coach into the water below.

'*Mon Dieu*, it's cold,' she gasped, catching her breath as icy water surged up around her thighs.

'He's too drunk to see, that's his trouble!' shrilled Lucette, following on. 'If we don't catch our deaths, this fool will break our necks for sure.

Why did we ever leave Paris?'

'Give over nagging, woman,' retorted Guillaume, a sloppy grin on his sweating face as he splashed into view. 'As I keep telling the mistress, we're nearly upon the sea. Those aren't crows aloft, they be sea birds. Taste the salt in the air.' Hermione glanced up at the noisy flock of grey and white birds and ran the tip of her tongue along her lips; they were gritty with salt. Within, she felt a quickening of excitement: what would the sea look like? Much the same as the Seine, she supposed, but without banks. And it was endless, carrying ships all around the world. According to the lawyer's instructions, when they departed La Rochelle on the morrow, the road to Du Chesne lay south, past the newly built town of Rochefort. Galvanized into action by the thought of arrival, Hermione dragged herself towards the back of the coach. No easy task as her skirt, billowing out behind on top of the water, quickly became like some great weight as she pulled it after her. At last, scooping up the sodden velvet over one arm, she waded into position behind the wheels. What had that dealer in dresses said as they haggled over price: 'worn by a lady close to the King!'

'Here I am, then,' she murmured, 'a châtelaine in velvet, and ready to push her coach out of the mire!' Suddenly the trials of the day evaporated, and she dissolved into helpless laughter.

'Zut!' Am I the only sober one here?' declared Lucette, taking up her position across from Hermione. Together they prepared for the strain to come.

'Are you and the horses ready, Guillaume?' shouted Hermione.

'Yes!'

'Then let's go. On the count, my friends: one, two, three!'

'Get on with you! *Allez, allez,*' roared Guiilaume. There was a slight rocking motion forward, but beneath the water the wheels were stuck fast in the mud. Again, Hermione shouted the count, and once again Guillaume roared at the horses and used his whip. It was back-breaking work pushing and savage on the hands. After another all-out thrust, the wheels lurched forward as the horses moved off. It had been hoped for, anticipated, yet, caught off balance, both women were flung face-forward into slimy filth. The shock knocked the breath out of Hermione and, blind and deaf to everything, she struggled to raise her shoulders out of the muddy water.

'Keep going, don't stop!' she spluttered, desperate to keep the horses moving as she tried to regain her footing. Through slitted eyes, she glimpsed the coach lurching sideways, then it jerked forward up out of the mire.

'May I help your ladyship to her seat?' Lucette's tone was heavy with mockery. Hermione turned on her a sharp look and found her unrecognizable. A swift downward glance revealed that she too was covered with a thick brown slime. It had seemed so important to arrive looking decent, not to let André Du Chesne down. The travelling dress was the best she had, and it was ruined. Despair and weariness sought to bring Hermione back down to her knees, but the coach was already gathering speed, causing her and Lucette to lift up their skirts and chase after it.

Despite the vicissitudes suffered during the days of travelling, petty irritations like Lucette's constant fiddling with her hair and the unbelievably loud belching and farting of Guillaume aloft, their arrival at La Rochelle changed the mood to one of ecstatic euphoria.

'So many fine young men,' cooed Lucette, laughing happily. Hermione wrinkled her nose at the pungent smells as the coach rumbled into the harbour. There was so much to look at: a confusion of rigging, spars and yardarms, lobster pots and coils of rope, ships of all sizes, men pushing barrels up gangplanks, small boats plying back and forth between the larger ships at anchor. Hermione leaned out of the window, her spellbound eyes following the screeching gulls as they hovered over the high stone towers which protected the harbour. Nearby, a ship was disembarking passengers, and there was a great press of people and coaches.

'Are we able to turn round?' she called up to Guillaume.

'I can't ... there are wagons behind. We would have been best entering at another gate.' Hermione sank back in her seat, content to enjoy the scene. Little by little, they gained ground in the *mêlée*, till they were eventually brought abreast of the ship setting off its passengers. She wondered where the man moving swiftly down the gangplank had been to be carrying, in May, a fur-trimmed cloak. He had about him an air of great vitality and dash. The jostle of people greeting and awaiting friends again claimed her attention; in particular, there was an elderly man with a mass of snow-white hair who was pushing his way forward towards the gangplank. Tagging along after him and pausing now and again as if to apologize to those who had been pushed aside by the older man was a dark-haired youth of about fourteen. As the man carrying the cloak stepped onto the quay, his arm immediately went about the elderly man's shoulders in an exuberant expression of delight and affection. Then it was the young boy's turn to be embraced. There was something so spontaneous and intimate about the relationship between the three of them that Hermione had to look away, filled with a sense of envy. She had never known such closeness to anyone. It somehow made her want to lash out, but she couldn't understand why, or at whom. Instead, she vented her frustration on Guillaume.

'I realize we are not in Paris,' she called, thrusting her shoulders out of the coach, 'but do we have to move like country snails?'

Heads turned at the impatient tone. With those about him, Jacques Maurellet took in the filthy creature adopting regal airs in an old-style coach.

'Look what the sea's thrown up,' jeered a man in the crowd.

'It's a worm, not a fish!'

'No, it's a princess from Paris!' a fishwife shrieked. 'You tell him your ladyship. You and those fine nags should be shown more respect!'

Beneath their muddy covering, Hermione's cheeks flamed scarlet as catcalls and hoots of laughter came her way. She ducked back, snapping forward the leather curtain to shut out the smirking faces. Lucette, of course, was giggling, which put Hermione into a further state of fury against herself for behaving like a complete fool. When, at last, she recovered composure and judged, as the coach moved on, that interest in her had passed, she drew back the curtain, only to find that standing right outside was the trio who had caught her interest before. It appeared they were also waiting to enter the city. Their smiles towards her were kindly, so trying to forget the state of her face and clothes, Hermione inclined her head in acknowledgement and smiled back, whereupon the man with the fur-trimmed cloak swept off his ostrich-plumed hat in polite salutation. It was quite obvious, though that he was doing his utmost not to laugh, for his dark blue eyes were sparkling with merriment as he straightened from his bow. Then, to her relief, the three men were lost from view as her coach moved on.

Jacques Maurellet gazed with mild curiosity after the battered coach as it rumbled over the cobbles into the city. Then his amused smile widened to one of joy as he turned towards his brother André and his grandfather Henri. It was good to be back!

'Come,' he said, 'let us waste no more time, for I haven't eaten a good meal since leaving France!'

Fellow travellers had held there was no shortage of hostelries in La Rochelle, and so indeed it proved. Whilst the horses were being looked to, a porter carried Hermione's trunk up to a room whose tiny window looked out onto rooftops.

'That's good,' said Lucette, with a gesture towards two small trestle beds. 'It couldn't be smaller, but at least we don't have to share with strangers.'

A brisk knock on the chamber door announced a serving woman, who bustled in with a pitcher of water which she carried over to a basin on the dresser.

'Pardon, madame,' ventured Hermione, as the servant turned to leave, 'but would you dry out our clothes?'

'Yes, lady,' the woman said nodding. 'The roads have been bad with all the rain, but today has brought good weather. Where are you from?'

'Paris.'

'You will have seen the King, then?'

'Oh yes,' put in Lucette beginning to unbutton Hermione's dress, 'and Madame Montespan, and before her La Vallière.'

Liberated of her outer clothing and barely aware of the chatter, Hermione enjoyed the relief of rinsing away the dried mud from her face and fingers.

'We've a good fire for drying,' sang out the serving woman, coming over to pick up the velvet dress. 'Help your mistress into her clean linen, young woman, then bring her wet shift and your own skirt down to me. You can then tell me more about Paris.'

It was unnecessary and dangerous to wash often, but Hermione found the clean shift and the brushing out of her hair was reviving. After Lucette had also cleaned herself up, they went downstairs to eat.

'There is space by the fire, Mademoiselle Hermione,' whispered Lucette. 'It will warm us, for that muddy water has struck right through to the bone.'

'While you order spiced wine, I'll see how Guillaume fares.'

Outside in the yard, Hermione found the big man happily seated with other coachmen around a trestle table.

'Will you order your own meal?' she asked.

'I'll be happy to do that, Mademoiselle Hermione. We'll have good horses for tomorrow, so don't you be worried. A guide will put us on the right road.'

Hermione nodded appreciatively, for, just as Olivier had warned, there was often no guide to be had, and they had frequently lost their way, especially where the road had been washed away by rain or overgrown by some houseowner's orchard. On one occasion, the track they were following had finally petered out, and they had been totally surrounded by forest. Guillaume had taken the precaution of laying his sword across his lap to show that he would put up a stiff fight. Hermione had sat alongside him with a loaded pistol – not that she had ever fired a weapon before, but she had in mind Olivier's parting advice after he had explained its mechanism: 'Use it if you have to.' But, what with the coach being so old and Guillaume so big, they had not met with any trouble. They had also taken care at night to examine every cupboard and chest for false bottoms and the possibility of intruders. She wondered how Olivier was faring. Perhaps it would have been wiser for him to have kept the pistol.

The spiced wine was waiting when she re-joined Lucette, and together with the warmth from the fire, the blood soon flowed back into their toes.

'We shall have a feast!' Hermione laughed, following her maid's nod towards the huge bowls of steaming *moules* on the next table and the wench approaching with their own serving.

Some time later, after the discarded shells had been cleared away and huge helpings of *tarte à la crème* had been enjoyed, Hermione roused herself. It was tempting to remain snoozing with half an ear on the conversations going on all around, but tomorrow would be an early start, so she gave Lucette's shoulder a gentle shake to rouse her.

'Let us go and look at the Hôtel de Ville. The innkeeper says it is very fine.'

Lucette's mouth opened into an enormous yawn. 'There's nothing fine outside Paris. Besides, it is more interesting here, Mademoiselle Hermione,' she pouted, her sideways glance directed at a group of young men who had just burst into song.

'Even more reason to come,' scolded Hermione, pulling the young woman to her feet. 'If you stay here, you're sure to get into mischief.'

Even by Paris standards, the Hôtel de Ville was noble. The rays of the setting sun gave a pinkish glow to the cream castellated walls and the carving of the city's emblem set over its gate.

'It's a good likeness of a ship, Mademoiselle Hermione,' commented Lucette, pointing up to the stone carving surmounted by three *fleurs de lys*. 'And see him up there, looking down at us as if he were alive! He's a fine figure of a man! Who can he be?'

'Monsieur,' called out Hermione, thinking to find the answer from a passer-by, 'pardon my asking, but which nobleman might that be?'

'Why, Henri de Navarre, of course – King Henri IV,' exclaimed the man, going on his way with a despairing shake of his head.

'Ah yes, King Henri.' Hermione nodded, studying the statue more closely. 'I think he was a Huguenot before he became king. Guillaume said this was a Huguenot stronghold, right up until they rebelled against paying their taxes. Then the royal army laid siege and Cardinal Richelieu blockaded the harbour to cut them off from English help. So they were starved into being loyal to France. You can see *he* is a Huguenot,' she added, looking after the soberly dressed man who had answered her question.

'Their clothes are like the old times,' mocked Lucette, pointing out women whose dresses hung straight about their ankles without any flounce of petticoats. Beneath the porches of the rue des Gentilhommes they came upon another carving of the town's arms, which this time featured a tiny sailor climbing the rigging of the ship. It seemed, as they wandered, that every other person they passed was of the Reformed Church.

'They are everywhere,' hissed Lucette. 'Not a pretty ribbon in sight. But I'll count on not finding any down there – too much laughter!'

Hermione paused, also attracted by the merry din. With a conspiratorial exchange of smiles, they turned into the narrow cobbled street and, midway down it, found themselves before a hostelry. Through its open casements the room within was packed with parties of men eating at tables, while others smoking pipes were drinking and playing cards. The din was deafening as people shouted for attention, and huddled groups suddenly threw themselves backwards in laughter at jokes or gossip. After passing the door, which was closed, they came before the next window. A serving wench, whose bodice did little to hide her full breasts, was setting down a foaming flagon on a table. It seemed she must have made some quip against one of the drinkers, for there was a loud explosion of laughter. Then, as she turned to go with a swivel of her wide hips, one of the men swept her onto his knee and kissed her lips.

'Oh, I'd like to change places with her!' declared Lucette enthusiastically. 'I'd kiss him right back if it were me.'

As Jacques Maurellet playfully pinched Antoinette's plump cheeks, his eye caught a movement from outside. Between the open shutters were two women whose attention appeared to be directed at him. His glance moved quickly from the beaming servant to her mistress. Beneath the curve of a brown hat was an oval face framed by jet-black hair. It was an intriguing face, yet the expression in the beautiful eyes was of such disapproval that Jacques's lips spread into a laughing smile of amusement. Reaching out, he pulled Antoinette towards him again and gave her a lingering kiss. Then, with a rakish smile, he threw a challenging look back at the open casement, but to no avail. The two women had moved on.

Since such scenes were commonplace in Paris, Hermione was surprised by her reaction. It came as no surprise to find the young man with the fur-trimmed cloak behaving that way, so why did she feel so irritated?

'That man's confession must take hours,' giggled Lucette, with a wistful backward glance.

'He certainly is not of the Reformed Church,' commented Hermione dryly.

Morning found the day without sun, but, they were thankful to see it dry. In good spirits and with a few tasty things to eat along the road, they set off south in the direction of Rochefort. Coming towards them was a steady stream of travellers: carters, pedlars, women with baskets of eggs, waddling geese, wagons loaded with vegetables and cages filled with twittering birds. There were boys driving pigs and a man with dead rabbits swinging from lines on a pole. All were going to sell their goods at the busy seaport. Many hours later, when the sun was starting its downward journey to the west, they made what would be their last overnight stop. Up bright and early the next day, they found themselves in company with a straggly column of peasants taking the same direction until the turn off to Rochefort. Thereafter, the road was clear of geese and cattle heading for the naval town, and Guillaume was able to increase their speed a little. He was in good voice, and though every so often Lucette put her fingers in her ears and pulled a face, he entertained them as the countryside rolled by until, quite unexpectedly, the coach came to a sudden halt and it creaked and swayed as their driver's great weight shifted down from it.

'What's happening?'

'He's speaking to an old dame at the roadside,' reported Lucette, who had the view on her side. 'It looks as if she has collapsed, and it looks as if he is offering her a ride, if you please! He ought first to ask you, Madame Du Chesne,' she added indignantly. 'And before he asks me to help lift her up, I'll be about my own needs.' With that, Lucette leapt out of the coach and ran off towards a bush. Hermione sank back against the upholstery, pleased that Lucette had remembered to address her correctly as Madame du Chesne. It was difficult for her and Guillaume to think of her as anything other than Mademoiselle Hermione, but soon they would join the servants at Du Chesne and things would alter. She nibbled on one of the biscuits bought at La Rochelle and wondered what Rochefort was like. No doubt some of those geese being walked towards it would be in a pot by tonight. She remembered that the man who wanted to buy Du Chesne lived there. What a long way Monsieur Tilly's messenger had travelled to make his offer to her in Paris. Having now experienced the journey herself, she felt she might have been more hospitable towards him.

Lucette returned to her seat and from aloft came the chatter of voices and the cackling laughter of an old woman's voice. The low fiery rays of the sun flooded the coach with reddish light, and, occupied by thoughts and expectations of what was to come, Hermione closed her eyes. Somewhere along the way, they had dropped off their passenger and Lucette took her place up aloft beside Guillaume. Then Hermione fell asleep again until a loud shout awoke her.

'There is smoke coming from chimneys! This must be the village of Du Chesne,' Lucette called.

'Here's the church, just as our good dame said,' boomed out Guillaume. 'And see, here is the priest coming out to greet you.'

Glad of Guillaume's help, having been shaken and rattled about for most of the day, Hermione stepped unsteadily out of the coach.

'*Bonsoir*, Curé. Is the chateau of Du Chesne close by?'

The priest's expression became speculative on hearing her Parisian accent. '*Bonsoir*, madame. I am Father Grégoire. The château is but half a league at most. However, it is no longer occupied, except by elderly servants. The Chevalier Du Chesne died a little while ago at his home in Paris.'

'I am his heir, Hermione Du Chesne.'

'*Mais oui*! The notary in Saintes, who ran things for him, mentioned the Chevalier had adopted a daughter.' The cleric's smiling gaze was now sharp with interest. 'What a delightful surprise, for it seemed not likely that you, madame, would take possession of Du Chesne.' Hermione waited expectantly, but with a knowing smile the priest did not enlarge further. 'You will find Pierre Paultre and his wife Marie a kindly old couple, but perhaps a little ... er ... shy of strangers. If there is anything you need, my housekeeper will oblige. I shall look forward to receiving you for Mass – the chapel at the manoir was destroyed.'

Hermione's desire above all else now was to set eyes upon her inheritance. So, though there was much she needed and wanted to ask, she did not attempt to delay the curé as he nodded his farewell.

In the gathering gloom, Guillaume asked the horses for one last effort and, fortunately, the last stretch of the journey proved to be downhill. Suddenly, there came from Guillaume a great whoop of laughter.

'They're expecting you, madame!'

'Quite a crowd!' shrieked Lucette.

Hermione hurriedly put on her hat to be ready to nod and smile as the coach lurched at speed between high metal gates. Suddenly, all without the coach seemed to be chaos: goats bleated and hens squawked, with one actually flying in through the window to escape death.

'*Mon Dieu*, you madman,' yelled Hermione. 'You will kill us yet.' Through the window she glimpsed a boy racing after his fleeing goats, while those nearest to the coach tried to scramble over their companions' backs to get away from hooves and wheels. Above their frantic din, Guillaume's loud guffaws gave way to song as he cracked his whip to urge the two exhausted horses onward. In a fury, Hermione promised herself all manner of retribution against the two of them; it was always a mistake to allow Lucette to sit alongside him. Now the coach was passing under trees hanging so low that Hermione could hear their branches tearing along the leather roof. No longer laughing his head off, Guillaume's curses mingled with Lucette's screams. Then the tearing and ripping stopped as they passed through a stone archway. She opened her mouth to shout to Guillaume to stop, but he had seen, before her side view permitted it, what lay ahead, and was already reining the horses to a halt.

Hermione almost crawled out of the coach, so battered and stiff were her limbs. In the gathering dusk, the whole of her attention was seized by the dark outline of the château of Du Chesne. It was beyond anything she could have expected: towers, whose tops looked like witches' hats rose black against the violet sky. It was a fortress.

'Oh, let us go back!' whimpered Lucette.

CHAPTER 4

he harsh screech of a gull stirred Jacques Maurellet into wakefulness. His black lashes opened and his gaze took in the unfamiliar arrangement of the room. He wondered why Annette had taken it into her head to move his bed away from the window and replace it with the dresser. She had never moved furniture before and he didn't care for change. Even so, after months of hard travelling by land and sea, to have passed the night on a mattress free of spiteful fleas had been sheer bliss! Casting aside the blanket, he padded across to the casement window and flung it wide. A stiff breeze borne along the Charente from the Atlantic blew back his hair, exposing a scar collected in a boyhood fight. Jacques leaned out further to give himself a full view of the shipyard and noted with satisfaction a merchantman nearing completion. Its sturdy lines would shortly take it trading across the Atlantic for furs or sugar, perhaps to the East for spices. Would their yard ever build another class of ship; a man o' war for the king's Marine? If ever contracts were offered to private yards, he'd make certain they won one, and if that meant …

From below sounded the slam of a door. No doubt it was Perrette arriving to help Annette with breakfast. It had become one of those things his cousin insisted on doing since the death of his father and uncle. Not that Annette had asked for help. Indeed, it was plain the elderly housekeeper did not care for her kitchen being taken over. There had been tensions before he had left; on several occasions, he had expected Annette to lose all patience. It wasn't as if Perrette had nothing to do. There was her mother to care for, but she saw herself as mistress over here. The implication made him frown, so he thrust it out of his thoughts and considered the day ahead.

There would be much to catch up with at the shipyard, but he must first report to the Intendant, after which, hopefully, there would be an end of special missions for the Marine. They had certainly added an extra spice to life, and contact with men of influence had given him a glimpse of the workings of state, but now he wanted to concentrate on building ships. His skill in assessing timber had marked him out, and other, more sensitive duties for the government had followed. These missions would not have mattered so much had his father and uncle been alive, but for his grandfather, the running of the yard was hard, even though their workforce was large and experienced.

From below came Perrette's call to breakfast. Jacques's lips twisted into a rueful smile. For the moment, he must co-operate on other fronts —except, that is, for the moving of his bed.

The smell of bread and the sight of a flitch of bacon hanging from a wood beam made him smile as he entered the kitchen. The housekeeper was nowhere to be seen.

'What is this?' he said, stretching out his hands towards Perrette. 'You are left to prepare my homecoming feast all on your own? Is Annette not well?'

'I told her to have a morning in bed; she looked tired, for she cleaned and polished over here yesterday,' said Perrette, her heart-shaped face beaming with happiness.

'Over here?'

'Yes. She lives under Mother's roof now.' A faint blush had come to his cousin's cheeks as his eyes widened in surprise, but she gave him a pert look as if it were all quite natural. 'Maman and she are of the same age,' she rushed on, 'and she can still come here to clean.'

'Is Annette happy with the arrangement?' he asked uneasily.

'She'll get used to it. But she was so against my improving things here!'

'Like my bedroom.'

'Oh, don't you like it that way?' The question was asked in such a plaintive voice that Jacques's resolve crumbled

'I expect, like Annette, I'll get used to it,' he said, not wishing to hurt her feelings. 'But was Grandfather willing for her to go? She has been seeing to us here for most of her life.'

'He has been so busy, I think he hardly noticed,' replied Perrette, cracking eggs into a bowl. 'And Maman feels less lonely, isn't that so, Grandfather?' she added, as Henri Maurellet entered the room.

'How is your head?' Jacques asked, with a conspiratorial grin.

'Heavy – but not as bad as my bones! There was a time when I could sit on a saddle all day and every day.'

'You shipwrights become soft,' teased Jacques, as Perrette brought bread to the table.

'Still, it was good to stay on at La Rochelle – always useful to remind people we're still building ships.'

'The men will be glad to have you back,' commented Perrette, passing him butter. 'Though from your best coat and breeches, I suppose they are not to see you much today. They will be disappointed, as we all shall, on your first day back!' His cousin's tone was sharp, and despite his good humour, Jacques experienced a flash of irritation.

'When the Intendant expects my report it is not wise to disappoint,' he commented drily.

'So you will disappoint your betrothed instead, who has prayed every day for your safety,' responded Perrette, setting down a platter of ham.

'I fear, petite-fille,' cut in Henri swiftly, his tone jovial, 'you and I are far down the ladder when it comes to a relative of the Contrôleur Général.'

'But I did not think to bring that gentleman back a present.' Jacques laughed, his good humour returning. 'Whereas upstairs in my bag I have something of Riga's finest for you, Perrette, nor have I forgotten Aunt Marguerite or Annette.'

The tremulous note of a single bird announced the stirring of a new day. It was joined by another and another until the joyful clamour was so noisy it seemed impossible that anything could sleep. Yet Guillaume slept on. Hermione shivered and pulled her cloak closer about her as she looked at his huge frame sprawled across the seat opposite. He was still snoring but the sounds were soft, unlike the noise in the hours of darkness when they had put Hermione in mind of someone sawing wood. So unbearable had it been that she and Lucette had come near to hitting him. The cold had been intense; even so it had taken much persuasion to get him to take shelter in the coach, for while he was not above saucy raillery, at heart Guillaume was a shy man who was used to working only with Olivier. She moved upwards into a sitting position, and in doing so stirred Lucette into wakefulness.

'Are we going back to Paris?'

'No, of course not,' answered Hermione, responding to her unhappy expression with a bright, cheerful smile. 'You'll see; things will be much better in the daylight. We'll be warm and comfortable once we're inside.'

'They must have heard the bell. Why didn't they let us in?'

'It was dark, and I do not suppose they have people calling very often.'

Hermione opened the door and stepped down from the coach to take in their surroundings. When they arrived, Du Chesne's towers had been black silhouettes against a dark sky. With the rosy rays of the sun touching the cream stone, the building seemed friendlier.

'It's falling down,' mumbled Lucette, who had come to stand beside her. 'Over there it looks as if it has been struck by lightning. That's a sign we should turn back! And them over there, they don't look very friendly.'

Hermione turned around and saw a huddle of men and women standing beneath the stone archway which the coach had passed under the night before.

'Go and ask those peasants how we get in!' called Lucette as Guillaume's burly frame stumbled out of the coach. Hermione quickly averted her eyes as he bent and loudly cleared out his nostrils, then stomped away. The group of peasants watched his approach in silence, but then, as his hands moved upwards, no doubt to adjust his black eye-patch, the watchers hurriedly withdrew from sight. Not being put off, Guillaume carried on and disappeared under the stone archway. After a short time he came back, shaking his great shaggy head.

'You would think I was the Devil! They bolted the doors of their shacks and all I got for an answer was a baby screaming.'

Hermione walked across the bridge which led over the small river to the gate of the keep. At one side, fixed into the stonework was a rusted bell pull. And just as Guillaume had done on arrival the previous night, she tugged on it to bring attention to their plight. Guillaume, who had finished harnessing the horses to the coach, joined her.

'Either they are deaf or there is no one there,' he said, moving towards the gate.

'The curé said the servants were here,' said Hermione, giving another tug. She sighed as Guillaume leaned his great weight against the latch.

'Well, aren't I the fool!' he exclaimed with a note of surprise. 'It isn't locked!'

'Not locked?' Hermione repeated in disbelief. 'You mean to say it was open all the time?'

'I thought it was locked last night, but it just needed coaxing – the wood is swollen and catching on the stones.' After another shove, with a cracking and groaning, the gate suddenly moved inward. Leaving Guillaume to push it right back to the stone wall, Hermione walked forward towards an inner courtyard. At the far end of the courtyard was an archway flanked by horse troughs, which presumably led to stables. To the right was a well, and behind it what must have been a wing of the château, though now it was little more than a burnt-out shell. Hermione stared at the blackened timbers, filled with dismay. Across the courtyard to her left was that part of the building which had escaped damage. It was of such consequence she could hardly believe it could belong to her; even Olivier would be impressed.

The rumble of wheels from behind announced the arrival of Guillaume with the coach, and Lucette joined her. All save one of the château's shutters were fastened, and though she could not be certain, Hermione thought she glimpsed through its opening a movement within. At the main door another rusty bell-pull produced the distinct clang of a bell somewhere within the house. Had liveried footmen once attended upon visitors, Hermione wondered as Lucette sneezed and shivered beside her. The priest had spoken about an elderly couple, shy of strangers. Hermione gave the rusty handle another pull and pressed her ear to the door. There sounded the faintest shuffling of feet, shortly followed by the grind and slamming back of bolts. With a great groan and creaking the door swung inward, but only sufficiently for Hermione to glimpse the person within. He was a man of many years, with a rough blanket draped around his bony shoulders. Squashed low over rat-tailed grey hair was a ragged hunting cap, which trailed a broken dusty feather. The eyes which squinted out beneath the cap's pointed brim glared black at her with hostility.

'It's a woman,' the apparition growled, speaking to someone nearby. 'What do you want?'

'I am Madame Du Chesne.' The old man gawped at Hermione as if she were mad. 'I've come to live here – I am ...'

'Be off with you!' Before another word could be uttered, the door slammed shut.

'Well, really,' gasped Hermione. 'Open the door, monsieur – let me speak to you.'

There came no response, only the continued deep-throated bark of a dog. With a helpless gesture, Hermione turned to Lucette, whose answering expression was lacking in any sympathy and clearly said, *I told you so!* Filled with exasperation, Hermione again pulled the iron handle. 'Monsieur, madame,' she called, 'we have come a long way and need shelter. We mean you no harm.' Nothing happened, so eventually, feeling weary and deflated, she made her way over to where Guillaume had positioned the coach.'

'They won't open the door.'

'Why didn't those stupid peasants understand you are their mistress?' grumbled Lucette.

'Leave it to a one-eyed man,' growled Guillaume, stomping across the courtyard in his great leather boots. At his violent yank, the bell-pull submitted and fell with a clank to the ground, whereupon Guillaume resorted to his fist, making the timbers of the door shake.

'Open this door at once or it will be the worse for you!' he roared, pounding on the wood. For answer, a shutter above was flung open and down dropped a cascade of missiles. After a near hit from a broken stool, Guillaume became tangled up in an old curtain. Hermione found it hard not to laugh, but Lucette's reaction was very different. Her lips stretched upwards as she let fly ear-splitting screams of abuse, which had the small birds pecking about the courtyard immediately on the wing.

'Don't let them get away with that, Guillaume. They're up there, Mademoiselle Hermione,' she shrieked. 'Some old chap with a feather in his cap, and an old lady.' Guillaume had stepped out of the firing line, but his temper was up, and storming off in the direction of the coach, he returned with his axe.

'Now you're in for it,' he thundered, waving its metal head up at the open window.

'Do you think you ought?' asked Hermione, placing a restraining hand on his arm. 'It's a very bad start to things. Perhaps we should send for the curé.'

'It's your door!' chipped in Lucette. 'We could be out here again tonight if it's left to these turnips. They'll be setting the dog onto us next,' she added, as the deep-throated barking sounded alarmingly near.

Keeping hold of Guillaume's arm to restrain him, Hermione reached within for the names the curé had mentioned.

'Monsieur Paultre, you must open the door so that I can speak to you and Madame.' Nothing, only silence. After five minutes or so, Hermione nodded the go-ahead to Guillaume.

'You won't open up for your mistress, so I'm going to break the door in, and after that your miserable skulls!' With a great shout the powerful man let fly a massive blow against the centre of the door, which immediately provoked a furious din of barking within. Undeterred, Guillaume swung another great blow which sent splinters flying, causing Hermione and Lucette to fling up their hands to protect their eyes. Suddenly, from overhead, the wooden shutters were once again knocked outward. They looked up and instantly were engulfed in icy water. Spluttering and gasping with shock, Hermione tried to speak, but before she could collect her thoughts, a second icy attack was thrown down upon them.

'Go away, you devils!' quavered a high-pitched woman's voice.

'Madame,' Hermione managed to gasp, 'we have come to live here … live here!' she yelled, as two enormous wooden buckets came flying down. Mad with rage, Guillaume ran back to the door and again set his axe to work.

'Be off! We don't want you here,' screeched the old dame, shaking her fist as she leaned right out of the open casement.

'But André Du Chesne wished it so! See, I wear his ring.' Hermione thrust her hand upward and the effect on the elderly pair was dramatic; the man's ancient sword, which had been waving murder, became still. The defenders of Du Chesne stared down in mute silence, then drew back from sight. 'That's enough, Guillaume.'

'A few more blows.'

'It is enough. They're coming down.'

'And I for one will run them round in circles till they drop,' shivered Lucette. 'They near drowned me.'

From the other side of the splintered door came the sound of what seemed to be a barricade being removed, and then the old people appeared. Hermione stretched out her hand so that they might see the gold ring with its engraved initials and surrounding cluster of oak leaves.

'Monsieur, Madame Paultre, I am honoured to meet you.' They replied not a word, their eyes fixed, spellbound, on the ring. Hermione kept her hand outstretched. She realized that for them it meant far more than verifying her identity. The heavy, masculine ring was linked with their past, a time when they had served the Chevalier. 'The curé told me you have looked after the château for many years.' At the mention of the priest, Madame Paultre's wary expression softened, though friendliness had still no part of it. Both servants now seemed at a loss; there was no invitation to enter. If anything further was going to happen, Hermione could see it was she who would have to initiate it.

'My coachman will unload the trunks, monsieur, and then please show him where to feed and stable our horses.' Turning towards Madame Paultre, Hermione gave an encouraging smile. 'We would be grateful for a fire, as you see,' she murmured. 'My maid and I are very wet.'

It was impossible to gain any impression of the house, for the candle the elderly retainer carried shed little light. A dark corridor led eventually into an enormous kitchen, where, as the smoke from the chimney had promised, a fire was roaring. Hermione and Lucette rushed towards it, for the deluge of icy water after a night of cold misery had set their teeth all a-chatter. Gradually, as life returned to frozen fingers and feet, a steady drift of steam began to rise upwards off their wet clothes. Through this mist Hermione wistfully eyed a pot of porridge set on one side of the hearth. It was obvious for whom it was intended, but when the old lady took it up and motioned them to the table Hermione made no objection, only asked if her portion could be divided into two so that their coachman might have some also, to which the housekeeper muttered and shook her head.

'What did she say?' whispered Lucette. Hermione raised her eyebrows and gave a slight shrug, for it was difficult to understand the rough patois. She watched the old lady hobble over to a swinging larder suspended from the ceiling to guard against rats.

'I think she means Guillaume to eat with her and her husband,' she murmured as the woman took out eggs.

With the warmth, Hermione's spirits rose, for the huge spit suspended across the wide fireplace conjured up an image of venison and boar prepared for feasts. Would she ever have cause to celebrate? she wondered, as she rose to introduce herself to the rest of the château.'

*** *** ***

The bell summoning Rochefort's workforce to another day of toil at its royal arsenal had not long ceased when Jacques arrived at the Hôtel de Cheusse. To his surprise, after he had announced himself to an officer of the Marine, he was summoned almost instantly into the bureau of the Intendant. The air within was stale, heavy with the smell of burnt wax, and a swift glance at the spent candles suggested the official must have worked throughout the night.

'How was your trip?' he enquired, without bothering to raise his head from his writing. With a degree of sympathy for the official, Jacques set down his report on the only part of the desk which was not already covered with similar rolls of parchment. When it came to wielding an adze, or a sword, his hands were fast, but holding a quill … Another good reason to make no more excursions – no more of these wretched reports!

'The area, monseigneur, is in a continual state of flux,' he ventured, when eventually Honoré Lucas de Demuin took up his report and began to read. 'The port of Stettin, since the Swedes have taken over, is practically decimated; its merchants are desperate. Trade has totally collapsed.'

'Riga?'

'Fares much better, but as the Russians have control of the inland waterways, they can stop timber reaching its destination whenever they choose.' Jacques watched the lips of the official pout as he leafed through the pages with the speed of a gambler handling cards. 'It does not make good reading,' he added, to distance himself from what he had written.

'No, it is very bad,' murmured Demuin, with a dismissive gesture of displeasure. 'It confirms the view of the Minister of Marine and the Contrôleur Général that we should exert every effort to make France self-sufficient on as many fronts as possible. Ask yourself, Maurellet, what happens whenever war breaks out with the Dutch or the English, or both? They blockade our supplies, and we are forced to transport timber hundreds of miles overland. Land transport costs are exorbitant and they know it!

'With due respect, monseigneur,' ventured Jacques, alert to where the conversation was leading, 'our own timber cannot match the quality of the northern forests. Their firs are of immense height, and,' he persisted as the Intendant attempted to say something, 'this means they have fewer knot holes. The wood is extremely close-grained. I do not understand why this is so, but it is my feeling that it may have to do with the extreme cold of the climate.'

Demuin leaned back in his chair, his outrage at being spoken down by the young master-shipwright mollified by interest.

'Your observation is extraordinary! You believe the colder the climate the more finely grained is the wood?'

Jacques nodded. 'I believe so, monseigneur.'

'You interest me, monsieur, for that is what the Contrôleur Général believes makes the wool of English sheep superior to our own! The English keep their animals outside in the cold. The Contrôleur Général has ordered English rams be imported for breeding, for if we could supply wool of equal quality, our stocking manufacture could capture the market. So must it be for our Marine! Louis Froideur and other commissioners have done excellent work to implement Colbert's *ordonnances* on waters and forest management, but there is still much to be done. Perhaps we should send you off, monsieur, to the Auvergne or the Pyrénées to look at their firs.'

Jacques's lips set in a stubborn line, but then, as the official went back to reading his report, he relaxed. It seemed for the moment he had escaped the hostile peasants of the Pyrenées.

'Your writing is poor, Monsieur Maurellet,' murmured the Intendant, clicking his teeth with irritation, 'but your observations are valuable, especially those on how our exported wine is being kept. But we must leave that to another time. I have much to occupy me with the Minister's intention to visit in a couple of months. He even hints the King himself may come. I have alerted our master-shipwrights to provide a spectacle. On your way out, arrange with the clerk to bring your grandfather, Maître Maurellet, to see it.' With a wave of dismissal, the official took up his quill, and, uttering a sigh, returned to his mountain of paper.

As a consequence of his special duties, which had been first instigated by Demuin's predecessor, Charles Terron de Colbert, Jacques was at liberty to come and go in the royal shipyard as he pleased, so before going into the town, he took a stroll. Within minutes, he became caught up in the familiar swirl of urgent activity. Of particular interest were two slipways on which towered ships of the First and Second Rate under repair. And once these great warships had been made seaworthy, two merchantmen presently riding at anchor downstream would take their turn. There was a constant traffic of small boats plying back and forth carrying supplies and sailors out to them, and smart little gigs ferrying back their officers after shore leave. Jacques's attention moved away from the river to the impressive length of the *corderie royale*, and though he had seen it many times, he nevertheless gave a slight shake of the head in wonder at its spectacular design.

'The elegance of these rope-works never fails to please the eye,' he remarked to a clerk who had just finished checking a large consignment of hemp into a storehouse. The man returned Jacques's smile and half-turned to look towards the long stone building with its distinctive grey-tiled roof.

'They say it is the longest building in Europe; over twelve hundred feet by twenty-five. You need that length for rigging, of course. I cannot think the English have a ropewalk as beautiful.'

'At least our Marine has the sense to buy in stores of the first quality,' quipped Jacques. The clerk raised his sparse sandy eyebrows and took from his pocket a handful of hemp.

'What do you think of that, monsieur?'

Jacques took up some fibres and rubbed them between his fingers, then pulled a slight face. 'There's better to be had.'

The clerk nodded in agreement as they moved closer to Mansart's building.

'It's no longer permitted to buy from Piedmont and northern Europe. Our spinners are now supplied from the Auvergne, Orléans, Burgundy, Dauphine and Bretagne.' Jacques remained visibly unimpressed, and the clerk was about to say more when a loud shout claimed both their attention. On turning to see who was calling his name, Jacques gave back a pleased response.

'Forgive me, monsieur, my brother,' he murmured, and took his leave.

'Shouldn't you be at school?' he asked as André came bounding up like some puppy.

'We were brought ashore early this morning to see how they cast the iron cannon at the foundry. I spotted you a little while ago, so instead of joining the others for dinner, I thought you might oblige. We would need to go now though, as I have to be back on board this afternoon for dance instruction.'

'Dance?' echoed Jacques, taking hold of his brother's arm as he broke into laughter. 'You didn't say anything about dancing when you came to meet me at La Rochelle.'

'I am to be a gentleman, Jacques,' rejoined his brother, flushing. 'And it keeps us warm, for it is freezing out on the river. Tomorrow we are practising gunnery: how to bring down enemy rigging.'

'Untidy.'

'But very effective if a mast topples. When the Minister Seignelay visits the arsenal, he is to come aboard our school to see us at our studies, and the great Admiral Duquesne will be with him!' Jacques smiled as they side-stepped two sawyers carrying a plank. He lengthened his stride as they went through the gateway of the arsenal, hoping to reach the Golden Dolphin before it became crowded. 'We've been told,' chatted on his brother, 'that the master-shipwrights are planning a spectacle; a galley is to be built before spectators in record time. The master-shipwright at Marseille is the great expert, but he refused to talk about his methods until they threatened to throw him into prison!'

'I hope no one ever asks Grandfather about his methods,' Jacques chuckled as they entered the Golden Dolphin and took a table. 'Great-grandfather taught him the Maurellet way of doing things, Grandfather taught Father and Father taught me.'

'And you will hand it on to your son after you and Perrette wed.'

'It is the tradition for shipwrights,' Jacques heard himself respond as a waiter set down a carafe of Bordeaux. His brother's words had effected within him an immediate tightening, and a note of ... of what? With a dismissive gesture, he reached out for the wine to bring him back to the pleasure of the day.

'Hard to think Rochefort was but a small village fourteen years back,' he commented as he savoured the full-bodied grasp of the grape. 'There are all sorts here now, all hoping to make their way; skills in every trade.'

'And greybeards like Grandfather who hold on to their secrets and stifle progress,' chortled André.

'It has always been the way of things,' commented Jacques, surprised by his brother's lofty manner.

'Our teacher this morning explained how the set Tables of Dimensions will help master-shipwrights like you and Grandfather to build better ships.'

'Is that so?' countered Jacques with heavy irony, becoming slightly irritated.

'The calculations were based on the best features of all the different Rates.'

'So?' Jacques raised a black eyebrow of enquiry and waited with an air of expectation, but with a slight shrug the young cadet looked away as if suddenly losing interest.

'Some of us think imposing fixed dimensions stifles experiment and innovation. Though I do concede,' Jacques added, chiding himself for bridling at what was only eagerness to show off new-found knowledge, 'these regularised standards could save lives; a sprung mast out in the Atlantic could then be replaced by a spare from any passing ship.'

'If there was a passing ship,' joked André. 'Of course, Grandfather would say ...' As one, they both held up their hands and spoke in quavering tones. 'I build with my eyes, my boy. I build ships with these!' They burst into laughter, and as André's hands were within reach, Jacques touched the palm of one, his blue eyes sparkling with amusement.

'Soft as a girl's! You'd best improve on the dancing, for you'll be no good in the yard if the Marine throw you out.' Mindful of the need to return before André's absence was noticed, they fell to eating, then immediately headed straight back to the arsenal.

'I did overhear this morning,' murmured Jacques as they reached the river where he had left his skiff, 'a most exciting rumour: contracts may be offered to private yards for the King's new fleet.'

'Your dream frigate?' grinned André, his eyes dancing with mischief. 'Tell me, would you abandon the official dimensions, or abandon Grandfather's lifetime of experience to build it?'

Jacques jumped down into his skiff and with swift hands released the sail.

'Well, how would you do it?' demanded André, throwing down the mooring rope.

The wind caught the sail and beneath the small boat the current of the river pulled. Jacques gave a wave and shouted back his answer.

'I would ask my little brother because he knows everything!'

CHAPTER 5

u Chesne seemed of a time when a lady might wave from one of its towers to her knight as he rode away to war. A small river named the Bruant wound a lazy course around the pentagonal rock upon which the fortress stood. These natural barricades would not have held off an army, but for pillaging raiders they would have presented an irksome challenge.

The devastation wrought by fire and years of neglect had left it in a sorry state. Hermione felt at a complete loss ... how did you set about rebuilding rooms whose walls were open to rain and sky? How to go about finding masons and carpenters, and having found them, how would she find the means to pay? Even the running costs would be beyond her resources. As for the garden about her ... Hermione grimaced as her ankle twisted on the uneven ground. Beneath the tall, coarse grass, every so often her feet had an impression of shallow steps. Someone, perhaps in the Chevalier's time, had begun to set out a garden just as the King was doing at Versailles. She sank down onto a mound of moss and stared ahead at the stretch of water which faced the house. This lake was fed by the river which flowed beneath the bridge of the Keep, and like a mirror, its waters displayed the fortress rising up behind her. For a moment, Hermione studied the various reflected windows and the soaring towers. Then her attention came back to what lay before her, and in particular two stone pavilions whose position at each end of the frontage of the water suggested a possibility of more stone formality beneath the high grass. Hermione stretched out, deciding curiosity must wait till another day, for there was still much to do indoors. Yet she remained where she was enjoying for a further few moments the cooing of woodpigeon and the soft breeze playing over her face. How far away Paris seemed; no grinding of wheels on cobbles, no street vendors shouting their wares, no one to disturb this gentle peace. The thought had no sooner formed than an outburst of furious scolding on the terrace above was followed by Guillaume's answering shout. Hermione burst into laughter; some things had not changed. With a rueful smile, she raised herself from the ground and walked back to restore peace.

Whatever the dispute had been about, by the time she arrived at the top of the steps leading on to the terrace it seemed to have been resolved, for there was neither sight nor sound of Lucette or Guillaume. Nor were they in the hall or the Painted Room. Until today, it had been impossible to see the full beauty of this room, but bit by bit, as Guillaume and Pierre had cleared away furniture saved from the fire-damaged wing of the château, the walls of the chamber had been exposed. In her entire life, Hermione had never seen so many coloured images painted on wood. In Notre Dame there was the wonder of the vast, coloured windows which offered a shimmering glimpse of heaven; what stories were all these painted panels telling? As for the portrait above the carved chimney-piece, here she needed no help, for the young chevalier was André Du Chesne. The familiar face was free of wrinkles, and the hair which hung either side of a white jabot was jet black, and the brilliant black eyes cast downwards on Hermione a bold look filled with youthful energy. How sunken and racked with pain those eyes were to become in his final days, yet, even so, how they had gleamed with contentment when she accepted his ring. Hermione looked down and touched her fingertip against the cluster of oak leaves on the gold band.

'I have arrived, my dear Chevalier. I am here.'

At that moment of Hermione's reverie, Lucette came bustling into the room.

'What a rat-infested dump this is!' she exploded, her expression filled with resentment and her eyes slits of spite. 'And that Guillaume, cosy as you like with the old man! They've gone off to check snares, leaving me to do everything. As for the old dame, I can't get a sensible word out of her.'

'I think her ears trouble her,' said Hermione, trying to find an excuse, for she could not get much out of Marie Paultre herself. When it came to answering questions about the village or the days of the Chevalier, the old woman's expression immediately closed over and she silently carried on with whatever she was doing. Even more infuriating was when she just shuffled away, leaving Hermione talking to an empty room. 'Guillaume says,' she added, 'Marie and Pierre can't understand what we say either.'

'Didn't I say they were stupid?' retorted Lucette, staring round at the painted panels. 'They're no older than Agnès' mother and father, and just think how sharp they are to hear and understand – everyone is quick in Paris. The longer we stay here, madame, the slower our wits will become. Imagine if Master Olivier were here. He'd forget how to add up his numbers.'

The mention of Olivier suddenly reminded Hermione of her promise to send Guillaume back to him when things in Paris became safer, though it was best to keep this from Lucette, or she would be fretting every day to leave with him. However, it could be months or years before that happened, and in the meanwhile, Guillaume's bulk and cheerful ways made her feel safe and secure. Even the old servants had opened up to him, for she had glimpsed Marie playfully shooing him out of her kitchen with a broom, amid cackles of laughter.

The clearance of the Painted Room had taken two whole days, but now, with selected pieces of furniture returned, she had a room to live in and a bedchamber within the tower nearest to the keep. Guillaume, with his usual independence, had installed himself down at the stables. The reorganization had taken a great deal of effort on everyone's part, but now Hermione felt ready to explore the rooms above her bedchamber. Dismissing Lucette, she made her way to the tower and ascended the steps which gave entrance through a door to the higher levels. The blackness swallowed up the feeble light of her candle, but as she brushed aside dusty cobwebs, she saw a door set into the stone wall on her right. With a thrill of anticipation, she lifted the latch and went in.

The circular chamber was flooded with light, as the shutters on the window which overlooked the lake had not been closed. Hermione walked over to the other window, which presumably, like her own chamber below, faced out towards the Keep. After opening up its dusty shutters, she turned about and regarded the four-poster bed which was the principal piece of furniture in the room. Its faded, embroidered curtains of green were closed as if a sleeper lay there still. Indeed, the longer her gaze held upon it, the stronger became her sense of some presence within. Treading softly on the balls of her feet, she moved forward, and taking hold of the rotting fabric she cautiously drew back one of the hangings. The face of a young woman stared towards her, but this was no long forgotten sleeper. Captured in oils, set within a dark frame, was a brunette whose beautiful brown eyes danced with mischief. So fresh did she look in her dress of silvery grey, so untouched was the canvas in contrast to the sad decay in the rest of the bedchamber, Hermione experienced a surge of delight. Her glance swept over the rumpled bedcovers towards the bolster; it was dented as if the occupant had just arisen. Was this the young woman's chamber, or had someone else lain here? Could it be that someone had shut themselves away with the portrait ... as with a lover? Whoever the noblewoman might be, and whatever her history, Hermione wasn't going to leave her buried away within the confines of the curtains.

'Come with me, beautiful lady. I have the very place for you!'

With a further small adjustment to the position of the portrait, Guillaume clambered back down the ladder.

'You'll find that level now, madame. Always best to ask a one-eyed man to do a job like this ... two eyes lead to argument.' Hermione smiled appreciation as the big man lifted up the ladder and clomped away out of the room. Lucette, who had been watching the hanging, gave Hermione a saucy grin.

'Has her ladyship told anyone where her jewels are kept? Little wonder her fingers are checking her neck to see no thief has nicked them.'

'That will be all, Lucette. Please ask Marie to come here.'

With a sulky flounce at being dismissed, Lucette left, banging the door behind her. Hermione turned her eyes towards André Du Chesne's portrait, then looked back at the lovely young woman on the opposite wall.

'You're reunited.' She smiled, feeling somehow certain that the two beings were now as one. She leaned back, resting her hands on the table, enjoying a sense of accomplishment. Lucette's caustic remark about the jewels returned to her. She studied with interest the cascade of diamonds suspended around the slim white neck; to possess just her eardrops would make a new roof possible. 'I wonder what happened to them?' she murmured.

The door into the Painted Room creaked on its hinges as Marie entered. Hermione turned her head so as not to miss her reaction to the portrait. The old lady, following her gesture, looked upwards. She remained in complete silence, not uttering a single word. Nor did her brown mottled face register a flicker of emotion.

'Am I right in thinking this is where the portrait should hang? Who is she, Marie?'

The hard black eyes settled on Hermione.

'Aglaé Saintyon.'

'Oh, so she is not a member of the Du Chesne family?'

The elderly housekeeper's lower lip pouted, making the flesh of her chin pucker. Then she gave one shuffling sidestep, and that was that as far as the conversation went. There seemed no point in trying to delay her; no doubt her reserve was bound up with having a stranger from Paris asking questions. Hermione had been little more than a stranger to André Du Chesne, yet for some reason he had chosen to leave his former home to her. As on other occasions when she wondered what had passed between them to warrant such extraordinary generosity on his part, she drew no answer. Maybe if she knew more about Aglaé Saintyon, she would find the clue. Her eyes fastened on the diamonds again; the large tear-like droplet in the centre of the necklace would solve all her problems!

The curé's acceptance of Hermione's invitation to dine at Du Chesne on the coming Sunday had a profound effect on Marie. Her shuffling steps became almost sprightly as with her broom she attacked the dusty, dark corners in the dining room. While the vermin ran for their lives, poor Lucette, trembling like a leaf, was dispatched to the woods in search of hens which had escaped from the coop. Then, early on the Sunday morning, Lucette again had to lend a hand to gather mushrooms away from the safety of the château. Hermione understood the girl's anxiety, but she needed to become more confident in her surroundings. And to try and learn some of Marie's ways of doing things. By the time Hermione was ready to go to Mass in the village, Lucette had returned with her basket but partially filled and her face set in a sullen expression. Would there be peace in her absence? wondered Hermione as Guillaume moved on the horses.

However, on her return from church, all seemed calm as she entered the house. There was no sign of Lucette, but Marie was in the dining room. What had been achieved in the wood-panelled dining-room in the last few days was truly praiseworthy; the dresser, the chairs and the long oak table were all gleaming from hours of polishing. Plates and pewter had been washed, and there were even flowers from the meadow arranged in a vase.

'You have tired yourself, Marie,' commented Hermione as she touched the gleaming wood. The old lady gave a shrug.

'The Chevalier would wish it to be right. And it is right for me to show our curé in to you. I told the girl that it was not for her to do – I took the stick to her and laid it on firm for she shouted and swore so.' Hermione swallowed with shock. 'She's blubbing by the well, madame,' continued the housekeeper with a nod of satisfaction. 'She has to learn her place here.' Hermione swallowed again, hesitating to extinguish the progress that had been made between them, but alarmed by what had taken place.

'Lucette has a hasty temper, Marie, but she is a kind girl. And she has always been used to looking after me herself. Everything is strange for her here, especially going to the woods, where she fears she might meet goblins. And she misses her friends in Paris. If there are problems between you, tell me, but do not lift your hand to her!' Hermione's tone was firm. 'Do you understand?'

The hard black eyes staring at her seemed to be making their assessment. At last, with a grudging nod, the old lady turned and walked out of the room. Filled with anxiety as to how hard the old lady had wielded her stick, Hermione hurried outside to the well, where she came upon Lucette sobbing into her apron.

'I want to go,' she wailed as Hermione gently touched her shoulder. 'She is a devil! Look how she hit me.' The young woman pushed up her sleeve and exposed three bright red weals on her flesh. 'I told her that I showed people in to see you in Paris, but she would not have it. You will have to tell her, Mademoiselle Hermione.'

'Marie said you swore at her.'

'Because she was being stupid; not listening to me. '

'Well, you must not swear at her again!' Hermione took up the pail and dropped it into the well, and upon withdrawing it dipped her kerchief into the icy water. 'You must make allowances for her,' she said, pressing the linen against her maid's arm. 'Remember, Marie has lived here with only Pierre and the dog for many years. She was housekeeper for the Chevalier Du Chesne, and that must mean something special to the villagers. It would be a kindness not to begrudge her her place.'

'Well, if she is to show people in, she is not to look after your clothes or to dress you,' snapped Lucette, 'or I shall walk back to Paris right now.'

'I wouldn't want that; at least,' teased Hermione, 'not before you have helped me dress for dinner!'

The welcoming fire in the great fireplace of the dining room gave a cheery feel. From the window which gave a view onto the marshy land along the river, the rough-haired Rouge could be seen bounding along beside his master. From this distance, Pierre's wiry figure made him look quite boyish. By the appearance of the bulging bag slung over his shoulder, he was returning from hunting. Hermione wondered how he would react when he saw his wife, for Marie was no longer wearing her moth-eaten, woollen dress and shawl. She was waiting to receive the curé in a crisp bonnet and a grey bodice and skirt, which from the smell of camphor appeared to have been stowed away with care for many a year. The clang of the bell sounded, and moments after voices and footsteps could be heard approaching the door. Then, seeming at least an inch taller, with grave dignity Marie led in Hermione's first guest.

'So...' the priest smiled after soup had been served and they were alone, 'you survived your inspection this morning?'

Hermione laughed ruefully. 'I felt like an evil goblin; everyone looked at me with great suspicion.'

'It will take many months, Madame Du Chesne. You are not only new to the village, but you are the adopted daughter of André Du Chesne. It is quite a shock for everyone.'

'Did you know the Chevalier, Father?'

'He lived here long before my time. I have only been here two years myself. It takes a while to accustom oneself to the patois, and one is never accustomed to being abandoned in such a backwater. But let us not cloud the day,' he added, dispelling the bitter note which had crept into his voice. 'Am I not most fortunate to have a lady of education as my neighbour? And, if you will permit me to say, one of such natural beauty? From time to time, I receive books and *La Gazette* from a friend. You are most welcome to them afterwards.'

Hermione coloured with discomfort. 'My thanks, but I read very slowly,' she said, unwilling to admit she was unable to read at all.'

'Time passes slowly here,' rejoined the curé as if sensing her reticence. 'I always enjoy hearing the sound of my voice, so whenever you would like me to read to you, I will be much obliged, especially if there were the offer of such fine fare,' he added as Marie, with Lucette following on her heels, entered with serving platters. After rabbit terrine had been served and the women had departed, Hermione wondered if she might steer the conversation towards Aglaé Saintyon. She glanced across the table, but as her guest was absorbed with his food, she judged it best not to distract a fat man when his tongue was occupied. At length, the curé looked up with a pleased, greedy expression on his chubby face.

'Exceptional, madame. Your *parisienne* influence, no doubt … the delicacy of the chervil.'

'It is Marie's work,' Hermione assured him with a smile. 'My mind has been occupied more by the house than by food. I have hung a portrait of Aglaé Saintyon. in the Painted Room, opposite that of the Chevalier. Do you know anything about her?'

The priest gave a shrug and shook his head. 'I heard there was some terrible accident in the woods. But as his adopted daughter you surely would know more than me?'

Hermione gave a vague smile and felt relieved as he scooped up several mushrooms and popped them into his mouth.

'Marie clearly knows where these flourish best,' he said, half-closing his eyes, 'but she is a good age and God may call her any time. Get her to instruct that young woman of yours, for it is easy to pick poisonous ones. I wouldn't wish to see you writhing in pain like some victim of La Voisin.'

The name swooped at Hermione like a bat out of darkness. She leaned back in her chair, sickened by what it conjured up.

'There, there, I have put you off your food,' fussed the prelate, looking contrite.

'It is nothing,' murmured Hermione, recovering her poise, though feeling icy cold as the priest gossiped on.

'Fortunately, Madame Du Chesne, I am not kept in total ignorance of what is happening in Paris. My dear friend the Marquis passes on all the news in his letters. For whilst he is an outcast like me on his estate in Burgundy, his friends at court do not forget him. You know about the *chambre ardente*?'

Hermione nodded, beginning to feel the pleasure of the occasion dissipate.

'Yes, of course you do; such things cannot be kept secret. The crowds that flock to the Place de Grève see for themselves the evil which the secret court is uprooting. And it is not hearsay, for the Marquis writes the names. Last week two poisoners, La Pottereau and Durand, were hanged and burnt. A witch and a fortune-teller named La Chéron were burnt at the stake; fire is, of course, the only hope of purification for such evil hags. On a lighter note, the Marquis's observations on Madame de Montespan's rivalry with the young favourite, Madame de Fontanges, are especially entertaining. But, Madame Du Chesne, can you believe what the Montespan's losses at Hoca were in March ... they say she lost fifty thousand *écus*. Though I'll warrant it was the King who settled her debt.'

Throughout the rest of the meal, his tongue seemingly loosened by the wine, the curé chatted on. Somehow, the mention of La Voisin had drained away Hermione's energy, and though she had intended to obtain a feel of local affairs, she now only wanted to escape into the sunshine. Her wistful glance towards the window as they rose from the table did not go unnoticed.

'But I must not tire you, and I have the usual duties awaiting me. A glimpse of your Painted Room will have to wait until my next call. Will you walk a part of the way with me?'

After exchanging her precious second-hand silk shoes for outdoor ones, Hermione accompanied the priest out into the courtyard.

'It seems your man fits in here,' remarked Father Grégoire, with a glance towards Guillaume and Pierre who were laughing together at the horse troughs. 'Will you start the rebuilding soon? I can find you reliable workers.'

'I thought I'd settle in first ... take regard of everything,' Hermione demurred, thinking of the costs involved.

'Of course,' Father Grégoire nodded, his podgy hands patting his stomach with an air of content. They strolled towards the keep, pausing to look out on the rough ground which led down towards the lake.

'You and the Chevalier had a garden in Paris, of course?'

The questioning, inquisitive eyes of her companion once again made Hermione feel uncomfortable, torn between being open, as was her customary way, and treading warily until she knew the priest a little better.

'What would we do without herbs?' she smiled.

'Certainly Marie Paultre can't, for if any of the villagers are ailing, it is she who tends them.' Their steps had brought them to the large barn and the cluster of miserable little shacks just beyond the stone archway.

'How do they manage?' murmured Hermione, eyeing the ragged children playing with stones in the dust.

'The journeyman picks up what their parents weave and they have their strip of land,' replied the curé matter-of-factly, inclining his head as some of the boys sprang up and bowed to him. 'Under a new system, the men in this area have also been conscripted into one of three classes for the Marine. Some serve for six months and are on half pay for the remainder of the year. It's an innovation which at least provides a basic subsistence for the men while they are not at sea, but they welcome any other means to bring in money.'

Together they set off down the drive, which with the encroachment of the woods on either side was little better than a track. Then, as the rusty iron gates came within sight, they parted.

'I hope, Father Grégoire, you will visit again very soon.'

'I shall find it hard to keep away,' said the prelate beaming, 'and I hope,' he added, half-turning as he started to walk on, 'that we shall find some means of speeding up your reading.'

It had been a great success. Marie had given of her best for the curé, as well as to honour her former master. Hermione realized she herself had not been in the elderly housekeeper's thoughts, but, she sensed the occasion had brought about some acceptance of her presence at Du Chesne. Most of all, she had gained a friendly neighbour, and one whose friends kept him abreast of what was happening in Paris. This was a new life, and it was a great pity the tranquility of Du Chesne had been disturbed by the vile name of La Voisin. Yet for Olivier's sake, she supposed she ought not to cut herself off from what might serve or even one day save him.

The moon, which had been masked by clouds, must have slipped its heavy veils, for the circular bedchamber became bright with light. Hermione rolled onto her side and continued musing about Father Grégoire's gossip; what sum was it that had been lost at Hoca? Ah yes, fifty thousand écus! Such as Madame de Montespan inheriting a Du Chesne would have fifty, a hundred, workmen swarming over scaffolding to return it to its former glory. Hermione sleepily pulled her blanket higher, wondering why that man - Monsieur Tilly - should send a messenger all the way to Paris to buy a château that was in ruins. The image of the cascade of diamonds about Aglaé Saintyon's neck floated into her mind until it changed into a moving, glittering stream, and she slept.

CHAPTER 6

t had proved a wise move to buy the two livery horses on the last stage of their journey to Du Chesne, for its stables were empty and in a sad state of disuse. Guillaume had mended one of the old wagons, and with the stronger of the two horses hitched up to it, he was ready to take Marie and Pierre to market at the nearby town of Saintes. As the wagon rattled forward beneath the hayloft and out into the courtyard between the two horse troughs, Hermione gave Guillaume a meaningful look.

'And remember,' she murmured, as Pierre and Marie approached, 'don't hurry back!'

The fine slats of wood sewn into the cambric of Marie's bonnet made it stand out proud, so it was not easy to judge her expression. There was no need, as Lucette had reported the old servant was well pleased to have an outing. As to this local style of bonnet, any mention of adopting it by Lucette to help her fit in locally had instantly been dismissed.

'I'll not be able to see right or left, madame.'

'More like,' Hermione had teased at the time, 'you think you'll never catch a kiss.'

Lucette, who had been at the well drawing water, came over to stand beside Hermione.

'I wish I were going,' she groaned, as Guillaume and Pierre helped Marie up on to the wagon.

'Another time,' promised Hermione. 'Some of the villagers are going with them today. And when we will go, we shall explore Saintes. Even more exciting will be a visit to see the new town of Rochefort ... think of all the sailors you will see there!'

With a crack of his whip and an outburst of song, Guillaume set the little party on its way. Lucette gave a snort of laughter.

'Look at the old dame – how she's holding on to that basket of eggs ... she might as well toss them over the side the way Guillaume drives.'

'Don't forget my candles, Guillaume!' Hermione called after them. 'Wax ones!' It was an extravagance, but whatever the future held, for a time, she might at least enjoy feeling like the châtelaine.

'And now,' she said smiling, her surge of excitement finally lifting away the sulky look from Lucette's face, 'our hunt for the diamonds begins!'

They had tapped panels, lifted carpets, clambered beneath the rafters of the roof from one tower to another, and by the time they emerged from the wine cellar, their hands and faces were covered with grime which cut into the flesh. Only what remained of the former wing of the château had got to be searched.

'Praise to the Saints this part burnt down,' gasped Lucette, as they paused to take a drink from the well. Hermione looked upward towards the one small part of the ruin which was still intact. How safe would it be to look there?

'It's all right for them,' grumbled Lucette, as birds flew back and forth out of the blackened shell. 'Likely they've got the diamonds in their nests.'

'I doubt we'll find anything,' commented Hermione as they picked up Pierre's ladder, 'but if I don't look, I will always wonder.'

Once through what formerly had been the entrance, they were confronted by fallen masonry and broken, blackened timbers. It was a grim scene, softened by the hold Nature had taken; green life was pushing and sprouting forth from every crevice. Hermione moved through the weeds and high grasses towards a flight of stone steps which gave access to an upper floor.

'The rooms up there may have escaped the fire,' she murmured. 'Help me with the ladder, but then come back down. It is too dangerous for you, Lucette!'

'What about staying down here on my own? Isn't that dangerous? What if you fall, and I'm left here, with Guillaume? Besides, I know I'll be the one to find those huge eardrops!'

Hermione flashed a smile and lifted up her end of the ladder. With great care not to lose their balance, as there was no balustrade, they ascended the wide stone steps. On gaining the top, Hermione hesitated, for just two arms' length away to the right was an open drop to the ground.

'What is it, madame?'

'I'm not sure whether the planks will take my weight,' responded Hermione. With considerable care she tentatively put down one foot. 'I think it's safe,' she murmured, as she took one cautious step and another to the left.

It was as Hermione had supposed. The rooms were intact, but empty save for dust, cobwebs and debris. As they retraced their way back along the passage Lucette, who was in front, suddenly paused and looked upward.

'What about through there?'

Hermione peered up at a trapdoor, and with a nod of agreement, she set her end of the ladder up against the wall. Once again, she climbed first, and one strong push had the trapdoor open. She had anticipated needing to ask for the candle, but even before she had fully emerged into the attic, she saw there was no need; bright sunlight flooded through what remained of the rafters.

'What ruin!' she exclaimed, staring up at the blackened timbers. The smell of rotting wood, together with the realization that they had wasted hours on this silly venture, made her swear under her breath. More out of frustration than the thought to linger further, Hermione swept aside a thick veil of cobwebs to her left. Beyond it was no bright sunlight; of course there couldn't be, as the roof along there was still intact, she remembered. With care she edged forward in the dim light until something ahead made her gasp with excitement. It was a high, ghostly draping of something. When she reached it, it turned out to be canvas. Hermione dragged it away, and there beneath was a collection of hat boxes and two large wooden chests.

'We've struck gold!' shrieked Lucette, who had followed on behind. With a further shriek she seized a box, and as a man's tricorne dropped out, she set it on top of her cap. Turning towards Hermione she made a comic bow. Smiling with excitement, Hermione, raised the lid of the chest nearest to her. Her fingers pulled away a layer of thick paper, and unbelievably, the air became imbued with a faint waft of lavender. Its delicacy somehow made her conscious of the filthy state of her hands, so before touching the pale pink silk folds of the dress beneath she wiped her fingers as best she could on her own skirt. Shortly, however, as she lifted up velvets and brocades of differing weights, she realized mildew had spoilt everything. She let drop the lid with a sigh of weariness; this was not a case of jewels. With no great expectations she opened the second chest. On first sight, it appeared to contain only woollen cloaks until in-between the thick layers she came upon a length of linen. It seemed some care had been taken to protect whatever was within. It was impossible not to feel mounting expectation as the linen unwound, but she cautioned herself against further disappointment as she carefully pulled apart the final layers. It was indeed just another dress, but her cry of wonder and joy brought Lucette to her side.

'Oh, Madame Hermione, that's the silvery dress in the painting! It's wonderful!'

'First the dress,' Hermione said with a laugh, 'next the diamonds!'

It was ridiculous to think valuable jewels would have been abandoned so, but her words drove them on to frenzied activity until, quite exhausted, both of them sank back on a great mound of old curtains.

Lucette flung back her thin arms over her head.

'Oh, I hate it here, mademoiselle! Can't we go back to what we know? We've found nothing but whalebone and ancient fans!'

'We'll go and take a glass of wine; you'll feel better then,' soothed Hermione, wishing she also was back in Paris. Her mouth was dry and gritty, and from head to toe they were caked with dirt. 'You did remember to light the copper? Good, then while I finish here you fill the tub.'

As Lucette made her way back to the ladder, Hermione began to select the few things which time and weather had not completely spoilt. She shook out a riding habit which she thought might do for herself, but as the folds of the skirt fell open, to her dismay she saw the entire front and back was darkened with dried blood ... a great deal of blood! Hermione shuddered and held it away at arm's length. Why, she wondered, had it been wrapped in a man's cloak underneath the beautiful silvery dress?

The harsh voice of a man shouting from below threw her into an absolute panic. She dropped the riding habit and softly crept back towards the area where the beams were open to the sky. Out there in the sunlight, the floorboards stopped short of the open drop to the ground. Hermione hesitated, considering whether it might be safe to slither forward on her front to peep over the edge. Fortunately, there was no need to take the risk, for another loud shout demanding attention came from the courtyard. No doubt Lucette had chosen not to hear if this visitor had rung the bell. Hermione considered ignoring whoever it was herself, but curiosity getting the better, she climbed down the ladder and made her way back through the tumbledown stacks of masonry out into the courtyard.

'Ah, there you are!' declared the rider of a brown stallion. 'The house servants seem not to hear the bell. Have someone tell your mistress that Monsieur Tilly calls upon her, and look lively! I've wasted enough time here.'

'Then you need not waste a moment longer,' flung back Hermione, indignation at his brusque manner smothering her embarrassment at been found in such a filthy state. 'I am Hermione Du Chesne.'

The impatient glaring eyes widened with shocked amazement. Then, quickly recovering himself, the small man sprang down from his horse and executed a jerky bow. With a sorrowful expression, he half-turned towards the blackened shell.

'It must be truly dreadful for you, Madame Du Chesne, dreadful! To travel so far, then to find such ruin! Now you see why I sent my man to you in Paris, to save you from all this.'

Her visitor was now all friendly bluster, and his taut, bony features expressed concern, but Hermione could not fail to see the contempt in the greenish eyes. It was, in truth, hardly to be surprised at, so shocking must be her appearance. Her mind raced as she decided how she should react. She must not appear too down-hearted, for if she sounded desperate, he would reduce his offer.

'Your manservant did explain the château was in a state of disrepair, although I did not imagine such ... 'she made a gesture towards the destroyed wing. 'However,' she continued with a smile, 'all can be made beautiful. One only has to see how our King has transformed a hunting lodge into a palace.'

Claude Tilly's answering smile was indulgent.

'If you will permit me to say, a beautiful young lady such as yourself should not have to endure even one single day here. You should come to Rochefort and buy one of the new houses without delay. Madame Tilly and I would be happy for you to stay at our town house. It would be an honour to introduce you to our friends. You would find life most agreeable; fêtes and social gatherings to keep you pleasantly occupied. While here ... such solitude. As for finding skilled labour to rebuild, why, the arsenal at Rochefort takes it all!' He shook his head and sighed heavily.

'You are too kind, monsieur, but I could not think of imposing on your hospitality,' she said. 'Before you set back, might I offer you refreshment?'

'Most kind, but let me not keep you from your … *diversions*,' rejoined her visitor, his eyes travelling over her filthy clothes. 'As for your coming to stay with Madame Tilly and myself, it would be no imposition, no imposition at all!' The tight trap of his mouth snapped shut as if that was final. Hermione remained silent; here was a bully, and she would have none of it. 'At least say you'll dine with us,' urged Claude Tilly, flicking the riding crop impatiently against his riding boots. 'My wife has never visited Paris, and she is most anxious to hear about it. You will marvel at our new town. The Minister of Marine, Colbert's son, the Marquis de Seignelay, is to pay a visit on the nineteenth of next month. That would be the best time to come; the whole place will be *en fête*. When you see the fine houses that have been built, you will not want to return even to Paris, and especially not to this hamlet! Should you decide to rid yourself of this sad place, I feel sure we could arrange things to our mutual benefit. I shall live in expectation of your visit, madame.'

With another stiff bow, the short, ungainly man walked across to his horse and with unexpected nimbleness threw himself up on to the saddle. 'Adieu, Madame Du Chesne.'

Hermione watched rider and horse pass out under the keep. It seemed she still had a prospective buyer!

After the discovery of the beautiful dress of the portrait, any prospect of finding jewels ended. There was silverware, and pewter, mirrors, moth-eaten tapestries and books, but nothing of more than moderate value. From the Chevalier's lawyer in Paris, she knew monies came into the estate from the toll travellers paid at the crossroads and the dues from the peasants. After the dispersal of the greater part of the Chevalier's money to charity, there was nothing like enough to run things. Now that she had found out how things stood, it was time to talk things through with the lawyer in Saintes who had kept an eye on Du Chesne and paid the wages of Pierre and Marie. To sell would undoubtedly break faith with the Chevalier, who had wanted her here, but why had he not left her the means to look after the house? With downcast heart, mindful of her promise at his deathbed, Hermione let time drift by. Common sense told her to take the easier path, which would be to sell and live in comfort in a small house, but a visit with the curé to meet the families who lived in the shacks near the barn showed her where her duty lay. Nevertheless, she needed to keep all options open.

On the day Guillaume had set off to deliver Hermione's acceptance of Monsieur Tilly's invitation to Rochefort, the weather was stiflingly hot. For a time, Hermione wandered beneath the trees along the edge of the lake, but so irksome were the clouds of tiny flies that she sought escape in the orchard. With a sense of satisfaction she saw Pierre had made a start on scything back the long grass. The scent of it was sweet and inviting, and she was about to sit down when the shady green peace was shattered by high-pitched screams. Then a horde of children, following on after a dark-haired boy who appeared to be their leader, rushed into view from behind a tree. At the sight of Hermione, they pulled up, their expressions changing from laughter to alarm.

'It's all right,' she reassured them. 'What are you playing?'

'We are hunting boar,' declared the older boy, whose brown eyes gleamed with mischief.

'They can be dangerous!' advised Hermione. 'Be careful when you find one.'

The black-haired boy regarded Hermione with interest. Then, raising his wooden sword, he turned on his heel, shouting in a fierce voice as he ran off.

'We will kill the boar for Madame Du Chesne! We will kill the boar for Madame Du Chesne!'

The small gang raced away in pursuit, their whoops and screams even louder than before. Hermione smiled, feeling deep within the pleasure of being called Madame Du Chesne; for the first time, it felt right. She settled down on the ground, but quickly realized the young hunters had placed her at the centre of their sport, for their shrieks and calls continually encircled her. It was not really what she wanted, so she moved on, enjoying the sight of the small green apples that would be ready come September. What a pity they had not arrived here in time to see the branches beautiful with blossom, but the seasons soon changed ... though would she be here next year? Hermione gave a sigh of frustration and tried to comfort herself with the thought there could be other apple trees, and in more manageable gardens. The village children, she sensed, were now following her, for every so often there was stifled laughter and whisperings. Then, as she passed through a rusty iron gate, it seemed as if they had abandoned their tracking game.

The trees here outside the orchard were small-leafed and perhaps were the mulberry which Marie had mentioned? Beyond them tall beeches beckoned, offering shade and cool rest. They looked beautiful, though, even as a parisienne, she knew she must be on the alert, for in woods there were greater dangers than wild boar. Only three days past, when Marie had sent Lucette looking for stray hen eggs, a roaming party of goblins had beckoned to her from the trees. Lucette's wits had been sharp; she had instantly closed her eyes and turned her back on them before they could entice her to them. Now, Hermione felt no threat, only delight in her surroundings. If she sensed things altering, then she too would take to her heels. This walk was so different from the noisy world of the faubourg Saint Antoine and its workshops. There was a feeling of being away from everything, even more so than at the château, where there was always intermittent noise: Marie calling to the hens, Pierre chopping wood, Lucette singing or scolding Guillaume. Here, the outpouring of birdsong seemed for her ears alone, and when every so often the singers fell silent, the sudden rustlings of small creatures through the undergrowth claimed her entire attention. In between these distractions was something else: a silence that seemed watchful, all-enveloping. Under the glare of the sun, the green leaves of a beech above were almost transparent, while underfoot last year's leaves made a carpet of rusty bronze. The crunching of the leaves shattered the silence, and her progress, seemingly ever noisier, began to make her feel self-conscious. It was even worse when she stood still; then the silence surged all about her, isolating her within the tall stands of the trees. She began to have the feeling that she was being watched and wondered if the children were still following her, but she knew they had tired of that way back. No, the feeling she had was of something else. Yet, to right, left and forward, all that she could see were the soaring stands of oak stretching far into the distance. Deciding she ought to retrace her steps to the orchard, she turned back.

She walked for something like an hour, but there was no sign of the mulberry trees she had passed earlier. Like ranks of silent soldiers, the oak stands stretched all around. It was like some great army waiting for night to fall. Hermione halted, feeling increasingly anxious, yet filled with the growing certainty that here was more than a wood … this was a huge forest! Flinging aside caution, she forgot about finding the orchard and walked swiftly on as if to make certain the trees would not suddenly peter out into open land. Steadily her hope and excitement mounted as she began to see a way to stay at Du Chesne. Coopers needed oak for barrels. People needed benches, tables, floorboards, bowls, beds … oh, the list was endless. How could she have been so slow, so stupid? It wasn't stumbling upon family jewels that could rebuild Du Chesne. The answer lay here, and this had to be what that unpleasant man Tilly wanted! Hermione's eyes sparkled as she looked about.

'Dear Chevalier! This forest is your treasure!' Hermione's whisper of wonder exploded into a shout of triumph for every creature to hear. 'Mine! This is all mine!'

Heedless of anything else, Hermione raced forward, wild with excitement until the toe of a shoe catching in roots hurled her forward. She flung out her arms in a desperate attempt to break her fall and shouted out in pain as her wrists jarred against stones. For a few moments, she lay as she had fallen. Then, bit by bit as she recovered, she cautiously raised herself up into a sitting position and rested her back against a tree. Her left ankle, which she had recently jarred in the gardens around the château, was throbbing so badly that she was hardly aware of her grazed hands. She glanced upwards, wondering what time it was, but so dense was the canopy above her that it did not offer a view of the sky. Even so, there had come about a change; the air was heavy and ominous with that hovering expectancy that bodes thunder. 'That's all I need,' she gasped, tears of self-pity and pain flooding her eyes. She dragged herself along towards a fallen branch, and using it as a stick pulled herself onto her feet.

Which way back? From which direction had she run? All about there was a darkening, and as the birds' singing intensified, Hermione knew she was in for a soaking. From some nearby tree, a mistle thrush let forth a glorious outpouring of notes. Following on came the subdued rumble of thunder. So close and dense was the forest's canopy, only the rain's rapid pitter-patter striking the overhead leaves could at first be heard. Then a heavy drop plopped against Hermione's cheek, and others soon followed until a steady flow broke through the leafy shield. At least the hot, oppressive tension of the day had been dissipated. So, despite her pains and predicament, Hermione offered up her face and enjoyed the cascade until the speckled body and white wingtips of the mistle thrush darted past, its warning, strident cry urging her to be on her way. It was an omen! The bird's insistent, harsh call sounded again and, catching another glimpse of its winged flight, Hermione hobbled after it.

Time was passing, and the light was fading. She peered through the downpour in an agony of pain, but it was impossible to tell where she was. At least she was not going round in circles, for the trees about had altered in size and shape. Their trunks were twisted and grotesque. Their spreading branches dipped low like swaying black arms whose cruel twigs tore at her face like crooked, grasping fingers. The mistle thrush had disappeared and so had natural light, replaced by jagged strikes of lightning. With every flash, the black outlines of trees rushed at Hermione like huge witches trying to bar her way. Childhood tales of werewolves and people taken away by evil spirits flooded back into her memory. Hermione felt for the crucifix around her neck and gabbled a prayer out loud. Now there was barely a moment between the deafening crashes and the brilliant flashes which flooded the entire scene in a blue, shimmering light. Barely able to think for the never-ending pulsating pain of her ankle, Hermione leaned back against a tree. Suddenly, something of great weight came crashing through the undergrowth towards her. Hermione screamed out in terror and in trying to hobble away lost hold of her stick. Her full weight bore down on the injured ankle. Her hand grabbed for support, but instead of finding the bark, it felt as if she was falling through a hedge as twigs tore at her face and hair.

Part-winded from shock and fright, her groping hands revealed she was wedged within the hollowed-out trunk of a tree. As she tried to shift and ease her position, from without sounded a fearsome grunting. In desperation, her hands searched on the ground for a stone but found only wet leaves. All that seemed to separate her from the snuffling, grunting beast outside was a barricade of what felt like twigs and ivy. Mute with fear, Hermione leaned forward, and with trembling fingers parted the wet undergrowth. Another strike of jagged lightning illuminated a boar. It was standing side-on, showing the outline of a large, dark body and one of its huge tusks. Hermione shrank back, petrified, but she somehow remained calm enough to wrench off a shoe to hit the brute on the snout with if it tried to get at her. Then all thought ceased as a crash of thunder shook the tree and it seemed the earth beneath her would split open. Hermione clapped her hands over her ears and closed her eyes tight as the storm intensified. Then, as if there was no more water left, the downpour suddenly stopped. All that remained was a steady drip, drip from the leaves of the tree working their way down into her cubby-hole. At least the thunderclap had seemingly driven away the boar, but it was still night, when Satan's creatures roam free. With her crucifix clasped tight in her hand, Hermione repeated the holy words to protect her from the terrifying world outside.

Despite the hours of cold and wet misery, sleep eventually must have come, for when she awoke it was getting light and Hermione was in an agony of stiffness. Outside her lair it sounded as if the whole of the bird world was rejoicing. She also gave thanks with a prayer for her deliverance from danger. No need for caution now. She thrust aside ivy and weeds and dragged herself through the gap in the trunk. Meeting her eyes was a scene of mystery which reminded her of her crystal at those moments when swirling mist clouds the sphere until, like a curtain wrenched aside, the scene was revealed. So the warming rays of the sun were lifting upward a misty veil from the ground. It suddenly cleared, revealing the sparkling delight of a stream across a huge expanse of sward, and dominating all were two monstrous oak trees. Hermione's gaze lifted as if she expected more. There it was, like some great stag straddling the top of the stream's bank: the King of Oaks! She could feel the magic of the place. Yes, here was the vibrating heart of everything! Deep within, Hermione knew what it was she must have glimpsed in the crystal when the Chevalier had sought a reading. For here before her was a tree she knew!

CHAPTER 7

he adze swung back and forth, its sharp cutting edge missing Jacques's toes each time by a hair's breadth. Not that Jacques feared any mishap; he had wielded the long wooden handle since boyhood, and his eye was true. He laughed softly, recalling his father's only instruction: 'Look out for your toes, lad!'

One following after another, gossamer fine slivers of oak curled away to set the curve for the rib of a frame. With tender little movements, Jacques eased away minuscule stray fibres of the creamy wood, a happy smile on his lips. He breathed in the fragrant scent and ran his hands along the silky smooth surface of the oak; this was truth, unlike negotiating with slippery-tongued officials who couldn't tell the difference between their lies and truth. One false move here with an adze and there was no disguising it. Best of all, a man was in total control. Though when it came to winning contracts for the shipyard, that was different. It was back to politics, and quality of work was not enough.

He looked over to where his grandfather was directing a group of men who were sliding great sticks into the mast pond. All was calm now, but it had been a hell of a morning. An apprentice had sprained his wrist tripping over the coaming around a hatchway. Then, unexpectedly, two officials from the royal arsenal had dropped by to cast a look over the yard. Whilst doing so, they had demanded to know how much deal and other naval stores were held … as if it was any of their business! Jacques's gaze rested on a long, heavy section of timber being raised to set into the frame of a schooner. As it swayed back and forth, to his horror he saw that the rope around the hoist was coming adrift. Shouting out a warning, he darted forward towards it, arriving at the same moment as his grandfather and others standing nearby. With up-stretched arms they took the strain of the massive timber until it was set back down onto the ground.

'Just as well it happened now and not when that interfering Maître Ladurie and Joubert were here,' grumbled Henri Maurellet. 'What right had they to come poking their noses into our affairs?'

'Versailles wants the shopping lists of private yards as well as its royal arsenals.'

'Bah! Such interference never happened when I was your age. There are too many officials now. I was building ships when that Joubert was still at the nipple. How patient you were with him, grandson!'

Jacques pulled a face and shrugged. 'Pierre Joubert has a seat on the Council of Construction at the arsenal. We need to keep him on board if contracts are to be offered to private yards.'

'Why you want to set us on this course, I can't fathom. We should stick to turning out fine merchantmen as Maurellets have always done. Then we wouldn't need to get mixed up with all these strutting officials. We would be in charge of our own affairs. If your father and uncle were here, they would agree with me. Ever since the moment you became entangled with the Intendant, we've had no peace.'

Unprepared for such an outpouring, Jacques watched Henri stomp away. The old man had never been open to taking on the challenge of building a man o' war. Maybe the truth of it was that he had never really taken it seriously until this visit from Ladurie and Pierre Joubert. His grandfather didn't like any changes, but things had to move forward. A builder of ships shouldn't just accept that timbers would eventually be eaten away by worm; Jacques's own generation must find a way to protect them. And if private yards were needed to help build a new fleet, they must seize the opportunity to expand the shipyard.

'You're making a fine job of it, Matthieu.' He nodded appreciatively towards the frame of the sloop as the worker approached with a new rope. 'After tomorrow, it can be left to weather.'

'The lads thought you did well not to give those nosy clerks a ducking, Master Jacques,' said the workman with a wink. 'Sniffing and poking about into every corner!'

Jacques's lips spread into a smile, for he had come very near to it. 'It's a big splash in the river I'm after, Matthieu ... a great man o' war opening up the waters on this side of the Charente. And Maître Joubert has influence at the arsenal. How is the boy's wrist faring?'

'He'll live to be more careful,' said the workman grinning. 'Master Jacques, I see you've another visitor.'

Jacques glanced over his shoulder and his smile disappeared as he recognized the rider manoeuvring his way around carts and gangs of men.

'Monsieur Tilly,' he said coldly as the entrepreneur reined in his mount. 'I am surprised you should visit here.'

'It is I, monsieur, who should be surprised,' retorted Claude Tilly, casting down on Jacques an angry look. 'You put my men to some trouble, refusing to take delivery of the timber you ordered. And the means you employed to force them to lift the first load back onto the barge was outrageous.'

'As I recall, there was no bloodshed.'

'I understand it was threatened!'

Jacques did not care for a man who remained mounted during a dispute, but he let it go; the sooner the scoundrel left, the better.

'Do you think we are so green as to accept diseased wood?'

'There was nothing wrong with the consignment ... you yourself chose the lots at auction,' shrilled the timber contractor in a fury.

Jacques Maurellet's face darkened with anger. He moved in close towards Tilly's horse and reaching upward yanked the man downward by his coat till their eyes met.

'You are a cheat!'

'The wood was stamped and entered into the records,' gasped the timber contractor.

'I'm not interested in *how* you cheat,' snarled Jacques, 'but I advise you to mend your ways. Now get out of my sight.' With that, he released his hold on the coat and thwacked the rump of the brown stallion. As the horse reared and raced away, his rider was nearly thrown, but, ungainly as Claude Tilly appeared, he managed to regain his seat. Through narrowed eyes, Jacques followed his retreat. There were a lot of men like Tilly who had flocked to the new town of Rochefort. They were eager for profits at any cost. Could it be that Tilly was connected with those who had spread the tale that the trees around Rochefort should be chopped down because they were the cause of disease? There was a lot of money to be made in growing cereals, especially now when there were so many mouths to feed! Whatever the cause of the sickness that had taken so many to Rochefort's cemetery, it hadn't come from the trees; he'd stake *louis d'or* on that. Neither did he give much credence to his cousin's belief that the fevers were God's way of testing faith.

No sooner was Perrette in his thoughts than he suddenly caught sight of her hurrying towards him, and by her purposeful walk he could tell that she had something serious to say. He considered escape, but it was too late.

'I thought you should know, Jacques, that you have upset Grandfather with your silly talk!' Perrette's pale blue eyes fixed accusingly on him as she closed in. 'Why did you make him so angry?'

'We only differed on matters concerning the yard,' responded Jacques defensively.

'Well, you should know I agree with Grandfather on this matter,' she said. 'We should only build ships for trade ... what we know and understand. If there were some great man o' war out here, what would happen if you were sent off on one of your adventures? Would that be fair on Grandfather at his great age?' Jacques closed his eyes as Perrette's anger overflowed. 'And there is another thing: would we ever get paid? By all accounts, the Sieur de Cheusse is still waiting for his money from the King for his land over at Rochefort.'

'Isn't it enough for you to worry about your mother and the running of our two houses, Perrette?' he put in mildly, meaning to keep her out of his affairs. The effect of his words was like a spark to gunpowder.

'Let me remind you, my father, your uncle, had a share in this shipyard which I shall bring to you as a dowry. If it were not for Grandfather, I would not know anything. I did so much while you were away: ordering stores, checking payments ...' To Jacques's great relief, he spotted a blackrobed figure in the distance. Help was on its way!

'Ah, look, Father Jean is heading over here,' he said, interrupting her high-pitched tirade. 'You always have something to say to him, cousin. Make my apologies, but time presses.' As Perrette's lips opened to protest, he slipped away behind the steaming shed and headed at speed towards the stables. Once there, he saddled up his horse, and as they moved out of the yard, he felt the instant relief of escape. Like some errant boy he glanced back towards the river to see if Perrette had spotted him. There was only the lone figure of the priest standing looking about him. Jacques raised himself onto the stirrups for a better sight; Perrette was nowhere to be seen. Then a flash of white caught his eye and there was her bonneted head peeping round a stack of timber, looking after the priest as he retraced his steps towards the orchard. Jacques shook his head, at a loss to know what it could mean. Then the thought of putting space between him and other people was irresistible and he set the stallion into motion.

Supper that evening was to be taken at Aunt Marguerite's house. The ride had left Jacques feeling invigorated and relaxed. On the contrary, he found his grandfather subdued. He assumed that Henri was still angry about their clash earlier, but, thinking about it, he realized it wasn't about what ships they should build. It went much deeper. Probably he was thinking about his two dead sons, and that would in turn open up the older wound of his lost wife. As they took the path towards his aunt's house, Jacques paused as if to look at the setting sun in the west.

'I think it best, Grandfather, if we don't mention anything about the rope slipping earlier … it will upset Aunt Marguerite.'

Alongside him, Henri gave a deep sigh. 'It's brought that dark day back to me, and I've not stopped thinking of it since. If only I had been there, it might not have happened.'

'But you weren't,' said Jacques, speaking firmly, just as he had spoken at other times of regret and remorse. 'If Father and Uncle could have chosen between ending their lives in the shipyard or lying wasting away on some sickbed …'

'I know, it would be down there,' acknowledged the old man with a gesture towards the river.

'The yard is our quarterdeck, Grandfather,' Jacques continued as they carried on walking. 'Just as sailors lose their lives at sea, men can be killed building ships.'

They entered the house through the kitchen door so as to be able to fuss over Annette, who was still feeling put out about the change in her circumstances.

'I'm wearing the petticoat, Master Jacques,' she beamed in a girlish way, raising the hem of her skirt, 'though it is only for Saints' days and Sunday best.'

'Then I shall have to go away again to get you another,' Jacques laughed, in passing slipping a kiss on her wrinkled cheek.

In the dining room the women were waiting, and, after they had all taken their customary seats around the table, Jacques began to pour out the wine.

'Did you know, Grandfather, they are starting to cast iron cannon in the mould at the arsenal? Apparently, huge subsidies have been paid to entrepreneurs to produce naval stores. At Vienne the factory has somehow managed to turn out an order for over 300,000 ells of sailcloth in one year!'

'Enough, Jacques! Can you not tell us more about your travels?' pleaded Marguerite Maurellet. 'Describe to us again the wonderful clock in Riga … and tell us more about the people there?' Jacques made a face of apology for boring the women with talk of ships, and throughout the meal he tried to be as entertaining as possible, exaggerating a little about the houses of the wealthy merchants. When it came to Riga's women, none, he declared, could touch the beauty and wit of those in France!

'You say things only to please.' Perrette smiled.

'To make us laugh,' cut in Jacques's aunt, trying to ease her bodice. 'Your tale about the lady at La Rochelle with fine airs and a face plastered with mud has near made me split my dress. Was there a coat of arms perchance on her coach?'

'I seem to remember, Aunt Marguerite, a mermaid with a crown of seaweed.'

'And a large shell for a fan?' tittered his aunt.

'I hope Annette will be able to manage without my help tomorrow morning, Jacques,' Perrette said seriously as their grandfather, declaring the talk was becoming too silly, scraped back his chair to leave.

'She will welcome being left to fuss over Henri as she was used to before you interfered,' put in Marguerite Maurellet, rising with the aid of her stick. 'You've more than enough to do here, daughter.' Jacques noticed a sudden blush stain the apples of his cousin's cheeks. Her reply to her mother was hesitant.

'I have to leave early, Maman. I have some miles to walk.'

'Leave early? Miles to walk? To where, pray?' returned Marguerite sharply.

'I don't know where the minister of the Reformed Church is preaching, but I shall be with Louise and her husband so I shall be quite safe.'

A dead silence fell on the room. The bewildered, shocked expressions on his aunt's and grandfather's faces reflected Jacques's own incredulity.

'Does the curé know of this?' he enquired in a whispered undertone. Perrette hung her head and stared at the table.

'What in heaven's name, Grand-petite, has brought this on?' Henri Maurellet's voice was filled with horrified outrage. The young woman looked up and Jacques saw that her pale blue eyes were swimming with tears.

'I am only going to listen, Maman,' she pleaded, looking from her mother to her grandfather as if for understanding. 'Please, Grandfather, don't say anything to the curé, I am only curious.'

'You ask me not to tell the curé when you need him to save your soul from mortal danger?' gasped the old man. 'I shall go right now and bring him to you.'

'Oh no, please, Grandfather. For pity's sake let it be!' Perrette's eyes were pleading as she turned to Jacques for help. So unprepared was he for this extraordinary outburst that he could hardly think what to say. He had no hostile feelings towards Huguenots; indeed, they had many on their workforce. Nevertheless, for a member of the family to have become embroiled in their way of worship was alarming!

'The decision must be yours,' he returned slowly, 'but I believe Grandfather is right; better to seek guidance and help in such a grave matter.'

The pale heart-shaped face crumpled, and Perrette's narrow shoulders began to shake.

'Come, daughter, let us hear no more about such foolishness,' interjected Marguerite Maurellet with a note of firmness. 'We shall go up to the church first thing in the morning, and you shall seek forgiveness.' While Perrette answered her mother with a docile nod, Jacques observed that her expression was clouded with disappointment.

On the way home, Jacques thought to change the subject, but Henri was still bristling with indignation at what had just passed.

'It is as well my son is dead rather than hear his own daughter speak heresy.'

'Perrette is only curious,' returned Jacques mildly.

'Then it is as well that we have brought a halt to it,' growled his grandfather as he paused at the gate. The elderly shipwright turned to Jacques and his glance beneath his jutting eyebrows was filled with meaning.

'Isn't it time you got on with things?'

'Things?'

'Don't play the fool with me, boy ... you know full well what I am getting at! And afterwards, with babies coming along, we would have no more nonsense about going to hear what heretics say!' So fierce was his grandfather's expression that Jacques looked away, for his reluctance to marry would surely show.

***

Since Hermione had been carried by Pierre and Guillaume from the forest to the château, Lucette had been all fussing concern.

'If anything happens to you, Madame Hermione, what would become of us stranded in this wilderness? You must stay in bed until you have got your strength back.'

It was now Hermione's fifth day of rest and, apart from feeling wretched with a cold, she was able to put weight on her ankle, and her wrists no longer hurt. So as the door of her chamber opened she looked to tell Lucette she would take breakfast downstairs. But it was Marie who entered, carrying a tray.

'You are feeling better, madame?'

Hermione nodded. 'I don't know what you give me at night, Marie, but my ankle does not keep me awake, and I sleep so soundly.'

'It is only valerian, madame,' murmured Marie, setting down the tray on a stool beside the bed.

'I could have been there for days but for Pierre,' Hermione reflected as she took up the mug of milk. 'Lucette does not know how he found me.'

Within the confines of her bonnet, the old woman's dark eyes gleamed.

'He knew where to go, like before.'

'Before?' Hermione dragged herself higher in the bed. 'Someone was lost in the same place?'

'Not lost … *taken*! They let you stay, but they claimed her.' There was a fierce intensity to Marie's voice which Hermione had never heard before.

'Who are *they*?'

'The Spirits,' hissed Marie. 'It is their place since long ago. Did you not see the sacred mistletoe sharing the life of the great oak?'

Hermione gave a slight nod of the head for reply. There were questions she wanted to ask, but Marie's expression and manner of speaking held her spellbound. She reached inwardly as if by conjuring up the massive oak it would help her understand the past. Sometimes it is not possible to hold a memory, but there it was; the mighty bough entwined and hidden beneath a great mass of slender green leaves. Marie was not exaggerating the mystery of the place; even here in the warmth of her bed, Hermione could recall the mystical atmosphere in the glade.

'Beneath the bough bearing the mistletoe is where Mademoiselle Aglaé died,' added the old servant, her voice hoarse with emotion.

Hermione's face clouded with sadness as she thought of the happy young woman captured forever in oils in her lovely dress; not to know that she would die well before her time. Thinking of the silvery dress, Hemrione glanced over to the chest in which Lucette had put it away. Lying on top of the chest was the soiled habit.

'Ah, a fatal accident explains the bloodstained riding habit we came upon in the attic. Poor lady, she clearly lost a great deal of blood.'

Marie's jet black eyes flashed with furious hostility. 'You have been going through Mademoiselle Aglaé's clothes?'

'Well, I did not know they belonged to her, not until I came upon the dress painted in the portrait.'

'What have you done with the riding habit?' Marie's tone was so harsh that Hermione's eyes widened in surprise.

'I meant to leave it where it was, but Lucette brought it down later not knowing it was spoilt. It is there on the chest.' Sensing she had done something wrong, Hermione watched the old lady hobble across the bedchamber. Reaching the chest, she hesitated, seeming reluctant to pick up the dark green garment.

'It is so heavily soiled, I did not think it could be cleaned,' explained Hermione, feeling more than ever that she had committed some outrage. For now Marie's face had darkened with anger as she turned about with the habit held protectively in her arms.

'It shall be burnt on the fire, for no one else shall wear it. And you must not mention to any living soul what you have seen!'

Hermione sat mute as the elderly servant went away, shutting the door behind her. What could it mean? Was there some dark secret, and did Pierre also know about it? For the remainder of that day, Hermione was preoccupied by the old servant's violent reaction and to whatever might have taken place in the forest.

On the morrow, feeling rested and filled with energy, Hermione rose early. Even had she thought to dwell on what had passed between herself and Marie on the pregvious day, Lucette gave her no chance, for she never left off talking about the forthcoming trip to Rochefort.

'Oh, I can't wait, Madame Hermione! There will be shops and lots of people ... sailors and the like. Are we to stay the night?'

'We have been invited to stay with Monsieur Tilly's family, but I would prefer to return.' The expression on Lucette's pale, angular face became one of disappointment. 'That means you are not going to sell up as Guillaume thought you would, or you would stay on to please Monsieur Tilly. If you do not mind my saying so, you could have a comfortable life in Rochefort with many fine suitors.'

'I do mind!' returned Hermione sharply, 'I am conscious of your feelings, Lucette, but I am now certain of finding the way to stay here. If you are truly unhappy, it may be that you would prefer to find another place, but for the time being it is safer for you to live here quietly. Whilst Catherine Montvoisin lives, you are in danger ... only a few days ago, the curé talked about more executions in Paris. So, should Madame Tilly's servants ask questions, be careful ... remember, we lived a quiet life in the Marais with the Chevalier Du Chesne.'

As well as giving some thought to what questions might be put to herself, Hermione decided to ask the curé if he knew anything of Claude Tilly. Father Grégoire had been very solicitous during the days she was recovering from her ordeal in the forest. When he next called in, as she offered sweetmeats, she took the opportunity to raise the matter.

'Have you knowledge of a Claude Tilly, Father?'

'Certainly. He often calls in at the forge, for as well as a house in Rochefort, he recently bought a fine house at Saintes. I came upon him once at the gates of the château. He was deep in conversation with the lawyer who looked after the affairs of Du Chesne. Perhaps that explains Monsieur Tilly's interest in the estate.'

'He sent his secretary all the way to Paris with an offer for Du Chesne.'

A knowing smile settled on the jovial face of the priest. 'That comes as no surprise. Did you know he is a timber contractor?'

Hermione gave a wry smile. 'It wasn't until I was lost in the forest that I realized his offer for Du Chesne was not so very generous.'

'Our small community will be glad not to exchange you for Claude Tilly,' murmured the priest, rising from his chair to wander over to the table where Hermione had set out some of the Chevalier's books which she had brought from the house in the Marais. 'To spend a night alone in the forest and return unharmed makes you very special to them.'

'I never let go of my crucifix and prayed all night,' said Hermione simply. 'Marie told me Aglaé Saintyon died beneath the great oak.'

'A sad business, by all accounts,' murmured the priest as he took up one of the books. 'She was thrown and trampled by her horse. She and the Chevalier were to be married ... very sad. My dear lady, these books are precious! This is a sixteenth-century edition of *Le Roman de la Rose* ... with this in winter Du Chesne shall become our *hortus deliciarum*. And here are Aesop's Fables. Ah, and a little more up-to-date almanac ... ever useful to a priest. The one I own is a later edition. Someone is always wishing to know when the next feast day is, or when the new moon will rise.' As he set the almanac back on the table, a loose sheaf of paper fell out. He bent to retrieve it. 'Some symbols of alchemy!'

Hermione rose swiftly, casting frantically about in her mind for how to explain what must be some of her childhood drawings, somehow gathered up by Lucette in the rush to leave Paris.

'I used to draw them when I was young,' she explained, arriving at Father Grégoire's side.

'You certainly had a steady hand,' commented the priest, his eyes alive with surprised speculation. Hermione glanced downward and saw that the drawings were not in charcoal, which she had always used, but finely done with a quill. However, she was now compromised. Her visitor's plump, rosy face was avid with curiosity. 'A keepsake I put out for my maid to pack ... she must have slipped it between the covers of the book to keep it safe. Done so.' The curé interrupted with excited impatience.

'You drew symbols used by alchemists as a child!'

Hermione pursed her lips; she wanted to blurt out her whole story, but though she liked Father Grégoire, deep within she felt a need for caution. For the present it seemed wiser to be vague about things, and, if necessary, to elaborate a little.

'A learned gentleman who cared for me in childhood was interested in such things. He travelled a great deal to meet other wise scholars in Prague and London.'

'Alchemists?'

'Men of natural philosophy,' replied Hermione, using Olivier's oft-repeated words.

'Does this gentleman still reside in Paris?'

'I don't think so,' responded Hermione, for truth to tell she could no longer be certain.

'Did he have his own laboratory?'

'It is necessary for the art,' responded Hermione, hoping he would not ask where it was.

'Let me guess,' murmured the priest, pointing to two parallel wavy lines on the sheet of paper. 'This one represents water?'

'Yes.' Hermione smiled, relaxing a little.

'And the triangle with its point at the top and a line passing through it … is?'

'Air.'

'Yes, quite right. You see, I am familiar myself with such symbols. Your friend and I would have had a mutually absorbing interest. I might, of course, with your help, write to him. It is always such a joy to receive stimulating letters.' Hermione remained silent. 'But of course, I am forgetting: you said your reading was slow. Your writing, however, is excellent, for I have seen you sign your name with a bold flourish.'

Hermione flushed with embarrassment. 'I have practiced it many times, but I have not learned all my letters … just those needed for my name.

'Then we are perfectly suited.' The curé smiled. 'I will help you learn your letters and in return you shall spoil me with little treats to excite my palate! And you shall tell me all about your life before the Chevalier adopted you. As for Claude Tilly,' he added, moving to pick up his hat, 'he obviously anticipated seizing the estate on the cheap. Your decision to take up residence must have been a great surprise. He is but a tradesman, and, like so many who now strut the streets of Rochefort, he thinks money will make up for his inferior birth. Be warned, dear lady. I think you will find he will not give up so easily.'

CHAPTER 8

he streets of Rochefort were exceedingly fine. Not only was Guillaume able to pass coaches coming from the opposite direction, there was space enough for others to stop either side beneath the shade of the lime trees. The wooden houses were modest, single-storey buildings with a window set each side of a central door. Clearly, the garrison town was *en fête*, for festoons of brightly coloured bunting fluttered from rows of little stalls, as well as in the branches of the trees. The air was mouthwateringly fragrant with the smell of newly-baked sweetmeats. Lucette brimmed over with happiness, unable to suppress her beaming smiles of approval.

'Oh, this is the place! We should come to live here! Look at all the people, madame.'

'Just don't get into mischief,' Hermione warned, as her maid cast a second look at a group of youths entering a tavern. 'Shall I remind you of the things I need?'

'I shall remember everything,' answered Lucette, her expression changing to sulky resentful as she turned back to face Hermione. The bony shoulders lifted beneath her calico dress as she uttered a despairing sigh. 'We're used to having people, lots of people about us, Guillaume and me. It's so dull in that hamlet.' With downcast eyes, the young woman caught at a stray strand of fair hair and wound it around her finger. Hermione's cheeks dimpled with a smile as a yet more harrowing sigh was loosed upon her. And when this proved to have no effect, with a toss of her head, Lucette turned her attention back to the street. It was not long before she let out a shriek of excitement.

'Pardon me, Mademoiselle Hermione, but just see how fine and beautiful those noblemen look in their uniforms!'

Hermione clicked her teeth with exasperation. The two officers walking beneath the trees did indeed look magnificent in their red jackets, large black hats, white breeches and glossy black boots, but other than casting an admiring glance, she was not interested in any man. There was no time for anything but her plans to sell timber. It would take years to return Du Chesne to its former glory, and she would be as wrinkled as Marie by then.

'This is the house, madame,' boomed Guillaume from aloft. The horses had slowed before iron gates which fronted a two-storey house built of stone.

'Off he goes.' Lucette giggled, as the coach groaned and creaked under Guillaume's weight. 'Just look at the size of him ... his fat behind is near bursting through those breeches! He's been eating his head off since he got his knees under the old woman's table.'

Hardly aware of Lucette's chatter, Hermione gathered up her bag and fan in readiness as Guillaume returned and hoisted himself back up to his seat. With the guidance of the servant who had come rushing out, horses and coach made the turn into the courtyard; no mean feat, as a coach was already occupying the greater part of the space. Every advance thereafter was minimal, for what with the clucking and cries of alarm from the servant lest contact be made against the glossy paintwork of his master's coach, the neighing of horses and Guillaume's oaths, it hardly seemed worth the trouble to save but a few paces to the door. At last it was time to alight. With exaggerated ceremony, Guillaume arrived to drop down the step of their old walnut of a coach. His broad face was dripping with sweat, but his expression was full of bravado.

'They don't make coaches like they used to, madame,' he declared in a booming voice. Hermione stepped down, and as she glanced upward, she saw that her arrival had provided a source of merriment. To her mortification, three onlookers at an upstairs window were shaking with laughter. Seeing they were discovered, the woman and the two girls immediately withdrew from sight. Then, claiming Hermione's attention, Claude Tilly hurried out of the house towards her.

'Madame Du Chesne, I have been impatient for your arrival! I trust you had a pleasant journey. What think you of our town?' He ushered her up the flight of steps into the house. 'Isn't it the most exciting place you have ever seen – so many new buildings, such potential for men who know how to go about things! Let us go up to meet my dear Angélique and our two daughters. The town's foundation stone,' he chatted on as he led the way from the hall, 'was laid in 1663, and now they say we have over nine thousand people within the walls! Today,' he said, turning towards Hermione as they reached a landing, 'we have the privilege of entering the royal arsenal to watch the launching of a ship. My family has been honoured with an invitation to attend a reception afterwards, and I have arranged affairs so that you are included on the guest list.'

'That was very kind of you,' murmured Hermione. 'On such an important occasion that cannot have been easy.'

'No, it wasn't.' Claude Tilly laughed, leading her past a newish-looking tapestry. 'It is not every day the son of the King's Contrôleur Général visits. Every port official wants to attend with his family in the hope of glimpsing the Marquis de Seignelay ... even so, money always finds a helpful palm.' He laughed, flashing her a look of cunning pride. Hermione inwardly cringed, beginning to wish that she had not come. He stepped forward briskly and opened a door.

'Ah, there you are, my dear wife,' he exclaimed, as he led Hermione forward into a salon hung with more tapestries. Three pairs of curious eyes stared towards Hermione. Madame Tilly, holding her position on a chair as if for a portrait, gave an immediate impression of gaudy disorder. There was an over-abundance of curves and curls and all bedecked and caught up with a profusion of ribbon and French point lace. Standing on either side of her were two slender girls of some twelve and thirteen years, wearing simple gowns of white.

'Madame Tilly, dear daughters, receive into your bosom our most special guest, Madame Hermione Du Chesne. Now I beseech you, dear ladies, do not tarry too long, for we must take our places as soon as possible at the arsenal. I shall join you in ten minutes' time when we must be on our way.'

After the salon door had closed on Claude Tilly, there was an awkward silence. Then the ample bosom of Hermione's hostess heaved as she launched into speech.

'Monsieur Tilly has told me a great deal about your terrible sufferings. It must be so hard to live in a house which is open to wind and rain, and so soon after your poor dear father, the Chevalier, departed this life. But I must not delay you,' she added, with a nervous glance towards the door. 'My girls will show you to the boudoir where you may refresh yourself, though I urge you not to take too long, madame, for though I have a million questions to ask about Paris, we must make sure we have a good place at the arsenal.'

With her two shy escorts leading the way, Hermione was taken to a bedroom. The girls remained outside, and mindful of her hostess's anxiety about time, Hermione soon rejoined her giggling escorts.

'The rosewater was very refreshing,' she said, smiling as she touched the inside of her wrists to her nostrils.

'Maman thought you might like lavender, but we said you would like rose.'

'Come along, ladies. The horses are impatient,' called up Claude Tilly from the hall below.

'And so is Papa too' The fairer of the two girls giggled, whose name was Adèle. Once outside with the Tilly family, Hermione saw with some relief that Guillaume had taken the coach off to the stables. Lucette apparently had gone with him.

'It must seem very dull here in the provinces.' Angélique Tilly beamed, her curls nodding with every jolt of the coach as it moved out from the courtyard into the street.

'Not at all,' replied Hermione, her smile encompassing the two wide-eyed girls who had not for a moment left off staring at her. 'Rochefort seems very lively, and I have never entered a royal arsenal before.'

Angélique Tilly gave a pleased nod and simpered. 'Monsieur Tilly, I am bound to say, has great influence here because he supplies ...'

'No need to bore Madame Du Chesne with talk of business,' Claude Tilly cut in sharply. The rounds of Angélique Tilly's cheeks flamed red at her husband's impatient rebuke, and she simpered this time with embarrassment, casting apologetic eyes towards Hermione. Having been put in possession of the facts of her host's livelihood by Father Grégoire, Hermione was seized with mischief.

'I wouldn't be bored, Monsieur Tilly,' she enthused. 'How does your work bring you into contact with the arsenal?' The merchant's narrow lips forced a tight smile as, along with Angélique Tilly and the two girls, Hermione looked to him for his answer. But then, distracting all of them, the coachman aloft shouted down.

'It would be quicker, Monsieur Tilly, for you to step down here on the rue d'Arsenal. There seems to be some hold-up at the arsenal gate.' Madame Tilly gave a sigh of disappointment, but the merchant seized upon the interruption with alacrity and rose from his seat, and almost before the coachman had lowered the step, he was outside urging the women to follow.

'Hurry along, ladies, hurry along! It won't do to cause a stir after the Minister and the Intendant take their places.'

Like a mother hen, Madame Tilly guided her girls before her and, in a most friendly way, offered her arm to Hermione. Straight ahead of them, on the other side of a wide street, was the impressive gateway into the royal arsenal. To its right was a large stone house set behind a wall.

'That beautiful house used to belong to the Sieur de Cheusse before

139

he sold it and his land to make way for the arsenal. I never thought to ever see inside.' Angélique giggled, her excitement spilling over as she beamed at Hermione. 'I don't expect even in Paris you have seen anything finer than our Hôtel de Cheusses?' Hermione smiled but did not reply, for while the house did promise elegance, it was of course, nothing to the Palais Royal, the Louvre, or the Hôtel de Guise and other great palaces of Parisian nobles.

With so many coaches waiting to enter through the open gates of the arsenal, walking had clearly given them an advantage. Joining the throng, they headed towards the river. On the grey waters of the Charente were vessels of every size, but the spectators' attention was directed towards a huge ship supported by props on a slipway. By degrees, Claude Tilly pushed and elbowed them forward through the ranks of onlookers to the front. A little apart from the press of people was a raised stand over which was a sumptuous canopy of crimson.

'Those seats are for the Minister and other high officials,' explained Claude Tilly, peering around his wife's ample breasts towards Hermione. As his head ducked back, Hermione heard him give a short laugh, and his tone when he spoke was boastful. 'You'll see, Madame Tilly, one day that is where we will sit, and then your parents will think you have not done so badly to marry a merchant.' Hermione turned her attention towards the swarm of workmen moving about the upper deck of the enormous ship.

'It's magnificent!' she exclaimed, taking in the frenzy of activity, 'but what chaos and confusion!'.

'Not so, mademoiselle!' countered a deep voice alongside her. 'Every man knows what he is about. The master-shipwrights are completely in control.'

'And the different-coloured uniforms,' contributed Madame Tilly, poking her head forward, 'are to identify different workers ... caulkers, joiners, riggers and the like. Am I not right, monsieur?'

'Indeed you are, good lady,' Hermione's neighbour agreed jovially. 'They built a galley in one day here yesterday ... just as a spectacle.

Leave galleys to the King's shipwrights at Toulon. Making ships of the line seaworthy is more what Rochefort is about.' As Hermione listened with interest, the mass of white hair pushing out beneath the elderly man's large hat reminded her of something: a time, a place? Something she had seen a little while back. As she mused on where it might have been and watched the comings and goings of the men aloft on the ship, the answer eventually came: the port of La Rochelle. From his weather-beaten complexion, she surmised he must work at the arsenal, for he was too old to be a sailor.

'What is a caulker?' she asked, wanting to keep up conversation with him.

'The men who make a ship watertight; they push oakum between the planking with their irons and afterwards coat it with hot pitch.'

'This ship looks so much bigger than those out on the river,' murmured Hermione, her gaze straying along the waterfront to a man o' war with closed gun ports.

'It only seems that way,' responded the elderly man, glancing her way with a slight smile. 'Because out there on the river you only see the ship from the waterline upward. Here, you are looking upwards from the keel. Step inside before the planking of the decks is put in ... it's as vast as any cathedral!'

'For incense you have tar!'

'Cordite in battle! For a master-shipwright such as me, it is the smell of oak!'

'And did you go much to Versailles, Madame Du Chesne?' Angélique Tilly's interruption implied there had been enough talk of ships. Reluctantly, Hermione turned away from the elderly shipwright to answer her hostess.

'No, I did not, madame.'

'But you have surely seen the King, the great courtiers ... the royal ladies?' There was no mistaking which of the ladies Angélique Tilly was hinting at.

'I have been as close to Madame de Montespan as I am to you,' answered Hermione, thinking of the time the royal favourite's carriage had come to a halt near Notre Dame. 'Her eyes are brilliant – she has the most piercing glance.'

'And Fontanges?' The merchant's wife giggled with a knowing wink. 'I see your hair is dressed in the style we hear she favours.' The plump woman's expression was avid for gossip, which was beginning to irritate, so Hermione did not answer. She was relieved when a ripple of excitement all about and trumpets heralded the arrival of the Minister of the Marine, the Marquis de Seignelay.

'I hope the Minister knows it is Claude Tilly who supplies the finest timber here!' Angélique Tilly's boastful shriek sounded for all to hear. Hermione could not see Tilly beyond the bulk of his wife, but his snarling riposte to her outburst, though delivered in an undertone, still carried to Hermione's ears.

'Now she, that Parisienne knows my business! If your loose tongue costs me a *livre* more than I've offered for her estate, you'll feel my cane!'

The threat made Hermione tremble with fury within. She could not comment from where she was, but she relished the thought of telling this bully that she was not going to sell! With a shake of her head as if to dismiss something unpleasant, she turned to the elderly master-shipwright with a smile.

'It must take a great many trees to build a ship?'

'Some two and some four thousand,' he said nodding, 'one of the reasons why Rochefort was settled on for the arsenal. There is no shortage of timber in the forest for refitting ships, though compass pieces are becoming harder to find. As for masts, well, my grandson will tell you the best come from the Baltic.'

'You know a great deal about it, monsieur!'

'These hands, young lady,' said the elderly man, holding up hands which were swollen with age, 'have been building ships for most of my life.' Hermione met the fierce, proud expression of the shipwright with a smile of delight, and she lowered her voice so that only he would hear.

'Then I am most fortunate, for you, monsieur, are the very person I had hoped to meet. I need to understand everything about selling timber.'

'Tilly there could tell you all about that.' Hermione arched her brows and gave a look. The blue eyes beneath the fierce eyebrows glinted with understanding. 'Aha ... of course, you need someone who is not a timber contractor! You must meet my grandson Jacques. No one knows more about such things than he. Do you have an invitation to the reception at the Hôtel de Cheusses?'

'I believe so.'

'Jacques made certain of one for me, but I'd feel like a fish out of water. He is dancing attendance over there with the Intendant's party. But I'll delay setting back home to introduce you to him.'

'Oh, there is no need for help.' Hermone smiled. 'I believe I shall be able to seek him out.' Before Henri Maurellet could put his surprise into words, proceedings on the slipway took his attention.

'Get ready mademoiselle! They've finished greasing the rails each side of the keel to help the launching cradle slide more easily into the water. Next they'll knock away those props at the stern ... the blocks went early this morning.'

'What about its masts?' Hermione queried, with a gesture towards festive flag poles and branches of oak.

'They'll be stepped in along with the fitting of rigging after she is afloat. There's still a lot to do before she's really finished.' The elderly shipwright nodded. 'Nor did they start it today, but eleven months ago!'

'I hope you are finding it diverting, Madame Du Chesne?' Claude Tilly said, leaning towards Hermione. 'Ah, I see it is Maître Maurellet from Soubise who is explaining matters to you ... no better instructor. He is not only a master-shipwright, but one of the finest makers of models in France.'

Tilly's ingratiating tone had the effect of making the elderly man beside Hermione turn away, his expression stiff with dislike. 'Little toad,' she heard the old man mutter.

The last prop now being gone, all that held the ship were ropes. A buzz of excitement rippled around the huge crowd of spectators and a man shouted out, 'Only the cable from the hawse holes to the bollards holding her!' As the command to release rang out, along with everyone around her Hermione emitted a great 'Ah!' as the launching cradle with its towering burden slid downwards into the water. A great cheer went up, almost drowning out the trumpet fanfare. 'Magnificent!' murmured Hermione. 'Like a huge swan.' Beside her, Maître Maurellet nodded, his eyes alight with pleasure.

'Wait for the day when the swan is given great white wings to spread,' he replied, having to shout as the arsenal boomed out a salute.

Though it was the first time Hermione had ever been invited to attend such a gathering, she felt completely at ease at the Hôtel de Cheusses, for the reception rooms were as nothing in comparison to those of Versailles, which she had visited on public days along with hundreds of other Parisians. After being announced, Claude Tilly hovered around uncertainly, with his wife every now and again letting out a nervous giggle. Then, on spying someone with whom he was acquainted, the timber merchant sped away.

'So many important matters to discuss,' faltered his abandoned wife, her plump cheeks reddening with embarrassment. 'I expect you are used to such gatherings, Madame Du Chesne.' Biting on her lower lip, Angélique Tilly snapped open her fan, her eyes stricken with fright. Hermione realized both she and the two girls were waiting expectantly for her to take command. She glanced about and, spotting an unoccupied window seat, started towards it before it could be taken by anyone else. Then she beckoned Madame Tilly and the girls to join her.

'This will give an excellent view around the *salon*,' she said, gesturing for the girls to sit. 'Would you prefer to stay with Matilde and Adèle, or to move amongst the guests, Madame Tilly?'

'I think here with my girls will be just right. And there is a seat for you, Madame Du Chesne.'

'Thank you,' Hermione said smiling, 'but there is someone to whom I need to speak. However, I will make sure a servant brings you refreshment.'

'Oh, will you?' exclaimed Angélique Tilly, the tension slipping away from her overheated face. 'How brave of you!' Had Hermione declared she was about to kill a king's musketeer on their behalf, she could not have received greater looks of devotion from the three. So, whilst she did not know what the custom was, she headed towards a servant who was carrying a large platter of tiny cakes.

'Be sure not to neglect Madame,' murmured Hermione close to the man's ear, as with an air of authority she pointed out the trio, 'Madame Tilly is *most precious* to the Minister!' Then, as if spotting someone, Hermione gave a flick to her fan and glided away into the throng. Now, of course, she did not feel so at ease among the groups of lofty officials and officers of the Marine and the army, but she wandered about as casually as she could eyes alert for Maître Maurellet's grandson. The crush of people was oppressive, but she was in no doubt that she would recognise the man who had disembarked from the ship at La Rochelle. Jacques Maurellet, she murmured, repeating the name. She sipped her champagne and examined various groups of men as they talked and laughed, pivoting slowly as she considered whether to ask for help. Then, in a corner, she glimpsed a man with broad shoulders. Inexplicably, she felt an immediate quickening of breath as she moved towards him.

'Jacques Maurellet?'

At the sound of a woman's husky voice, Jacques swung round with a start.

'Mademoiselle, you have the advantage of me,' he apologized, making a gesture to the officer he had been talking to as he moved away.

'I am Hermione Du Chesne. Your grandfather said I would find you here.'

'Of course.' Jacques nodded, rapidly considering a variety of possibilities as to where they might have met. Certainly it was not in Rochefort, and positively not at Soubise. There was something that struck a chord … something, something? Jacques's shoulders lifted into a little shrug and Hermione laughed, appreciating his dilemma.

'La Rochelle. I saw you in passing from my coach. You had stepped down from a ship, and your grandfather was there. People were laughing at me,' she added to assist him more, giving a rueful smile. Jacques's eyes settled a penetrating look upon Hermione, and then his lips opened into a wide smile. 'You were looking in at the tavern. And before that, the lady smothered in mud! Was that really you?' Their eyes met and mutual laughter burst forth as both conjured up the scene. 'You live here in Rochefort?' Jacques asked eagerly.

'No, Du Chesne; it's on the road to Saintes. Maître Maurellet says you know important people at the arsenal. I have timber to sell.'

'I see. You are asking me to use my influence to obtain a contract?' Jacques's tone was cool. He felt piqued.

'I would not ask you to do that,' Hermione said quickly, sensing he was about to move away. 'I just need to know how to go about things. Your grandfather said you know a great deal about forestry. Could you recommend someone to look over my forest, to offer advice on what should be done?'

The wary expression on Jacques Maurellet's face disappeared. Suddenly, irked by the heat and din of the room, he glanced about, wanting to escape. 'Let's walk outside. You can then tell me about your estate.'

A swift look to where the shy trio were seated reassured Hermione that Angélique Tilly and her girls were happily eating. There being no sign of Claude Tilly, it seemed she would not be missed.

'It would take the whole of a day to show you everything,' remarked Jacques Maurellet as he led Hermione away from the reception. 'And there is still much construction going on. But if it is your first visit to the arsenal, you should see a little more, especially as trees are its life blood.'

'I was told Rochefort was chosen for a royal arsenal because of its forest.'

'Partly … it also has deep anchorage. Most importantly, the river's entrance is protected by the Iles de Ré, d'Aix and d'Oléron. The Dutch and English will find it impossible to threaten our ships here. Soubise was also considered,' he continued, as they walked past a windmill, 'but at the time, the Grand Seigneur Rohan refused to sell his land. The Sieur de Cheusses, however, dared not say no to the King. Now, look ahead, Madame Du Chesne, and let your eyes delight in Jules Mandouin Mansart's design for the royal ropeworks. It is elegant, don't you think?'

'It is the longest building I have ever seen. Why so long?'

'Lengths of yarn spun from the hemp have to be the best part of a thousand feet because so much is taken up in the twisting of the ropes. Look at that ship on the river,' he said with a gesture. 'Do you see the cables running from the hawse holes? They must be over six hundred and fifty feet in order for her to weigh anchor in two hundred and forty feet of water. On a ship like that the riggers will need something like seventeen miles of cordage.'

Hermione studied the intricate spider's-web of rigging. 'Is it my imagination or does that ship seem to be tilting to one side?'

Jacques Maurellet laughed. 'I think it is your imagination. But it can happen when the frame of a ship has been left to weather on the blocks. We're not absolutely certain what causes it, but it might have something to do with the sun shining mostly on one side of the timber.'

Hermione's gaze took in the busy scene on the river, the number of ships hauled up on the slipways for repair.

'Two thousand oaks … even four thousand,' she murmured, casting her mind back to Henri Maurellet's words. 'A load of timber weighs a ton.'

'A ship of the Third Rate takes one thousand tons of timber.' Jacques grinned, instantly following her drift.

'How much does a load of timber fetch?'

'It varies. Compass timber commands more … think along the lines of nine livres a ton.'

'Oh, marvellous … nine livres a ton!'

Jacques's eyes sparkled with amusement, and his laughter was unrestrained at the blaze of excited avarice showing in Hermione's dark eyes. 'It needs to be top quality for the Marine,' he warned. 'Royal yards and private ones like my own family's also look for the most attractive tender.'

'Can I count on your advice … for a fee? I would not expect you to come to Du Chesne for nothing.'

'Madame Du Chesne, I shall be happy to visit for the sheer pleasure of seeing you again.' The words were polite enough, but vibrant with flirtation, and Hermione had to look away to hide her reaction. Nor should she forget how this man had swept the tavern wench onto his knee at La Rochelle. Suddenly, the figure of a short man clutching at his wig came into view, approaching from the direction of the Hôtel de Cheusses. As he drew nearer, Hermione saw it was Claude Tilly.

'Madame Du Chesne! Madame Du Chesne! Madame Du Chesne, we are going home soon!' called out the timber contractor. Jacques Maurellet turned with a look of surprise towards Hermione, and his deep voice was tinged with disappointment.

'Claude Tilly is a friend of yours?'

Hermione shook her head. 'He is not a friend, though I am indebted to him for bringing me here today.'

'But he could tell you everything you need to know about trees.'

'That's true, Monsieur Maurellet,' countered Hermione teasingly, 'but then I would not have the sheer pleasure of seeing you again! Shall we say, three days hence?'

CHAPTER 9

irm to his promise to visit the château of Du Chesne, Jacques set forth before dawn. He had more than enough to attend to at the yard, but he was well pleased to get away from his grandfather's grumbles and his own suspicions about Perrette. On reflection, it was strange she had not wanted to go to the fête at the royal arsenal. At the time, she had pleaded a headache, but now he wondered whether her interest in the Huguenots had had something to do with it. He returned the greeting of a journeyman walking towards him and reined in his horse to exchange a few words. Then, as he eased the stallion back into canter, his thoughts returned to his cousin. There was no daintier woman, yet often she seemed in her ways more like a boy. He had noticed how she would hover behind apprentices as if impatient to snatch away their chisel to perform some intricacy, just as she excelled with her embroidery needle. After the dreadful accident of eighteen months ago, she would find any pretext to visit the yard. He understood her grief; he felt it himself. He would look up expecting to see his father and uncle at work, and their absence hit hard. So, when she had asked to do the bookkeeping whilst he was away on his travels, despite Grandfather's disinclination to have a 'woman's interference', Jacques had accepted her help, mostly because the accounts would end up in a hopeless muddle if they were left to Henri. Since his return from Riga, Perrette had not wanted to give up the cubby-hole which served as an office. More than once she had reminded him that her dowry would be that part his uncle had formerly owned in the shipyard. Jacques's lips compressed, and, as was increasingly his habit, he cast his mind away from promises made to think of something else.

'Come on, show me what you can do,' he urged the stallion. 'You've been getting fat standing about in your stall!'

There was no certainty when Jacques Maurellet would arrive, but that he would come on the day agreed Hermione never doubted. So she was dressed for riding, and Pierre had saddled up one of the old horses. Her mood was one of excitement and anticipation; what would he think of the forest? Could it bring in regular income to Du Chesne? An inner part of her mind wondered also whether there would be that feel of flirtatious banter on which they had parted. As soon as Lucette dashed into the Painted Room with news that a rider was coming through the Keep she hurried out to greet the master-shipwright, but as he dismounted and they exchanged greetings, she sensed a quiet reserve about him. With a shy smile, she made a wide sweep of her arm to take in the whole of the château.

'What do you think?'

Jacques's gaze took in the creamy stone of the towers, then the encroaching green of the forest below which, like the trees on his approach, guarded the château like a palisade. He swung about, his attention dwelling briefly on the massive tower of the keep, then around and along to where ivy and ferns had taken a strong hold on the blackened beams and stonework of the ruined wing.

'It looks as if Du Chesne has been slumbering for a long time.'

'Perhaps I am wrong in wanting to awaken it?'

They walked towards the tumbled-down piles of masonry, and Jacques idly pulled out a weed from between two blackened slabs of stone.

'Neglect leads to eventual death: the house will be happy when you have restored it to life.' His deep voice expressed such calm certainty that Hermione suddenly felt less overwhelmed by the immensity of the task ahead; all was possible. She was about to ask his opinion on how to set about rebuilding when a furious outburst of barking made them both turn around. Pierre's great hound came bounding towards her visitor in attack.

'No, Rouge! Stop!' shouted Hermione in alarm. Rouge took not the slightest notice till two piercing whistles from Pierre brought the hairy assailant to an immediate halt. Uttering a grumbling, dismissive growl, Rouge flopped down a body's length away from Jacques and began to lick at one of his paws.

'You'll have to learn to whistle.' Jacques laughed.

'Pierre has been in service here since he was a boy,' explained Hermione, as the elderly retainer came forward leading the old horse, tacked up with an equally old side-saddle. 'He has knowledge of the forest and will guide us. Can I offer you breakfast before we go?'

'I am happy to set off now.'

'I am riding for the first time,' she confessed as he offered his hands to help her up onto the saddle.

'You are nervous?' The blue eyes beneath the thick black brows were quizzical as he looked up at her. Hermione shook her head and laughed as he swung himself up onto his stallion.

'This poor old thing can barely walk. I am nervous about what you might have to say ... so much depends upon it.'

'Some proprietors faced with your problems would take a quicker path to profit by planting wheat,' he said, as they passed beneath the keep and followed Pierre and Rouge over the bridge towards the forest. 'Fortunately, Colbert's ordinances forbids such practice.'

'You mean I can't do what I like on my own land?'

'Mostly you can, but conservation has priority. We need trees for the Marine.'

'How can that be?' Hermione urged her mount onward as she

lowered her head to nibble grass. 'From here to Paris are thousands of trees ... I have seen them with my own eyes.'

'And yes, throughout the whole of France,' agreed Jacques, motioning her to go ahead of him as he pulled aside ivy and brambles. 'Unless exploitations are controlled and forests properly managed, in fifty, a hundred, two hundred years France could have no timber reserves for her shipyards. Can you imagine how serious it would be if we ran out of wood? The whole of human existence depends on trees!'

Hermione glanced askance at him.

'You think I am mad when we have so many great forests,' he continued, 'but consider how long it takes to grow a mature oak ... over two hundred years. Yet people chop them down without a thought.'

'Two hundred years,' murmured Hermione, trying to take in the scale of things. 'Only these saplings, not we, will know what life will be like then.'

'And not many of them,' intervened her companion, with a teasing note in his voice. 'Of twelve thousand sown to one acre, thirty years into their cycle two-thirds will have disappeared. By the time the crop has fulfilled its life cycle of two hundred and twenty years, it will carry only fifty-five trees to the arpent ... eleven thousand two hundred and sixty cubic feet of timber.'

'Stop, stop,' protested Hermione, clapping her hands to her ears in laughter, 'it is too early in the day!'

From the initial shy formality on his arrival, conversation between them had gradually become an easy flow, but not wishing to distract him from what she had asked him to do, Hermione gradually fell back so he could concentrate on what was about him. After some two hours, he halted, resting a hand behind on the saddle as he faced about.

'You have a good number of stands ready for felling this autumn.'

'Why wait till then?' she asked, impatient to sell as soon as possible.

'Autumn is preferable because the sap isn't rising. The first thing is to make a start on clearance ... you are overrun with weeds and hornbeam.'

'So the shoots have more space to grow?'

'Yes, but only from the weeds. Too much space and you'll rear *gourmands*.'

'Greedies?'

Jacques smiled. 'So called because they stretch out their branches.' Excellent for compass timber, but what you're after are stands which are straight, with good length before the first branches. The introduction of a dense undergrowth of hornbeam and sometimes beech prevents branches forming and spreading low down. Another really important thing to do is clear out rabbits ... tender green shoots are their favourite dish. Does your man, Pierre, know much about forestry?'

'He hunts, mainly.'

'What about the village ... isn't there someone who worked here for the Chevalier Du Chesne?'

'It is unlikely. He was a good age when he died, and he was young when he lived here.'

'Time was green then when he rode amongst these trees.' Jacques Maurellet's tone was tender, and Hermione liked him for it. She looked upwards to the canopy above and imagined how it might have been in the Chevalier's day.

'These trees perhaps would have been just saplings. His father would have planted some, perhaps even his grandfather.'

'Planting oak requires a generous heart.' Jacques Maurellet's expression was challenging, but Hermione did not flinch. That she would not see the trees she planted reach maturity mattered not.

'Do you want me to call Pierre back to ask about a woodsman?'

'No need,' replied Jacques. 'Let him lead us to the boundary. I'll talk to him then.'

They continued on at a faster pace in order to catch up with Pierre, who had disappeared, though every so often an outburst of barking kept them on the right line. Then, as if he had been sent to round them up, Rouge crashed through the undergrowth and urged them forward with deep barks.

'Can that be water?' asked Hermione, glimpsing a sparkle ahead.

'It will be the Charente. So, Madame Du Chesne,' exclaimed Jacques, enjoying Hermione's obvious excitement, 'not only do you have timber, but the means of transporting it!'

Leaving Jacques to speak to Pierre, Hermione sat on a fallen branch of a tree and looked at the sunlight sparkling on the blue waters of the river. Rouge came bounding up to her carrying a great stick clenched between his jaws.

'The first of the exploitations.' She laughed as he dropped the wood at her feet. The rusty-haired dog growled and wagged his tail as if waiting. Not really knowing what she was supposed to do, Hermione picked up the stick and threw it beyond Rouge and was rewarded with a joyful bark as he chased through the undergrowth after it.

'It's been a glorious morning,' she enthused, as Jacques Maurellet strode back to her. 'You will enjoy Marie's special way of dealing with rabbits; our curé swears she is the best cook in Saintonge. And afterwards, I will show you the beautiful painted panels in the study.'

Jacques's black eyebrows drew together in an expression of regret as his hands made an apologetic gesture. 'There is nothing I would enjoy more,' he declared with warmth, 'but if I am to be here the day after tomorrow to meet the men Pierre has in mind, there is much I must attend to at the shipyard.'

'Won't you at least come back and take a piece of bread in hand?'

For reply, Jacques swung himself up onto the saddle. 'Try not to worry,' he said, covering the dark tangles of his hair with his hat. 'You say your means are slender. I shall return in two days time and tell you how you might save money, and make money.'

'Oh, tell me now!' pleaded Hermione. 'I cannot wait two whole days!'

Jacques gathered up the reins, his lips lifting in a wide smile as he glanced into her dark eyes.

'If you are going to work with oak, you will have to learn to be patient, Madame Du Chesne.' Then with a cheery wave he rode away through the trees.

On the following day, a letter arrived for Hermione, brought to the door by a journeyman. Bidding Lucette take the man to the kitchen for victuals, Hermione settled herself on a chair in the Painted Room with the letter. Father Grégoire had helped her make a good start on reading. She only hoped there would not be too many long words to struggle over. To her surprise, on breaking the seal she saw the paper was only marked with symbols. The way they were drawn was familiar; clearly the letter had come from Olivier. Could he be in some kind of trouble to contact her in this way? She rang the bell for Lucette.

'Ask the journeyman who gave him this letter.'

'Those look like Master Olivier's squiggles,' commented Lucette, as her eyes glanced down at the parchment.

'Yes, but not a word to anyone. Just find out as much as you can before the man leaves. Ask what is happening in Paris.'

While Lucette was away, Hermione studied the symbols. A bird flying up into the air with fire and earth below she knew very well. As a child, she had copied the bird many times. It was Olivier's sign for separation: 'the division of bodies, Hermione.' At the time, his words had meant little. What was he trying to say here? Two wavy lines also needed no thought, for they represented water. The next symbol, a square with two lines and a circle on the left, she knew not what to make of. The final drawing, a rectangle crossed diagonally by two lines, meant a month. What was Olivier trying to say? Outside the room, she heard Lucette's feet splash through water where it had rained in during the night.

'Were you able to find out anything more?'

'He says the man was bundled up in a hooded cloak so he couldn't see his face, except he limped slightly.'

'Then it could be Olivier,' murmured Hermione. 'What news of Paris?'

'Oh, that's different; he had plenty to say and couldn't tell it quick enough. The crowds were enormous on the day the witch La Cheron was burnt. But La Voisin and her old boyfriend Le Sage are still in prison … they must be talking their heads off by now. No one, high or low born, is safe until they find the ones who tried to poison the King.'

'Poison the King,' gasped Hermione in horror. 'How could it be possible? Who would dare? It is unthinkable!'

Lucette shook her head. 'Guillaume said it is not the first time the King has been in danger. When he was a small boy, he and his mother had to run away from the Fronde. Oh, it makes a change hearing all the gossip.' Lucette's sigh was heart-rending. 'Olivier's house was small, but I wasn't paddling in water.'

'It was the thunderstorm last night that brought it in. We'll soon have everything fixed,' responded Hermione cheerfully, buoyed up since Jacques's visit. 'Monsieur Maurellet is coming tomorrow.'

'Pierre told me so,' commented Lucette with a sly smile. 'Monsieur is very manly and dashing, don't you think, Madame Hermione?'

Hermione gave her a stern look. 'Find Pierre and send him to me!'

'Certainly, *milady*,' flashed back Lucette, adding with a twist of her narrow hips as she flounced away, 'even Pierre and Guillaume look interesting in this farmyard.'

While she waited for Pierre, Hermione looked at her letter again: separation and water. Could it mean Olivier was going on a journey across water, a river or the sea? Could he possibly be coming to Du Chesne … and by the other symbol, in a month's time? What if he was still in Paris and needed help? There came a tap on the door and she looked up, expecting Pierre, but instead it was Guillaume, and she saw that his expression was anxious.

'Might I speak to you, Madame Hermione … Lucette says there is a letter from the master?'

'It seems like it,' replied Hermione, making a gesture for him to look at the parchment.

'That's the master. I've seen enough of those in the laboratory to know his hand,' agreed the big man, 'but what does it mean, madame?'

'I think it means he may be leaving Paris and travelling by water somewhere.'

'Here?' asked Guillaume with a glad note in his voice.

'That I am not certain of. He may not have been able to get away.'

'I must go to him,' said Guillaume, looking to her for agreement. Hermione nodded, feeling a mixture of relief and anxiety.

'I should not ask you … it could place you in danger, especially if he has been arrested.'

'I'm not afraid, nor will I lead any police back here,' said Guillaume with a meaningful glint in his one good eye, 'but I'll not sleep for worrying about the master. I should have gone back to him before.'

'That is my fault,' nodded Hermione, 'I've relied on you so. When will you start?'

'Within the hour, if I can take one of the new horses you bought?'

'Of course, whatever you need. I'll go and get money for the journey. Take Olivier's pistol too.'

Guillaume's hurried departure caused a great stir, especially with Lucette, who never left off begging him to take messages to her friends. Though Marie kept quiet, she busied herself packing up cheese and sausage.

'Will he come back to us, madame?'

'I hope so, Marie,' said Hermione, trying not to let her own anxiety show. 'Duty calls him, and God willing, he will return with my dear friend Monsieur Olivier. Ah, here he comes now with Pierre; they have become good friends, do you not think?' There was a slight nod of the old lady's bonneted head, and though it was not possible to see her expression sideways on because of the proud curve of the material, Hermione just knew a smile was softening her wrinkled face.

On the morrow, with Guillaume gone, Pierre set off up the hill to the village where he was to meet Jacques Maurellet and take him to see two possible woodsmen. For some reason, he left Rouge behind and the dog's mournful howls never ceased until, on her way to the *pigeonnier*,

Hermione glimpsed Marie dropping a bone over the stable door. Then, thankfully, there was only the soft clucking of chickens and snuffling of the sow. The *pigeonnier* had fallen into disuse, though a few birds were fluttering about in alarm at the disturbance as she mounted the rickety steps outside. In the dismal light, she squinted up at tier upon tier of nesting ledges set around the circular walls. She calculated there once could have been near a thousand birds nesting on them.

'And they shall again. A job for Guillaume when he gets back!' Hermione instantly bit on her lip as she retreated from the filth, lest the Devil, heeding her words, bring disaster on Guillaume. Her fingers caught at the crucifix round her neck, and she murmured a prayer to Saint Michael to protect him from harm on the road. Would he find Olivier still in Paris? she wondered, and Agnès and her parents, what of them? As she came opposite the stable door, she heard Rouge give an impatient whine.

'It can't have been a very big bone.' She laughed, crossing over to give him a pat. The moment she opened the door, his big body nearly knocked her over as he rushed out, streaking away like an arrow up the slope towards the house. When she followed on beneath the hay loft and under the stone archway, sure enough, Pierre had returned. With him was Jacques, whose stallion was drinking from one of the two troughs. Its master was talking to two young men, who were being studied with obvious interest from the doorway of the kitchen by Lucette. As he spotted Hermione, Jacques left the two young men and strolled over to her.

'Is all settled?' Hermione asked eagerly.

'They are ideal,' smiled Jacques, 'strong and willing to learn. Naturally, Pierre is content because he suggested them. So, I've given them a rough idea of how to start things off. For some reason, someone introduced a few lime trees, but they must go. Lime is invasive and does not mix well with oak. It won't take them long to remove it, and its bark will sell for twine. I'll come back in two weeks' time to check their progress.' Hermione nodded, and the shipbuilder's blue eyes suddenly narrowed. He stretched forward and plucked at her hair. 'You seem to have abandoned mud for cobwebs, Madame Du Chesne.' He smiled again, holding up dusty threads and a feather.

'I've come from the *pigeonnier* … it hasn't been used for years.'

'Then no doubt soon you'll be offering doves on your table,' he teased. 'Impatience here is a virtue.'

'I don't like wasting time,' Hermione laughed, 'and you have kept me waiting two days to hear how I might save money when I might have already put it into practice.'

'Then I'll not lose another minute. Take me to your stables.' Tiny laughter lines marked the corners of Jacques's eyes as he cast an amused glance at Hermione, and, filled with curiosity, she led him towards the stables.

'Ah, that brings back a memory of La Rochelle,' he commented as he opened double doors and the battered walnut of a coach was revealed. 'We really will have to find you something more up to date.'

'First, you need to tell me how I would pay for one.'

'The answer lies in here,' said Jacques, walking along into the next building, in which was a row of empty stalls, beside those occupied by her three mares.

'I don't understand. You mean keep more horses? How would that save money?'

'Not just any horses. You would keep a stallion for the King. I'll explain.' he smiled, amused by her shocked reaction. 'Fifteen years ago it was usual to buy horses from abroad for the army's needs. Most owners of coaches prefer horses from Holland and Denmark because they are big and strong. France's horse-rearing enterprise started in sixty-five. Colbert's aim is to make us independent of other countries. So anyone importing now, for example, an English horse has to pay twenty *livres* tax on it.

'But I know nothing about horses.'

'You have stables ... the rest can be learned. And you have a farrier in the village.'

'So, would I keep horses for the army?'

'On the contrary ... once there is a stallion in here, you'll be exempted from providing lodgings for soldiers. It is one of the reasons why I registered.'

'Rearing stallions *and* building ships?' Hermione teased. 'So,' she continued as they walked back down the row of stalls, 'you say it will save the expense of the billet, but how do I make money?'

Jacques closed the door of the stables behind them and they walked up the slope back towards the house.

'You'll be eligible for the thirty *livres* reduction in taxes and a fixed rate thereafter. Once the colt is four years old, you will be able to charge for every mare he covers.'

'How much?' asked Hermione, her eyes gleaming. Jacques inclined his head, and by his expression, she felt he was implying she was avaricious. 'Look at that,' she countered with a wide sweep of her arm which took in the ruined wing of the château. 'I need a great deal of money!'

Jacques walked away from her and for a while considered the stark, blackened beams rising up against the blue sky. Continuing his assessment, he entered into the ruin and looked upward to what remained of the upper floors. Shortly afterwards he re-emerged, and pausing by the well he took up a ladle of water from the bucket. As he quenched his thirst, his eye ran again over the ruined exterior and to the undamaged wing across the courtyard. Then he re-joined Hermione.

'Why rebuild? Just pull it down. Anyway, something for you to think of,' he added, seeing her reluctant expression. 'So, shall I put your name forward for a horse?'

'Yes! What will happen?'

'The Sieur Garsault is in charge of distribution; he, or more likely one of his officers, will come and inspect your facilities. So, the sooner you get Pierre to clean and paint the stable walls, the better.'

'Must you go so soon?' she asked, as he began to pull on his riding gloves.

'Like you, I have much to do,' he said with a wry smile, 'but I'll be back in two weeks. Be prepared,' he added, as he took his seat on the saddle and looked down on her. 'It won't be a heavy horse; they go to Brittany and Guyenne. The Sieur Garsault distributes horses from the Barbary to Poitou and Saintonge. So those ancient mares of yours had best prepare for an Arab stallion!'

CHAPTER 10

n his return to the shipyard, Jacques came upon Henri in the mould loft, and in a great state of irritability.

'What has happened?' he asked, staring down at letters and accounts scattered about the floor. 'Where is Perrette ... how did these get here?'

'They got there because that bad-tempered girl threw them there. And for the past half hour I have been trying to pick them up and set them in order,' Henri thundered, his face red from stooping.

'But why did she do it?' asked Jacques, gathering up all the papers.

'Because I told her to stop interfering, that's why! She believes when you are not here she is in charge of everything.'

'She means well,' said Jacques, calmly sifting out letters from bills.

'That might be so, but Matthieu has worked here for a good ten years.'

'Matthieu ... how does he come into it?'

'He was late back from his dinner, and she scolded him good and proper in front of the men.'

'How did he take it?' asked Jacques in alarm. His grandfather gave a shrug of his shoulders.

'He let it pass out of affection for her father, but he didn't like it, nor did the men. There's been some grumbling. I know it lightens your load, Jacques, her looking after things in the office, but the men don't care for it. For one thing, it means they have to watch their language for fear

165

she will hear.'

Jacques nodded and gave a sigh. 'Where is Perrette now?'

'Gone home to Marguerite I expect. It is time you got round to honouring your pledge; she needs babies to occupy her, like other women.' Henri Maurellet's expression was stern as he looked towards his grandson.

'I'll speak to her,' promised Jacques, and he walked through into the tiny office and sat down at the desk.

'Go now!'

Jacques swallowed hard and sighed with vexation. The earlier part of the day at Du Chesne had passed well, indeed, it had been very entertaining. With a resigned expression, he got to his feet, picked up his hat and left the mould loft. Outside he paused, debating whether to go and seek out Matthieu, go up to the inn for a drink, or speak to Perrette. He grimaced, and, steeling himself for the less appealing of the options, he turned in the direction of his aunt's house. On the way he considered the problem in hand. Perrette would take it very badly if he told her not to come to the yard anymore, and what if the Intendant sent him away on some other fact-finding mission? Who then would see to checking things?

As the gables of the house came into view he slackened his pace, wondering how he could soften the blow. At least it was not as difficult as that time two years ago when he had been the one to break the news. There had been no way of softening what he had to say then: that Antoine had been crushed. What a damned business it had been; Father had been killed outright, while his uncle died two days later. Had they lost their lives in a battle at sea, both men would have been remembered as heroes, but there was nothing heroic about being crushed under so many tons of oak.

Jacques found both women sitting out in the garden enjoying the soft warmth of early evening. On seeing him, Perrette put down her embroidery and gave a wave.

'Aunt, Perrette,' he smiled, looking down on them. 'Has your tooth stopped aching, Aunt Marguerite?'

'It has, nephew. I've had a clove wedged in the hole … just four teeth left and I wish they'd all drop out in my sleep.'

'Then you wouldn't be able to eat,' put in Perrette.

'I'd live on soup, and have you make it, mademoiselle, instead of leaving the cooking to Annette and me while you go off adding up figures at the yard. I hardly ever see her,' complained his aunt, darting an accusing look at Jacques.

'And now I am going to take her away – only for a little while,' Jacques added hastily, as the eyes of both women brightened with anticipation. 'It's a pleasant evening. I thought perhaps Perrette and I might go …'

'There's no need to go anywhere,' snorted his aunt, heaving herself onto her feet with the help of her two sticks. 'I've things to mind in the kitchen if you and your grandfather are to have supper.'

'Call me, Maman, if you need me,' said Perrette, gesturing for Jacques to sit beside her. His intention had been to talk about the trouble at the yard, but her obvious expectations had thrust his mind into a chaos of indecision. Since his return from the Baltic, he knew she was expecting him to speak. He averted his gaze, unable to respond to the love which shone in her eyes. What was it that held him back? Was it his freedom he feared to lose … the right to jump on his horse without explanation of where he was going or when he would return? Since coming home, he had felt trapped. He took a deep breath, deciding one thing at a time was the best way. Deal first with the immediate problem. Things could not go on with her upsetting the men. Their future together was better left until the moment was unclouded, for she would be sure to take badly what he now had to say.

'I hope Grandfather is in a kinder mood than when I left him,' Perrette said, breaking the silence. 'I had occasion to speak to one of the men about timekeeping and grandfather chided me, as if I were at fault! He quite lost his temper. I believe it is best to nip things like that in the bud, or all the men will take advantage, don't you think?' Perrette's touch for his full attention was light, and her pretty heart-shaped face looked for a return to her smile. 'I will put the papers in order first thing in the morning,' she added with a slight air of embarrassment.

'There is no need,' responded Jacques, wishing he were somewhere else. 'I sorted them out … it was no trouble. Now that I am back and you have so much to do here for Aunt Marguerite … I do not know what grandfather and I would have done without your help, but now …'

Perrette's look became cold with accusation. Used to facing down the strongest bully with fist or sword, Jacques shifted with discomfort.

'You don't want my help. Is that what you are trying to say, cousin? You are telling me to stay away?'

'I have to think what is best for the men. Grandfather feels they do not like a woman being in the yard. It is not against you personally. '

'They hardly see me,' flashed back Perrette.

'But it means they have to watch their tongues lest you overhear when they blaspheme.'

'Learning restraint is good for them! Christian men should not blaspheme!'

Jacques's expression hardened with exasperation. 'They are not maids embroidering!'

'And is that what you will have me do after all I have done when you were away?' Perrette gasped, her eyes brimming with angry tears. 'I enjoy being a part of it, and now you and Grandfather want to take it away from me.'

'It is best.'

'Pray, am I to carry on with this?' She reached into her embroidery bag and pulled out what looked like a bolster cover. 'Or would you have me unpick it?'

Jacques stared in bewilderment, not understanding, till her fingers jabbed at one of the corners of the white material. His breath caught with shock as his eyes took in intertwined letters of P and J set within

168

a circle of blue silk knots. Perrette's face was scarlet with emotion. Uttering a heart-rending sob, she flung down the material and from her pocket took out small embroidery scissors.

'No, no don't,' he cried, restraining her hand as she made to cut at the embroidery. 'Don't spoil your lovely work.'

'I should not have worked it until you spoke,' she blurted out, wiping the tears from her eyes. 'But when they told me you took father's hand and said you would always look after me, I thought you meant it.'

'I meant what I said,' he said gravely. 'I will always look after you, Perrette. Leave it as it is ... the P looks well beside the J.'

'You mean it? I can begin others for a trousseau?'

Jacques experienced a shrinking within, but, taking hold of her small hand, he raised it to his lips. 'I have much to catch up with.'

'I know,' she said, her pretty face glowing with happiness.

'So let us wait just a little while.'

'Oh, my dear Jacques, you have made me so happy. Shall we go in and tell Maman now?'

He gave her a fond smile. 'Why don't we wait for Grandfather and tell them both before supper.'

It was hard not to be infected by her gaiety, but even so, as she offered up her pale lips, Jacques felt something akin to despair as he kissed them.

Since Guillaume's departure to Paris, Du Chesne seemed an emptier, quieter place. It was not only Hermione and Lucette who missed his merry outbursts of song, but noticeably Marie and Pierre. Other than to say he had had to go to Paris to offer help to her friend, it had seemed to Hermione wiser to say no more. But Guilluame, she discovered had not been so reserved, for as she accompanied Marie to visit a sick boy in one of the cottages, the elderly housekeeper spoke about Olivier.

'Pierre says, madame, that Guillaume's master will be coming to live here.'

Hermione's dark eyes widened with surprise, and she wondered uneasily what else Guillaume had said.

'It is possible,' she replied, as they arrived at the cottage door where the young boy Michel lived. 'Would you like me to help change the boy's poultice?'

For the first time ever, Marie looked up directly into Hermione's face, and her expression was softened by a faint smile. 'It would make them uneasy, madame, but your pot of honey will help him bear the pain.'

The room was an eye-smarting mist of grey smoke. And what with the heat of the day and the smell of animals from the adjacent stall, Hermione had to swallow hard not to physically react. Then the pale face of the child watching her from the trundle bed claimed her attention.

'Bonjour, Michel.' She smiled, nodding respectfully to his mother, who, like the boy, was staring at her wide-eyed. 'Marie is here to help you, but first, I want to give you a small present from the bees. Their queen has spared you a little of her honey.' The uncertain eyes of the boy and his mother widened even more as they fixed on the pot in Hermione's hand. 'I shall give it to your *maman*,' said Hermione, 'and perhaps when Marie has finished, she will give you a spoonful.'

'Thank you, madame,' mumbled the woman, shyly stepping forward. As her hand touched Hermione's to take the earthenware pot, though they were of about the same age, Hermione noticed that her skin was as rough as a file and blackened from work. By her awkward expression, Hermione sensed she likewise was aware of the contrast. Just as Marie had said, it was best to leave her alone to get on with her healing.

Waiting outside the door was now a cluster of children. 'Are you coming to see us also, madame?' one of the girls asked.

'No, silly, she'll be seeing yonder man!' shouted a boy, pointing down the driveway. The boy was Julien, whom Hermione had formed a liking for since the time she had encountered him playing at hunter in the orchard. His bow was obviously still in favour and slung across his slender body. At the approach of the horseman, he raced away down

170

the driveway, and lifting the bow free, planted himself in the line of the rider. Hermione's gaze held on the black-haired boy as he let off dozens of imaginary arrows. Then her eyes slid towards the oncoming horseman and she saw it was Claude Tilly. His coming to Du Chesne was a complete surprise. For whilst at Rochefort he had behaved with cool civility at her decision not to sell Du Chesne, she had sensed his frustration and anger. Perhaps Angélique Tilly was the cause of his visit, for she and her girls had been most anxious to see Hermione again.

'*Bonjour*, monsieur. It is a hot day to ride from Rochefort.'

'*Bonjour*, madame,' rejoined Claude Tilly. He doffed his hat and in an ungainly yet agile way, dismounted.

'My dear girls and Madame Tilly are enjoying the country air at our house at Saintes. You must come and see our fountain, and shortly we shall have a small orangery! Just one or two pots ... not quite as many as Fouquet showed off to our King!' He gave a braying laugh at his joke. Then he lifted away his hat and raised his wig as if to let in a flow of air. 'Have you thought of an orangery here?'

'A little ambitious for me,' commented Hermione, with a gesture towards the weeds and brambles.

'It must be difficult to know where to begin,' mused Claude Tilly sympathetically. 'That is one of the reasons why I rode over ... any advice or help which I can give. Do remember I would be more than happy to handle your exploitations. Everything will be taken care of; the felling and transport to auction. I am one of the Marine's major suppliers of timber, as well as private shipyards.'

'It is thoughtful of you,' replied Hermione with care. She was not keen to include him in her affairs, but she needed to sell, and one couldn't always pick and choose in business. 'May I let you know in a day or so? At the moment, my head is full of plans for clearance.'

'Start with the rabbits. Drive them out!' advised Claude Tilly with a brittle laugh. 'Now permit me to complete the small commission entrusted to me by my dear wife, and I'll not trespass further upon your time, madame.' With a flourish, he produced from the inside pocket of his coat a prettily wrapped box. Hermione received it with surprise. 'Do not forget,' he said, waving aside her thanks, 'my workmen will make things easier than anyone else!' With that, he executed one of his jerky little bows and walked back to his horse. Viewed from behind, his hat and full-bottomed wig completely dominated his body and short bowed legs. Hermione wanted to laugh and pressed her lips together so as not to. Perhaps, after all, this strutting little man was only trying to help.

172

CHAPTER 11

or the purpose of helping Hermione Du Chesne, Jacques made the journey upstream towards Tonnay-Charente to visit Charles Terron de Colbert. As Demuin's predecessor, the former Intendant had brought to fruition the building of the royal arsenal and the development of Rochefort. It was he who had drawn Jacques into using his eyes and ears to help the King under cover of buying naval stores.

As Jacques was ushered into the bureau of his unofficial master, he wondered whether there would now be a distance between them. To his delight, the nobleman greeted him with a kindly smile.

'I am indebted to you, monseigneur, for receiving me,' murmured Jacques, making a respectful bow. 'I trust your health improves, monseigneur?'

'I like to think so,' answered Terron de Colbert, setting aside the book he had been reading. 'The doctors have their opinions, but I believe we are all in agreement; the decision to pass responsibilities on was appropriate.' The elderly nobleman motioned for Jacques to move closer. 'It suited my own intent to see you again: whilst seeing to my affairs, I have recommended you for a pension for the intelligence you gathered during the Dutch war.' Jacques's eyes widened with surprise, and he acknowledged his good fortune with a nod of the head. 'Despite your youth, you had a swift grasp of affairs. More importantly, you were trustworthy and not prone to exaggeration ... look upon it as my parting gift. If you should think after a time His Majesty's Treasury has forgotten you, be assured it will come through eventually. I have received good report from the Seigneur Demuin of your recent visit to Riga … such *ad hoc* arrangements as yours serve France well.'

'Your pardon, monseigneur,' put in Jacques, thinking this an opportune time to influence matters before he became more deeply entangled as a spy, 'my inclination is to concentrate solely on shipbuilding, especially as gossip has it contracts may be offered out to private yards for the building of a new fleet.'

'Then all the more reason to oblige His Majesty when your services are required elsewhere,' rejoined Terron de Colbert with *hauteur*. 'Now, why have you come to see me rather than the Intendant?'

'Because, monseigneur, it concerns a matter that I trust will be of some interest to you. I have discovered empty stables but a few leagues from here. They would be ideal for the raising of horses.'

'*Alors*, even in this, Jacques, the eyes and ears of the King,' observed the Contrôleur Général's cousin with a faint smile on his lips.

'I seek your influence for Hermione Du Chesne, who is most eager to acquire a royal stallion.'

'Du Chesne?'

'Following the death of her father, André Du Chesne, she has come from Paris to live at the château, which is in a great state of disrepair.'

'Du Chesne. I do not recall the family; no doubt country squires with chickens and empty stables. I'll warrant the young lady is poverty-stricken, but pretty?'

'I hadn't noticed,' demurred Jacques, refusing to be drawn by the nobleman's mischievous smile.

'Your eyes are usually so sharp, Jacques! Should a valuable animal be entrusted to this *très jolie* lady?'

'I believe so,' replied Jacques, trying not to react to the raillery.

'Then, for Mademoiselle's sake alone, let us brook no delay,' said Terron de Colbert good-naturedly. 'The Sieur Garsault shall be asked to place a feisty stallion with the lady. As Rouen's Intendant Le Blanc said of the scheme, "It is a worthy way for people to attract money for their subsistence and the payment of their taxes". Even so, people seem reluctant to register. Your own stallion must be four years now … has it served many mares?'

'There has been some reluctance,' conceded Jacques. 'People are afraid when the colts are born they will belong to the King. I've tried to reassure them it won't happen.'

'Saint Leger shows the way forward. Yet even so, a few years back, they had many miscarriages because of the long frosts. Now they are raising first-rate stallions. Royal colts at the fair at Guibray were snapped up. What exciting times I have lived in! So many grand schemes: the hospital of Saint Louis at La Rochelle, the arsenal at Rochefort. They robbed me of sleep many a night, not least the marshy ground at Rochefort. But as Paul-Pierre Riquet has demonstrated, problems are there to be solved.'

'It is hard to believe his tunnel under the hill d'Ensérune was completed in eight days,' contributed Jacques, 'over five hundred feet! Such a feat as the Malpas tunnel seems as improbable as being able to ship goods from the Atlantic to the Mediterranean.'

'Yet with the Canal du Midi completing the link, it will be done,' said Terron de Colbert, rising up from his seat and leading Jacques to a table on which was a model of the section of the canal linking Toulouse to Sète. 'These one hundred and fifty miles will help to save many a dangerous sea voyage. Henri IV was one who dreamt of doing such a thing. What apparently inspired Riquet was the ancient tunnel dug in the Middle-Ages to drain the Étang de Montady.' The nobleman turned to Jacques with an expression of supreme pride. 'As my cousin once said, "We are not in a reign of little things; it is impossible to imagine anything too grand."'

*** *** ***

The sturdy youths taken on to work in the forest had made an energetic start on cutting back the undergrowth in preparation for the mast. It was not only Pierre with whom they had found favour, but in particular, Lucette, who declared Georges had the kindest eyes and strongest legs she had ever seen.

'Are they working nearby, madame?' she enquired one morning, as Hermione was setting forth with Pierre to see how the work was progressing.

Hermione looked down into her maid's eager eyes and laughed.

'Too far for anyone to just bump into ... but, Guillaume being away, Georges is going to drive Pierre and Marie to market.' Such was Lucette's beam of delight, Hermione seized the moment. 'You can go with them. If you wear the bonnet of Saintonge, it will make you seem less of a stranger to everyone.'

'Oh, do you think so? It does hide the face so.'

'I expect a lad like Georges knows how to peep into one for a glimpse of a pretty lass.' Hermione laughed, nudging her horse forward. As she passed through the keep and out over the bridge after Pierre and Rouge, she reflected on how in their various ways each of them was adjusting to life at Du Chesne. Yet just one encounter by Guillaume with the police in Paris and everything could fall apart!

Throughout their ride along the river bank, Hermione contemplated the château. The towers, with their pointed, witch-like hats, no longer seemed frightening as they had done on that first night. Over her horse's head beckoned the sunlit trees of the forest. This feeling of having something important to do was new to her. It really mattered what she did in her lifetime. It mattered so much, Jacques Maurellet had said, owners who did not look after their forests could be sent to prison. There were heavy fines also for allowing trees to encroach within ten feet of the King's roads, which Du Chesne's clearly did! Pierre had stopped to wait for her, and as he wiped his forehead against the heat of the day, Rouge raced back to her.

'Be quiet,' ordered Hermione as the hound leapt upwards, barking for attention. 'I have to remember the way back without your master, isn't that so, Pierre?'

'Rouge shall stay with you till you become familiar with the way, madame.'

'But will he stay? Won't he run off to find you?'

'He does what I command!'

Hermione nodded gravely, hoping Rouge was heeding him. They carried on for another half hour until the faint sound of voices grew gradually louder. Then Hermione glimpsed movement through the tall stands of trees.

'*Bonjour*, Georges, Victor ... you've cleared a great deal of ground,' she called out in greeting.

'There's a lot to be cleared, madame,' replied the sturdy Georges, shifting uneasily as she came alongside and sprang down from her horse. Hermione ignored the men's shyness. They would have to get used to dealing with a woman.

'Are you about to fell?' she asked, seeing spiked boots lying on the ground.

'Yes, madame. The oak over there is dangerous,' said Victor, the slighter of the two men. 'Maître Maurellet explained how first we need to lop off the branches.'

'Wouldn't it be wiser to wait for him?'

'Don't fret, madame,' interjected Pierre. 'We don't need a master-shipwright to tell us about our trees. I will guide them. If my legs were younger, I'd show them how to climb. The sooner it is done, the better, for a falling bough could kill, and we don't want more deaths!'

Hermione nodded gravely as the elderly man gave her a meaningful look. Silence followed, and she waited expectantly for the men to get on with things. The two muscular peasants shifted uneasily from foot to foot, and finally, Pierre came up close to her.

'It would be easier for them, madame, if you were not here. It is dangerous work.'

'Then I will ride awhile,' conceded Hermione, hiding her disappointment. 'Don't be concerned,' she added as he whistled for Rouge, whose head was deep in a hole. 'I will return when I am ready to go back. And I shall not go beyond the sound of your voices.'

With a shake of his head as if dealing with someone who had lost her wits, Pierre stooped and offered his hands to hoist her up onto the saddle. No doubt he and the other two put her different ways down to being a Parisienne, but her friends in Paris would also think she had lost her wits, especially if they knew what she was about to do. When weeds and creepers were choking new life out here, there was no time for dreaming about fountains or constructing trellis walks with roses!

As soon as she was well out of sight, Hermione dismounted, and from the saddlebag took out a leather apron, gauntlet gloves, and a sickle and spade which she had come across in one of the outhouses. Jacques Maurellet had said the forest floor should be clearer for re-seeding in the mast; there was no reason why she could not take on some of the weaker species which stood between acorns and soil. Filled with bravado, Hermione strode into bracken which came up as high as her shoulders. She laughed out loud as she began to slash and hack back and forth. If the men were to see her now, they would be mortified. Most likely they would take to their heels, thinking she was possessed by the Devil. It was madness to behave so, but she didn't care! Just this once she wanted to actively make things better. At least it was not likely the curé would drop by, as he was prone to do at the house. Though what a letter he would have to write to his Marquis about the châteleine of Du Chesne behaving like a labourer! It was foolish to take the risk, but deep within, she needed to work the earth.

Cutting back bramble and nettles turned out to be astonishingly hard work made worse by swarms of small black flies which buzzed about her head. Hermione crushed the flesh of a dock leaf between her fingers and wiped the juice over her face to see if that would keep the hateful things away. The one thing she must not do was to measure what she cleared against what lay about her. Bit by bit must be the way of things, till every clump of bracken she had condemned, including this particularly obstinate one, was gone. In an outburst of frustration, she grasped the thick fibrous stems with both hands. 'Hateful, hateful!' she gasped, twisting them back and forth in a frenzied attempt to work the roots free. They wouldn't budge. Maddened by insects biting at her eyes and mouth, she dug her heels into the ground and with the whole of her body pulled on the unyielding roots until, her balance lost, she toppled onto her back. Utterly spent, her face pounding with blood and oozing sweat, Hermione stared up at an ivy-covered branch overhead. Somewhere close by she was vaguely conscious of a horse whinnying and her own responding. Soon after followed a crunching of leaves, and suddenly the dark green of the ivy above was replaced by the face of Jacques Maurellet. Open-mouthed with shock, Hermione could only gaze silently upward at the tanned face. She could see that he was finding it hard not to laugh. We are back to the quayside at La Rochelle, she thought ruefully, wiping soil and sweat from her face. As she scrambled onto her feet, her gaze swept over the worked ground … it looked like a cottage garden. She must seem a complete fool! Blushing to the roots of her hair, she made a face of self-deprecation as she looked at Jacques, but he raised both hands.

'I'm impressed … truly!' The master-shipwright's lips were restrained to a whimsical smile, Hermione saw, while his eyes sparkled with laughter. 'Let me give you a hand.'

Without more ado, he slid off his coat and waistcoat, untied his cravat, and draped everything over the branch of a tree. 'Shall I take the spade?'

Hermione hesitated, for his white cambric shirt was trimmed with lace, but already he was rolling back its sleeves. With an uncertain smile she handed over the spade and took up the sickle. They worked on in silence, she slicing through vines which were cutting deep into the trunks of trees, he slashing and digging up riots of brambles. At one point, he paused and looked in the direction of the ringing sound of axes striking against wood, then, catching her eye, he set to work again.

In the whole of her life, Hermione had never worked so hard. The insides of her gloves had become sticky and uncomfortable. She tore one off and saw that a blister had appeared between her thumb and forefinger despite the leather protection.

'It would be a pity to ruin your hands,' observed Jacques in a mild voice as he glanced her way. 'The men from the village are getting along quite well.'

'But there is so much ... and besides, I wanted to ...'

'Work the soil?'

They were the very words which expressed how she felt, and Hermione smiled at him. She gazed around her at the differing greens, the dancing delicacy of two butterflies, and sought for words.

'Come on.' Jacques laughed, cleaning the blade of the spade with grass. 'Your time would be more profitably spent learning about selection: identifying trees which are showing signs of disease, spotting those which are growing too close.'

Hermione turned towards the enormous mound of branches and weeds created by their efforts. 'I feel I belong now.'

'When you build ships,' commented Jacques, stretching to pull down his clothes from the tree branch, 'you feel the same. No matter how large or skilled the workforce, there is the need to shape some of the timbers that bring a ship alive.' His upward reach had made the air pungent from his sweat; inevitably Hermione's attention was drawn to the muscular body visible beneath the damp clinging shirt. The effect upon her was so disturbing she was inwardly thrown into panic. She turned away and hastily busied herself with putting the gauntlet gloves into the pocket of the leather apron.

'I know you build ships,' she managed to say with studied calm, 'but I don't know what it is you do for the Marine?'

'Some would say I was a connoisseur.'

'Of trees?'

Jacques' dark blue eyes were speculative as they swept over Hermione. 'Sometimes.'

Once more, Hermione experienced a sense of panic. With a soft laugh, Jacques draped the cravat loosely around his neck and slipped on his waistcoat.

'I have spent exciting times wandering about forests ... owners are not always friendly.'

'Why should they not be?'

'Trees reserved for the Marine can be forgotten for years. If rot sets in, profit disappears.'

'And there is nothing one can do?'

'Men or trees ... once conscripted, there is no escape. Don't look so worried: that is not going to happen to your trees. Entrepreneurs like Claude Tilly are much too greedy to permit delay.'

'He has asked to handle the exploitations here.'

'Then he will need watching. Tilly's one aim is to come out on top, but he could also put a lot of business your way.'

'I will be careful,' said Hermione, gathering up the tools. 'Would you see how the men are faring ... don't tell them about this.'

'For both our reputations.' Jacques chuckled.

While he was away, Hermione endeavoured to understand the feelings he had aroused within her: in one instant, the easy companionship between them had been threatened by something uncontrollable, wilder than the flirtation she had had with the actor Robert in Paris. Despite the heady thrill, she sensed that if she did not act with more constraint, she would soon be overwhelmed.

Upon Jacques's return, they moved slowly through the trees, leading their horses by the bridle. Throughout their progress Jacques drew her attention to trees which should be allowed to complete their natural cycle.

'Once you select, should you remove the others?' asked Hermione.

'Always remember,' responded Jacques, pointing upwards to the canopy, 'first take that into account ... remove too many at one time and you open up a gap to snow and wind-strike. It's advisable to do three light thinnings. I'll explain the intervals in the cycle when you're less tired. Let's see what you've learned today. What think you of this tree?'

'I am not sure ... it's a bit spindly, and it has no smell ... is that good?'

'We call it *bois passé* ... lack of vitality. Find me one you think should live to a ripe old age.'

Looking to right and left, Hermione strode through an expanse of nettles until she found a tree of height and sizeable girth. Coming close up to it she believed she identified a faint smell of tannic acid and gave the reddish-brown trunk an approving slap.

'Vigorous growth ... should be allowed to complete its cycle AFTER WE ARE DEAD!'

'Excellent! School is over.' Jacques laughed. 'I think, Madame Du Chesne, it is time for something interesting from your wine cellar!'

Feeling the day had really made a difference, Hermione remounted her horse.

'We shall be back well before dusk and the evil ones,' she said conversationally, riding ahead since the space between the trees was narrow.

'Do you mean witches and such?' Jacques's loud hoot of laughter behind her rang out through the trees. Hermione drew on the reins and turned to face him, her expression grave.

'This forest is no different from others; evil spirits roam at night. You are foolish to laugh,' she persisted, not discomfited by his reaction. 'Your sword would not save you ... the Devil has his creatures just as God has his angels. You are Catholic?'

'Yes.'

'Then you must believe there are dark forces.'

Jacques delayed his reply. Outwardly to family he gave every appearance of being devout, though within he was often troubled.

'One of our great scholars, Descartes,' he said at length, 'suggested we must first understand everything in order to believe. I think therefore I am.'

Hermione shook her head, not understanding. 'Everything flows from God. Surely, the closer we are to God, the more we will understand. You were brought to show me the way of doing things by his good grace.'

'Is that so?'

Jacques's expression was part-amused, part-mockery. He took in Hermione's wild mass of black hair, no longer held up from her face but swinging loose about her shoulders, and nudged his stallion forward alongside her mare. With slow deliberation, he plucked away broken bits of twig and a green oak leaf caught up in the glossy tangles.

'So, how am I to know,' he asked, staring deep into her gleaming brown eyes, 'that you are not a witch who has lured me here?'

'Never say it,' whispered Hermione, her expression clouding with fear. 'Such words could lead me to the fire.'

'I jest,' said Jacques contritely. 'Anyway, witchcraft is no longer proscribed. The stake and the burnings are cruelties of the past.'

'You may be right,' murmured Hermione, 'but they do not seem to know that in Paris!'

CHAPTER 12

he din of laughter and talk in the Cheval Blanc made it barely possible to hear what his brother was saying. Along with the others around the table, Jacques leaned forward towards André so as not to miss a single word.

'You ask me who Paul L'Hoste is, Grandfather! Why, he is Professor of Mathematics at the Royal Seminary of Toulon. The treatise he is preparing on evolutions at sea will be the first of its kind. It will set out for the Marine how ships might best manoeuvre to guard a passage or a strait ... the most effective positioning for them in attack and in defence. His work will determine how ships are designed.'

'Determine ship design!' growled Henri Maurellet, his expression a mix of disbelief and scorn. With slow deliberation the white-haired master-shipwright set down his tankard and raised both weathered hands, thrusting them before his grandson's girlish face. 'What has mathematics to do with these? These fingers, and ... ' he pointed to his eyes, 'these are what design a ship; isn't that so, lads?' For answer came an enthusiastic banging of tankards on the table. Seeing his brother flush scarlet with irritation amid the raucous laughter, Jacques offered an encouraging nod. André responded with an upward roll of his eyes in mock despair, then launched into further debate.

'Would you agree, Grandfather, that shipbuilding is an art?'

The naval cadet's insistent tone cut through the laughter. There was immediate silence around the oak table, then expressions of keen expectancy as Henri Maurellet drained his ale and set down his tankard with a bang.

'I'll grant you that, lad.'

'But wouldn't you say it is an imprecise art?'

'I part with you on that,' retorted the old man. 'My work is precise and that goes for all our lads.' There was an immediate murmur of assent.

'Well, that's just it,' persevered André Maurellet. 'Can you remember a time when two ships of the same plan, for no apparent reason, performed differently?'

'It sometimes happens,' butted in one of the men.

'Well, that's *it*,' exclaimed André triumphantly, turning to the man who had spoken. 'Nicolas, you've worked as a caulker for many years, and you know some ships sail better than others, yet you can't tell me why. A man like Paul L'Hoste will.'

'As the Councils of Construction are trying to do,' put in Jacques, enjoying his young brother's intensity and enthusiasm. 'They have been examining ships of different rates and summoning *experts* like Grandfather to give testament, after which the best sailing points of the ships are recorded to compile the Tables of Dimensions for construction. It is one way of doing things.'

'But Jacques, you know that is not what I am talking about,' protested his brother. 'Paul L'Hoste is examining the action of bodies moving through fluids and the effect of wave and wind power upon the hull of a ship. Until such things are understood, the design of ships will not progress.'

'I'm glad this lad isn't at the yard,' commented the caulker. 'He'd give us all a headache and himself jaw-ache.' Jacques saw André's lips compress as an angry flush stained his cheeks.

'Time for a refill,' he said, standing up. 'Then my brother and I have to go.'

There being no sign of the serving lad, Jacques threaded his way through the tables to place his order. Upon his return, he caught the eye of a master-shipwright from the arsenal and would have passed by with just a nod, but the man half-rose as if wanting to delay him.

'Have they run out of ale on your side of the river?' joked Jacques.

'Oh, we came to look for the Maurellets' First Rater, didn't we lads?' returned the man, raising his voice for all around the table to hear. 'But all we could find was a little sloop.'

'Don't forget the rowing boats, Joubert!' jested another man. Amid the outburst of laughter and advice on building a man o' war, Jacques tried to remain smilingly impassive, but within he was fuming, mostly with himself. He had obviously talked too much about his ambition and word had got out about the arsenal. With a cursory nod, he returned to Henri and the others, who of course wanted to know the cause of the merriment, but he passed things off lightly, not wanting to bring on a fight. As soon as the drinks arrived for the men, he and André made their goodbyes and set off to meet friends for a game of *pétanque*.

'Speed ... how to make a ship travel faster,' mused Jacques, his determination not in the least diminished by the shipwrights from the arsenal. 'A component is to find the centre of gravity ... that is right?'

'So our teacher says. He met Paul L'Hoste when he was in Toulon.'

'Well, if Pierre-Paul Riquet can manage to carve a way to the Mediterranean, it shouldn't be beyond our wit to improve the sailing ability of French ships.'

'What a pity his canal won't take sea-going ships. It must have cost Riquet a fortune, even so.'

'As contrôleur of salt for Languedoc, I expect he was not short of *livres*,' retorted Jacques, narrowing his eyes as he looked towards the line of shady trees near the church where they were to play. 'It's certainly not going to be popular with the Barbary pirates ... goods being moved inland! *Zut*!' he exclaimed, seeing no sign of a game in progress. 'Those rascals are not here and all we find is our curé, who is the last person I want to see.'

'Then I'll leave you to him...' André laughed, 'for I should anyway get back to the ship. Give my warm wishes to Perrette. Grandfather says you are to be married this year. I hope I shall not be away at sea.'

'Nothing is certain,' answered Jacques.

'That you are to marry or that I shall be at sea?' teased André. 'You'd best hurry, brother. Perrette is pretty, and someone will steal her away if you tarry too long.'

As André made good his escape, Jacques sighed as the priest descended on him with his black gown flapping in the wind.

'Good day to you, Father,' said Jacques, removing his hat. 'Forgive my brother for rushing away, but he must return to his floating school.'

'It is not André that concerns me, Jacques, but your cousin, Perrette.' Jacques's heart sank as he anticipated a lengthy discussion on the gravity of the nuptial mass, for no doubt Perrette had lost not a moment in telling the curé of their pledge to marry.

'Perrette does not come to confession, Jacques.' The priest's questioning eyes bored into him, and though he was caught off guard, Jacques refrained from displaying his astonishment.

'She has not been herself lately,' he murmured, not sure of what else to say.

'And yet I see her visit the butcher and about her other duties.'

Jacques was silent for a moment. 'I will speak to her,' he said at length. 'The death of her father is still a cause of anger and sorrow.'

'Ah, you think it is that,' said the priest eagerly. 'But for seeing Brigitte Richet, I would call upon her now to help bring her to a state of acceptance. Grief is no reason to shun God, and I shall tell her so tomorrow. The sooner you young people are joined in matrimony, the better. Let's take this opportunity to ... '

'Forgive me, Father.' Jacques was keen to evade a lengthy discourse. 'I have a pressing matter which cannot brook delay ... For the parish,' he added, hastily handing over some coins as he hurried away. After the laughter in the Cheval Blanc, he was in no mood to be bored, and he certainly needed to be alone to consider what the priest had just said.

He had hoped, as had Henri and Aunt Marguerite, that the nonsense about wanting to know more about the Reformed Church had passed. Now the priest was saying she was missing confession! Furthermore, he had the distinct impression she had not mentioned anything to the curé about their marriage, which seemed strange. What was alarming, and yes, shameful, was his own reaction to this: an immediate overwhelming sense of relief!

Jacques walked briskly downhill and continued along the shoreline of the Charente. Could it be that Perrette had doubts also about their future together? Yet whenever she looked at him, her eyes shone with happiness. With idle interest, he noted that a line of barges moving downstream were exceedingly low in the water, the reason, of course, being that they were loaded with stone. He walked on, closing the distance between him and the dark shapes of masts and spars at the shipyard. Certainly after that first angry outburst about no longer helping at the yard, Perrette had complained about not having enough to occupy her mind, but latterly she had seemed less resentful. Sometimes he caught her looking at him with a questioning expression … a kind of anxiety. Then there was that time in the shipyard when she had seemed to be hiding away from the priest. Whatever it was about, he had best warn her the curé intended to call upon her on the morrow. Cutting up from the river he ascended the slope to his aunt's house, where he found Marguerite alone at her sewing in the salon.

'Would you like me to light a candle, Aunt?' he asked, for it seemed dark within after coming in from the light.

'Perrette asked me the very same thing five minutes ago. Didn't you pass her on her way over? She said you needed help with your bookkeeping.'

Jacques's eyebrows lifted in surprise. 'I came here from the Cheval Blanc,' he explained, thinking it best to keep things brief.

'Then you'll find her when you get home. I thought this nuisance of her helping at the yard was done with!' So had he, Jacques thought, but he made no comment, and after spending a little time consoling the old lady over the pains in her swollen knees and hands, he said goodbye. On his way to the shipyard he wondered how best to tell Petrette that she really must not interfere, but when he entered his office in the mould loft, one glance at his desk revealed that nothing had been disturbed. With a sense of relief, he went to the house, expecting to find his cousin sitting with Henri.

'Did Perrette call in?' he asked, finding her not there.

'I've only just got back,' replied Henri. 'You changed your mind about *pétanque*, then? If you want Perrette, she will be at home with Marguerite.' For a moment, Jacques considered going out to look for his cousin, but deciding she had probably called in on a friend he sat down to talk about André. Even so, in the back of his mind, he was pestered by the shadow of a suspicion.

*** *** ***

In the tower, Hermione's bedchamber moved between darkness and dazzling blue-white light; the thunder was deafening. Each massive crash reminded her of the night she had crouched in terror in the forest. Since then, the months had passed swiftly, and there had been no time to return to the glade and its stream. Hermione snuggled deeper under the blanket and promised herself a ride out if the weather was fit by morning.

A sullen sky with glimmers of gold showing behind grey clouds the next morning was invitation enough to have the mare saddled up.

'You should not go riding alone, madame,' Marie chided, as Hermione waited at the mounting block.

'Rouge will look after me. The hens have done well despite the storm,' she commented, glancing at the wicker basket of eggs on the old woman's arm. 'An omelette when I get back would be welcome … empty your basket and I'll fill it with mushrooms.'

'It is not fitting for you to do such!'

Hermione's cheeks dimpled as she laughed, and the old servant clicked her teeth with annoyance. 'Do not eat any before I see them, madame. We don't want you poisoned!' Marie's brusque manner of speaking, Hermione realized, was out of new- found concern. So she nodded her head compliantly, and while Marie went into the kitchen to empty the basket, Pierre appeared leading the old riding mare. The leather of the ancient side-saddle was cracked from lack of care but that didn't matter so much as the difficulty of fitting her left knee under the rising head. The previous owner's legs must have been shorter than her own. Would she be allowed to put a saddle on a King's stallion, she wondered? Jacques Maurellet's warning about a likely visit and inspection of the stables by royal officials had set Pierre into a flurry of activity. More than ever, Guillaume's help was missed. A good quantity of lime to make a wash for the stable walls had been brought in, which Pierre was presently sifting. Perhaps she ought to do without the omelette, as the additional mix of paint he was to use on the *pigeonnier* walls required a good quantity of the white of eggs. But, as a delicious omelette with mushrooms was now eagerly anticipated, Hermione reached down for the basket from Marie without saying anything. With Rouge bounding along beside, she rode under the keep and out onto the bridge. All along the river shallows down below, excited children were carrying out their search for the white stones which Pierre needed to break down into a powder for the lime mix. When it came to painting the *pigeonnier*, crushed glass and egg whites would also be added to the mix in order to make the walls shine and sparkle so that birds would be spellbound to return to it. Or so Olivier de Serres' receipt in his great book promised! Hermione called down to the children, and looking up they returned her wave, wishing her a good day. Black-haired Julien, of course, had to go one better. Scrambling back up onto the bank he lifted high a stone which was really large.

'Too big!' Hermione laughed, thinking how audacious and lively he was.

Since spending days visiting Georges and Victor in the forest, she was beginning to absorb the feel and layout of her land: its various rocks and inclines which served as landmarks. She passed under a beech whose leaves were still letting fall drops of water from the downpour of the night. Their colour was darkening, and by autumn, green would have changed into rusty brown. Marie had told Lucette they would then gather the fallen leaves for re-stuffing the mattresses.

Suddenly Rouge rushed away in pursuit of a rabbit, taking not the slightest notice of Hermione's command to stay. She laughed for thinking he would. But as Pierre had promised, within minutes the rough old thing bounded back through the ferns, barking as if to say, 'I am here, madame!'

The tall ranks of trees began to thin out, and as the spaces between each tree grew wider, so increased the girth of their trunks. Their green crowns were no longer soaring up to the sky as in the High Forest, but their branches spread sideways, making grotesque shapes. At times, the network of exposed roots protruded so high it was easy to see how she had lost her footing in the dark. Unexpectedly, as a shaft of sunlight broke through the clouds, the glint of water sparkled through the greenery. It was momentarily obscured by a dense screen of holly, but when Hermione gently wheeled her horse between it and a high thorn bush, she emerged onto a green expanse of turf across which was the stream. A party of hind drinking from it lifted their heads sending sparkling droplets scattering as they looked her way. Then, probably scenting Rouge who was snuffling at a rabbit hole, they leapt away and rushed up a rocky incline.

Hermione sighed to see them go, vowing never to bring Rouge again, for he had such a way of disturbing everything about him. She lingered on the saddle, content to watch butterflies dancing back and forth over the daisy-strewn stretch of green sward. It was hard to understand how she could have been so afraid here when now the air resounded with warbling song. Her life at Du Chesne was giving her a new-found confidence about being on her own. In Paris, she had been rarely alone. Even though there were many places to experience solitude, it just would not have occurred to her to do so. Now she was beginning to feel at ease in the forest, not to feel self-conscious at being unaccompanied or to imagine she was being watched when riding through the ranks of trees. She dismounted and stood quite still, marvelling at the size of the three oak trees dominating the scene. Her memory had not served her badly; they were indeed noble giants.

'The Prince,' she murmured, with a gesture towards the smallest of the oaks. 'Then we have the Queen, and last of all the King looking down on his subjects!' Between each vast tree was some fifty metres, and to approach the mighty spread of the King, Hermione took the way the deer had fled up the steep rocky incline. When she'd reached the oak, there was a rustle of leaves and a small bird darted out and landed at her feet; it was a wren.

'Ah, is that you, *roitelet*, little king of the glade?' Hermione's eyes gleamed with pleasure to have a bird of such good omen greet her. Her attention went upward from the bird to a mass of mistletoe whose leaves were entwined around one or two enormous branches. Beneath the soles of her boots the sharp edges of roots pressed uncomfortably, but Hermione did not bother to shift her position. All she was conscious of was the beating of her heart, the soft inward take of each breath. There was magic here beyond human understanding. The life of the woodland sounded all around, yet underlying it was this silent, sacred force, reminding her of the vibrations before a storm. This great oak seemed the heart of all. With due reverence, Hermione stretched her fingers upwards to touch the slender green leaves of the mistletoe, and afterwards those of the oak. It was beneath these vast boughs, the curé had said, that Aglaé de Saintyon had been trampled to death by her horse. Her blood had soaked the earth. Hermione reached into her mind, and, as if he were with her, the face of André Du Chesne appeared.

'Dear Chevalier,' she murmured, 'your love ended here, and so shall mine for Du Chesne begin!'

On Hermione's return to the château, she found Pierre still at work, helped by the father of the boy Julien. While Pierre shovelled crushed glass then stirred it with a wooden paddle into the second vat of lime, Gaspard was steadily grinding down the stones which the children had collected. Both men were covered from head to toe in white dust.

'You've been working hard,' gasped Hermione, as she coughed and sneezed all at the same time, for the air was thick with the dust. 'I see the wash for the stables is ready.'

'Yes, madame.' Pierre nodded. He pulled away his cap and in flapping it against a bony leg set them all a-coughing in a further cloud of dust. 'We'll mix the special wash for the *pigeonnier* tomorrow,' he croaked. 'The extra hands can paint the stables.'

Not sure who else was being brought in to help, Hermione gave a nod, and so as not to interrupt Pierre, she started to unsaddle her horse. The old man, of course, immediately came across to her.

'Leave it to me, madame. You'll be wanted indoors.' Wondering why he gave her such a pleased smile, Hermione walked up to the house. Marie's basket was filled to the brim and the thought of the meal to come was tempting, but even so, as she entered the kitchen, mushrooms and omelette were promptly forgotten, for spooning up broth as if he were a starving dog was Guillaume.

'What in heaven has happened?' gasped Hermione in horror.

'I got into a fight.'

'I can see it,' she said, quickly looking away from the blind eye, which was normally covered over. Of even more concern than the loss of his patch was the black and purple swelling around his good eye.

'You poor man,' she murmured, noting other bruises and scabs. 'Any news of Master Olivier? But finish your food first,' she urged, as Guillaume's attention wavered between her and the broth. His great shaggy head bent again over the bowl and at speed the last drops of the contents were spooned up.

'Forgive me, Madame Hermione. I haven't eaten for days. There was no sign of Master. Being as the gate was open, I went to the laboratory thinking he would be there. The furnaces were not lit, but I put that down to my not being around to help, or Master having one of his learning times. The next thing was that something hit me on the head, and I was flung pell-mell against the wall.' Guillaume paused and tentatively touched the centre of his broad nose. 'It's since had time to heal, but a few leagues from here was it not freshly opened again by rogues!'

'But who was it in the laboratory?' demanded Hermione, seized with anxiety and not caring what Marie made of it all.

'I can hardly say. A man who looked as if he'd be at ease with the archers of the King; I'll warrant some agent of the police. Though he didn't reckon with me, for while he had the advantage, my being near insensible as I lay on the floor, my hand found an iron and I slammed it hard against his ankle. Oh, he yelled out good! And on my feet like a cat, I brought my knee up well and truly ... let's put it this way: if he bears children, he'll be fortunate, for I left him weeping like one.'

'What then?'

'I didn't delay ... got down to the Seine and took a great leap onto a barge. They were going to throw me off into the water till I showed them a handful of coin.'

'They got you away.'

'No, they took the money then threw me back into the water.'

'Filthy pigs,' spat Marie, who had been avidly following the conversation.

'I was about to go under for the second time when like true Christians they fished me out with some long hook. They were merry rogues.'

'So you have not a word of Olivier? You did not think to ask Agnès?' Guillaume shook his great, shaggy head, then after a nod from Hermione he set to on Marie's offering of sausage.

'It is so good to have you back,' Hermione said with a fond smile.

'Lucette missed you every day, didn't you?' she added as her maid rushed in.

Leaving Guillaume to enjoy recounting his adventures, Hermione went and changed out of her riding clothes. Shortly afterwards, Marie carried into the salon a golden omelette. As she ate, Hermione went over everything Guillaume had told them about his encounter with the stranger in Olivier's laboratory. Were the police keeping a watch on the place? If Olivier had run away, were they then expecting him to return to rue de la Cocotte? Yet his message to her clearly meant he was travelling by water. Had he, like Guillaume, found passage on a ship on the Seine? Any day he could arrive … the thought made her feel excited, as well as anxious as to how he would fit in, not only with her small household but also with Father Grégoire.

On the morrow, the atmosphere down at the stables was boisterous, with Guillaume letting forth snatches of song as he painted the stalls. Rouge had obviously been rushing in and out to him and presumably had wagged his tail so much it was entirely white with paint.

'Do you need more white wine for the mix, Pierre?' asked Hermione, as Gaspard took over the paddle to carry on stirring.

'With the water it is enough,' answered Pierre, 'but that wench of yours is holding us up, madame. Ah, that looks like her dawdling now.'

'It is subtle work separating the whites from the yolks,' explained Hermione. 'I see Guillaume has a new eye patch; he said Marie made it for him.'

'She sat by the candle late, madame; said we couldn't have the poor man showing that terrible eye.'

'I would have sewed it myself,' chipped in Lucette, catching onto the talk as she approached carrying a leather pail, 'for the sight of that staring white thing is enough to make me heave up. I hope this is the last,' she sighed, tipping the transparent goo of egg whites into the vat, 'or me and the hens will take flight!'

'There'll be no flying away when this is painted on the *pigeonnier*,' put

198

in Pierre, not deigning to look at Lucette. He stepped towards Hermione and made a gesture towards the high circular wall. 'I remember in the Chevalier's time how the pigeons loved the sparkle of the walls. They came to it in flocks. And inside the paint makes the walls slippery and stops the rats getting up to the eggs.'

Leaving the men to carry on undisturbed, the women went back to the house. As they parted at the entrance into the kitchen, Lucette turned on Hermione a coy look.

'Are you content with Georges and his brother?'

'Yes. I had not realized how strong a man's legs must be to lift him high into the canopy.'

'The spiked boots give grip.' Lucette nodded, airing her new-found knowledge with a pleased expression. 'A forester needs thighs like Georges's.'

'Is that so?' teased Hermione, sending her maid scuttling away in a fit of giggles.

The stable walls were clean and white, and each of its ten stalls was deep in new straw. They were ready for any official inspection, and just in time! The following week when Hermione was sitting reading about the management and care of pigeons, Lucette came running into the Painted Room.

'Oh, Mademoiselle Hermione, come and see … such a fine carriage. Guillaume is guiding the coachman over the bridge into the courtyard. It is a Monsieur Basville, and he wishes to see you. He has been sent by the Sieur Garsault, and oh, there is something more than his coach to marvel at!'

Hermione's brown eyes widened with speculation, then she gave a cry of excitement.

'Have they brought a colt?'

'Black as Satan with eyes like red coals. The old mares will collapse with fright.' Lucette giggled.

'Tell Monsieur Basville I shall be with him in an instant,' said Hermione, setting a bookmark in Olivier de Serres' *Le Théâtre D' Agriculture*.

Just as Lucette had described, the stallion was a fearsome sight, and dark as a raven's wing. It was highly agitated, lashing out with its back legs and tossing its mane violently from side to side. A lackey in a braided blue uniform was trying to calm it whilst trying to keep clear of its plunging hooves. Standing a little apart overseeing the scene was an impressive figure. The royal official's clothes were of the newer style; the breeches were narrower than of yore though still adorned with an abundance of ribbon at the knee, as were his shoes and one shoulder of his brown coat. At each failed attempt on the lackey's part to calm the horse, Monsieur Basville's silver-topped cane tapped against the ground with impatience. On catching sight of Hermione, instantly he swept away his hat, and presented a graceful salutation.

'Madame Du Chesne, I am honoured. You have doubtless been expecting my visit?'

'It is my pleasure, Monsieur Basville, to receive you at Du Chesne. I was not anticipating the arrival of my ward so soon,' replied Hermione, her attention drawn back to the colt as it reared high over the head of the groom. 'It is … more spirited than my horses.'

'Indeed, madame; an Arab with the speed of the wind. It is customary before such a valuable horse is placed to make an inspection of the stables. But we had it from a trusted source that Du Chesne's were suitable.'

'You shall see they are,' said Hermione, hoping Guillaume likewise would pass the inspection. In solemn procession, with Guillaume leading the way, she walked beside the royal official towards the stables. Once they were beyond the hayloft, the white, sparkling walls of the *pigeonnier* gave a hint of what was to come, and so it proved. The newly whitened outer walls of the stables and within its line of freshly painted stalls, deep in sweet-smelling straw, drew from her visitor a distinct murmur of approval.

'It is good,' he said, with a quick glance inside the tack-room, where ancient harnesses and saddles had also received hours of attention. Hermione released a breath of relief, whereupon one anxiety was replaced by an absolutely terrifying thought! What might happen to them if this colt died!

'We are not very experienced in the rearing of horses,' she ventured as they regained the yard. Monsieur Basville pursed his lips as he flicked some speck of dust from his lace cravat. Then, after offering Hermione a polite smile of reassurance, he directed a stern look towards Guillaume.

'The rules on care are exact! They must be followed to the letter, without deviation! Is that understood?'

'I understand, my lord,' mumbled Guillaume, shifting uneasily from foot to foot.

'Under no circumstances must water that is icy cold be given to the stallion. Nor must it be ridden by anyone! I have written instructions with me which I shall give to your mistress.'

With a brisk tap of dismissal from his cane, the royal official turned back to Hermione, and together they returned to the upper courtyard. During their absence, the stallion had been quietened and was now drinking from one of the two horse troughs. Monsieur Basville called across to the groom.

'Take him to Madame Du Chesne's stables, lad.'

As the colt lifted its head from the trough and was led away, Hermione gave a cry of surprise. Branded on its nearside thigh was a crown and the letter L.

'It is true...' she laughed with delight, 'it is indeed a royal horse!'

A faint smile softened the expression of Monsieur Basville's thin lips. 'That, of course, madame, is why it is forbidden to take him to fight at *assemblées*.'

'Are many people registered to stable horses?' asked Hermione, feeling a rising sense of awe to be entrusted with an animal of such breeding.

'The numbers slowly increase,' replied Monsieur Basville as he followed her into the hall. 'We have farmers in Brittany, innkeepers, notaries, a priest and ...' His voice died away as they entered the Painted Room. Hermione let him stand silent, without distraction, as he stared at the beautiful panels. When at last he looked at her, the expression on his hawk-like features was alive with interest, and his grey eyes gleamed with pleasure. 'These panels are very fine. If you forgive my saying so, a great contrast to what lies outside.'

Hermione gave a rueful smile. 'That wing of the château was destroyed by fire ... another reason I was so happy when Monsieur Maurellet offered to put my name forward for registration.'

'Reduction in taxes is always attractive.' Monsieur Basville nodded. 'Likewise, exemption from the billet will save much expense. As to the ruination outside, why not just remove it ... fountains and parterres are more desirable now than loopholes and fortifications.' Once more, the tall man took to moving leisurely around the room to study the panels, but at last Hermione was able to shepherd him into the *salle à manger*, where Marie and Lucette had somehow contrived at short notice to put together a passable offering of cold meats.

'I hope in the future to develop a garden here,' explained Hermione, as the royal official went to look out of the window,

'André Nostre would certainly approve of your landscape,' he observed, with a gesture towards the lake and the rising ground behind. 'Nature has provided you with water and trees.'

'I would like parterres filled with narcissus, red and yellow tulips ... but I fear a garden will have to wait.'

'Then you should make the acquaintance of Jean-Baptiste Monnoyer,' rejoined her visitor, returning with her to the table. 'He has filled Versailles with baskets of tulips, hyacinths, and honeysuckle. They look so real you think you can smell their scent. He is a painter,' he explained, dipping his spoon into the *potage*. 'He also designs the borders for the tapestries of the Gobelin. I understand you lived in Paris, madame?'

'In the Quartier Marais,' replied Hermione. Then, before he could ask another question, she offered him pâté and took the conversation back to the raising of horses. It was not only because she did not wish to talk about her life in Paris, but also because she wanted to know, while he was here, as much as possible about looking after her royal ward.

'I have your written instructions, Monsieur Basville. Is there anything more I should heed?'

'To show restraint, madame,' replied the official, taking a sip of wine, his grey eyes reflective. 'One disobedient owner in Brittany gave us much trouble. Her avarice drove her to put colts of only two years to serve mares.'

'Of what age must they be, monseigneur?'

'Over four years. And don't forget,' he added as if making a little joke, 'as well as the five *livres* charge you make, you should demand a pint of oats from the owners of the mares.'

From the direction of the village, the church clock struck the double hour and Monsieur Basville made a little gesture of apology. 'I fear as soon as we have finished this delicious repast, I must leave you, Madame Du Chesne. But we will go through the instructions to make certain you understand everything ... imperative to remember is that mares which are defective in any way should be refused. Please to remember, fillies and colts bred from the stallion are to bear the royal brand!'

When it was time for Hermione to accompany the royal official to his coach, her mind was taken up with a whirl of facts, excitement, and anxiety. As she moved to return indoors, so he might enter his coach rather than be forced to walk ahead of it until out of her sight as etiquette required, Monsieur Basville presented her with a graceful bow.

'It is a solemn responsibility you have taken on, Madame Du Chesne!' he said, with a grave smile. 'These horses bought in Cordoba are going to provide our cavalry with a turn of speed that will save many lives on the battlefield. It is a great thing you are doing for France!'

CHAPTER 13

he greater part of Jacques's morning had been spent watching apprentices at work. As he climbed down from the sloop, an amused smile touched his lips, for a lad who barely knew the day of the week was blessed with the nimblest of fingers, whereas another, whose cunning eyes betrayed a swift grasp of affairs, had no handiness at all. Jacques stretched out his arms and turned away from the part-constructed ship to face the grey water of the Charente. It was good to be caught up once more in the bustle and noisy din of building ships. Further along the shoreline, two men were burning old tar off the bottom of a boat. With barely a breeze, conditions were ideal for handling the breeming hook and the flaming reeds within its iron head. Even so, the second of the workers who was using the scraper kept dropping it ... clumsiness seemed the order of his day! He was no youngster, either. Curious to know something about him, Jacques called over to Henri, who was nearby talking to one of the caulkers.

'Who is that at the fishing boat?'

'You might well ask,' called back Henri, breaking off his conversation to walk over to Jacques. 'We've never had a clumsier pair of hands.'

'When did you take him on?'

'I didn't,' replied the old man. 'It was Perrette. She felt sorry for him.'

'You let Perrette do what?' exclaimed Jacques in astonishment.

'Well, you know how things were when you were away. Besides,' his grandfather's watery eyes glinted, 'just because this Huguenot isn't permitted to practise law doesn't mean we can't ask for a little advice now and again!'

Jacques' attention went back to the slightly built man scraping at the tar on the bottom of the boat. He had once again managed to drop hold of his tool. As he bent to retrieve it, Jacques saw how he glanced furtively about, his expression a mixture of anxiety and embarrassment. It was a hard way for a scholarly man to earn his bread, and Jacques felt a surge of sympathy.

'We need to order tallow ... we've used a fair bit for graving this week,' he murmured, his eyes narrowing a little as he continued to study the newcomer. For no reason, a faint inner disquiet, which till now had been nameless, manifested itself, taking his thoughts off stores. 'Tell me, Grandfather, on the day the Minister of Marine visited the arsenal, did you think it odd Perrette did not want to go with us to the celebration?' His question so startled the old man that Henri just stared blankly back. Then he gave a shrug of indifference.

'Didn't she have a headache or something? If I think anyone is odd, it is that young brother of yours! Telling us oldsters how we should build ships ... "bodies moving through fluids" ... we laughed ourselves hoarse! What did you make of his impudence?'

'Oh no, you're not going to draw me into that one,' responded Jacques with a chuckle. 'Consider only the honour your grandson will bring to the family; the first to become an officer of the Marine!'

'And I hope he and others who strut the quarterdeck will remember it is we shipwrights that give them their ships.' Jacques smiled as his grandfather waved his large weather-beaten hands, and he could not resist teasing.

'Did he tell you about their dancing classes?'

With a snort of exasperation, and muttering something about the sooner André was packed off to sea the better, the old man stomped away.

Jacques chuckled. Henri might protest, but he knew the old man was bursting with pride. He looked again towards the two men working on the shoreline and in particular at the sandy-haired man. There was something about him which aroused in Jacques feelings of disquiet.

It seemed unthinkable to spy upon his own cousin, yet, distasteful as it was, Jacques found himself keeping watch outside his aunt's house the following evening. Nor did he have long to wait before the dainty figure of Perrette emerged. She was clearly in a hurry, for she set off at a fast pace uphill in the direction of the town. Jacques followed, maintaining sufficient distance to take cover if she looked back. When his cousin reached the cottage of Matthieu and Louise Dubois, she went to the door. So, there was no mystery after all! She was simply calling upon a woman friend. Jacques chided himself for behaving so badly, and he was about to turn back when from the corner of his eye he glimpsed movement. Evidently, there was no one at home, but instead of turning back, his cousin was continuing on uphill. Where was she going and with such urgency? Anticipating she might look back when she reached the little lane which led through to another cottage, Jacques pulled back behind a tree, but without any hesitation Perrette turned into the lane and disappeared from sight. A frown creased Jacques's brow as he recalled who it was Henri had said was renting the house, which had been abandoned by a Huguenot family the previous year. It was that hopeless labourer on their workforce, Martin Migault. With a grim expression, Jacques set off along the rough track, his thoughts in a whirl of suspicions. Maybe she was just befriending a stranger? He laughed out loud, his voice harsh with angry affront … *only calling upon a man*! Surely, out of consideration for her own good name … for the family honour … what was she thinking of visiting some newcomer? Like a sudden violent flurry of wind, fury overwhelmed Jacques; that she could so brazenly humiliate him! Moments ago he had felt ridiculous and ashamed as she knocked on Louise Dubois's door. Fired now by self-righteous anger, he strode forward. Once through the gate to Migault's cottage he made no attempt to lighten his footsteps on the paved pathway. Despite there still being daylight, he noted with a swift intake of breath that the shutters of the lower windows were shut. At such flagrant impropriety, Jacques's lips compressed with anger, and he was impatient to confront the two inside. His hand grasped hold of the door's iron knocker, but as he was about to bring it down, from within came the sound of singing; men and women singing together! Jacques's hand fell away from the knocker. He stared blankly at the oak panels of the door, his anger engulfed by dismay. This was worse than any lovers' tryst! With a restless shift of position, he leaned his back against the stone portal, vaguely conscious of the scent of roses overhead. How long had it been going on ... while he was away in Riga? Whatever the answer, there was nothing for him but to get her out of there. Get her away from the psalm singers before they brought disaster on her. Jacques turned and seizing hold of the knocker brought it down against the oak timbers. Immediately, the singing within ceased. He imagined the apprehension and fear amongst those inside, but he slammed the knocker down again and twice more. Within a minute or so the door was opened by Martin Migault. The expression on his scholarly face was calm and composed.

'Good evening, Maître Maurellet,' he said respectfully. 'Are you here to join our meeting?'

'Certainly not,' retorted Jacques coldly. 'I believe my cousin is within!'

'Our dear sister is indeed,' rejoined the former lawyer with a smile, 'but don't stay outside, Maître Maurellet, please do come in.'

'I have no wish to enter nor to join your meeting. Tell Mademoiselle Maurellet I wish to speak to her ... *now!*' Martin Migault gave a respectful nod and, leaving the door ajar, he disappeared within the house. Moments afterwards, Perrette appeared in the doorway, her face expressing a mixture of anxiety and happiness.

'So Perrette,' said Jacques gravely, 'you have deceived me and Aunt Marguerite ... it is with Huguenots you spend your time?'

'But I do see Louise! She comes here also with her husband. Will you join us, dearest cousin, open your heart and mind to the Reformed Church?'

Jacques clenched his teeth and shook his head. 'We are leaving.'

'But the prayer meeting has only just begun.'

'Perrette, I have no desire to exchange angry words here. Make your goodbyes to those inside and do not tarry!' His voice was heavy with angry disapproval and his cousin paled, for he had never spoken to her in such a way before. Tears sprang to her eyes, and she made a helpless gesture with her small white hands as she retreated back into the house. From within came the rise and fall of voices, then the return of footsteps. Just short of the door, Jacques heard the hushed tones of Martin Migault.

'Let me persuade Maître Maurellet to join us so that you can be united in worship.'

'It is too soon, Martin … he is angry to find me here. But I will help him understand that this is the path for us both, and that I am being prepared for baptism.'

'God go with you, sister!'

Jacques nearly choked at the outrageous words, and lest he lose control he walked away down the path. Inwardly, he was seething with anger and alarm. Behind him the door of the house shut and light hurrying footsteps soon brought Perrette to his side. They walked back to the road in silence. He was half-aware that his cousin had started to cry, but all he could think of were the words he had overheard: *prepared for baptism*. It made him feel sick to contemplate what she had become involved with … little wonder she was hiding from the curé!

On reaching his aunt's house, Jacques was relieved to find both she and Annette had retired to bed. It would break his aunt's heart to know what had just taken place. The fast pace of their return had burnt up much of his anger, and though it was by no means diminished, bewilderment was what he now predominantly felt. He poured himself a large cognac, took a deep draught, and faced Perrette.

'I can hardly believe you would visit the house of a bachelor ... a labourer on our books.'

'I was not alone,' responded Perrette defensively.

'You think that makes it better? From where I was standing I could clearly hear a party of some twenty, amongst whom were *men*. Who were these men?'

'I don't know. Some come from a great distance.'

'Do you think it modest to meet – even worse, to sing with – men you do not know? Have you lost your mind?'

'They are Christian brothers,' she sobbed, her pale blue eyes spilling tears.

'I want to understand.' He sighed, flinging himself onto a chair. 'What induced a good Catholic like you to ...'

Perrette moved closer, and Jacques noticed her hands were holding her shawl as if something precious was within. 'The reason is here,' she whispered. With reverence she revealed a black, leather- bound book. 'It is the New Testament. And Jacques, the words are in French! I am able to read and understand what Jesus said to his disciples. I don't *need* a priest to tell me!'

'They are teaching you to turn away from the Saints,' rejoined Jacques, reaching for the first thing to say as his mind reeled with shock. 'What is it, Perrette, that persuades you to renounce all which not so long ago you held most sacred? Do you no longer kneel before the statue of our holy mother Mary?'

Perrette flushed red with discomfort. As she sank down on a stool, the expression on her face was intense and anxious.

'The minister says Christians have no need of idols. Of course I have doubts, but through preparation I begin to see that as humble as I am I can speak directly to God. I can speak to him anywhere ... in a garden, in a field. If you would only come to a prayer meeting ... we are given a text to read, and we all talk about what it means. Sometimes, it is a *woman* who reads it, and the *men listen with respect.*'

'You are singing and kneeling beside men whom I do not know … it is *shameful.* I won't have it, Perrette!'

'You said you wanted to understand.'

'There is nothing to understand,' retorted Jacques, rage and consternation overtaking him. He stood up and looked down at her. 'Do you want to bring on us a thousand *livres* fine? Must I witness your upper lip being slit for blasphemy, and when you don't heed that, see your lower lip cut away? You've lost your wits, and before you ruin yourself, you'll not go anywhere without my permission or I shall inform the curé that your soul is in peril.'

*** *** ***

'Is that you, Hermione Lefèvre … she who lived in faubourg Saint Antoine?'

The question which was hissed near to her ear sent a thrill of alarm through Hermione. All about her, people were open-mouthed and wide-eyed as they stared at the wondrous stonework fronting the entrance into the cathedral of Saint Pierre. It being Wednesday, one of the two market days of Saintes, the square was packed solid with people. Such was the crush as people pressed forward to enter the cathedral, Hermione could barely move, let alone turn around. However, as she twisted her neck to the right, she encountered a man wearing the large-brimmed hat of a pilgrim.

'Dear little Hermione! It is indeed you.'

'Olivier! We need to get out of this press!'

By pushing sideways, both of them eventually managed to escape from the passage of people surging in and out of the cathedral.

'Why didn't you make yourself known sooner?' asked Hermione. For, despite the hundreds of pilgrims, she had been conscious of one who had hovered about her when she was studying the tower of the

Benedictine convent on the other side of the river. Then, again, on this side of the Charente, when she was descending the staircase after visiting the shrine and church of Saint Eutrope. She took Olivier's hands and pressed them with affection. 'Oh, it is so good to see you,' she went on, realizing just how much she had missed him. 'I received your message and had not forgotten what your symbols meant. Did you leave because of La Reynie's men?'

'Yes. A lad from the street ran in and told me the archers were coming. So, fearing the worst, I made my escape. I arrived here yesterday evening, and by an amazing stroke of good fortune, I saw you at the Abbaye aux Dames, this morning.'

'Why didn't you approach me then? For in truth, I do believe you have been following me ever since.'

'I have,' confessed Olivier, 'but I was not *certain* it was you. The brim and feathers of your hat cast your face in shadow. But when you knelt as the bell announced the arrival of the Holy Office there was that scuffle as a man near you wouldn't take off his hat. Men snatched it away and trampled on it.'

'He was a Huguenot.' Hermione nodded, recollecting the man's blasphemy.

'You picked his hat out of the dung after the priest had passed and took it to him. It was then I knew it really was you. But I decided to speak to you where none would notice.'

'Are you hungry?' asked Hermione, thinking how thin and gaunt was his face. Olivier shook his head.

'I eat when I remember. It has been the most interesting journey from Paris, Hermione. The church at Poitiers was of particular note. But for my wish to see you I was greatly drawn to travel on to Spain. I even bought a pound cake for the journey.'

'Oh no, you must come to Du Chesne! Guillaume would expect it. You will not know he returned to Paris and found you not there. My coach is to take me home within the hour. Do you have belongings at the inn?'

'I do.'

'Then collect them and meet me at the Arc de Germanicus.'

'But my room is paid tonight, and I have not yet seen the Roman amphitheatre,' protested Olivier. Hermione groaned with exasperation; nothing had changed. Olivier was as unworldly as ever. He was supposed to be on the run, yet all he was concerned about was looking at wonders.

'There will be other times,' she said firmly, 'and there being so many pilgrims the inn can let the room twice over. Oh,' she added, suddenly thinking of how she would explain him when she returned to Du Chesne, 'do you have other clothes?' Olivier shook his head. 'That is a pity. It would be better for you to arrive looking like a gentleman taking up residence with a chatelaine rather than a pilgrim dressed for the road. Have you money? Good, then see what you can do within the hour.'

For her own part, Hermione needed to buy scissors, both small and large, as well as ink and paper. After making her purchases, she suddenly caught sight of a highly bedecked Angélique Tilly entering a shop which sold silks and ribbons. It would have been amusing to bid her good day, but with Olivier to meet there was not time enough.

Good to his promise, Olivier arrived on time, his reserved nod of greeting drawing no attention to them. Guillaume's joy, however, was not to be suppressed; he swept off his hat and brushed it across the step of the coach as if it were for the King himself. Then he almost lifted his master into it. As Olivier took his seat, Hermione nodded with approval at his elegant black coat and breeches.

'What became of your pilgrim's hat and cloak?'

'The good woman took them in part exchange,' answered Olivier, setting down a small leather satchel and a brown paper package beside him.

'That smells wonderful.' Hermione sighed, suddenly conscious she had not eaten since dawn. 'Is it your pound cake?'

'Steeped in cognac; would you care for a piece? It is the specialty of the town.'

'I can't wait.' She laughed as he took out a small knife from his leather bag.

'So!' she said, happily settling back and breaking off a piece from her slice as they left the town behind. 'How did you escape?'

'I have a means to pass through a store cupboard in the laboratory.'

'I know that, Olivier. You showed it to me.'

'Ah yes, so I did.' He nodded. There was only time to snatch up the money I kept in a bag for such a catastrophe, though I never thought to use it.'

'Did they try to follow you?'

'I do not think so. As the furnace was hot, they may have expected me to return. Perhaps when I didn't, they searched and found the hidden spring ... who knows? It was the worst day of my life.'

'It would have been your worst day if they had caught you!'

'How am I to live without my work ... how can I work without my laboratory? Everything is lost to me, my manuscripts, my notes ... years of work. It is a disaster!' he snapped, his eyes intense with anger. 'And all because of filthy hags who peddle poison and ignorant minds who do not know the difference between charlatans and men of learning ... even with our king's *Académie des Sciences*.' The atmosphere became heavy as Olivier slumped back, his slice of cake forgotten.

'Dearest Olivier,' said Hermione softly, wondering how she might lift his spirits. It was indeed a disaster, in terms of not only losing all his valuable equipment, but the days and weeks, the months and years ... how could they be given back to him? 'And you so close to finding the Elixir of Life,' she murmured, feeling she would also weep if she thought on it any longer. 'Well,' she said, forcing a bright note into her voice, 'there are dusty manuscripts and books at Du Chesne to divert and occupy you. And the parish priest is very learned.'

'His thinking no doubt shackled by superstition! I cannot wait to meet him,' quipped Olivier. He gave a heavy sigh, and with a dismal expression stared out at the passing countryside. For a time, they continued so in silence, and having finished her own portion of cake, Hermione let her eyes stray downwards to his, as yet untouched. She considered helping him out, but then, when he had seemingly digested her words, his fingers began to pick at it and absently deliver up morsels into his mouth. 'What nature of books are they?' he asked in a grudging tone.

If Olivier's arrival was met with restraint and suspicion by Marie and Pierre, Lucette's joy and that of Guillaume made up for it.

'Fancy your spotting the master,' remarked Lucette as she made up a bed in the chamber above Hermione's in the tower, 'and him on his way here. Is he here to stay?'

'I think so. He had to leave everything behind.'

Lucette met Hermione's eyes and nodded with sympathy. 'He was kind to me that night when Guillaume brought me in ... do you remember, mademoiselle?'

'How could I forget?' murmured Hermione, turning from the narrow window where she had been watching Olivier wandering about beside the river.

'Have La Voisin and Le Sage been burnt yet, madame?'

'He did not say ... you know the master never interests himself in such things. Though the sooner they are put to death, the better .... lest they talk about the *lady*.' Lucette's eyes stretched wide as she sucked in her breath in alarm. But, any terror on her part of being hauled back to Paris for questioning was exceedingly short-lived, for within minutes of being sent to tell Olivier all was ready, she was heard to burst into song as she clattered away down the stone steps. Within these thick stone walls it was easy to feel safe, thought Hermione as she began to scatter dried lavender amid the rushes on the floor. Paris was leagues away, and they had all found sanctuary from its troubles. Olivier might be aloof from the daily happenings of life, but his kind generosity was out of the ordinary. How many unmarried men would have taken in a baby?

And when Guillaume had brought a terrified kitchenmaid to the house, without hesitation Olivier had provided a place at the kitchen table for Lucette too. It had then been left to herself to listen to the other girl's gabbled story about the Queen of the Witches. Hermione brushed her hands together to rid them of the dust from the dried flowers and sat down on the bed. Stretching out fully, she cast her mind back to the girl's tale.

La Voisin's maid, Margot, had taken Lucette to do rough work at the villa on the outskirts of Paris. At first, all had gone well. Lucette worked hard and kept strictly to the kitchen and some niche in the attic where she slept. She knew visitors came to the villa for predictions and potions, but after some time, she became aware also of callers arriving long after dark. On such a night, she was awakened by a frantic ringing on the bell. Having become less shy and more curious about what went on in the early hours, she disobeyed the rules and stole downstairs to watch from a dark corner overlooking the hall. The caller proved to be a woman who was enveloped in a long cloak. Beneath its large hood her face was concealed by a black mask.

'There was no need to ring, madame,' La Voisin had said, as she ushered in her visitor. 'I am as anxious as you that your visit here remains secret.' As the mysterious caller was led away, Lucette had then run back up to her mattress. She supposed she had drifted to sleep when it seemed in the next instant she was sitting bolt upright clutching at the blanket as a piercing scream shattered the silence. It was followed by another of spine-chilling agony and then one more, subdued and muffled. Shaking with fright, Lucette had crept down from the servants' quarters to her hiding place. There was but time to squat down before a door opened and three figures stepped into the soft candlelight of the hall. With La Voisin was a woman whose apron was stained with blood. Almost hanging between them was the caller, who was still masked. Her cloak had been thrown around her shoulders in some haste, for in the dim light her dress showed the glint of jewels. It was clear from whom the screams had come, for the woman was in excruciating pain as she was half-dragged towards the door.

'God forgive me,' she panted, emitting a terrible groan as she staggered and collapsed onto the floor. Without pause, La Voisin and the abortionist hauled her back onto her feet, and as they did so the black mask slipped away, allowing a clear view of her face.

'Attention, madame, heed what I say,' the woman in the bloodied apron had hissed. 'Lie down in the coach and take to bed the instant you get home. Drink the potion … it will stop the bleeding. You should have stayed longer.'

'I can't,' quavered the woman, as the door opened onto the courtyard where Lucette could just see the wheels of a coach. 'I must not be discovered … even now I may be undone.' Then the door closed on La Voisin's client.

Terrified that she might be discovered, Lucette had scurried away. Although mysterious happenings sometimes woke her thereafter, she stayed hidden away under her blanket until one morning, overcome by curiosity to know where chanting had come from the previous night, she had ventured into the garden before the household was about. What she found in a small pavilion was so horrible that she took to her heels and did not stop running till she was through Porte Saint Denis. Hermione shivered and made the sign of the cross to rid herself of the horrors of the Devil. So absorbed had she been recalling her maid's terrible past she had not heard Olivier enter, and when she opened her eyes, she found he was looking down at her. Hermione smiled up at him and was glad that he did not carry the burden of knowing about the foul, evil deeds of Satanists.

'I hope you will stay with us, Olivier,' she said, rising up from the bed. 'We are safe here. The peasants have very little, and they are depending upon me to make their lives easier. Will you help me?' The baffled look which settled immediately on Olivier's intelligent face made her burst out laughing. 'The most I will ask is for you to help me make sense of the King's tax laws.' Inwardly, Hermione acknowleged that the most effective way for Olivier to help was to keep away from everyone.

On the following day, Guillaume carried a chest of ancient manuscripts up to his master's room in the tower. Thus, with a table set up before one of its windows, Hermione hoped Olivier's restless mind would be content ... at least for a while.

CHAPTER 14

here seemed not a breath of air. Summer's blistering heat sapped energy from young and old alike. Every face showed the fatigue of hard physical work, but also something else: relief that a plentiful harvest was assured.

At midday, Marie would ring the bell in the courtyard to let the field hands know it was time to break off. If any were working close by, it would bring them to quench their thirst at the well and eat bean soup set out on a trestle with rough hunks of bread. Any thoughts on Hermione's part of offering more had instantly been dismissed by Marie.

'It won't do to alter the way of things, madame,' the old lady had said with a stern expression. 'It will excite them. Next year, they will want more, and when you don't give it, some will be disappointed and others angry.' So Hermione had to be content to look on, deriving at least some satisfaction whenever she saw the plodding team of oxen. She had bought them to replace those which had been seized two years ago by tax-collectors. These valuable beasts would not go the same way, she vowed.

Gradually, as evening shadows lengthened, the barn began to fill with cereals. There was much to occupy her thoughts; even so, she often found herself wishing Jacques Maurellet would call in at Du Chesne. He had no real need, of course, other than to see how the men were getting along in the forest. Perhaps, as he had expressed an interest in buying in Du Chesne's timber, it was time to remind him of it.

So early the next day, with a real sense of adventure upon her and a saddlebag packed with pots of honey as a gift for Henri Maurellet, Hermione set off on the new mare which Guillaume had bought at a horse fair. One of the things she had come to love about living in Saintonge was the special light of its sky. There was a brilliance which she had never noticed in Paris, and its appearance could change so fast. One moment it would be dark with rain clouds, then within hours the sun would burst through. Hermione put her mount to a low hedge and experienced a thrill of excitement as it lifted with ease and cleared the ditch on the other side. With the Charente to guide her, there was no danger of getting lost, so she let her horse have its head. At the sound of pounding hooves, rabbits raced away to their burrows and birds pecking at the ground lifted upwards in great flocks. In comparison to her progress, the flat-bottomed barges on the river taking their loads to Rochefort, or maybe as far as La Rochelle, were causing no disturbance. All seemed calm, though no doubt the fish would not agree. Hermione laughed at her foolishness, but she was excited by the adventure. There were not many travellers on the road, so upon spotting a man ahead she decided to check if she was nearing the shipyard. As she gradually closed the distance between them, she saw he was carrying an enormous bundle of kindling across his shoulders; perhaps he lived nearby.

'*Bonjour*,' she called out, slowing the mare to walk beside him. 'Would the Maurellet shipyard be near here, monsieur?'

'Always has been,' grunted the man, not looking up. 'The path over yonder is quicker.'

After making her thanks, Hermione rode along the rough track which brought her through willows directly alongside the river. She saw she had almost reached her goal; the shoreline ahead was completely taken over by the shipyard. Masts thrust upward like trees to the sky and small boats lay idle on the water, while others were hauled up onto the beach. Further away from the river, she could glimpse row upon row of stacked timber. The main gate leading into this vast area, Hermione guessed, could be reached along the top of the rise of land to her left. She urged her horse up the bank towards a clump of small trees whose branches had been driven sideways by strong winds, so it was not until she arrived at them that she saw the young woman they had hidden. Over one arm of her grey dress the stranger carried a basket, but by her bearing and the quality of her clothes, Hermione concluded she was not a servant.

'Good-morrow, madame,' Hermione greeted her. 'Is the entrance to the shipyard along this lane?'

'Yes.'

'Can you tell me where I might find Maître Maurellet?'

'He is probably down at one of the slipways,' replied the young woman stiffly. The cool gaze of her eyes was studying Hermione's riding habit. Then it was the feathers and ribbons of her green straw hat which were being assessed. Perhaps she was being over-sensitive, but the expression on the heart-shaped face looking up at her was a mix of curiosity and disapproval.

'I am Maître Maurellet's granddaughter. Are you seeking help for a charity?'

'I am here on business,' explained Hermione, experiencing a shrinking feeling within as the woman's pale blue eyes widened with shock.

'Then it seems I must show you the way, madame.'

Hermione gathered up the reins. 'My thanks, madame, but I shall manage without incommoding you. Your basket looks heavy.'

With a curt nod, the petite woman moved away and continued along the track until she turned upwards towards a largish house fenced off by an orchard. Hermione stirred her horse forward with a sense of relief. Those eyes had been pretty, but their expression had not softened in return at her own parting smile. To be fair to her, though, everyday callers going to the shipyard would not usually be flaunting green beribboned hats! For no real reason, the joy of coming here seemed to have evaporated a little. She felt foolishly overdressed.

Once through the great wooden gates into the shipyard, Hermione guided her mount with some care past high stacks of planking set upon beds of cinders. Following on from these neat rows came areas crowded with grotesque cuts of trees. Every moment the bustle and clamour of men at work grew louder. To right and left sawyers wielded their long saws; a blacksmith at a forge was hammering out a red-hot length of metal. Hermione needed constantly to calm her horse, as unexpected, ear-splitting outbursts of hammering broke out or heavily loaded wagons swayed past them. Her interest and concentration were so intense that she had almost forgotten whither she was bound until Jacques Maurellet suddenly called down to her from the uppermost deck of a ship.

'I've come to look at your ships.' She laughed, returning his wave.

'Why, young lady, what are you doing here distracting my workforce?' growled a familiar voice.

'Maître Maurellet, you have not forgotten me then?'

'I never forget a pretty face, Madame Du Chesne,' declared the elderly master-shipwright, offering up his hands to assist Hermione to dismount. 'My grandson has given such good account of your timber that he has persuaded me to take in several loads.'

'Oh, I am pleased to hear it, for I had begun to think it was forgotten,' rejoined Hermione, wincing as she moved, for she had never ridden so far before.

'Should you return in our coach?' the elderly man teased, as she pulled a face and stretched out her shoulders.

'Indeed no,' she said with a smile, her eyes on Jacques as he swung down from the scaffolding at the side of the ship.

'We are honoured,' he said, his blue eyes gleaming with pleasure as he reached Hermione. 'A long ride for you. I see you have a new mare … not bad! But how fares the royal stallion?'

'You already know?' she gasped in surprise as he nodded. 'I would have been here in half the time if I were allowed to put a saddle on him.'

'And likely not arrive in one piece,' he said with a grin.

'Enough of horses,' interrupted Henri Maurellet, 'boats and ships are what we are about! So, while I show you around, Jacques shall tell my granddaughter to set a place for you at the table, for she calls upon us at this time.' It was a kind suggestion, but realizing whom he must mean, Hermione shrank from all that would go with it.

'It is a kind thought, Maître Maurellet, but I would not wish to trouble your granddaughter. I believe it was she who was kind enough to point out the way here. Truth to say, I am not at all hungry!'

Beneath his mane of white hair, Henri Maurellet's weather-beaten face became a picture of astonishment, and his fierce black eyebrows flew upwards. 'Not hungry ... I have never heard of such a thing. I've known people who don't eat because they have no food, but when we have at hand a fine cook! What say you, Jacques?'

Jacques' eyes interrogated Hermione, and she flushed lest he divine the root of her discomfort.

'I say,' he responded, his eyes thoughtful, then glinting with amusement, 'we will follow Madame Du Chesne's bidding and seek not to delay her longer than she desires. Come, Grandfather,' he went on, as the elderly master-shipwright snorted with vexation, 'show off the fine carving you completed yesterday.' In company with the two men, Hermione walked towards a small craft riding at anchor on the river.

'The barge is for Paul de La Grange Jordan, de Sury,' explained Jacques. 'It is for the Marquis's personal use to visit friends along the Charente when he comes to stay in Rochefort. Come aboard.' Hermione walked up the gangplank behind him and her nostrils pricked with the smell of paint as they made their way past the rowing stations towards a raised opensided cabin. 'Of course a canopy of green has yet to be fitted. It will look quite splendid when its gold tassels are fluttering in the breeze. And there you have the Marquis's coat of arms,' he added with a gesture.

Hermione turned inquisitive eyes towards a wooden partition on which was a carved heraldic device. A crown surmounted by nine balls had been gilded to dazzling effect, and she smiled. 'How the gold catches the sun. A crown I know represents seigniorial authority, but the two stars beneath … what do they symbolize? And a goose! What can that mean?'

'Foie gras?' offered Jacques mischievously. His expression of amusement became thoughtful. 'The stars symbolize celestial goodness … a noble person, and by all accounts such is the Marquis. The goose I believe represents resourcefulness. How do you like Grandfather's carving of the seats for the Marquis and his lady? So many daisies and leaves it seems like a bower for lovers.'

'I suppose you would have had crabs and gaping fish,' snorted Henri as he arrived to join them. Silently, Hermione stared at the flowing lines of the letter P centred in the back of one of the two seats. Even her inexperienced eye recognized that the carving was masterly. Yet there was something more … like a force or energy which went beyond mere replication. 'I think the Marquis will be pleased.' The elderly shipwright gave a nod of satisfaction.

'Is the decorative work what you enjoy most?' asked Hermione as her attention left the delicate furled petals of a rose set along an armrest to be caught by the hands which had executed it. Henri's fingers were swollen, their knuckles painfully enlarged, yet they could turn wood into such beauty! As if picking up on her thoughts, the master-shipwright chuckled.

'Yes … my hands are not as nimble as they used to be. And this eye seems misty of late and bleedings don't seem to help.'

'You could carve roses and dolphins with your eyes blindfolded!' Jacques told him with a note of pride.

'Do you carve, as well?' Hermione asked as moments later she accepted Jacques's arm to step down onto the gangplank.

'I haven't Grandfather's patience.'

'It is the length of a keel that fills his daydreams nowadays,' mocked

Henri Maurellet. 'And questioning God's forces which he and other upstarts hope to outwit with mathematics.' Jacques Maurellet pulled a face as he exchanged a look with Hermione, and she fought to smother her laughter.

Their tour had taken something like over an hour when the clang of a bell sounded in the shipyard. All about there was an instant bringing to an end of what men were about.

'Are you sure you will not stay?' questioned Jacques in a low voice. 'No? Then I'll take you back to the road.'

'There is no need.'

'But there is,' he retorted with a smile. As he walked away to the stables where her horse had been taken, Hermione followed Henri Maurellet to a high wooden building.

'Will you be coming to select the stands you want in October, Maître Henri?'

The elderly shipwright led the way into a small cubby hole, which from ledgers and piles of papers seemed to be an office.

'No, I shall leave that to Jacques, who is content with the price you ask. The merchant Claude Tilly can handle the transport … he needs watching on price, but that will be for us to negotiate. Now, what am I looking for?' the old man murmured as he looked into boxes on a shelf. 'Ah yes, here we have it. A little keepsake for you.' Hermione's eyes took in the proffered model of a ship. It was quite small, yet seemed complete in every detail, even to tiny coils of rope on its deck.

'It is perfect,' she exclaimed, smiling, as she took it from him. 'Did you make the sails also?'

'No, my granddaughter Perrette sewed them … she is a kind girl. Let me put it back in its box. It will be easier for you. Come back here any time, but only if you mean to stay to break bread with us. Now, if you will forgive me, I must to the house, for my granddaughter does not like to be kept waiting, and you would oblige me by reminding Jacques of that.'

With a feeling of fondness, Hermione watched Maître Henri depart. He was of a great age, yet his limbs seemed only a little stiff. She wondered about his dim eye and thought that Marie might know of some herb to cure it.

When Jacques returned leading her horse, he was mounted on his stallion.

'But your meal!' she urged as she quickly exchanged the pots of honey in her saddlebag for the carving of the model ship. 'Maître Henri asked me to remind you not to delay.'

'It can wait awhile,' he flashed back with a grin. 'Come, follow me.'

They set off at a fast trot, leaving the now silent shipyard and heading uphill towards the town. Reaching a wayside inn Jacques indicated for Hermione to rein in her horse. Judging by the number of men sitting at the roughly hewn tables outside and the hubbub from within, there was a great deal of eating and drinking going on.

'Are we to eat here?' Hermione asked hesitantly. Despite her hunger, it seemed no place for a woman. With a boyish grin, Jacques leapt down from his horse.

'Stay here,' he directed, tossing his reins up to her. Ten minutes or so passed and then he re-emerged carrying a small basket. As he reached her horse the air became pungent with the smell of bread and something delicious. Offering no explanation, he raised the flap of her saddlebag and stowed away the basket. Then he was up onto his saddle and reaching to Hermione for his reins. Their eyes met, his gleaming with laughter.

'Do you always tell lies to elderly men?'

'Lies?'

'I am not at all hungry, Maître Maurellet!"

'Now, Madame Du Chesne, all you need on your ride home is a shady tree to spread your meal beneath. I wish I could join you, but further delay will make another lady very angry!'

Jacques wheeled about his horse and with a cheery wave he raced away. Hermione stared after him. Not once had he asked why she had declined the invitation to eat at his home. It seemed he had understood what she herself could hardly make sense of.

CHAPTER 15

aving spent a good part of the day with Pierre in the furthermost part of the High Forest, assessing the number and quality of trees, Hermione had decided to return to the château. Pierre, in company with Rouge, had stayed on to set traps in his ongoing war against rabbits. It had been a tiring but satisfying time spent within the forest's green calm. In contrast, the sound of uproar coming from the stables filled Hermione with alarm. It sounded as if murder was being done ... to the piglets! Could a fox have got to them? It was unlikely, yet something was making them squeal. Without pausing to dismount at the block, Hermione carried on under the stone archway and through the courtyard, putting hens to flight right and left. As the gleaming walls of the *pigeonnier* came into view, so too did Lucette. She was standing outside the wash-house door doubled up with laughter as squealing piglets raced back and forth between the legs of the royal stallion with Guillaume lunging after them. Unbelievably, the stallion was drawn up close behind the hindquarters of a bony mare. For a split second, Hermione's lips puckered in laughter, but then the terrifying implication of it all struck home as Lucette screamed out, 'Catch them, Guillaume, so he can get to it!'

Just as Lucette danced forward to join in the sport, it seemed she was forewarned of Hermione's arrival by the approaching clatter of hooves. Not even bothering to look, she whirled about and darted back out of sight into the wash-house. With horrified eyes, Hermione gazed at the mangy looking mare, which she recognized as the one usually tethered outside the smithy. Indeed, as the bony creature skittered sideways, there was the blacksmith, his bulging muscular arm holding its halter.

'*Mon Dieu*!' gasped Hermione, as she slid down from the saddle. 'What is happening here?' .

'Ah, madame,' replied Guillaume with a sheepish smile, 'we've had a spot of bother getting the stallion to mount Raoul's mare. Somehow the piglets got loose … and I fear one got kicked.' Following Guillaume's tentative, guilty gesture, Hermione saw the victim. The small, lifeless form was lying in a puddle of muddy water. With its eyes shut and its tiny ears resting backwards, it might have been asleep except for the crimson gash splitting open its belly. Hermione bit on her lip to control her reaction. This loss alone was a blow, but as nothing to the trouble she would be in over the stallion. Then, as Guillaume's gabbled excuse came back into her mind, she experienced a surge of overwhelming relief.

'The stallion hasn't mounted the mare then?' she asked, to make absolutely sure.

'Not yet,' answered Guillaume, with a grovelling smile.

'Then lead the colt straight back into its stall. This is no place for such a purpose. And you should know, Guillaume,' she added, trying to control the anger that had taken over from relief, 'this is certainly no mare for a stallion belonging to the King!'

'Oh, we've had her staring at the stallion all day so her foal will take after it, just as the King's man told us to do.'

'Guillaume,' flashed Hermione, 'this mare could stare for a year, and it would not help!'

'My money is as good as any man's, Madame Du Chesne,' snarled the blacksmith.

'I have no doubt of it, Raoul,' returned Hermione, trying to remain calm, for his clenched hands were as big as hams and his expression was defiant. 'The King's orders are clear and *must* be obeyed. Only first-rate mares of quality are to be led to the stallion when he is four years of age, he is but two.'

'And who is to judge my mare besides you, madame?'

'I am sorry. If your mare were the finest in the land, the stallion is too young.' It was not a good thing to upset such a man, whose skills were essential to them. By his black, belligerent stare, Hermione could see that despite her explanation the man had taken her refusal personally. 'When you have finished, Guillaume,' she directed in a severe voice as she looked away from the blacksmith, 'come straight up to my bureau.'

The door of the wash-house was still shut, and Lucette was either still working within or had escaped back to the kitchen. With a final look of regret at the dead piglet, Hermione began to walk away. As she did so, the blacksmith's muttered oath behind her was obviously meant to reach her ears. Hermione took no notice. In a week or so, he would have forgotten all about it.

*** *** ***

The atmosphere within the salon bristled with the aftermath of the loud exchange of angry words which had brought Jacques into the house. On one side of the polished beech table stood the curé, and facing him were Perrette and her friend Louise Dubois. Oblivious of everything was Louise's baby, fast asleep in the Maurellet family cradle, apparently brought down into the salon for its use. As Jacques moved to stand beside the women, he tried to grasp what had passed before he arrived. By the silks and linen spread out across the table, the women had been embroidering, so what could have occurred to anger Father Francis so much, and why was he here?

'Monsieur Maurellet, I appeal to you to bring your cousin to order! She refuses to desist from practising heresy against the Virgin and the Saints.'

At a loss, Jacques turned a questioning look on Perrette.

'There has been no heresy here, cousin,' she answered in a calm voice. 'I did not think you would mind my bringing Louise here. The baby was crying so much it was disturbing Mother. While we sewed, we sang the songs of David. How can that be heresy? How can joining together to sing the praise of God in my grandfather's home be wrong?'

'Because it goes against the teaching of the Catholic Church,' snapped the priest, his eyes hard with anger. 'I call upon both of you to desist from this practice. You must promise here and now that you will not sing psalms in the house, not in the fields, nor in the streets.' The women remained mute. 'If you disobey, if I have to enter here or your mother's house to ask you to stop singing, I shall bring you before the courts.'

Though inwardly he found the whole matter more than aggravating, having more important matters to think of, Jacques bridled at the priest's bullying tone.

'Father,' he said respectfully, 'I beg to remind you that you have entered a private home ... my grandfather's home.'

'I have the right!'

'Only an Officer of Justice has right of entry into a private home to question; otherwise, it might be regarded as trespass.' The word hung heavy in the room, and clearly inflamed by Jacques's reaction, the priest's gaunt face reddened.

'I shall pray for you all,' he muttered, trembling with rage. Then he swept out of the room, muttering as he went.

'Thank you, cousin,' said Perrette, turning with a relieved smile to Jacques.

'I don't want your thanks,' he snapped. 'He is not going to give up. Sing psalms here again and you'll bring down on Grandfather and me the burden of a heavy fine.'

'I am sorry to have brought trouble on you, Monsieur Maurellet,' put in Louise Dubois. The young mother's stricken glance showed she was ill-at-ease and anxious to leave. She quickly gathered up her sewing materials and put them into her bag. Then, turning to Perrette, the young mother's white-capped head bent in prayer.

'May I live in the world as if I were beyond it,' she murmured reverently.

'May my conversation,' continued Perrette, 'be that of a citizen of Heaven.' The women embraced and then, moving across to the cradle, Louise lifted out her baby. With a polite nod to Jacques, she hurried from the room. There followed silence as Perrette tidied away her scissors and silks. Jacques watched her finger a prayer book which evidently had been hidden under the embroidery when Father Francis had entered.

'You told me I should not visit certain friends,' she said defensively. 'As this room is not used when you and Grandfather are working, it served us well.' Jacques strove to calm his irritation, and then their moment of intimacy was suspended at the sound of footsteps approaching the door.

'If the priest takes this to the courts, I will not be able to protect you,' warned Jacques, his voice urgent, taking it to be the curé returning. The door swung open, and happily it was their grandfather, though by his expression, it appeared a storm was about to break.

'I am glad, Perrette, that you are still under my roof,' he thundered, 'because I would not wish your mother to hear what I have to say.' Perrette glanced to Jacques for help as the old man launched into his attack. 'Can it be true what the curé has just told me?'

'You let Huguenots work in the yard,' whispered Perrette defensively.

'But I'll not have some Huguenot in my family ... my own flesh and blood taking up with heretics!'

'It is a matter of conscience,' intervened Jacques half-heartedly in an attempt to shield Perrette from Henri's hurt and disappointment.

'You'll mend your ways if you do not wish to break your mother's heart. It is not hard now to see why Jacques has hesitated so long to wed thee! I don't want to see you here when I get back!'

The cruelty of the old man's words as he flung them out with a dismissive gesture proved too much. As the heavy oak door slammed shut, his cousin burst into tears. Jacques took her in his arms. 'There, there,' he soothed, as to a child, 'Grandfather did not mean it … his hurt will pass,' though in his heart he could only envisage things becoming worse.

The arrival of a summons on the following day, ordering Jacques to attend at the royal arsenal, was a welcome diversion from the happenings of the previous afternoon. There was no mention of his grandfather also going, but Henri showed only relief as he walked with Jacques down to the river.

'You know I don't like dressing up. Besides, you'll be running things after my death … though if that stupid Perrette does not come to her senses, I'm not likely to see grandchildren in my lifetime.' The bleak note in the old man's voice tugged at Jacques's heart. He tried to make light of things.

'She'll come around,' he murmured. 'You yourself said women are changeable.' With rough affection, he put his arm around Henri's shoulders, which once had felt so compact. 'I'll sort things out, don't you worry.' Without much conviction that he would be able to do so, however, he stepped into the boat that was to take him upstream. He gave a wave to his grandfather as the young apprentices took up their oars.

'What cargo do you think that barge is carrying, Maître Maurellet?' asked one of the lads, as their boat lifted on the wash caused by the passing vessel.

'It'll likely be bringing sugar from the refinery,' he observed, 'I've heard Colbert is now bent on building refineries in the West Indies, as well as two on the Ile de France and three on Guadaloupe.'

'Places I'd like to see,' said the youngster with a grin. Jacques smiled, and they continued in silence until eventually, rounding the curve of the river, they moved past the line of battered barges and old vessels which served as makeshift homes for some of the workers at Rochefort.

'It can't be easy living,' observed the lad with a nod towards them.

'Shall we stay aboard while you're away, Maître Maurellet? Jacques nodded. As he stepped ashore, he offered his password to a sentry and then strolled along the wharf, for he was in good time. Ahead, a man was sitting on a capstan staring downstream. There was a desolate air about him, and when Jacques closed the distance between them and identified who it was, the reason for the gloomy demeanour became apparent. The Companie du Nord had virtually gone into liquidation in 1671, with most of its ships, including the one built by their own yard, now sold off. Here was one of those who had invested his hopes, and a great deal more besides, into the Company. The Maurellets too had invested money, though nothing on the scale of Monsieur Pages, who was one of the Company's principal directors. Jacques touched the businessman's shoulder in friendly greeting.

'What good fortune to see you here. How goes it in La Rochelle, Monsieur Pages?'

'Beaten ...' the man sighed as if speaking his thoughts aloud, 'I'm a beaten man, Maurellet ... no use in pretending any longer ... I'm ruined!'

'But the Company is still bringing in masts and continues to trade with Spain and Portugal.'

The entrepreneur answered with a bitter laugh. 'What is that when we were formed to compete with the Dutch, to carry France's wine, the sugar from her refineries, cognac, silk from Lyon, exports of every kind, to the markets in the north? We were to bring back stores for the Marine. Even after selling off many ships, our debts are enormous. Your father invested before he was killed ... you'll not see back a *livre*.'

'I grieve only for him,' rejoined Jacques, in a voice flat with sadness. The disillusion on the weary face of the other man was hard to bear. 'What went wrong?'

'What went wrong? The Dutch ... they are what went wrong.' Even Pages's accusation was lacking in energy. 'Right from the start they saw the Company as a threat aimed against them. And, as you know, they simply glutted the markets here and everywhere else with cheap goods. We couldn't compete, even with all the backing from Colbert and the King himself. What finally did it, of course, was the war. Colbert made every effort to get agreement over neutrality for our ships, but despite passports and flags, Company ships were captured, while the rest lay idle in port at La Rochelle. Forgive me, Maurellet,' he said with a sigh, 'I'm not telling you anything you don't already know.' In silence they followed the progress of a merchantman heading upriver, and, as if something had amused him, the entrepreneur laughed, but there was no joy in the sound of it. 'Now Colbert's interest has switched to private merchants,' he said, his voice loaded with bitterness ... 'it seems it is they who are to carry French goods to northern markets.'

'He's also encouraging the building of sugar refineries in the West Indies, I'm told,' remarked Jacques. 'It makes sense, of course; labour costs on the islands will be low, and refined sugar is less bulky to transport.'

'It is not making investors in the refineries happy here,' said the other man. 'Best stick to shipbuilding, Maurellet.' The entrepreneur's smile stopped short of his unhappy eyes, and with a brusque nod he moved away. The disappointment and sense of betrayal which had exuded from Pages still lingered, and feeling his own spirits affected at a time when he needed to be positive and buoyant, Jacques lengthened his stride to shake free of the encounter.

After first meeting the Master Maker of Masts and spending time assessing firs, Jacques was brought before a company of officers and master-shipwrights of the Marine. His entrance, in company with the Master of Masts, went by unnoticed, as everyone was much occupied with the draft of a ship laid out on the floor of the mould loft. Jacques was more than happy to remain overlooked as he studied the black ink drawing of a First Rate whose inner construction was delineated in red ink. Could they perhaps be going to offer his yard a contract to build a man o' war? He smiled with irony at his overweening ambition and returned to considering the design of the ship. There came a light touch against his arm, and the Master of Mast's whisper diverted his attention.

'I think we have been spotted, Monsieur Maurellet!'

'Ah, there you are, messieurs,' called out the Intendant, bringing a halt to the murmur of discussion. 'As some of you may know, Maître Maurellet is acquainted with the timber markets of the Baltic, and in particular that of Riga. My question to you all is, are we in France going to run out of trees?' The question brought an immediate outburst of laughter. 'You laugh,' said the official, holding up his hand for quiet, 'but the well-being of France's forests is of concern to the Contrôleur Général. The *ordonnance* of 1669 introduced much-needed controls, and since the appointment of Louis Froideur and other *inquisiteur-commissaires* their inventories have revealed that many of our royal forests are seriously depleted. The practice of *jardinage* has resulted in mature trees being cut down on a whim with no regard to forest management. Why, even here at the arsenal, shipwrights regularly take up large cuts of timber when a smaller piece would suffice. The Contrôleur Général believes we are squandering what sustains life on every level throughout France. Whenever we are at war, we find ourselves at the mercy of the English and the Dutch, who seem able to cut off supplies from the north whenever they wish. Transport costs overland are exorbitant, so it is crucial to make certain our domestic supply is conserved for our Marine. Jacques Maurellet has just inspected the sticks which have been brought down from the Auvergne. Let us have your opinion if you please, monsieur.'

'I am honoured to offer it,' said Jacques, making a bow as the Intendant gestured for him to speak. He knew full well what the Master of Masts wished him to say and what the officials, influenced by their desire to please Colbert as Master of Forests and Waterways, would want him to say. But thinking of sailors in the teeth of a storm out on the Atlantic, Jacques decided it was they who had to be his priority.

'So, monsieur, what do you think of exploitations in the Auvergne?' the official repeated with some impatience in his tone. 'Would you say numerically the province could meet our desire for a domestic source of masting sticks? You have visited the region in the past.'

'I have reservations,' replied Jacques, 'and what I have seen today does not persuade me to alter my mind. The wood is sapless and dry, and therefore very brittle. I fear most masts would last but a year.'

'There seems not to be the height, either,' put in a captain of the Marine.

'Quite so,' agreed Jacques. 'Polish and Russian trees have all the virtues: fine, close-grained wood and enormous height, and free of knot-holes where it matters in the lower trunk area.'

'We can remedy lack of girth and height by bringing together twelve or thirteen lesser trees around a spindle,' put in a man who looked as though he should be confined to a high chair in a counting-house. No doubt the Clerk of the Chèque, decided Jacques, catching the eye of a ship's captain, who gave an ironic smile.

'There are the Pyrénées, of course,' suggested the Intendant in a somewhat glum tone, after Jacques's obvious dismissal of the Auvergne. 'The minister still feels confident that where la Provence has disappointed, they could be one answer to a cheaper domestic source. The first inspection, regrettably, had to be abandoned because of vicious attacks on our officials, but force can put down these hostile peasants next time. The greatest problem is how to move sticks of great length through the locks to Bayonne. But problems, messieurs, are to be overcome!'

As the discourse veered towards ship dimensions, Jacques sensed his own part was over, but he was more than happy to stay and learn, and even, if called upon, to put forward a view. Then he saw one of the arsenal's master-shipwrights, Maître Joubert, look directly across at him, and moments later a clerk hurried to his side.

'Thank you for your attendance, Maître Maurellet. You are free to go

240

now.' With a sense of injured dignity, Jacques stalked out of the room, but as he reached the anteroom, his mood took a different turn, for coming towards him was the great hero Admiral Duquesne.

'I am honoured,' said Jacques, sweeping off his hat and making a deep bow to the great hero. In their exchange of glances there was something which made Duquesne pause.

'And who might you be?'

'Jacques Maurellet, grandson of of Henri Maurellet. Our shipyard is nearby on the Charente. I was invited here to give my opinion on firs from the Auvergne.'

'And?'

'One cannot better masting sticks from Riga, monseigneur. If the King's cavalry are to have the swiftest horses from Barbary, do not our sailors also deserve the best?'

'You speak boldly, Monsieur. Yet it is the truth,' conceded the admiral, his eyes sharp with interest. 'The army's grip on royal circles has always been strong. We must pray that Jean-Baptiste Colbert's vision for France to dominate world sea-routes will continue to interest the King. And to that end, our arsenals are constructing large-scale models to send to Versailles for His Majesty's instruction.'

'I am happy to hear it, monseigneur,' said Jacques, feeling a stab of envy, 'though it is a pity that private yards such as ours are not called upon to lead the way.'

'You are not lacking opinions, Maurellet. What, pray, should a model offer to capture a king's interest?'

Jacques's blue eyes gleamed with his inner vision.

'Artistry, but above all else, speed!'

'Artistry and speed … is that so? Then perhaps we should put your high-flown words to the test!' And without uttering a further word, the great man strode away.

*** *** ***

It was too soon to claim Olivier was happy, mused Hermione, as she watched him pace restlessly back and forth before the bookshelves.

'You read too swiftly,' she teased, reminding herself that Olivier had never expressed happiness, only restless curiosity. Now it seemed he had devoured every book of interest and was reduced to one written by Antoine de Pluvine on the art of horsemanship. 'Why don't I ask Father Grégoire to dine with us tomorrow?'

'I never mind his company.'

'I shall send Guillaume right away,' said Hermione, laying aside the ancient fan which she was mending.

'I feel time is slipping away,' Olivier sighed in a plaintive voice when she returned to her sewing after summoning Lucette. 'I had reached a phase in my work which was critical ... which I may never reach again ... months and months of distillation. I need my papers, I need my equipment. The only course is to return ...'

'You can't!' she gasped, horrified he had so soon started to imagine it was possible. 'We'll think of some means to get what you need. Meantime, we could plan where you might establish your laboratory. And you could make a start by drawing up a list of all the equipment it would require.' She had spoken as if to a bored child and it worked, for Olivier's miserable face immediately took on an expression of interest.

'But how would it be possible?'

'First, make the list, and afterwards, we can take the next step.'

The embroidered rose, now complete, had artfully disguised the moth-hole in the old fan. With a smile of satisfaction, Hermione carefully examined the rest of the silk for other holes. Moments like this, sitting with Olivier before the fire, had been rare at rue de la Cocotte. He had always been immersed in his work, except for occasional moments when, in-between experiments, he took a fleeting interest in the world about him.

'Tell me how you found me, as you used to,' she murmured, making a start on another flower. Olivier stood up and threw a log onto the fire, for the chamber was chilly.

'I've told it to you more times than your own years.' He sighed, settling into his chair as there came a cracking and flurry of brightness.

'I always like to hear it,' rejoined Hermione. 'Don't leave *anything* out.'

'It was snowing.'

'Olivier!'

'It had been raining, and I was returning home after taking a walk.'

'After meeting with a learned scholar of astrology!'

'Quite so.' Olivier nodded. 'I was tired and looking forward to supper. As I arrived at my house and passed through the gate, just a few strides within was a trunk with its lid slightly raised. From within came a mewing sound.'

'A kitten.' Hermione laughed, taking up a paler skein of pink and cutting a length for her needle.

'A baby,' continued Olivier, beginning to sound bored. For him, the story was a well-worn path, but it was all she had of parents.

'It was a baby of the firmament, for the mewing bundle was covered by stars which sparkled and gleamed in the moonlight. I carried the chest into the house and set it before the kitchen fire. The stars on the bed of black velvet were embroidered in silver, and as I lifted the baby out I saw remaining inside a crystal as used by seers.'

'And you tried to feed me on sausage?'

'Something like that,' said Olivier, running his hand through his grey locks. 'It certainly altered my life. It was about that time, when my work as an engraver was ending, that I was led on the journey of purification to find the Elixir of Life.'

Hermione stood up with a wistful expression and went to the window to look up at the moon and the scene beneath as it sailed in and out of clouds. There was the darkness of the rocky outcrop and the silvered ribbon of the Bruant wending its path round the front of the château. The stony rise of the land opposite glowed with moonlight till the darkness of the surrounding forest absorbed it. The effect was dramatic, and she was reluctant to leave it for her bed, but Claude Tilly was calling on the morrow. So, after a few more words with Olivier, Hermione bade him goodnight. Shortly afterwards, his feet passed by her door as he climbed to his room above. Moonlight cast its light over the oak planks of the floor, and the scene she had seen from the window of the salon refused to leave her.

On the following day, awaiting the timber-merchant's visit, Hermione walked with Guillaume along by the river and looked across the lake towards the rocky outcrop that rose above.

'When you worked at Versailles, Guillaume, you saw how they did things. Would it be possible for us to have a fall of water tumbling down to the lake?'

'I can't say. At first, I was only digging the wolf plunges. Then later on I was up on scaffolding and lost my eye and got sixty *livres* from the King because of it. If you break an arm or leg, you only get thirty livres. I wouldn't know about fountains. Though, just after I left, I heard from some of the lads that they were starting to dig in a new wooded area. These court officials think such as we have no ears as they prattle about their plans. I've never seen the *bosquet du Marais*, but I can tell you it has a metal tree in the middle of the pool and water springs out from all its branches, twigs, and leaves. Just like your oak trees over there.' He laughed, pointing towards the dark edge of the forest. 'And you don't need fancy metallic reeds either, Madame Hermione. You've enough of your own!'

'I suppose it is a bit too soon to think of water effects,' she agreed. 'Ah, and indeed, here comes Monsieur Tilly searching me out.'

'*Bonjour*, Madame Du Chesne,' called out the timbermerchant, raising his hat in greeting as he rode towards them. 'I hope my men are not causing trouble.'

'Not that I am aware of, monsieur. I hear the ringing of their axes and that makes me happy.'

'We are fortunate September was dry … heavy rain, and the oxen would have had difficulty reaching the river bank. There is some fine timber out there,' he declared, jumping down from his horse.

'It will fetch a good price?' asked Hermione, as they walked towards the Keep.

'Undoubtedly. While my men are here, they might as well carry on felling, and what is not transported can be left over winter to weather on the ground. It will be cheaper for you.' Hermione made no comment until they reached the small room which served as her bureau. At the forefront of her mind was the advice of Jacques Maurellet.

'I don't think it is a good idea leaving the timber to weather,' she ventured, as she gestured for him to take a seat. 'It might open the logs to infection and rot. Take as many loads as is possible now, but better to continue felling next year.'

'You seem to have become an expert already, madame,' commented Tilly, his tone edged with sarcasm. 'I hear you have acquired a royal stallion also. What a responsibility ... let us hope no harm befalls it!' Hermione ignored what she felt was childishly meant to alarm her. With cold restraint, she went through the number of loads to be taken, and when their business was done, she had to concede he was very efficient. Everything had been supplied: men to do the felling, drivers and teams of oxen to pull the wagons to the river and barges to take the logs upstream to Rochefort.

'You say Maître Maurellet will also be selecting timber for his yard?'

'Yes,' replied Hermione. 'I have received a letter confirming his visit.'

'Will you come to the auction, madame?'

'Would it be appropriate?'

'Highly inappropriate,' responded Claude Tilly, with something of a sneer.

'Then, monsieur,' said Hermione, deciding not to offer him any hospitality, 'it is best I stay away.'

Jacques was in a buoyant mood as he entered the salon. Hermione listened attentively as he told her about his visit to the arsenal, and how, within twenty-four hours, a tight-lipped Maître Joubert had brought a letter instructing him and his grandfather to build a model of a frigate for the instruction of the King.

'And it was signed by Admiral Duquesne himself!' Jacques accepted a glass of wine from Hermione. 'I should not even be here today. The arsenals have already begun work on their models, so we will have to work flat out during the winter.'

'Is Maître Henri as excited as you?' Hermione teased.

Jacques laughed. 'He pretends not to be, but he is, and it has made up for other worries. It is to be no ordinary model, Hermione,' he went on using her name for the first time. 'These models are to be bigger than anything made before ... a tenth of the real thing, and to precise scale in every detail.'

'And to sail down the Grand Canal,' she laughed, repeating what he had said several times already, to please him with the sound of it. 'I think, perhaps, you are too light-headed to go up to the roof?'

'If I fall I shall fly.' He finished his wine with a flourish and stood up. Hermione led the way upstairs until by way of the roof space they gained a small ledge which offered a view out over the High Forest. 'Why did you want to be up so high?'

Jacques's excitement had abated a little, so he put his mind to what he had come to explain before going into the forest to select trees for the shipyard.

'I wanted you to understand how careful you must be when opening up a new stand for thinning. What do you see?'

'Sky ... treetops.

'What strikes you about the trees?'

Hermione pursed her lips as her gaze skimmed over the green canopy. 'I can't say,' she said. 'They all have leaves ... green leaves! Some are taller.'

'Exactly.'

'Some of the crowns are well above the rest, which means,' she said, thinking it through, 'they must be the more vigorous trees.'

'Too vigorous,' responded Jacques. 'We call them wolf trees. They outstrip all, grab for everything in order to survive. It is best to fell them so as to give the trees around them more space and light.'

'It's very exciting ... there is so much to learn.'

'*Exciting* ... you are strange,' murmured Jacques, studying Hermione's animated face. 'This is more than making money to rebuild and buy hangings from Lyon?'

Hermione continued to look at the swath of green which stretched away to the horizon. 'Part of it is realizing that in two hundred years the acorns I plant will replace many of those trees out there.'

'You don't have to sow every one by hand,' teased Jacques with a smile in his voice. 'The forest only needs a little help; Nature will do the rest.'

'If you were offered some high office at Versailles, would you give up building ships?' she asked, the dreamy expression in her brown eyes changing to curiosity

'Play politics at Versailles?' Jacques grimaced. 'I like what I do, especially now, here with you.' His words were spoken without thought, but they immediately produced an intense feeling of intimacy between them. Hermione returned his smile with warmth, but as if she had threatened him, the expression in his blue eyes suddenly became remote, and he turned abruptly away. 'The ideal time to assess the canopy is while the trees are in full leaf,' he went on, deliberately making his tone cool and businesslike, for he was shocked by the heat of his feelings. 'After the leaves fall and the whole trunk is exposed, that is the time to assess the tree.'

Conscious of the altered mood between them, and feeling somehow rebuffed, Hermione led the way back inside. They moved beneath the rafters of the roof till they reached a door which led through to the stone steps in the tower.

'You have not asked about my royal guest!' she said as they began to descend, her tone of voice reserved. But once begun, the tale of what had near taken place between the royal stallion and the blacksmith's bony mare quickly restored the easy informality between them until their merriment brought Olivier to his door. Whereupon, on seeing Hermione with a stranger, his cross face disappeared as he slammed his door against them.

'I laugh now,' continued Hermione, not bothering to explain Olivier, 'but what if I had arrived ten minutes later?'

'There might be a royal colt on the way with crossed eyes and crooked legs,' responded Jacques. 'And your man Guillaume would find himself wearing a royal brand and sitting at the first chain of a galley.'

In the courtyard, Hermione watched as Jacques mounted his horse.

'I am sorry I can't attend the auction for you,' he apologized.

'It is enough that you are buying some timber,' she replied firmly. 'I wish you God speed with the model!'

'Hermione ... it would make a pretty name for a ship!' said Jacques, looking down at her as his stallion pranced, restless to move off.

'My name in golden letters to go before the King!' she exclaimed, taking immediately to the idea. 'I'd like that ... will you name it so?' Jacques gathered up the reins.

'I may need more than your name, Madame Du Chesne,' he said with a rakish smile, 'but, like the King, you will have to wait to see.'

*** *** ***

During this busy time of gathering in before winter there was much to occupy Hermione's thoughts. Olivier's safe arrival had banished all former feelings of fear and anxiety. She gave thanks to the Saints for the peace that all of them had found in Saintonge, and perhaps for her maid something else was blossoming. Lucette's shrill peal of laughter sounded from the orchard and Hermione smiled, having spied Georges but a moment before heading that way. At this time of the year, the scent within the walls of the storehouse was delicious, and she could not resist picking up an apple from a rack and biting into it.

'That one will be sharp, madame, and you will be asking later for something to soothe the cramps,' chided Marie, looking towards her. The light which filtered through the open doorway lit the housekeeper's face with soft gold, softening the wrinkles which showed her years. There was beauty in the moment and about her capable hands as they reverently took up each apple.

'How many times have you done this, Marie?'

The hooded eyes closed slightly with the old lady's smile of remembrance. 'Since this table was above my head. Mother worked for the Chevalier's father ... there is not a stone I do not know hereabouts.'

'Tell me a little of him when he was young.'

For a while, Marie stayed silent, her eye and hand continuing their work of selecting and transferring fruit onto the racks.

'Our royal stallion would have recognized the master,' she said at length. 'There was not a rider or hunter braver than he. And he was learned ... he would read first thing, sometimes all through the day like Monsieur Lefèvre. And he would try different things. We all had to help plant trees to feed silk worms.'

'The mulberry trees by the orchard.' The old lady nodded and discarded an apple into a sack.

'The cocoons were to go to the spinners and weavers in Lyon. Sometimes visitors would arrive and stay for weeks. They would boil things up in his cauldron ... we were not allowed to see, though the furnace would be kept alive for days on end.

'And you never peeped?' pressed Hermione, her interest beginning to increase. Marie's lips worked as if she were thinking about it, and then, having decided, she spoke in almost a whisper.

'He was trying to turn lead into gold ... Pierre hid under a sack.'

'And did he ... make gold?'

'One of the visitors did. Pierre saw it with his own eyes ... a small speck gleaming in the bottom of the crucible after they had gone.'

'This is amazing!' declared Hermione, thinking how excited Olivier would be when he heard of it.

'But just as the silk worms did not come for the master, neither did the gold. Then everything was forgotten when at his cousin's wedding he met Mademoiselle Aglaé, and he became consumed by a different fire.'

'The furnace, is it still here?'

'Next to the stables. The Chevalier's strange things are still within, although not as he left them, for we needed to store things there during the fire.' Hermione was tempted to rush away to tell Olivier the good news, but her interest about the Chevalier was strong.

'And Mademoiselle Aglaé's family ... did they not keep in touch with the Chevalier after she was killed?'

'They came for her body. They blamed him, you see, for the accident ... the horse was too strong for her. But when the spirits called her to that part of the forest, any horse would have been too strong. Now you are here for them instead.'

CHAPTER 16

he construction of a vast model for the king had fired the imagination of shipwrights, joiners, and apprentices at the Maurellet shipyard. Even Henri gave a smile of approval when Jacques announced his intention to go and see the Master of Decorative Works at Toulon's arsenal. 'There is no finer sculptor than Pierre Puget. If he will offer advice, even a stubborn one like me will heed him, lad.'

Time being precious, Jacques decided not to delay in making the journey south. After stowing a few clothes into a bag, he left the boy to saddle his horse while he went over to his aunt's house to make his goodbyes. He found Perrette at the open kitchen door knocking a nail into the latch. Her deft fingers handled the hammer with such skill it made him laugh. 'You should have been born a boy!'

'I'd gladly help you build the model,' countered Perrette with a happy smile as she stood back to look at her work. It was their first exchange of warmth since the visit of Father Francis. Jacques moved across to her and tested the latch.

'First rate,' he murmured, 'but petticoats and Grandfather don't mix.'

'Then I'll wear breeches!'

Jacques took hold of the small hand which had held the hammer and pressed it to his lips. 'If I thought it would keep you safe from other influences … but it won't, will it?' he added, letting go of her hand as her eyes hardened with a stubborn expression.

'I wish only to worship the same God. How can that be so wrong?'

Jacques gave a sigh of exasperation. 'If you have no regard for me or Grandfather, at least consider Aunt Marguerite. She still mourns your father, and if you turn away from your faith, you too will be lost to her. To us all!' Grim-faced, he turned away in frustration, sensing that his words to Perrette were just that ... words. How could he get through to her the harsh reality of what would happen to her? Perhaps if he had not been so hasty in bringing an end to her help in the shipyard, she might not be so drawn to the company of those wretched people. He hesitated, hating to leave with discord between them. However, this was their chance at the yard, and he would not let it slip through his fingers. With a grave expression, he took her hands and kissed her. 'If you love me and your family, think carefully before you do anything that will bring hurt to yourself,' he murmured. Then he walked away, filled with misgivings.

On arrival at Toulon, he found a room and at once sent a messenger to the Royal Seminary. He had judged it best not to mention to Henri that in addition to calling upon Pierre Puget it was his intention to seek an interview with the professor of mathematics at the university. With no letter of introduction, he half expected to receive no response to his request, so, he would at least enjoy the day by taking in a few of the sights and treating himself to a splendid meal. Several hours later, in a happy mood, he walked back to the inn and to his delight found an invitation to call upon Professor Paul L'Hoste the following morning.

Early by half an hour, inwardly buzzing with anticipation, Jacques waited on a stone bench for the professor of mathematics to return to his rooms. After what seemed like the passing of an hour, though in reality no more than twenty minutes, the silence was disturbed by a sudden outpouring of students from a doorway further along the corridor. For a short time the stone walls resounded with chatter and laughter, until as the group moved off, peace was restored. Now, however, the silence began to irritate. Jacques stood up and paced back and forth. As he wheeled about for the umpteenth time, he saw a gowned figure hastening toward him.

'Monsieur Maurellet?'

Jacques took a step forward and made a bow of respect.

'You have asked for my help.'

'It is generous of you, Professor, to see me at such short notice.'

'I am intrigued, monsieur.' Paul L'Hoste smiled as he opened the metal-studded door alongside the stone bench. 'Also, much heartened that a master-shipwright wishes to discuss my theories. What is the exact nature of your problem?'

'I wish to know how a ship might travel faster and what I must do to bring it about.'

'Then you will have to stay here for a year or so,' returned the learned man with a wry smile. Seeing Jacques's expression cloud with disappointment, he relented. 'But there are principles we might discuss. Let us see what we can do in the time I have at my disposal. Are you familiar with the Principles of Paracelsus?'

'I fear not,' replied Jacques, beginning to feel inadequate.

'Then come into my chamber and let us discuss his law that *matter* on its own is passive unless an outside force affects it.'

Within the sparsely furnished room, untidy with books and scrolls of parchment, Jacques accepted the stool set opposite the professor's chair.

'So, monsieur, I know from your letter that your family has been building ships for generations on the Charente. For you to construct a large-scale model of a frigate for His Majesty must be an acknowledgement of the skill of your shipwrights. Yet ... a man o' war, albeit a model, is surely a challenge for you?'

'Yes.'

'Who directs you Maurellets when you construct your ships?'

'No one. We do things our own way.'

'But now you will be building for the Marine, which has its approved Tables of Dimensions. Why then have you come so far to see me? Surely you must adhere to the conclusions and findings of the officers of the Marine.'

The dark intelligent eyes fixed on Jacques for his answer. Their expression was challenging, yet not without a gleam of amusement. Jacques pursed his lips and gave a slight shrug as he considered how to answer the question which latterly had robbed him of sleep.

'Our shipyard was asked to construct a large model of a frigate exact in every detail, but no mention was made of official dimensions. I am used to being my own master, but I am not so proud as to believe I know everything. Even though the marine based its findings on the opinions of shipwrights and the experience of sailors, it is in the end hearsay. What makes a good ship is still part chance. I want to understand the mechanics. If this means a departure from the official dimensions in order to improve performance, I am willing to take the risk. When my frigate sails down the Grand Canal, its superior sailing qualities will defend any innovations on my part. I want it to be the finest frigate ever built.'

'Then to the basics,' said the professor, taking up a piece of charcoal and swiftly drawing an outline. 'What have we here?'

'A fish,' answered Jacques, somewhat put out by such a childish approach. The professor gave a faint smile.

'The swiftest of fish are fuller before and slender behind. For hundreds of years these considerations have confirmed us in our opinion that the large end of a body moving forward opens a passage through which the rest slides with ease.

'For which reason,' put in Jacques, 'it is best to take the *heel* of a mast in tow.'

'Quite,' the professor said with a smile. 'Experience teaches us that a body divides the water with less resistance when the greater end thereof is pushed forward first. The difficulty that the moving body meets with, in passing through a medium, increases in the same ratio with its velocity. Therefore, the resistance and velocity of the moving body increase in the same ratio that the time decreases. Of course, above the water a vessel must be able to cut through a wave.'

'How do waves affect a ship that is heavily loaded, Professor?'

'Since the wave raises the ship, notwithstanding her weight, it every moment communicates to her a motion greater than that of her gravity; therefore, it communicates to her an acceleration in proportion to her weight. So everything else remaining the same, the ship will rise equally above the wave however she is loaded.'

The discussion continued, and the hour passed too swiftly, but with it had come an appreciation that a professor of mathematics could determine with calculation how best a vessel might move against wind and wave. It was a novel way to go about things. It meant a further departure from the massive decorative upper works of the ships of former times, whose splendour had brought glory to France. For if they placed a ship's point of gravity too far forward, making her top heavy and thus slowing progress, they should be stripped away.

'So it is the ship that captures the wind which has more chance to win glory for France!' concluded Jacques as Paul L'Hoste brought the session to an end. 'Sculptures must be subservient to length of keel and breadth of hull.'

'Don't let Maître Puget persuade you otherwise.' The professor smiled, leading Jacques out into the corridor. 'I have much work to do before my treatise will be ready for the printer. After that, perhaps traditionalists will be open to new ideas.'

As he made his way to look at Pierre Puget's acclaimed caryatids at the town hall, Jacques mused on Henri's likely reaction to what had just been discussed. In his grandfather's world, you made a stout ship with seasoned wood and sailors put their trust in God, whereas someone like the professor aspired to counter the force of wave and wind so that they served rather than impeded the vessel. Some might consider that the professor was setting himself up above God, whereas he was simply trying to understand the world around him. If that saved sailors' lives and meant a journey took less time, Jacques was all for it.

At the Royal Arsenal, on the understanding that he would not distract Maître Puget, Jacques was permitted to watch the great master at work. The young apprentice who stayed at his side whispered that the work in progress was a representation of Milon de Crotone. The composition was of an athlete with a hand caught fast in the cleft of a tree stump while being attacked by a lion. It was a truly powerful portrayal of suffering: the twisted torso under stress, the man's head thrown back as he cried out in agony at the savagery of the claws sunk deep into his thigh. Jacques's eyes moved over the bulging calf muscles, the tension of the toes bracing against the ground, the raised sinews of an arm under stress ... it was as if Puget could see what lay beneath a man's skin.

As if he himself were wielding the *burin*, Jacques became totally absorbed as the lion's fur materialized beneath its sharp edge. He was eager to meet the sculptor, yet when at last the master left off and stood back to take in the whole of the block of white marble, Jacques experienced a pang of regret. Pierre Puget accepted a towel offered to him by an assistant and, after wiping his face and hands came over to Jacques.

'So, Monsieur Maurellet, you have travelled a great distance to ask my advice on decorative work for a model of a frigate. Perhaps you do not know that I am no longer in charge of decorations for His Majesty's ships.'

'I am sorry to hear it,' ventured Jacques, trying to offer sympathy for what he knew not.

'Do you know,' continued the sculptor, flinging down the towel and taking up a jug to pour out a draught of water, 'in Genoa I was fêted ... appreciated for the great artist I am. In Genoa my patron provided me with all the Carrara I wanted. Here, in my own country, I have been given but these three blocks.'

'I suppose money is in short supply after the war,' murmured Jacques.

'You are a diplomat, young man. So, let us see what you say of this: do you prefer my Milon or my Persée?'

258

Jacques followed Puget's gesture and walked away to the other end of the workshop where there was another work in progress, not so advanced as the Milon de Crotone. The helmeted Persée, arm outstretched as he snatched Andromède clear of danger, was in heroic stance.

'When I sent my two drawings in for the King to see, I heard he preferred this,' murmured the sculptor, who had followed him.

'I can see why,' commented Jacques, 'for it could be a king performing a glorious epic deed, whereas,' he added, turning back towards the Milon, 'that could be any ordinary man bearing pain and suffering.'

Pierre Puget smiled and gave a nod. 'So, you have a swift feel for things, young man. But to the purpose of your visit?'

'My grandfather's yard has been singularly honoured. We are to construct a model of a frigate to interest the King and his Marine. That is why I am here to seek your advice, for your carvings on the poop of the *Dauphin-Royal* are legendary. Are you able, Maître Puget, to set aside your work awhile to offer guidance?'

'My guidance would be to find other employment if you want to keep your good health.' Pierre Puget sighed, motioning Jacques to accompany him to his office. 'But at a glance I can see you are a stubborn fellow. Have you thought that others may not be so happy that a private yard has been so singled out? When a king is in question, jealousies are quickly aroused. Have you ideas for the frontispiece ... Apollo and his chariot, perhaps, or Poseidon ruling the waves?'

'The blazing rays of the sun in homage to the King,' said Jacques. 'I like the idea of Apollo with his horses and chariot because I want the frigate to be fast, but perhaps such a composition is best suited to a ship of the First Rate.'

'Then Hippocampus abreast of the waves,' put in Pierre Puget, swiftly sketching a horse with the hindquarters of a fish stretching forward over turbulent seas.

'Marvellous!' exclaimed Jacques with delight, as the sculptor drew in dolphins, also breaching the waves.

'You are easy to please.' Pierre Puget smiled, his good humour restored.

'Only because you bring forth the essence of each subject ... but not my figurehead. You do not know the face I have in mind.'

'Then show me,' directed the older man, passing over paper and charcoal. For a moment, Jacques hesitated as he reached into himself to call up the image, then at speed he created the compelling features of a woman's face. He slid the drawing across the bench. The sculptor nodded, and when he looked up, his eyes were bright with approval.

'You are not without skill yourself, Jacques Maurellet. Do you consider you have captured the essence of the lady?'

Jacques shook his head and laughed. 'I hardly know her.'

'Even so,' said the sculptor, taking in the energy of the work, 'if you are to make this image a plaything of the King and his courtiers, best to safeguard her identity in a laurel bush and name your frigate *Daphne*.'

'Perhaps,' nodded Jacques, taking a critical look at what he had drawn. Where had the expression come from? Very likely on the day they had looked out on Du Chesne's canopy of oak ... the wind had seized her hair as she spoke of her hopes for the forest. He had not been conscious of committing her face to memory, yet here it was: the full lips lifted into the beginning of a smile, the lovely eyes alight with eagerness. As he took in the whole, there surged within him such a rush of desire that he turned the sheet of paper over, and as if to regain control and make light of things, he casually crumpled it into a ball.

*** *** ***

As had become a regular habit, the curé and Olivier sat in quiet intensity over the chess table. Hermione sat writing out a long list of things she needed. She glanced towards the men as Olivier uttered 'Checkmate'.

'Can I get anything for you in Rochefort, Father Grégoire?'

'A knife to sharpen my wits ...' the priest sighed as he stood up. 'I have been too long in this parish with only my friend's letters to provoke and amuse.'

'And what news has your marquis of Paris?' asked Hermione, who had herself begun to count upon this line of communication.

The priest's eyes gleamed as they did when he was about to toss out a juicy scrap. 'The King is now content to sit with a breviary in his hands before the fire with Madame Maintenon ... it is said she rules supreme. The lady is bent on reclaiming all those who have strayed, and any in her family who follow the Reformed Church risk the Bastille. Through her influence, the King seeks to restore religious unity throughout France. Furthermore,' he added, lowering his voice near to a whisper, 'anyone with spare *livres* should have them ready in the coming months. It is likely there will be bargains a dozen in Poitou and Saintonge!'

'Bargains? I don't quite follow,' murmured Hermione.

'You will soon,' responded the curé with a knowing smile, as Olivier reappeared from his visit to the pot behind the screen, 'and pray God I shall have at such time the opportunity to demonstrate my fervour to the King.'

'Would you like a lantern to guide you home?'

'Thank you, dear Hermione, there is moon enough. I shall sail back up the hill with the pleasure of the evening.'

Leaving Olivier to smoke his pipe after Father Grégoire had left, Hermione retired to bed. While waiting for sleep to take her, she considered what the curé's marquis might mean about bargains in Saintonge. It was beyond understanding, and of more importance was the sale of timber on the morrow.

It felt like a day of celebration. Today, Du Chesne's forest was making its own survival possible. With a contented smile, Hermione settled back in her seat as Guillaume prepared to lift up the step of the coach.

'You will not go to the auction, then?' he asked.

'You think I should?' she asked, instantly feeling anxious.

'Best to keep an eye on things, I always say!'

'It is not customary for a lady to attend.'

'That's as may be, madame, though there would be nothing to stop me mingling with the merchants.'

'Oh, Guillaume, what would I do without you!'

'You'd have a servant with two good eyes within the hour,' he said, his broad face beaming with self-conscious pleasure. 'Best keep the curtains of the coach drawn, madame, so as not to be seen. I will need to whip up the horses most of the way, for the auction will have an early start.'

In the entrance of Claude Tilly's timber yard there were a number of abandoned coaches, their drivers standing idly about chatting in small groups. Through the chink in the leather curtain, Hermione could see that the only available space would place her coach far away from the centre of action. She tapped with a stick on the roof to attract Guillaume's attention.

'Go further into the yard,' she urged. Despite the call of some lackey shouting for Guillaume to check his horses, they moved onwards and stopped beside an enormous stack of tree trunks. The coach gave a lurch as Guillaume hauled himself down, then his dirty fingers pushed the curtain inward a fraction.

'I can't go closer without drawing attention. There are not as many here as I would have thought.'

Hermione felt a stab of disappointment. She recalled Jacques's warning about keeping an eye on Claude Tilly, but surely at a public auction he would have to do what was right with all eyes on him. She raised the leather flap and leaned out a little, but all she was able to see was a group of men, although she could faintly hear the auctioneer's voice taking bids. The words were indistinct, but they sparked off excitement at the prospect of returning home and telling Georges and Thierry what their hard work had achieved ... Jacques Maurellet also. She would invite him and his grandfather to a splendid dinner to thank them.

Suddenly, from the other side of the coach, Guillaume's urgent whisper seized her attention. She moved sideways to lift the other curtain, and as she did so saw by the big man's expression that all was not well.

'Madame, you did say you expected your hardwood to fetch nine *livres* a load?'

'I did.'

'It went for four *livres*. The bidding seems very slow.'

'Four *livres*,' gasped Hermione, staring back in dismay. 'But he can't let it go for that!'

Guillaume shook his head and looked miserable. 'Perhaps the wood was not –'

'Not anything!' snapped Hermione. 'It is top quality. I had that from Monsieur Maurellet. Has other timber gone under the hammer?'

'Yes, from Angoulême. That reached eight *livres* the load.'

'Then something is wrong,' said Hermione, putting her cloak around her shoulders and opening the door.

'Madame,' cautioned Guillaume, as she didn't even wait for the step to be lowered. 'It will look unseemly. Think of your standing hereabouts.'

'To hell with that!' exclaimed Hermione, the blood rushing to her face. With Guillaume lumbering after her, she headed towards the group of men. The auctioneer was raised up on a dais, and standing below him to one side was Claude Tilly. As there were so few people standing about, Hermione's approach drew forth instant murmurs of surprise. A man in close conversation with the timber contractor, Hermione suddenly realized, was the messenger who had called upon her in Paris seeking to buy Du Chesne. He cast on Hermione an impudent look, then, reacting to something Claude Tilly whispered, he burst into unpleasant sniggers.

'Monsieur,' Hermione said, facing the timber contractor full on, 'is it correct that my timber is being sold at four *livres* a load?'

Tilly gave a shrug of his shoulders, and his hands spread in a half-hearted attempt at disappointment.

'Is that my timber they are bidding for now?'

'Yes. Madame. This last load is a little improved … see, it has still reached four livres.'

'You mock me, monsieur! You are letting them give it away! It is not enough … *stop it*!' she cried, whirling towards the thin auctioneer as he brought down his hammer. 'Monsieur, you are *cheating* me!' Hostile mutters of disapproval broke out all around, and even worse, hoots of laughter. Hermione whirled on Claude Tilly. 'You said my timber was of the first quality … Jacques Maurellet said so too, and he settled on a price of nine *livres*.'

'Then he is a generous man. or perhaps madam, grateful in other ways,' smirked Tilly, exchanging amused glances with his clerk.

'Madame, come away,' urged Guillaume at Hermione's elbow. 'This is no place for you. It is useless … see, he is moving on to other lots now.'

Blinded with tears of humiliation and rage, Hermione allowed the strong, rough hand to lead her away. Once they had gained the coach, Guillaume helped her inside then hovered at the open door like some great hound waiting for her to give the word to go. Hermione looked to him for some explanation of what had happened. For days she had been buoyant; now all hopeful expectations had been crushed. 'How could he have led me to believe … Was there finer timber? Did no one want oak?'

'I don't think any of those things, madame,' commented Guillaume, adjusting the patch over his blind eye and making secure his coachman's hat. 'I am new to this, but it seemed to me that all those back there knew each other. It might be …. things had been arranged from the start.'

'But that is dishonest!' exclaimed Hermione, slamming her fist into the seat to release her fury.

'They took advantage of your inexperience.'

'He wanted the timber from the first,' cried Hermione, fighting back the tears. 'That is why he has been so obliging, even to taking away faggots to sell to bakers. Through my stupidity, he and his associates have practically got the whole lot free.'

'Not stupidity. It was trust on your part, Mademoiselle Hermione,' comforted Guillaume, speaking as if they were back at the rue de la Cocotte. 'It's a pity your friend Monsieur Maurellet was not here to put a stop to it.'

Hermione shook her head as Guillaume shut the coach door. She sank back against the cushions feeling completely deflated. It was a bitter blow, and she could not even find the relief of tears.

A week had gone by when, to Hermione's amazement, Claude Tilly called in at Du Chesne as if nothing unpleasant had passed between them. She received him with icy coldness in the bureau.

'I am surprised you should think to feel welcome here, monsieur.'

'Madame Du Chesne, I felt I owed it to you to come in person to hand over monies received in payment for your timber and to offer my profuse apologies for any disappointment suffered on your part.'

'I have been cheated, monsieur, and there are no apologies which can make up for that!'

'Madame, you are too harsh. The auctioneer cannot *make* people bid.'

'You led me to believe the market price would be higher.'

Claude Tilly pulled an apologetic face, but Hermione was not deceived. 'Nothing is certain in business, Madame Du Chesne. And fine though your timber is, you must remember that the banks of the Charente are thick with trees.'

'Why did you not instruct the auctioneer to set a reserve price?'

'Madame, if you had instructed me to do so … but you pressed your case with such urgency, I assumed any money would be welcome.' The small eyes cast a doleful look, but the pinpricks of malicious glee in their grey-green depths made Hermione tremble with fury. She turned aside not to give him the satisfaction of seeing it, but her reaction was not lost on Claude Tilly, who felt such exuberance it was as if he had come alive. He was hard put to it not to laugh out loud at the sight of the parisienne upstart near to weeping. 'Ah well, time presses.' He sighed, withdrawing from his satchel a heavy bag of coins. 'Now that we have a better understanding, I am sure you will be satisfied next time. We might renegotiate my percentage, to make up a little for your present disappointment.'

'There will be no *next time* for you, monsieur! I shall deal with another merchant.'

'Of course,' responded Claude Tilly with an understanding nod. 'Should you require a recommendation, do not hesitate ... we timber entrepreneurs are but a small band ... like brothers.' The malicious gleam was there again and his meaning plain enough to suck the anger out of Hermione. When the door closed behind him, she dragged the heavy bag of coins across the desk towards her. With a dispirited expression, she untied the leather thong and looked at the *livres* within, then turned away, biting on her lower lip to stop the tears. She had prevented him from buying Du Chesne, and now it would seem he could prevent her from selling its timber at a fair price.

As he rode down the driveway to reach the road leading up to the village, Claude Tilly felt exultation akin to that he experienced when chastising Angélique. He threw his head back, relishing every recollection: first there had been her happy expectation ... those brown eyes gleaming with hope as his oxen took wagon after wagon of timber down to the river; then her gushing praise for managing the extractions so quickly, her ridiculous concern when one of his men had been struck by a rotting branch. And in the auction yard he had thought he would die of laughter as those brown eyes had glistened with tears. Today the lady's expression so *cold*, and oh, the *pièce de resistance*, the gradual realization that he controlled the local timber trade! Claude Tilly laughed out loud. He dug in his spurs, and noticing on either side of the driveway the freshly dug earth which bespoke a planting, he dragged on the bit to set his horse's galloping hooves to churn up the soil. The feeling of destruction was glorious!.

In the following days, Hermione's mood moved from anger to depression. She recalled how she had ridden alongside the first of the wagons taking the oak stands to the river, feeling sure that the money they would bring in would allow her to make a start on so many improvements. Guillaume, of course, had told everyone what had happened, and all sorts of dire threats were mouthed against Tilly, although she had overheard Pierre shouting in his deaf way to Marie: 'It was not fitting for a woman to interfere in such things! The master would not have permitted it. She will bring bad luck on us, just you wait and see!' It was an old man's prejudice, but nevertheless, the pronouncement made Hermione shudder. Lucette was, of course, staunchly on her side. 'Georges is ready to give him a black eye,' she said as she brought Hermione hot chocolate to cheer her. 'I think you should tell the police about his cheating. What about Monsieur Maurellet? He would tell you what to do.'

As she sipped her drink, Hermione thought about Jacques. She wondered what his response would be and instinctively knew that he would be furious, not because he had paid twice as much again as the men at the auction, but because of the sheer injustice of it. There would be no more felling now the weather was starting to worsen, but what of next year, if the entrepreneurs were all in league with Claude Tilly? How would she manage? The next day Hermione set off for Soubise.

The atmosphere within the long wooden shed was of intense activity. The two master-shipwrights were so intent on what they were doing that neither looked up as Hermione walked in. There was no need of explanation of what they were about, for a keel laid out on wooden blocks showed that work had begun on the model for King Louis. By its length, Hermione calculated that its size upon completion would be much bigger than a rowing boat. Uncertain of whether she would be welcome at such a time, she moved quietly over the wood shavings which filled the air with sweet pungency.

'You do realize,' declared Henri Maurellet, his booming voice making Hermione jump as he called over to Jacques, 'the length of this keel, if it were built full size, would make the ship two metres longer than is customary!'

'So you keep reminding me,' said Jacques, not looking up from what he was doing, 'and that, with a decrease in width, would produce greater speed.'

'I'd like to see it!' scoffed Henri Maurellet. 'Have you thought you might rule yourself out because of these dimensions? You should stick to tried and tested ways.'

'We'll never move forward if we do that,' rejoined Jacques cheerfully, not willing to be deflected. He glanced over to his grandfather and was surprised to find they were being watched by Hermione Du Chesne.

'Are you here to lend a hand?' he asked, returning her smile with delight as he motioned her to come further in.

'*Bonjour*, Maître Maurellet,' said Hermione as she came first to Henri.

'Madame Du Chesne, it is a pleasure to see your lovely face,' exclaimed the elderly shipwright, looking up with a smile that was part apologetic as he continued with his work.

'I see you have made a good start on the model,' Hermione murmured as she moved alongside Jacques and glanced down at his work on the bench. 'How snugly those come together.' She passed a finger across where the two sections of wood met, and Jacques nodded as she looked to him to see if he minded her pulling them apart. In doing so, she saw that steps had been cut into each separate face which, when brought together, tightly interlocked the two sections of wood. There was not a hair's breadth of space; they fitted as one.

'A coaked scarph,' explained Jacques. 'A plain scarph is less complex. Where six lengths must form as one, say in the keel of a large ship, they have to fit to each other precisely. And where great stresses are brought to bear, as at the point where the stempost fits into the keel, a boxing scarph is used to prevent any movement.'

'Don't be fooled, Madame Du Chesne. Most of the time my grandson is thinking about professors of mathematics and wild theories!' called out Henri. Hermione burst into laughter at the expression on Jacques's face. She set down the two pieces of wood on the bench. 'My fingers could never be so skilled,' she murmured.

'Then we'd set you on as a trenail mooter … turning out these.' Jacques took up a long peg of wood from a nearby stack.

'It's what he'll have me doing, madame, when my hands become shaky,' called Henri, keeping up his banter.

'Pay no heed to him … Grandfather's hands are steadier than mine. Would you like to turn one out? The ones we use for the model are smaller, of course.'

Hermione watched attentively as Jacques took up a length of wood and a plane. Somehow she found herself studying his hands rather than what they were doing. The fingers were strong and supple, and while his hands were marked by past cuts and hardened by handling wood, they were of a beautiful shape … they were gentle hands. 'Now it's your turn!'

'Eight sides?' she said with a slight flush, as she tried to think how he had done it.

'Sometimes it can be sixteen,' he said, passing her the scuffer plane. 'Remember,' he added, as she received the length of wood, 'trim it first into a square. The oak needs to be really well dried so it expands when exposed to moisture.' Rather clumsily, Hermione began to move the scuffer plane along the length of wood. 'Easier if you hold it like this,' murmured Jacques, placing his hand over hers. The contact was warm, and again Hermione partly lost concentration.

'Not bad,' he grinned at length, as the eighth side was completed. 'We'll reserve it just in case we are asked to build the real thing!'

With the point of a blade he carved an initial H into one end of the trenail. 'Before I forget to ask, how did the auction go?'

The smile slid from Hermione's face, and she was unable to disguise her despair. Jacques stared at her, then turned away abruptly and went over to his grandfather. There was a brief exchange of words, and he returned holding his jacket over one shoulder.

'I need some fresh air. Let's walk beside the river, and you can tell me what happened.

They walked along the river bank in silence, putting some distance between themselves and the noise of the shipyard.

'Ah, that's good,' Jacques said, breathing deeply, 'and it's good to see you,' he added, turning to her with an expression full of concern, 'but not when your eyes are full of hurt. What happened?'

Quickly, Hermione related all that had taken place, and when she was done, though there came no explosion of anger from him, she could see by his expression that he was furious.

'You have enough to think of,' she said, feeling guilty for altering his mood.

'I'm glad you came,' Jacques said, his look serious and intent. 'I should have handled the sale for you.'

'I must learn for myself, though it was a bitter lesson! But what is to happen next year? Tilly boasted he has influence with the other entrepreneurs. "Close like brothers," he said.'

'More like collusion!' remarked Jacques, turning to her with a meaningful look.

'I made such a fool of myself,' she blurted out, her face flushing with embarrassment. 'I tried to stop the sale, and they just laughed.' Her self-deprecatory smile didn't quite work as the humiliation of the moment returned. Jacques's reaction at such impropriety on her part, as well as the tears now flooding her eyes, was one of dismay. His lips compressed with anger against Claude Tilly.

'Would you be happy to leave it with me?'

'Gladly, but I do not wish you to go to trouble.'

'No trouble … it will be a pleasure!'

CHAPTER 17

hroughout the latter part of October, heavy rains had made it impossible to ride out, so come the first dry morning Hermione had Guillaume saddle up her mare. With an uncertain sky it would have been unwise to contemplate any great distance, so whilst she would have enjoyed seeing Jacques and Maître Henri, she confined herself to a quick canter across a meadow. It was just as well she had not ventured further from home for her horse threw a shoe.

Since the incident involving the blacksmith's mare and the royal stallion there had been no contact with Raoul, but his greeting as Hermione led her horse into the smithy yard was polite enough, albeit sullen.

'Have you much work?' she asked, as he took up a shoe from a store he kept ready.

'I'm busy enough, madame. I've not long since shod the stallion of Monsieur Tilly. Now there's a gentleman who knows what he is about … was it not he, madame, who handled the sale of your timber?'

'Yes,' answered Hermione, showing no emotion. By now most knew how she had been duped. As if something had amused him, the burly man let out a snigger. He retrieved the now red-hot iron from the fire, and transferring it onto the anvil made swift adjustments to suit her horse. Then, after plunging the shoe into water, he stooped and grasped hold of the unshod hoof. There was the hiss of burnt hair, and as he began to hammer in the nails, he gave a quick glance over his shoulder.

'Now here come our curé leading his palfrey.' With impressive speed, the blacksmith finished the job. 'There you are, Madame Du Chesne, all finished.'

Hermione led her horse to one side, while the curé, after a brief exchange, handed over his mount. With his customary light steps, the portly cleric almost danced towards Hermione.

'*Bonjour.* How clever of our mounts to abandon their shoes so as to bring us together! Will you delay and give me your company? I will then ride with you to the château. Raoul will not keep us waiting long.'

Shortly afterwards, his palfrey being shod, the curé settled his ample quarters upon its saddle. As they rode abreast downhill, Hermione took the opportunity to talk about winter gatherings at Du Chesne.

'Father Grégoire, do you think the villagers would enjoy my reading to them at the veillées?'

Bending his head a little against the wind, the priest laughed. 'Dear Hermione, peasants make a great deal of noise sharpening their scythes and mending tools ... but no, don't let me put you off. It is a kind idea.'

'Olivier says reading to them from a book will stir up dull minds. What would suit, do you think?'

'They are used to Aesop's Tales ... and with the soup you are offering, they will think themselves fortunate you came here.'

Hermione flushed with pleasure. 'It is not much to offer. Do you know, Father, the workers building Pierre-Paul Riquet's canal get paid even when they are away sick? Monsieur Maurellet told me the labourers even have a paid holiday!'

'One can take things too far,' commented the curé. His evident disapproval was in such contrast to her enthusiasm, it brought an immediate halt to conversation. In silence, they negotiated the deep, waterlogged ruts. Hermione considered what it would be like to be rich enough to care for labourers in such a generous way as the Marquis. After Tilly's cheating she could barely find the means of paying anyone for their day's work. Recalling the blacksmith's sniggers, Hermione felt a flush of anger which stayed with her till they reached the keep. In single file, their mounts clattered onto the bridge over the river and out into the courtyard. Just as Hermione had seized the opportunity of dry weather to go for a ride, the labourers had arrived and were pulling down blackened timbers in the ruined wing.

'It will shortly be hard to imagine there was another wing to the house,' observed the curé, as he dismounted and looked towards the standing heaps of masonry.

'Not rebuilding will save money I don't have!' Hermione smiled as they walked towards the house.

Olivier was found in the salon, standing staring downwards into the fire, his hands behind his back. Roused from his preoccupation by their entrance, he stirred.

'Shall you join us at the table, Father?' asked Hermione, as the men greeted each other.

'It would be a pleasure,' responded Father Grégoire, 'but if I do I shall upset Matilde, and good housekeepers are not so easy to find.' After leaving them to change out of her riding clothes, Hermione returned to find that Olivier was in full flow, quoting something which she could not make sense of. She took a seat and waited for a moment to speak.

'Unless thou knowest the thing from the head to the heel, from the eggs to the apples; that is, from the very beginning to the very end, thou knowest nothing, and ... '

'*And*,' interjected Father Grégoire, holding up his hand to silence Olivier, while carrying on in the same intense tone, 'though I have told thee enough, yet thou knowest not how the Philosophers do make and break open the glassy seal of Hermes in which the Sun sends forth a great splendour with his marvellous-coloured metallic rays, and in which looking glass the eyes of Narcissus behold the transmutable metals.' Olivier's expression during this outpouring, Hermione observed, was flooded with rapt delight.

'So your reading is indeed wide!'

'I am open to all things,' answered the curé. 'My friend, are you close to transmuting base metals into gold?'

'You misunderstand, Father Grégoire. Those writings are not the path I follow. I strive to discover the Elixir of Life. Had I but had a few more months to keep my crucible fired! Now I am ruined … years of work, my manuscripts, my horoscopes, all that valuable equipment abandoned!'

'Your laboratory is still complete in Paris?'

'Yes.'

'Olivier has never harmed a soul in his life,' interrupted Hermione, beginning to feel anxious about the turn the conversation was taking.

'Surely it is simple enough to send for Monsieur Olivier's notes,' declared Father Grégoire, turning towards Hermione. 'Otherwise, how can he progress? His years of work would be as naught … the sequence of experiments wasted.'

'It is not possible,' said Hermione. 'Any person who owns a crucible in Paris is likely to be arrested.'

'Anyone offering cantharidin is destined for a dungeon,' quipped the priest with a worldly smile.

Olivier jumped up from his chair as if he had been stung. 'It is intolerable we men of learning should be cast under suspicion because of charlatans and hags peddling poison.'

'It is most regrettable for one blessed with the precious knowledge,' soothed Father Grégoire, as Olivier flopped back onto his chair, lost in distraction. 'If God has given someone the gift of understanding, he must mean him to find the way. Just think how it would change our lives … the sick, the poor . . . to have this precious secret held here in our humble parish.' Hermione stared at the curé uneasily as his eyes gleamed with something akin to greed. 'Hermione shall help you, dear friend, to fulfil God's purpose!' The curé's resolute tone shook Olivier out of his torpor. Hermione bit on her lip to stop herself saying *then why don't you go to Paris*, but the look of joy which lit up Olivier's gaunt face melted her heart.

'Oh, will you go, Hermione? Will it not be too risky for you … is it too much to ask of you?'

It was hard to measure the affection she felt for her guardian, but it ran deep. He had cared for her since childhood, and his work had always been everything to him. His curiosity and desire to understand came from deep within, and she knew he would wither away if he could not continue his personal journey. She stretched out her arms and moving across to him kissed him tenderly on both cheeks.

'Have no fear; it is settled. But you will have to be patient a little while longer, for I shall not go until after Christmas.'

Outside in the hall, Father Grégoire tied on his cloak, and then he took Hermione's hand and patted it.

'Well done, my child. With his book of calculations to hand, Monsieur Olivier will be able to accomplish much during the winter.'

Hermione could not help but feel an upsurge of anger. 'No one travels the roads in winter unless they absolutely need to!'

'Exactly! A question of need.' The curé nodded, settling on her the stern look he used for naughty children. 'To abandon notes on a whole sequence of experiments will set him back years.'

'But they may no longer be there,' protested Hermione, lowering her voice as Lucette glided behind them.

'I've made you angry!'

'It isn't that, Father,' sighed Hermione, as they walked towards his horse. 'I do not think you understand how dangerous Paris is.'

'Danger? For you, dear Hermione? How can that be? It is unjust that a scholar like Monsieur Olivier should have to answer for his work. It might have been to his benefit had he stayed in Paris to make a statement rather than to run away. Now he is compromised. But who would wish to arrest you?' Hermione did not reply as the priest heaved himself up onto the saddle. The two men had spent much time closeted together, and it seemed Olivier had spoken freely about his past. It was just as well he knew nothing about Lucette's involvement with La Voisin. Her own reluctance to confide in Olivier had served well. It wasn't that he would deliberately give things away, but anything other than his own work was of scant interest to him, and who knew what he might inadvertently let slip.

'Anyway, who am I to urge such an arduous journey upon anyone?' murmured Father Grégoire, his expression mild as he looked down on Hermione. 'The important thing is that Monsieur Olivier has *sanctuary* here. I shall be writing to my dear friend the Marquis in a day or so to keep him abreast of the great events in our little community. Naturally,' he added, with a conspiratorial smile on his fleshy lips, 'you can count on my discretion. I shall not be so imprudent as to reveal that we have an alchemist from Paris in our midst.'

Hermione's expression was grave as she looked into the eyes of the priest. Their hard stare remained unflinching, and she knew he would have his way in this. The affable smile which always brought a dimple to his rosy cheeks was still there, and it reassured her a little, but for the first time, Hermione sensed that beneath the jolly exterior was a different man.

'I will not disappoint Olivier,' she replied quietly. Immediately, the chubby face was wreathed in smiles, and the slightly bulbous eyes shone with pleasure. It seemed impossible those brown depths had but a moment before reflected a ruthless will. Father Grégoire tapped the palfrey with his crop.

'No matter how you try to shut the world out, Hermione, it will not forget you. And there is nothing like wealth to ease away troubles.'

Hermione watched after the palfrey's bouncing progress across the courtyard and wondered whether Father Grégoire's words had veiled a threat. She could not think he would make trouble for Olivier, yet a careless observation in one of his letters could easily bring disaster on them all. So, whilst it was madness, she would return to Paris.

*** *** ***

It was the last week in February. Wearing the clothes of a maidservant, Hermione approached the door of her friend Agnès. From within came the sound of two familiar voices. Hermione's heart lifted with pleasure. They were safe! Would it startle the elders to walk straight in as she used to? She opened the door, and there they were, still knitting, needles clicking away as always.

'Good morning, monsieur, madame. You are still knitting for France, I see.'

'Oh, it's you, madame. Come and warm yourself by the fire. You must get very cold sitting in that house hour after hour,' chirped the old lady, not looking up. 'I tell Agnès they won't come back, but I don't suppose you care, just as long as you get paid. Come and sit ... people coming and going all day long, wanting things made bigger, things made smaller.'

'Have you come to collect knitting?' quavered the old man, peering towards Hermione.

'It's the lady who watches,' put in Agnès' mother. Hermione moved closer towards the light of the fire so they could see her better, but it seemed to make no difference. She was about to tell them who she was when footsteps approached the door and Agnès entered. Her look of utter astonishment made Hermione burst out laughing.

'Yes, it truly is me,' she said, going over to embrace her friend. 'Your father and mother seem to have forgotten me.'

'They become confused,' explained Agnès. 'It is Hermione, Maman ... her eyesight isn't so good now, nor her hearing,' she added, dropping her voice.

'I think she thought I was a concierge,' said Hermione, a little ill-at-ease, sensing a restraint in Agnès' manner.

'They will soon be forgetting who I am! Won't you both ... *forget who I am*!' The knitters at the fireside tittered, and Agnès' mother nodded vigorously.

279

'I told her they will never come back!'

'That's *enough*!' snapped Agnès. Hermione looked at her friend in surprise, never having heard her speak so before. As if conscious of her harsh tone, Agnès gave an apologetic smile. 'Let's sit over in my corner as we used to. Nothing changes,' she said, as she pulled aside the old curtain. 'I am still plying my needle, though as you can see by this heap of clothes, it's alterations now.' Hermione thought back to when the cubby hole had overflowed with costly, delicate shades of velvet and silk. As if reading her thoughts, Agnès nodded. 'Here's a safer line of work than turning out pouches for powders and the like. I know where the clothes are going ... this dress here I let out for a friend whose waist is spreading.'

Hermione sat down on a stool and accepted a mug of cordial . 'I never liked that colour,' she commented, considering the vivid green of the dress as she sipped her drink. 'What name did the dyers give it?'

'Parrot green. I've heard a whisper the master-dyers will offer lettuce green this year.' Agnès' eyes settled fully on Hermione, and the resentment Hermione had already sensed was there clear to see. 'You left without even saying goodbye to me, or Mama and Papa!' The accusation came forth in a rush. 'If I had been in when you arrived, I am not sure I would have let you in, Hermione. We were worried for months about you. And Mama was so upset ... not even a message. And not to tell Monsieur Olivier where you were going, and to leave him without even Guillaume to help him.'

Hermione's hands lifted slightly as she tried to express her regret.

'I'm sorry. There wasn't time. You know how many arrests were being made. I was afraid to get caught up in it all.'

'And then Monsieur Olivier just took off ... we heard the police had come for him. Is he with you now?'

Hermione hesitated, wondering how much to tell. Her eyes contemplated the vivid green frills which edged the skirt of the dress on the table. She had seen it before ... but where? Agnès' face had now become all smiles and interest as she asked again about Olivier.

'I don't know where he is,' Hermione said at last, her mind still taken up with the parrot green.

'Where are you living? And how is Lucette?'

Hermione hesitated. It wasn't that she did not trust Agnès, but for her friend's safety, as well as that of the knitters by the fire, it was better not to involve them in her affairs.

'It is best you don't know details. I lead a quiet life in the countryside,' she said, with a motion to her simple wool cloak. 'You would think it very dull!'

'Well, dull or not, I want to hear about it. And why are you here?'

'Have the police sealed off Olivier's house?'

As Agnès opened her mouth to reply, a knock came at the door. Her friend's hand flew to her mouth as if she had forgotten something. In a trice, the green-trimmed dress was slung over an arm, and Agnès darted out of the cubby hole. A sudden rush of cold air had blown the curtain inward against Hermione's back. Mildly curious to see who might wish to wear such a gaudy colour, she peeped out towards the door, but Agnès' bulk hid the caller from view. The exchange between the two women had a note of urgency about it. Whilst it was not possible to distinguish what they were saying, something about the caller's voice struck a chord, especially her laugh as the door closed upon her. Agnès returned, clucking with irritation, her eyes seeming to avoid Hermione's as she settled herself on her stool.

'Sorry about that ... people coming to collect things all the time. Now, how long are you staying? We must give you a grand meal.'

'I've taken a cheap room at an inn until Friday. Will I be safe going to the house? There are just a few things I would like to have if they are still there. Did you keep the spare key?'

'Yes. I went over when I heard Olivier had run away from the police. If the police took anything, I could not say; it all seemed the same. So I locked up, hoping you would all come back.'

'Did the police ever come here?'

The expression on Agnès' fleshy face hardened, and her eyes glared with such resentment that Hermione was immediately filled with guilt.

'I was not as fortunate as you, Hermione! Not only had I to answer for my sachets and pouches, but when Monsieur Olivier gave them the slip, had it not been for friends, I would have been put in prison. But we'll speak no more of it,' she said, holding up her hand as Hermione was about to ask more questions. 'When are you going to the house?'

'I thought now.'

'Why not leave it until tomorrow? Your friend Robert is in such a funny play about La Voisin. It's been playing since November and is due to end soon ... it would be a pity to miss it. If you go to the theatre tonight and get your things tomorrow, it will give me time to make a good meal for the four of us. Is there anyone else you would like to come on such a special day?'

'Just the four of us,' Hermione smiled. 'Besides, my arrival in Paris is not so special.'

'Oh, I don't mean you,' chuckled Agnès. 'Tomorrow is special because they are burning the Queen of Witches on the Place de Grève!'

Nicolas La Reynie, the Directeur général of the police, contemplated his notebook, which contained passages of interrogation of which even the judges of the secret court at the arsenal were to be kept ignorant. Only Louvois, as Minister for War, and the King were party to certain dossiers likely to implicate Madame de Montespan. Catherine Deshayes Montvoisin, during her time on the stool, before the judges of the Cour Ardente, had refuted with vigour any links with members of the royal favourite's household. Even when put to the Question of the Boot, in the torture chamber at Vincennes, La Voisin had not confessed to delivering powders and potions to Madame de Montespan's maid Cato at the châteaux of Versailles and Saint-Germain. Nor had she admitted to poisoning the petition which she had wished to present to the King.

La Reynie's eyes were thoughtful as he recollected how the scribes had hovered close to La Voisin so as not to lose a single word as the adept, black-gowned team of torturers had progressed to the Question Extraordinaire, even to the Fourth, Fifth, Sixth, Seventh, and Eighth Corner … yet still nothing! He sensed some external order, and from the *highest* level! For while all seemed the normal intense application of instruments, as the silent master and his apprentices went about their business in the crowded chamber, the crucial agony had clearly been withdrawn to ensure silence! Was it Louvois, Colbert or the King who had interceded? Whichever it was, anything which might reflect badly upon Madame de Montespan was to be avoided.

La Reynie turned the pages of his notebook at random and shook his head with something akin to despair as he looked at the aristocratic names that had come before the secret court. It seemed as if poison had become the accepted remedy for any bored wife, any jealous rival … especially when the King's affection was the prize. La Vallière had been in peril, Mademoiselle Fontanges was clearly a target. What artists the poisoners were! La Debraye and La Delaporte were so skilled and artful with their laughing-death powders! Their evil art was only betrayed when some customers, becoming impatient with the delicacy of application, administered larger amounts which then gave the game away. What a filthy, evil business it was, disguised under the cloak of supposed witchery and magic! Sometimes he thought the poorer people had more common sense than these court ladies with their silly love potions to turn the King's head in their direction. More sinister and sickening were the accounts of the Abbé Guibourg: of Black Masses and pacts with the Devil, when not only live doves had been offered for sacrifice, but premature babies. The abortion trade and baby snatching for sacrifice made him grind his teeth with rage. It was an emotion he rarely indulged. His way was a careful sifting of evidence: matching statement against statement, appraising, evaluating, reading the hundreds of reports sent in by agents.

With this in mind, he snapped shut his notebook and began to read through the dossier of reports left for him that day by his assistant. One, concerning an Olivier Lefèvre in the rue de la Cocotte, took his eye. A young fortune-teller who read the crystal had disappeared together with two servants from the man's household. Months later, Lefèvre himself had fled from the archers when they were hauling people in for questioning. La Reynie picked up his quill and struck through the name of the fortune-teller, making a note of dismissal beside it. At the onset of this enquiry into a possible poisoning attempt on the King's life, it would have been prudent to bring Hermione Lefèvre in for interview. Now, with Catherine Deshayes Montvoisin but hours away from the scaffold and the dungeons of Vincennes holding bigger fish, there was no need for small fry. The eye of the Directeur général lit on the inventory of Olivier Lefèvre's laboratory. Ah yes, that was the reason for keeping the case on file. Such a well-equipped laboratory could well have supplied drugs and poisons for half of Paris, though to be fair to this Lefèvre, it also suggested he might be a serious man of natural philosophy. La Reynie noted that the place had been left open like a jam pot with a spy on daily watch for the likely return of the alchemist. Attached to the file was a message booked in but some hours ago. It was barely legible, reporting he, or was it she, would be returning to the house on the morrow. La Reynie tried to decipher the name through the ink-blots and snorted with contempt. With a degree of impatience, he rang for his secretary.

'Have the agent who wrote this told to do better,' he said curtly. 'Put that bright young man Michel Troude onto this case. I want Olivier Lefèvre brought in tomorrow for questioning. Tell him to use his own judgement in this matter ... he is no fool. Oh, and he is to escort me to the theatre tonight. I am safe nowhere since starting these investigations.'

Hermione's intention had been to make a start on packing away those precious pieces of equipment which were light enough for her to carry away in a large basket. Olivier's main priorities were his books of calculations and horoscopes, diaries of experiments, gold filings, and above all the glass jar containing the phosphorus. However, Agnès' suggestion of visiting the theatre to see the King's troupe perform was compelling. It was strange to be back amid noise and bustle, and while she would not exchange the world she had found in the southwest, a part of her readily embraced the sights she had known since childhood. As she lingered on the Pont Neuf, she contemplated going to look at the house in the Marais but knew that would make her sad. Besides, she now felt the Chevalier's presence at Du Chesne, so she also decided not to visit his grave.

With the news of La Voisin's execution on the morrow had come a sense of relief. According to Agnès, the maid Margot was still in prison, but it was more than likely the police would be questioning her only about her mistress's clients. It seemed the danger for Lucette was over.

As Hermione drew near the rue Guenegaud, she saw Agnès had not exaggerated. There was a huge press of people moving towards the theatre to see The False Enchantments. It was going to be difficult to get in, so she made her way to the stage door. It was the worst of times to ask for Robert, but within a minute of giving her name to a stage-hand she saw the tall, slender figure of her friend hurrying towards her. He was clearly agitated. Beads of sweat glistened on his narrow face, and whoever he had just left was already yelling for him to get back.

'I'm glad to see you are still alive, Hermione,' he said in a rush. 'It's a bad time … come back after the performance!'

'Can you get me a seat?'

A look of intense irritation crossed the actor's sensitive face, then he nodded. 'You are ever a trouble, beautiful one … I'll see if I can spirit you in!'

Spirit her in was the way of putting things, thought Hermione, as some time later wizards flew in and out of stone walls and skeletons danced across the stage. Her sides ached from laughing. Suddenly, along with everyone else in the theatre, she gasped with amazement when a man who had clearly been sawn in half somehow managed to put all his pieces back together again.

'Let La Voisin try that tomorrow!' shouted out a wag.

The ensuing explosion of laughter in the theatre brought a smile of satisfaction to the lips of the Directeur général of Police.

'There we have it, my friends, a seed on fertile ground!' Just as he had done on opening night in November, Nicolas La Reynie turned to express his thanks to Donneau de Visé, editor of *Le Mercure Galant*, and Thomas Corneille. 'Paris laughs at your charlatans and gulls and realizes your stone walls are but cardboard. They are small but important steps to lift people away from superstition.'

'The play was your idea, Nicolas!' declared the editor of Paris's society sheet.

'Which both you and Thomas made a reality. It will make people think.'

'That's what theatre is for,' replied Thomas Corneille. 'If Molière were alive, that is what he would say.'

'Then let us share a glass of wine to toast his memory afterwards. And you also, Michel,' declared the chief of police, turning to his promising assistant.

'I am honoured, monseigneur,' murmured the young man, tearing his eyes away from the beauty of a young woman squeezed behind a group of nobles occupying a front corner of the stage. Another theatrical explosion again lit up her face and made the jewels on the cloak she was wearing sparkle afresh. La Reynie, who missed nothing, laughed.

'I sense, Michel, that you would rather take a glass of wine with that interesting young lady whom you cannot take your eyes off. But we will save you from her, for she may well be a witch!'

At the end of the show, Hermione went into the wings to hand back the cloak which Robert had taken from the costume box. She felt exhilarated as familiar faces gathered about her, everyone asking where she'd been and what she thought of their performance. Then Robert was by her side, all smiles, his eyes dancing with laughter as he hurried her out onto the street with the rest.

'How did you enjoy it?'

Hermione was about to reply when an old woman shoved in between them. Instead of sending her on her way, Robert bent his curly head to listen. Then, with a nod, he fished some coins out of the pouch at his waist, and after passing them over, he gave the woman a sympathetic pat on her shoulder.

'Who was that?' asked Hermione in idle curiosity, as they hurried to catch up with others.

'That's Jeanne ... she works for one of the dealers in waste paper who supply us with papier-mâché. You've seen how we make the masks. The last of the poor woman's teeth have dropped out so she can't chew the paper. Her job has gone to someone else. I told her that her gums will soon harden, and then she'll be able to break the paper down again ... she's got plenty of spittle.'

'So, are you going to tell me how to saw a man in half and put him back together again?' asked Hermione, filled with a dozen questions. Robert looked down at her with a grin as they went into the tavern in which they were all to take supper.

'It would be more than my life was worth ... and I'd likely not work again. I'm more interested in what is happening to you. Where are you living? Why did you leave?'

With the bustle of finding seats and responding to friendly greetings, Hermione escaped having to find answers. Nor was her friend looking for them, as everyone around the table became caught up in laughing outbursts about the things which had nearly gone wrong during the performance.

'It was one of those nights.' said a young man with a sigh. 'Perhaps it was because the Directeur général of Police was watching us.'

'Nicolas La Reynie was there?' breathed Hermione in horror, more to herself than anyone else. Swiftly the conversation changed to vigorous debate over Thomas Corneille's brother Pierre's play *Tite et Berenice* and whether it really was inferior to Racine's *Berenice*. The argument went back and forth, and then suddenly all became excitement as Robert mentioned the plans for a theatre at Versailles. Time raced by till it was the hour to make her goodbyes.

'Won't you come and get a place outside Notre Dame to see if La Voisin will make the Amende Honorable?' asked Robert, as they stepped outside the tavern. 'I always think it is like theatre when the criminals kneel there ... and a different audience from the Place de Grève. I don't like to see the burnings even though they purify before Purgatory.'

'Tonight, Thomas Corneille made me *laugh* at wizards and witches,' reflected Hermione, 'but if I see La Voisin I will be filled with horror. So let me kiss you goodbye while I am feeling happy.' Hermione reached up and kissed Robert on his cheeks.

'You'll be back, beautiful one.' He smiled as he turned away. 'No Parisienne can stay away from Paris.'

Beneath the feet of an unrepentant Catherine Deshayes Montvoisin, the faggots had been set alight. The straw laid against the white gown of execution gradually began to billow smoke, and behind its grey-white screen the executioner's assistants, offering mercy, deftly ripped off the prisoner's head with hooks. Michel Troude had seen enough, and he hurried away to the honey trap to lie in wait for Olivier Lefèvre.

As Hermione had anticipated, the rue de la Cocotte was silent. Everyone had gone to watch the execution. Feeling no sense of threat, she approached Olivier's house recalling past happy times. She was but a few paces from the gate when as if from nowhere, just like a jack-in-the-box, an image popped into her mind: a woman whose vivid green skirt showed through the opening of her cloak! Hermione sucked in her breath and froze. '*Mon Dieu* ... can it be she?' Could Agnès' friend be the woman who had come to her for a second reading of the crystal, then had asked for a sleeping draught to get rid of a rival? Who had hurried away to the police? With a nervous glance over her shoulder to see if she was being followed, Hermione pulled back into a yard while she strove to make sense of things. The woman's laugh had sounded familiar, but the dress she could not be certain about. It could just be a coincidence. Whatever it meant, Agnès had said it was safe to go to the house.

The door into the yard was open, which put her again on immediate alert as she replaced the key in her pocket. Treading softly, she went down the yard towards the laboratory and eased open the door just enough to avoid letting in the light. She remained still and listened for any sound. All seemed quiet, so she eased herself round the door and gently pressed it shut. To be absolutely certain, she remained motionless and strained for sounds of breathing in the darkness, but the place was empty. Losing no time, she moved towards the desk where Olivier kept his papers and books and lit the candle. He had been precise about what he wanted and soon she had gathered up all and had them safe in her large basket. Heading for the storeroom she stiffened mid-step as from outside came the sound of a slammed door. In a flurry of alarm, she sped back to the door and opened it a fraction to peer out. Nor had her ears deceived, for hurrying across the yard from the kitchen was a woman. It was impossible to identify her from behind, but as she turned to close the door onto the street, a flash of bright green showed through the opening of her cloak. Her face was sideways on, but Hermione immediately recognized the woman who had gone to inform on her. She shut the laboratory door, her mind filled with speculation, but she would have to think on it later. She headed towards the storeroom, the light from her candle bringing to life the vessels and retorts which Olivier used for his experiments. On an upper shelf she spotted a favourite flask of his. It was high up, but by raising herself on tiptoe she could almost reach it. For one triumphant second, her fingers had it, then somehow it must have knocked against the edge of a metal tray, and all about was falling down to the floor. The commotion of breaking glass and the reverberating crash and clatter of metal was awful. It was as well there was no one to hear at the house.

As Olivier had described, the gold filings were concealed within a box of candles. It was a stout box, ideal for her purpose, so, after setting aside the candles, she added everything else he had asked for. There was just space enough left in which to wedge the jar containing the phosphorus. Hermione's lips lifted in a smile as she recalled the wonder of seeing it glow when Olivier had lifted it out of its watery balm. During the journey back to Du Chesne she had to ensure it stayed submerged under water at all times. Olivier had been particular about that!

Everything had been accomplished with such ease. If she was really quick she could run up to her bedroom and get the blue vase which Olivier had given to her when she was small, and, not least, say goodbye to the old house. For despite what Robert had said about Parisiennes, it was unlikely she would ever return to Paris. With a final check that the phosphorus was packed in tight, Hermione closed the lid of the box and picked up the candlestick.

Humming softly, she stepped back into the laboratory and near jumped out of her skin with fright, for sitting at Olivier's bench was a man!

'Is it Mademoiselle Hermione? Welcome back to rue de la Cocotte,' said Michel Troude, experiencing a thrill of elation to have caught a fish on his first watch for Nicolas La Reynie. 'I had hoped it would be Olivier Lefèvre who was making such a noise down here.'

'He is away, in Amsterdam,' lied Hermione. Despite the pleasant appearance of the young man seated on the stool, she was so alarmed she felt hardly able to breathe. Her heart raced, and her eyes went to the open door. There was no sound of archers in the yard. She knew she had to get away before anyone else arrived. 'He studies there,' she said, trying to sound casual. 'Sometimes he goes to Cambridge in England to meet other men.'

'So, if I wished Monsieur Olivier to make up certain potions, he would be my man!'

Hermione laughed, genuinely amused.

'He is not for sale to make the brews you are thinking of. He is seeking the Elixir of Life. The means to offer people *good health* within the span of life that God allows them.'

'It sounds fanciful ... almost as fanciful as The False Enchantments,' remarked the chief of police's assistant with a smile of recognition, as he identified the young woman he had lusted after at the theatre. 'Did you enjoy the play last night, mademoiselle?'

'Yes, I did,' replied Hermione, casually putting the box into the wicker basket. 'It made me laugh. I found it also disturbing and thought about it for hours.'

'The playwrights Corneille and de Visé would be pleased to hear it.'

'It made me wonder whether some of the things we believe in can be true.'

'So, if you are indeed Mademoiselle Hermione, does this mean you will throw away your crystal? Oh yes, I know all about your black velvet room with its silver stars.' Michel Troude laughed, recalling the statement he had written up after interrogating the seamstress Agnès Basset. 'Tell me about the clients who used to visit ... better still, let us go into the house, where there is a fire, and we can get to know each other. My chief would like to meet Monsieur Olivier. He thinks his work must be at a learned level. And you shall have plenty of time to *persuade me* of it.'

It was clear where things were heading. Hermione threw back the hood of her cloak and shook out her hair as if to make herself more attractive. While she was doing, so her thoughts raced as to how she might get away. She walked towards the stocky young man, responding to the excitement in his eyes with a smile of invitation. 'Let me *persuade* you of it *now*,' she murmured. 'But close the door; candlelight is softer for loving.'

With a shrug of his shoulders, Michel Troude walked away, thinking this was better sport than watching some murdering hag go up in smoke on the Place de Grève. While his back was turned, Hermione reached into her basket and raised the lid of the wooden box. Then, as the police agent sauntered back, she gave a flirtatious smile.

'So, you do not believe in magic?'

'No!'

'Then let me show you something no one in Paris has seen. Have you the courage? I must blow out the light.'

The eyes watching her across the bench immediately narrowed with suspicion.

'I promise not to turn you into a frog. I won't fly over your head as an owl,' teased Hermione. With a scowl of embarrassment, the police agent gestured for her to proceed. Hermione's smile was warm and reassuring, whilst inwardly she tried to recall all that Olivier had said when he had first shown her the phosphorus. She moved away from the bench and took up a glass retort. Her heart was pounding, her mind straining to remember: *sand, a little sand must be scattered in the base of the retort; a glass rod warmed.* 'Nearly ready.' She laughed, trying not to sound nervous. Returning to the bench she warmed the glass rod in the candle flame. Then, running over what she must do, no matter what happened, Hermione took a deep breath and steadied herself. Removing the container's stopper, she took up the tweezers and raised the wax-like lump out of the liquid. Within two breaths, the strange substance began to give off little puffs of smoke. Instinctively, Hermione sensed there was little time. She dropped the phosphorus down the neck of the retort onto the sand beneath. Tense with excitement, she inserted the glass rod and touched it against the phosphorus. The police agent cried out in amazement as bright sparks and white flame erupted within the sphere. Hermione withdrew the rod and finally thought to blow out the candle. The entire globe was now completely suffused in a shimmering white light. Never had she seen such a glow, not from fire or candles. It was like a small moon, here in the darkness. Terrified of burning her hands, yet urged on by curiosity, she tentatively touched the magical lamp. She cried out in shock. It was icy cold! Of course! Olivier had named it Icy Noctiluca!

'Has your magic burnt you?'

The policeman's laughter brought Hermione back to the peril of her situation. Realizing he had misinterpreted her reaction, she seized hold of the unearthly light and hurled it up in the air across the bench towards him.

'Here, catch. It's hot … don't drop it!'

Losing not a second, Hermione reached out and snatched for the handle of the wicker basket. Then, with her free hand, she managed somehow to thrust the heavy bench forward. Her sabots crunched on broken glass as she ran in the direction of the storeroom. Behind in the dark came shouts of alarm, then the shattering of glass, followed by a gasp of pain. Hermione's outstretched hand made contact with the storeroom door. She felt for the lock, her fingers all of a fumble as she pulled out the key and locked herself into the small space. Olivier had only once shown her how to open up the wall. With desperate speed her hand sought upwards in the dark for the shelf. From behind the door rattled as her pursuer shouted out terrible threats. Then his body crashed against the wood and still she could not find the catch beneath the shelf. Under the pounding assault the door was beginning to splinter. As it caved in, sharp edges of wood slammed against her back, and she gasped in pain. Then her fingers, making another sweep, had the catch. The click and whirr of mechanism began; the shelves began to move inward. Hermione turned towards the cold draught of air and prepared to slip through sideways. Suddenly, a hand grabbed for her shoulder and strong fingers seizing hold of her cloak began to pull her backwards.

'Let me go!'

'You're not going anywhere,' yelled Michel Troude. Hermione tried to force her way inward to the passage but the man held on tight, though he was unable to get nearer as the smashed timbers of the door were between them. Desperately Hermione reached at her throat and dragged on the cords which were choking her. Somehow she managed to untie them.

'You bitch!' shouted Michel Troude, finding himself now holding but a cloak. From the other side of the wooden barricade he heard a loud click, and then the flow of cold air was cut off. A muffled peal of laughter rang out from somewhere beyond. It was so joyful, Michael Troude's anger completely dissolved. He fingered the woollen cloak and sighed with regret as he caught the faint, intriguing scent of its wearer. Suddenly put in mind of what suffering would have come to this vital woman in prison, he was glad his fish had slipped its hook!

CHAPTER 18

hile retaining the inherent intricacies of a work in miniature, the model was proving a challenge because of its large proportions. The concentrated effort both Jacques and Henri were putting into its construction was exhausting, but at least it he distraction from worrying about Perrette. As if it were not enough to have personal problems, the ever-increasing hostility of the government towards Huguenots was affecting every trade and profession. With a sense of frustration, Jacques looked on as one of their valued craftsman headed towards the shipyard gate; Wilhelm and his family were going back to Holland. The Intendant Demuin's increasing influence in court circles had locally brought about a more rigorous approach towards the Reformed Church and its followers. A brooding expression settled on Jacques's face as he thought of Perrette. Was she still slipping away to prayer meetings at Martin's house? He did not know, and truth to say, he was guilty of not wanting to think about it. Should he sack the man? It was harsh to take bread from a man's mouth when he worked hard, albeit he had no talent. As to his own coming together with his cousin as man and wife, there seemed no possibility whilst she was in such a precarious state of mind. Even if she regained her senses and steered clear of this dangerous course ... what then, when he himself yearned for something else? Yet he had made a sacred oath looking into the eyes of his dying uncle. There could be no going back.

With a set expression, Jacques walked back towards the mould loft, once more to immerse himself in work.

'We shall miss Wilhelm,' grumbled his grandfather, as he and an apprentice set in place a plank of the miniature ship's deck. Jacques remained silent, thinking that it made no sense for France to drive such men away. 'Have they cast the cannon yet?'

Jacques raised his head from the gun port he was beginning to work on. 'Not yet,' he replied, contemplating what he had done.

'I don't like the sound of that!'

'You're too suspicious.' Jacques chuckled. 'We're nowhere near ready for them.'

'I know those upstarts at the arsenal,' growled Henri. 'They like to think the rest of us are only good for building fishing boats. Those dogs are up to something, I'll be bound, and it won't be to *our* benefit.' The furrows etched across his forehead deepened. How they would crow if he and Jacques made a mess of things. He had been slow to warm to his grandson's youthful ambition, but now it would be the last big project of his own working life. His customary practice for small-scale models was to make the hull from a single cut of wood, but this was for a King! The King of France! Every detail must be correct. It must be perfect! As for choice of wood, pear, cherry, and box, had been abandoned for elm. This model was not going to be admired upon some stand, it had to sail on water … nothing better than elm for that. As a working model there could be no short cuts; everything must accord in precise detail to the real thing for the King's instruction.

Over an hour had passed when the jingle of harness and grind of wheels announced the arrival of a coach outside. Jacques gave a casual turn of his head and near dropped his lathe in surprise as through the open doorway he saw who was stepping out of the coach.

'Grandfather, prepare yourself! We have visitors … it is Admiral Duquesne!'

'Duquesne … coming here?' gasped Henri, his expression a mixture of confusion and excitement. 'Why didn't you tell me? Perrette could have prepared refreshment. Our men might have been ...'

'I didn't know ... and I expect he planned it this way because he does not want any fuss.'

'Then at least let us greet him with respect!' exclaimed Henri, flinging aside his leather apron. But before either man could reach the entrance of the mould loft, France's great hero of the Marine crossed its threshold.

'Monseigneur, we are most honoured!' growled Henri, attempting a deep bow.

'No need for formality, Maître Maurellet,' pronounced the admiral with a dismissive wave as he walked forward. Scampering close on Duquesne's heels like some small fawning dog came Maître Joubert from the arsenal. His manner, while clearly anxious, was overridden by such a lofty air of *hauteur* it was bordering on the ridiculous. 'So,' commented the commander, darting a look at Jacques as he quickly strode around the length of the frigate, 'your claim about the competence of the Maurellet shipyard was not exaggerated. The workmanship is fine ... the lines very pretty. Explain the gun ports.'

'We've spread the main frames further apart.'

'To what end?'

'It has increased the length; it will give the gun crews more working space. And it will permit us to use larger guns.'

'I see.' The admiral nodded, his eyes keen with interest.

'What decorative work do you have in mind?' Jacques looked towards Henri to see if he would like to speak, but his grandfather shook his head.

'We have been most fortunate to have Pierre Puget's guidance.'

An immediate smile of approval touched the admiral's eyes and lips. 'Then all is assured for beauty and splendour! You have departed from the Table of Dimensions in part to achieve greater speed. You dangled that as bait when last we met ... and it got you this far. Before you illuminate me about your length of keel and breadth of hull, explain the points at which the model may be dismantled. For your work is so snug, I cannot straightway tell?'

If a boulder had dropped from the sky, Jacques could not have been more shocked. He could hardly believe his ears.

'Forgive me, monseigneur, but did you say dismantled?'

'I did, monsieur.'

'I do not follow you, monseigneur,' responded Jacques uneasily. He looked to Henri, but his grandfather's expression, as he ran a hand through his mane of white hair, matched his own blank state of mind. The only help he got from the royal arsenal's master-shipwright Joubert was a malicious smile. 'Were you anticipating the dismantling of the model?'

'You mean it is fixed?' asked Duquesne, halting dead in his tracks. 'It cannot be taken apart and afterwards re-assembled?'

'Indeed not!' snorted Henri.

The colour drained from Jacques's face. 'No, monseigneur.'

'Then how do you suppose it can be transported to Versailles? The Chevalier De Tourville's amended instructions to the arsenal were plain, and plainer still is the fact that I have travelled here this day for no good purpose! And we will have no frigate to offer to the King!' With an angry dismissive gesture, Admiral Duquesne turned on his heel and stalked away. Still reeling from dismay and shock, Jacques caught the smug expression of triumph on Maître Joubert's face and exploded inwardly with anger. Directing a murderous look at the official, he pushed past him and hurried after the admiral. No wonder there were so many knowing smiles and winks at the arsenal when he had last gone to see about the casting of a miniature anchor and cannons. It was futile now to plead ignorance … that they hadn't been told. Men like Duquesne were not interested in excuses, only in results. Nevertheless, he strove to put their case as he kept pace with him towards the waiting coach.

'Had we been told ... received instructions! Monseigneur, I give my word, you will still have a frigate, and with no delay.'

Duquesne threw on Jacques a look of cold scepticism as he paused before the open door of the coach.

'Do you really want me to hold you and that old man yonder to what is impossible?'

Jacques did not flinch under the penetrating stare. 'There is no one else for you to trust in, monseigneur,' he answered boldly. 'It will be constructed as the Chevalier De Tourville ordered.'

As the coach wheels turned and carried the visitors away, Jacques gave a scowl of fury as the full implication of what Joubert's spiteful omission had wrought on them. It was a disaster, added to which was the rash promise he had just made to the admiral. Jacques gave a desperate sigh, hardly able to bear the thought of going back in to face Henri. After all the hours of work ... his grandfather's pride ... how had he taken it? The bowed white head and slumped figure on a stool told it all. Jacques swallowed with emotion, having only once before seen him so, on the day his father and uncle had been carried away in their coffins. Without speaking, and wishing that Henri's reaction had been one of fury, he laid his hand on the old man's shoulder.

'I can't do it, lad. I'm finished. To begin again ... they've finished me.'

Jacques's fingers dug hard into Henri's shoulder. 'It is my fault. I should not have gone to see Pierre Puget. It would have been more politic to have sought advice at the arsenal. Instead of which, I stirred up jealousy.'

'It was a fine piece of work ... I was looking forward to carving your hippocampus.' Henri's voice was flat with disappointment. Jacques ground his teeth with anger as he thought of the petty spite and the injustice.

'By God, Grandfather, we will start again! I have given my promise to the admiral that the King shall have a frigate. And I need your old hands, for they are more skilled than any! If I have to stay up night and day, our model is going to sail down Versailles' Grand Canal!'

*** *** ***

Guillaume had walked the royal stallion up from the stables to show him off in the courtyard after his customary early morning grooming. Marie and Lucette had come to the kitchen door to render what everyone, including Hermione herself, regarded as due reverence to nobility of the first order.

'He is beginning to fill out, Guillaume,' she commented as she made a circuit of the stallion. 'It must be the aniseed in the bean mash. Have you mended the fence around the meadow?'

'It will be safe enough. I fixed a padlock to the gate to stop the blacksmith's mare getting to him.'

Hermione raised her eyebrows at Guillaume's cheeky grin, then could not help but laugh as she recalled the mangy mare shaking with fright before the royal colt.

'Speaking of Raoul, you'll need to get him to trim ... Hermione's attention was suddenly diverted from the stallion's hooves as the small figure of Julien came running out from the keep.

'Madame Du Chesne, Madame Du Chesne, there is a rider coming here ... it's a dragoon!' Hardly had the young boy spoken before the approach of a horse at gallop could clearly be heard. Hermione exchanged anxious looks with Guillaume as hooves hammered over the wooden bridge, and then a uniformed rider made a fast approach into the courtyard.

'Good morning, madame,' the soldier called, as his mount slithered to a halt beside Hermione. 'I am billeting officer for His Majesty's forces, lately returned from the Rhine.'

'Good day to you, officer,' responded Hermione with a cautious smile, as the dragoon drew a parchment from a leather pouch on his belt. 'How can we help?'

'You are required to provide bed and shelter within the château for the officers of His Majesty's Dragoons and stabling for their horses and as many troopers as your outhouses and barns can take.'

Hermione shrank within at the prospect of such an invasion. Unsettled by the dragoon's horse, the royal stallion snorted and wheeled sideways. Hermione thrust out her hand to fend him off, and in doing so her fingers made contact with the brand on his rump.

'I would like to assist you, officer,' she said, suddenly remembering with a surge of relief that she could refuse him. 'But as you see,' she gestured at the brand, 'Du Chesne is exempt from the billet, and so too its tenants. It is vital His Majesty's stallion is not disturbed in any way.'

The billeting officer's eye lingered on the crown and the letter L imprinted on the stallion's hide. An expression of disappointment and weariness showed on his gaunt face. Touching his gloved hand to his helmet, without comment, he wheeled around his mount and sped away.

'He didn't look at all happy.' Lucette, who had wandered forward from the kitchen door, giggled.

'I didn't ever think a horse would hold off dragoons,' put in Guillaume.

'It seems a royal colt can,' murmured Hermione, experiencing a huge sense of relief.

'What fun we've missed,' complained Lucette.

'Some fun!' snorted Guillaume back over his shoulder as he led the stallion away. 'You would be hard at it now serving them breakfast, and they'd have me cleaning their muddy boots.'

Hermione turned to Julien, who had stayed throughout and was now slashing about with his wooden sword. 'Thank you for coming to warn us,' she called. The small boy rushed towards her, laughing.

'I came to guard you, madame.'

'And so you did, and the soldier went away. How fares your new sister?' For a while, Hermione listened to the boy's excited chatter, until, announcing he was off to get his friends to guard the bridge against

303

other dragoons, he ran off. Hermione's lips curved into a fond smile. His jet-black hair and blue eyes put her a little in mind of Jacques Maurellet. How fortunate she was that Jacques had put her name forward to raise a stallion; otherwise by now she would be wondering how to feed a large force of men. It was likely that Jacques also had received such a visit and would likewise be glad not to have the expense and trouble of soldiers living under his roof. The recollection of him suddenly made her heart squeeze with a restless feeling of loss. It seemed so long since they had spoken. No doubt the winter months for him and Maître Henri had sped by; the model must now be near completion. For herself, the journey to Paris had interrupted the long winter days, and since her return rue de la Cocotte seemed part of a former life. With La Voisin dead, she felt there would be no pursuit on the part of the police for herself. As for Olivier, well, that was less certain. He was, of course, not at all concerned, for from the moment of being reunited with his book of calculations, most days he kept to himself. The only person he wished to commune with was the curé.

Hermione shivered slightly, for she had stepped out to look at the stallion without a cloak. Even so, she lingered as the bell down at the stables began to ring. Her eyes lifted to the grey, wintry sky where pigeons were wheeling, and others joining them in response to the bell's summons. She had put the winter days to good use reading about husbandry. Olivier de Serres's advice to feed birds in the morning and leave them undisturbed at midday seemed to suit them. As to the advice that their droppings should be cleared out every week, Pierre's reaction to this new way had been to throw up his hands and mutter '*Merde*!' as he stomped off with Rouge. So it was left to Guillaume who also couldn't see the sense of spreading it on the fields, but obliged anyway. Lucette had the impudence to comment: 'The men say better to stick to the old ways, madame.'

'Then you can tell the men, Lucette,' Hermione had responded, 'that Olivier de Serres wrote his book in 1600 … so these are the old ways!'

Hermione laughed as she thought of what other things the book had inspired her to do once the spring arrived. Until then, as the snows were now in retreat, she must heed Jacques's advice and, while there was still a lack of foliage, carry forward the selection of final crop trees. So she returned indoors to breakfast, and afterwards dressed for riding out.

The snow had completely cleared from the open ground around the château, but within the High Forest it held stubbornly on, its frozen expanse in stark contrast to the dark trunks of the trees. Rouge loved it, of course, leaving tracks of dark paw marks as he dashed back and forth.

'Begging your pardon, madame, but I told you it was still bad,' said Pierre, as Hermione dismounted into a drift which came above her boots.

'Are you cold, then, Pierre?'

'Not me, madame! I am used to all weathers, as is Georges here. But it is not work for a lady.'

'I'm sure you are right, Pierre,' murmured Hermione, as she examined fungus on the bark of a tree, 'but it interests me. I want the Chevalier's forest to be strong and vigorous. It's become overstocked through neglect. Maître Maurellet advised light and frequent thinning at this stage. Would you agree, Georges? The crowns in this part need more space to expand. We mustn't let too much light in, though, or then the weeds will flourish.'

Her woodsman did not immediately reply as he stared upwards and all about him. Then he looked towards Hermione and nodded, a faint blush staining his broad face as it did whenever he spoke to her, no matter how she tried to set him at ease.

'I think, madame, the tree yonder will need to come down. It's sound enough, but see how it towers high above the rest. And those close to it are but spindles.'

'One of the wolf trees Maître Maurellet told us to look out for,' agreed Hermione.

'Best leave it to Georges and Victor, madame,' put in Pierre, as he finished setting a snare. 'There are dangerous things in a forest.'

'The meadow is no safer,' put in Georges. 'When I was taking wood for Guillaume to mend the fence, what I took for a rabbit turned out to be a *hare*. The witch's long ears were twitching to my every move ... those bulging witch eyes of hers were sideways fastened on me. I was so afeared I drew behind a bush and hid for a good while. Your maid, madame, told Mother at the *veillée* how the goblins have tried to entice her into the forest. We fair trembled when she told us about their eyes, red as fire.'

Hermione nodded with a grave expression, wondering how the conversation had taken such a turn. She hesitated to dismiss what Georges was saying, but since seeing the False Enchantress, she didn't know what to believe anymore.

'I have confidence in you all,' she said, remounting. 'But riding here is nothing compared to the discomfort and danger the Queen and her ladies must face when they follow the King on his springtime campaigns. And,' she added, trying not to laugh as her eye suddenly caught sight of a heart pierced by an arrow and a G carved into the trunk of a nearby tree, 'I learn something new each time I come out here!'

It had been some four months since Claude Tilly had been summoned to account for himself at Rochefort against a complaint of rigging bids at auction. Apart from some natural anxiety he had, however, felt fairly secure, knowing the associates with whom he had colluded would back him up by testifying Du Chesne's timber had been wanting in quality. To his great relief, he received only a warning. Nevertheless, the gossip which would surely flow from this to lessen his standing at Rochefort and at Saintes left him with a festering sense of grievance. Come springtime, his need to punish the Parisienne had become overwhelming. Not that everyone had been unsympathetic towards him. Maître Joubert, whom he had bumped into in the billiard salon at Rochefort, had tipped him off that it had been the shipbuilder Jacques Maurellet who had lodged the complaint. Tilly scowled, then gave a snigger as he recalled Joubert's hilarious account of the Maurellets having to rebuild a model for the King, and how old Henri Maurellet was near to collapse with the strain. By the glint of malice in Joubert's eyes, it hadn't taken much imagination to guess who had brought about the misunderstanding! With the roads opening up with the warmer weather, and his horse in need of some attention, Tilly dropped by the smithy at Du Chesne.

'You've been in my mind over winter, Raoul,' he declared, eyeing the blacksmith's dog as it snatched up a large trimming cut from his horse's hoof and noisily began to chew on it.

'You've thought of me, monsieur!' exclaimed the blacksmith in surprise. 'Why should that be?'

'I could not forget about the insult done to you last year … how the châtelaine would not let the royal stallion cover your mare.' With a feigned expression of sympathy, Tilly noted with satisfaction the scowl darkening Raoul's face. 'She has caused me trouble also,' he continued. 'It is not seemly for a stranger to these parts to make fools of us. Were you to keep an eye on things at the château … where Madame Du Chesne goes, who calls upon her, that sort of thing … you would be doing me a kindness.'

With an air of uncertainty, the blacksmith stared at Claude Tilly, who, with a tight smile, set down three *livres* beside the money he had paid for the trimming.

'Madame Du Chesne rides out often into the forest,' ventured Raoul. 'People think it very strange.'

'Do they believe she meets with the Devil?' asked Tilly, inspired to plant the seed of the thought.

'Why no,' replied Raoul, his voice expressing shock. 'She has given work to Georges and Victor. The lads say she wants to improve the forest. There is the man who has come to live there, of course,' he added quickly, as the entrepreneur gathered back up the *livres*. 'They say his candle burns late into the night.'

Tilly jingled the coins. 'I'll call in again Raoul ... don't disappoint me.'

The Bon Chrétien pear given to Hermione by the curé had miraculously survived winter under its bedding of straw. Fruits during the winter months had been virtually non-existent, as Marie had got out of the way of preserving. Not that she had forgotten the art of things, for as soon as the beans were ready for picking, Lucette and Julien's mother were put to work transferring them into large, salt-filled vats of water.

'Those women have used more salt than they have in the pans at Brouage,' declared Guillaume, whose job it had been to buy it in.

'How much do they use?' asked Hermione, who had never preserved beans and peas herself.

'Enough to keep an egg afloat,' replied Guillaume, who seemed to know a bit about everything. 'The first batch has been in the saline now for ten days. Marie is lifting them out and drying them off now. I'll take the new wicker baskets up to her.'

Hermione looked with satisfaction at the lines of preserving jars which she had brought back from Saintes. This coming winter they would not go short of garden produce. Before returning to the house, she went across to the stables and spoke softly to the stallion. On the other side of the door which led into the Chevalier's former laboratory, she could hear Olivier putting questions to himself, just as he always had done.

'Does he tell you all his secrets?' murmured Hermione, running her hand down the black glossy neck of the horse. The proud Arab head pulled away from her. 'Don't you dare,' she scolded as the colt's teeth made a grab at her arm. 'If you don't behave, I shall bring the blacksmith's mare to share your stall!'

After a lengthy steeping in salted water, the beans and peas had firmed up, and their lovely green colour, according to Marie, would now endure throughout the months they were held in the syrup. First, however, the excess salt needed to be rinsed out of them. From where she stood on the terrace, Hermione caught sight of Lucette carrying one of the wicker baskets alongside the river. Helping her was not Guillaume, but Georges. The meandering pace at which they were both going seemed likely to take the best part of the day, for, as if the basket were too heavy, from time to time Lucette would set it down. Then shrieks of laughter ensued as Georges tried to kiss her, each attempt foiled by the stiff protruding shield of her bonnet. Hermione's smile became wistful. How sweet it must feel to be so head-over-heels and immersed with another. She had hoped for a visit from Jacques Maurellet, for he was often in her thoughts. Had it just been her imagination that there had been a special feeling between them? No doubt he enjoyed many flirtations. She had not forgotten his bold way with the serving girl at La Rochelle. Was there a sweetheart at Soubise or Rochefort? Hermione gave a dismissive sigh. She had more than enough to occupy her time. The wicker basket containing the beans had at last been set into the water, at a point where it was not too deep but its flow was lively. For a few minutes, Georges splashed about, making certain the basket was secure. Then, with a leap, he was back on the river bank, and in a swift move had tipped Lucette's bonnet backward. Hermione laughed with amusement to see him so assertive. It was just as well a wedding was in the offing! She turned away and returned indoors to the Painted Room. Automatically, her eyes lifted to the Chevalier's portrait and her lips curved slightly with a smile. Then she glanced towards Aglaé, and her smile deepened as she took in the cascade of diamonds. How excited she and Lucette had been, tapping on panels in their search to find them! If only she had received a fair price for the timber, it would have made a huge difference, but money was tight. At least with the forest abounding in game, and fish in the river, there would be no problem in providing a wedding feast. Hermione moved across to a carved chest in to which she had stored the materials come upon in their searches and raised its lid, her hand going to a sky blue dress which she had in mind to refurbish. Beneath it was a large packet of lace. Hermione pursed her lips as she opened it. Dare she take a chance and break the law? In Paris it would be noticed immediately, but here, would anyone care? The beauty of the collars and trimmings was irresistible. She gave a shrug and took out the lace.

It was a moonlit night when Raoul set forth for the château, and he was relieved to see that the door of the keep had been left open. To ensure that he had some news to please Monsieur Tilly, he went first to the river where he knew they were rinsing the fruits of the garden. It took him but minutes to tip over the wicker baskets, and as the contents sank or floated away, he could not help but shake his head with regret to see good food wasted. Still, it was getting one back for the insult to his mare. Retracing his steps, Raoul crept through the keep and positioned himself behind a pile of building rubble where he could listen and watch without being seen. There was not long to wait, for just as a nearby owl hooted, the château's door opened, and the châtelaine, in company with the old housekeeper and the maid, came out.

Hermione looked up at the moon, which was wondrously bright, and just right for their purpose. 'Ah, here comes the ladder,' Raoul heard her say, as Guillaume approached from the direction of the stables.

'You've got a good night for it, madame,' Guillaume said cheerfully, setting the ladder up against the wall. 'I put a hook earlier beside the door so it shouldn't take a minute. Hand me up the end, Lucette,' he added in a brisk tone, as he clambered up the rungs. 'Come along, girl … quickly, quickly!' Lucette went forward and stretching upwards handed over a thin cord supporting all the discoloured lace. Guillaume began to fiddle, and then as the flimsy material fluttered away to the floor, he let fly an oath. Lucette immediately shrieked with laughter.

'It is too dainty a task for a man, Guillaume,' soothed Hermione as she retrieved the end of the cord and raised it up to him. 'Let Lucette take your place!'

'It was her fault, madame. I felt her tug the other end.'

'I never did,' protested Lucette in an innocent voice. Hermione exchanged a look of despair with Marie as there was an explosion of fury from Guillaume and another shriek of laughter from Lucette.

'We're wasting time, madame,' said the housekeeper, as the moon passed behind a cloud. 'Hold it steady, you silly girl, until he has secured it. Now, walk across to the well and attach it to the post as I told you to do.'

'Do you think it will need another night out here?' mumured Hermione, as Lucette walked away, paying out the cord from her bundle.

'I think so, madame. It is very yellow.'

As soon as Lucette had completed her task, Hermione called across to Guillaume. 'Make sure you lock up the Keep. We don't want thieves getting us into trouble, or prying eyes telling tales on us!'

Within the shadows, Raoul realized he had to move before he was locked in, yet he was reluctant to leave without discovering what it was that trailed its narrow whiteness across the expanse of courtyard. There was only Guillaume left, and Raoul thought he might be able to get close enough without being seen, but as he crept forward from his hiding place there sounded the deep-throated bark of Pierre Paultre's hound. It was time to be gone before the brute had his scent.

Fired by the thought that he was on to something, Raoul was back in position the following night, armed with a knife. The moon was bright, and with no passing clouds to interrupt its power to whiten things it was likely the mysterious bunting would be hung out again.

The first person to arrive in the courtyard was Guillaume with his ladder. In the shadows of the Keep, Raoul smiled when only Lucette joined him. As soon as they were done, he would seize his opportunity. It arrived sooner than he had expected, for as Guillaume was clambering up the ladder to secure his end of the line, someone called the maid's name from the open kitchen door, causing her to drop the bundle she was holding onto the ground and run indoors. It might have been safer to wait, but impatient to get it over and done with, Raoul dashed forward noiselessly on the balls of his feet. With the blade of his knife ready, he reached what appeared to be lengths of lace suspended on a cord. By sheer luck it had fallen with its end towards him and as he sliced off what seemed a good length he realized his luck, for had he cut a section from the middle they would have known someone had interfered. Above his head, Guillaume's feet began their descent on the wooden rungs; clutching his prize, Raoul raced away to the Keep and out over the wooden bridge.

Returning to her position, Lucette picked up the bundle of lace.

'Are you going to lend me your arm when I walk into church?' she asked pertly as she sauntered towards the well, paying out the flimsy line.

'Oh, I don't know about that. After all, I had my eye on your goings on in Paris,' guffawed Guillaume.

'And which eye would that be … hopefully, the one under your black patch.' Lucette giggled. Suddenly she came to a halt and clicked her teeth with impatience. 'It's not going to reach,' she commented over her shoulder.

'If it reached last night, it will reach tonight,' boomed back Guillaume, as he picked up the ladder to carry it away.

'I tell you it won't. You must have tied a great big long piece round the hook.'

With a snort of impatience, Guillaume set the ladder against the wall.

'I've done no such thing!' He stomped over to Lucette and gawped at the white end held between her fingers. He wrinkled his broad nose, not knowing what to make of it. 'It's too short.'

'That's what I said, stupid. She'll be furious,' added Lucette, pulling on the cord to try to stretch it. 'I don't want to be the one to tell her … I left you with it.'

'I had nothing to do with it.'

'Do you think someone came and stole some?'

'How would I know? No one came when I was on the ladder; I would have heard them. Perhaps as the moonbeams whiten it they make it shrink.'

'I've never heard so,' said Lucette, giving another tug.

'Say nothing, and no harm will come of it.'

'Well, how shall I fix it?' demanded Lucette.

'You called me stupid. So how would I know!' Guillaume laughed as he walked off.

When next Claude Tilly paid a visit to the smithy, Raoul sent his lad off on an errand and led the timber merchant into the small cubby hole wherein he kept his money and accounts.

'I am very glad you called, monsieur,' he said, wiping a stool clean with a piece of sacking. 'I've been very busy keeping a watch on your behalf.'

'I am glad to hear it,' responded Tilly, sitting on the stool. 'Speak, man. I haven't got all day.'

'They have been whitening things under the moon.'

Tilly's eyes became green slits of contempt as he regarded the sweaty bovine face.

'Not linen or anything like that,' stammered the blacksmith, fearing from his visitor's expression that he was about to leave, 'and Madame Du Chesne was there herself and ordered the manservant to be sure to lock the Keep as she didn't want thieves making trouble for her.'

Tilly flicked his riding crop impatiently against his boot. 'What other news have you?'

'But there is more to it, monsieur,' persisted Raoul. 'She talked of not wanting *prying eyes telling tales on them*!'

'Telling tales?' repeated Tilly, ignoring the blacksmith's hopeful expression. 'Repeat exactly what Madame Du Chesne said.'

Raoul felt a surge of satisfaction. He pursed his thick leathery lips as if about to deliver the words, then scratched his head. 'You promised, monsieur.'

'Yes, yes, you shall have your money,' snapped Tilly, following his meaning.

'She said, "We don't want prying eyes telling tales on us."'

'Telling tales … telling tales,' repeated Claude Tilly softly. He reached into his jacket and from a small money bag produced a *livre* which he sent spinning on the table. 'Bring me a piece of what they were whitening and the second coin shall be yours.' Raoul's slack lips opened to reveal his broken teeth, and he nearly laughed, so overcome was he with his own cleverness. Without speaking a word, he opened a drawer and pulled out the length of lace. Claude Tilly stared blankly at the exquisite collar, then, suddenly, he understood what had come his way. Within, he felt a flood of savage joy.

'You've done well,' he murmured, flinging down the promised money. 'Very well indeed!'

CHAPTER 19

s Claude Tilly waited to be taken through to the magistrate, he could not recall feeling quite so elated since his wedding day when he had acquired Angélique's money. Now he really had the Parisienne! Let us see how she survives after a three thousand *livres* fine!

'Monsieur, please come through to His Honour.'

With alacrity, Claude Tilly sprang to his feet and followed the usher. From his business dealinsg in Saintes, Tilly was aquainted with the magistrate, and he saluted him with a low bow.

'It is good of you to see me, monseigneur.'

'Proceed, if you will, Monsieur Tilly.'

'It has been brought to my attention that the King's law is soon to be flouted!'

'Yes?' said the magistrate, waving him on with an impatient gesture.

'There is to be a wedding,' continued Tilly, 'at the church at Du Chesne. It is my belief the châteleine will defy the King's law by wearing proscribed lace.'

'Is that so!'

So excited was Tilly, the heavy tone of sarcasm went unnoticed.

'It is my belief that Hermione Du Chesne intends in some way to use *point de Venise*!'

'Monsieur,' returned the magistrate, with a conciliatory smile, 'do you not think it best on such a day of happiness to turn a blind eye!'

'It is against the law to buy, to wear, repair, or to clean *point de Venise* … only lace worked in France is permitted, is it not?' Tilly's green eyes bored into those of the official.

'It was forbidden in 1665, but things have changed. Times are now more relaxed.'

'But it is still the law?'

The magistrate grimaced with exasperation. If the tedious little man didn't get his way here, it was evident he would go elsewhere and make trouble for everyone. 'What do you suggest, monsieur?'

'It is not my place to suggest, Your Honour,' replied Tilly deferentially, 'but if an example is to be made, it would be best on the day of the wedding, before the whole village … lest others be led to flout the law.'

'Would it not be a courtesy to warn the lady? After all … '

'Not so, for she has made it known she holds *point d'Alençon* to be inferior, and not even the King will prevent her using the superior *gros point de Venise*.'

In response to Tilly's lie, a change came over the magistrate's countenance. In a severe tone and with an imperious gesture of dismissal he gave his direction.

'Leave the details outside with the clerk. The constable's men shall deal with this impudence.'

***

The new construction of the model, being in three moveable parts, brought additional work. There was the challenge of ensuring the snug fit of all three parts upon assembly at Versailles. The internal structure being visible when dismantled, albeit the King would probably only see the frigate when assembled, the highest degree of finish was nevertheless still required. Such was the pressure, they could barely take a break until Henri cut his hand just as André paid an unexpected visit to the yard. Parting from Henri, who was going to Aunt Marguerite to have his hand bound, Jacques and André headed home for something to eat. Their way took them past the stables, where a groom was washing down the legs of Jacques's royal stallion. Perhaps their appearance had spooked it, for suddenly it reared up onto its hind legs. All that power and muscle high above them was an alarming sight, and along with the groom they leapt sideways to escape the plunging hooves. André gave a low whistle as the groom sought to calm his charge.

'He'll bring a heavy purse if you let him fight, Jacques.'

'Not allowed. Besides, I don't like to see horses biting at each other. Did you hear Colbert is going to found a national stud at le Pin in Normandy? Mansard is planning it. It is going to be very grand ... a rustic Versailles.'

'France will not only have the best horses, but a Marine to strike terror into the English and Dutch,' crowed André, his young face flushed with pride. 'And your frigate will so capture the interest of the King, he will forget his army.'

'I believe that is Colbert's scheme of things.' Jacques smiled, wishing he could abandon work for the rest of the day. 'Come on ... a quick bite of bread and cheese and then you can turn out some trenails for us.'

'I'm not complaining,' the youth said grinning. 'It will give me another look at the figurehead ... Grandfather tells me it is taken from life. I'd like to meet the lady. She seems to have made a great impression on you!' Jacques's eyes crinkled with the smile he gave his brother, but as they entered the kitchen he remained silent, refusing to be drawn. While André set out plates and knives, Jacques brought bread and cheese to the table. He had just filled two tankards with ale when their grandfather burst in.

'Get up to Marguerite's straight away. Father Francis came to take Perrette to church, and she has refused to see him. She has locked herself away in her chamber.'

If Jacques had hoped things might be resolved by the time he reached his aunt's house, he was disappointed. Upstairs he could hear Perrette sobbing and Father Francis shouting for her to come out to him, whilst Annette was weeping into her apron and Aunt Marguerite sat sobbing in her chair. The din was frightful.

'Ah, dear nephew, what has come over the silly girl? Go up to her and make her see sense. To defy Father Francis! What will people think?' Jacques patted her plump shoulder. 'It will be all right,' he murmured, not knowing what else to say. He made his way upstairs and came upon the black-clad figure of the priest standing outside his cousin's bedroom. Father Francis looked towards him with a severe expression.

'Tell Perrette to come out immediately.'

'I fear she will not while you are standing here, Father,' replied Jacques, his tone respectful but firm. 'I think it would be best to leave her in peace to find her own way to you.'

'She shall have no peace from me until she comes back to the church. Her soul is in peril,' declared the priest angrily.

'Should we think instead, Father Francis, of her mother, who is suffering great distress?' said Jacques, marvelling at his own restraint, for he was actually outraged by the priest's behaviour. 'My cousin has the right of undisturbed sanctuary in her room. I will speak to her when she is ready to listen.'

The priest's expression was one of uncertainty, but then, as the wailing below grew louder, he turned away from the door and hurried downstairs. Jacques clapped his hands over his ears to shut out the noise. He was sorely tempted to saddle up his horse and get away from work and everyone. Tomorrow, he would go and visit Hermione Du Chesne and be damned to it all! From the other side of the stout oak door he heard the latch pulled back. The door opened a fraction, and Perrette stared up at him.

'Has he gone?' she whispered. Jacques nodded and his cousin pulled back the door for him to enter. Once inside, he put his arms around her as she cried. They remained so for a while, then she broke away, wiping her eyes with a kerchief and motioning for him to take a seat.

'What can be so wrong?' she asked in a tight small voice. 'I am worshipping the same God.'

'Our family has always been Catholic,' murmured Jacques, his tone grave. 'Our King is Catholic. You are a French woman. Why do you wish to be *different*?'

'There are other French women who are members of the Reformed Church.'

'And their temples are being pulled down! Over a hundred years has passed since Saint Bartholomew's Eve ... let us pray such terrible times do not come again. Consider how difficult you will make things for yourself, for all of us.' He believed his words had impressed, for Perrette's expression became anxious as she moved towards the window. In a moment of silence she remained with her back to him looking outwards. Her voice, when she began to speak, was firm.

'Listen to part of my preparation for communion and tell me that you are not moved by the words. "Let each person examine himself. If he believes Jesus his Saviour, if he fears God, serves and loves him and all his brothers with a true heart, if he knows and feels his misery and weeps bitterly because of it, if his repentance is sincere and he wants to live in holiness ... " I do want to live in holiness, Jacques. Oh, dearest, when I pray directly to God I feel *ravished with joy*! Can you not join with me so that we can enter the Church as man and wife?'

Jacques stared at Perrette in disbelief. It was the second time she had put this plea to him. Yet never so strongly or in such language: *ravished with joy*! He recoiled from her fervour.

'How can I?' he gasped, horrified on all fronts. 'It is a religion which brings division. And my feelings ...' He struggled, trying to find the right words, not wishing to wound her, but needing to release what was truly in his heart. She moved towards him and took his hand between hers and he bit on his lip. 'And children ... would you expect them to be raised in your Church?' As if he had plunged a knife into her bosom, a look of agony sprang to her light blue eyes. She gave a low, broken sob, and he pulled her gently towards him.

'I will do all I can to help you,' he said softly, 'but please do not flaunt your belief ... be discreet. It is not for nothing they are calling the dragoons the booted missionaries. Father Francis knocks on your door ... they will smash it in!'

*** *** ***

If Hermione was still something of a stranger to local customs, she would not be found wanting in hospitality on Lucette's wedding day. A great boar was turning on the spit, and two dusty barrels of wine had been brought up from the cellar.

When the festive procession arrived at the church of Saint Hilaire, Claude Tilly gave not a glance to the servant who was to be married. His eyes were fixed expectantly on the door of the battered coach. The first of its occupants to step out, he deduced, was Monsieur Lefèvre. With cold intensity, the timber merchant examined him. His clothes were plain and much worn but of good quality. Whilst his expression was vague, it was not the vacant expression of the fool, but more the look of a scholar whose mind is elsewhere. His skin, however, had something of a burnished likeness to Raoul's as if he spent much time before a fire, which seemed strange for a gentleman. Tilly compressed his lips and determined to find out more about what Monsieur Lefèvre did at the château.

With green hostility, his gaze settled on the Parisienne as she emerged from the coach. Despite his loathing, he acknowledged she would turn every head in Saintes or Rochefort! The dress was magnificent ... it was as well, he thought with a humourless smile, that his own womenfolk were not here to see it. His eyes swept over the bodice and the exposed petticoat between the sky blue silk. Such a profusion of lace would cost a fortune, and it was exactly what he was looking for ... indeed, hoping for! Within, he experienced a surge of fiendish delight which inspired

322

him to sweep off his hat and execute a mocking bow. In doing so, he glimpsed the flurry of his own lace, so white at his wrist, but then it was new, and, more important, had been worked in Normandy. 'Oh, Madame Du Chesne!' He laughed as the party disappeared into the dark entrance of the church. 'Enjoy your humiliation … perhaps the constable's men will strip you down to your shift!' It was a great pity that he could not stay to watch the fun, but he did not want any angry fingers pointing towards him. He had been but passing through and thought to give a bow of respect. With narrowed, expectant eyes he looked in the direction of Saintes for signs of horsemen approaching … what was keeping them? He was reluctant to leave the area until he knew for certain the police had arrived, so he walked his horse onward to find shelter at the forge.

The whole of the courtyard resounded to the merry sound of pipes and drum. As a dancer lost his footing, Pierre chuckled.

'This takes me back some years, madame. Marie and I danced just like them.' Hermione smiled; she had never thought of him being young, nor of Marie as a young bride. She tapped her toe to the rhythm of the drum and watched the chain of men and women advance towards Georges and Lucette. Then bride and bridegroom rose from their seats and, running forward, linked arms with the dancers.

'There has not been a day like it,' the curé sighed, repeating what was on all lips. 'Did you invite the merchant Monsieur Tilly? I saw him talking to Raoul on my way here.'

'Perhaps that is why Raoul did not come with the other villagers,' murmured Hermione. 'But no, I did not invite Monsieur Tilly.'

'And indeed, it is not he who is your latecomer,' observed Father Grégoire. Hermione glanced towards the Keep and, on seeing the rider was Jacques Maurellet, felt her heart leap with pleasure. She watched as he jumped down from his horse and walked purposefully towards Lucette and Georges, who were leading the line of dancers.

The exchange of words between them was brief, for, seizing hold of the master-shipwright, the couple led him into the dance. For some time, Hermione had been longing to join in, and now, despite all the reasons why she shouldn't, her feet could no longer be contained.

'Yes, off you go, my child,' the curé encouraged with a benevolent smile. With light steps, Hermione ran forward and, slipping in between Jacques Maurellet and the next dancer, she took up the step. Jacques glanced towards her with a smile as they went their separate ways with other partners, until, some dances later, breathless and elated, together they broke away.

'You did not reply to my invitation,' she chided. 'I did not think you would come.'

'Nor I ... nor should I have,' he riposted, his blue eyes sparkling with laughter. He took up a pitcher of water and drank it dry.

'Thank you for honouring their day,' she said, feeling such a surge of happiness within. 'Try Marie's pastries,' she urged, as a girl from the village approached with a platter. As if he were a child, she watched with concern as he ate. Giving her a sideways look, Jacques laughed.

'I should ask you about the forest.'

'I should ask you about the model.' Simultaneously, their hands reached out, and they ran to re-join the dancers. Then, after a time, as the pace quickened, Hermione broke free again, dragging him with her.

'Not possible in this dress,' she gasped. 'And I suppose my dancing this way is improper.'

'You are mistress here ... and this is not Versailles. Shall we walk a little?' Hermione nodded and led him into the house and out onto the quiet of the terrace.

'You have not begun your garden,' he commented, looking down upon the marshy ground.

'I spent hours in the winter looking at designs for parterres in Olivier de Serres's tome, dreaming of a cascade of water. But other things were more pressing. You will see much improvement in the High Forest ...

324

would you like to ride there now?' At such impetuosity, Jacques laughed with amusement. He caught up her hand to impart a playful kiss. As his lips touched against her skin they lingered, and the expression in his dark blue eyes became intent and earnest.

'I would like nothing more,' he murmured. Then abruptly, breaking the intensity of the moment as if something disagreeable had entered his mind, he released her hand. 'We have but weeks left before we have to hand over the frigate. You do not know how we were deceived. A second model had to be constructed, and it has been at a high cost. Grandfather is spent. But let me not spoil the day. Come and see the frigate before it starts on its journey to Versailles. I think, Madame Du Chesne,' he added, his eyes filled with laughter, 'there is about it something that will please you.'

Claude Tilly had hung around in a state of furious impatience for hours. He could hear the sound of music coming from the château, and his patience was near to snapping. What was keeping the constable and his men? Had that wretched magistrate failed to do his duty? As if to make something happen, for the fourth time that day he rode off in the direction they would come. Then, just as before, in frustration and impatience he wheeled his horse about and rode back towards the iron gates which led into the grounds of the château. At least on this occasion there was something to divert him, for coming towards him was a rider whom, as he drew nearer, he identified as Jacques Maurellet. They were not on good terms. Had he not Maurellet to thank for having to account for his part in the auction of the Du Chesne timber? Nevertheless, he positioned his horse to block the way through the gate.

'Good day, Monsieur Maurellet. You attended the wedding of servants?'

'It was my privilege,' retorted Jacques coldly at Tilly's sneering tone. 'What brings you here?'

'Ah, trouble with my horse earlier. Being so placed by the church,

I saw the bride ... very pretty. As for Madame Du Chesne ... such magnificence ... a dress surely meant for the famous Hall of Mirrors rather than some rustic celebration with peasants.' Jacques ignored the snigger as he speculated why the timber merchant was loitering in the vicinity.

'Do you intend to call upon Madame Du Chesne?'

'Ah no, I am not welcome as you are, monsieur. But spotting you on my way home, I wanted to offer you my commiserations.'

Jacques's stare was challenging. Claude Tilly floundered a little, but could not resist the jibe.

'I did hear that you and Maître Henri got the building of the King's model quite wrong. Quite a catastrophe, they say. What a tragedy ... so much work. Some say the Maurellet reputation is damaged forever.'

'If there was any mistake, it was not of our making!' snapped back Jacques. 'And our reputation remains unblemished!' He glared across at Claude Tilly and silently dared him to pursue the conversation.

'I meant no harm,' faltered Tilly. 'On a happier note, Monsieur Maurellet, was the beautiful châteleine still wearing that splendid blue dress when you departed the château?'

Still bridling from the merchant's malicious thrust, and knowing if he stayed longer he would not be able to restrain himself, without answering Jacques spurred his horse on.

So that was how they were putting it about at Rochefort: the Maurellet yard had blundered! It would suit Joubert at the arsenal to make it seem so. Such men as Tilly would eagerly keep the lie alive in order to discredit him. Jacques brimmed over with indignation. He should have knocked the insolent fellow from his saddle. What was he doing there hanging about? After swindling Hermione, he would not be welcome, and indeed, the man himself had admitted that. He was obviously up to some mischief. As great clods of turf flew out from beneath his horse's hooves, Jacques deliberated on what had passed between him and the merchant. Beginning to feel more and more uneasy, he slowed the pace of the stallion until he came to a complete halt. Should he return? But return for what? He shook his head and set off again for home. What was it Tilly had been saying about Hermione's dress ... was she still wearing it? What an extraordinary thing to ask. There was something not quite right. Once again, Jacques reined in, and this time he wheeled his horse's head round and at a gallop returned the way he had come. Just thirty or so yards away from the turn to Du Chesne, he spotted Claude Tilly riding away towards Saintes. With an exclamation of vexation for delaying his return to the shipyard for no apparent reason, he was about to ride off when he noticed a cloud of dust heading in the direction of the timber merchant. Through narrowed eyes, Jacques gradually identified a constable of the law with his men. Clearly Claude Tilly had been waiting for them, for he raised his arm towards them in greeting. Lest he should be seen, Jacques made for cover on the Du Chesne side of the road. He watched as the parties met, and after words between Tilly and the official, the timber merchant pointed towards the gates of the château. Then, to Jacques' surprise, Tilly rode off in the direction of Saintes. The constable, who had dismounted to relieve himself at the side of the road, remounted and moved slowly towards the château's large rusty gates. Whilst Jacques was still unable to fathom what it was all about, instinct warned him some kind of trouble was heading Hermione's way, so he set off at a fast pace by way of the woods back to Du Chesne. Although he would be well ahead of the official and his men, there would still only be minutes to warn her ... warn her about what?

Jacques's approach through the keep into the courtyard of Du Chesne was so reckless, it brought the coachman Guillaume running towards him.

'There are police coming ... your mistress ... where is she?'

'In the hall,' shouted back Guillaume, responding to the urgent tone. 'What do they want, Monsieur Maurellet?' Jacques did not stay to answer but raced across the courtyard towards the open door leading into the château. To his relief Hermione was there, her feet resting on a footstool and her eyes closed.

'Oh, I've been discovered.' She laughed, her expression one of surprised delight as his footsteps disturbed her.

'There is no time to waste,' he urged. 'A constable will be here any moment.'

'What for?'

'I'm not sure,' he said. 'It has something to do with Claude Tilly, for he directed them here.' He looked at her, his mind racing. 'Could it have something to do with your dress? He seemed unduly interested in it.'

Hermione stared back at Jacques, her face reddening with embarrassment and dismay.

'It could be the lace,' she said with a sweep of her hand. 'It's Venetian point ... forbidden.'

Jacques took in the profusion of decoration and sucked in his breath with understanding. Without comment, he reached for his dagger and with a few deft strokes cut away the trimming on the edging of both sleeves. Then, as her lips opened in protest, he put a hand to the front of her bodice and ripped it clear away. 'Is that all?' he asked, as he ripped away the skirt's front panel and gathered up the lace from the floor.

'Yes,' she gasped, shielding her breasts with her hands.

'I'll take it to the fire!'

Hermione nodded, her head reeling. 'Wait! There is Lucette. There is a little on the front of her cap ... she is dancing.'

Many of the villagers were merry with drink, which was just as well, for they were unaware of the arrival of the police. The noise and laughter allowed Jacques to approach the fire beneath the spit unnoticed. He cast his eyes over the dancers and saw that Hermione's maid was at the furthest end of the colourful chain. The pattern the men and women were stepping, he saw, would bring the bride and groom out right in front of the constable. The dancers were still unaware of the newcomers and were raising their arms to form a tunnel. Jacques slipped forward

328

and, bending low, pushed between two dancers. Then he moved forward under the archway of arms in time to confront Lucette and Georges. Their happy faces expressed astonishment at seeing him and then outrage as he snatched away Lucette's cap.

'Police ... keep quiet!' he hissed.

With the flimsy cap stuffed into his doublet, he was away and sauntering towards the fire. Just in time, for the drum and pipes had stopped and the dancers were breaking apart to see what was happening. Concealed by the flames, Jacques slid out the cap and threw it onto the fire just before Georges reached his side. The woodsman's face was dark with anger.

'Monsieur, you ... you had no right,' he stammered, his eyes narrowed, black with threat. Behind him appeared Lucette, her eyes flooding tears.

'My dear husband, hush,' she whispered, as the constable approached.

'I won't see my wife treated so,' replied George with vigour, standing his ground.

'Monsieur,' said the constable, directing his remark to Jacques, 'where is the châteleine?'

'Madame Du Chesne is within ... ah, I am mistaken,' replied Jacques, as Hermione stepped out of the house. 'Madame Du Chesne, you have unexpected guests.' At Jacques's tone, edged with the slightest mockery, Hermione came forward, looking calm in a green silk gown.

'Madame Du Chesne,' said the constable in a severe but respectful voice, 'it has come to the magistrate's attention that you have broken the law. That you have worn this day foreign lace ... *point de Venise.*'

'But surely, it is forbidden?' replied Hermione, looking as shocked as she could. The constable, who was accustomed to women's guile, was not to be deterred. All the while, his eyes had been roving over the dress of the châteleine, but he discovered not a scrap of lace. He turned to Georges, who was standing near by.

'I am told you are the bridegroom. Is this the dress that Madame Du

Chesne wore to church?' Jacques Maurellet noticed Lucette slip behind the young man, who suddenly gave a start as if nipped by an insect.

'It looks like it,' he stumbled.

'Looks like it … you are not certain?' exclaimed the official, his expression alive with interest.

'Well, they all look the same to me,' replied the young man, his face filled with misery.

'What he means is he only looks at me,' chirped Lucette, linking her arm through that of her husband. 'I helped lace the mistress into this dress myself.'

'Our witness, who was outside the church, said the dress was blue.'

'Perhaps he does not know his blue from his green.'

'Monsieur,' intervened Hermione in a soothing voice, for she could see the constable was becoming irritable as laughter broke the tension that had held everyone silent. 'Would it set your mind at ease if my maid took you and your men to make an examination of my dresses?' With a nod towards two of the policemen to follow Lucette, the official assumed an icy air of dignity. As if to reassert his authority, he moved around the villagers with the remaining policemen. Hermione tensed as he interrogated a woman who had never shown any sign of acceptance towards her.

'You will find yourself in prison if you lie,' threatened the official to the woman. 'Is that the dress Madame Du Chesne wore at the wedding?' Hermione held her breath, fearing the worst.

'I watched Madame go and come back in it,' replied the woman in a sullen voice. One after the other the answer was the same. Such a show of loyalty brought tears to Hermione's eyes.

'Even if you were the Devil, they would not give you up to officials from Saintes!' Jacques's teasing whisper made Hermione smile.

'And there was I believing they had begun to love me.'

'It would not be hard,' he replied. She glanced up, anticipating mockery in the blue eyes, but they were serious.

The return of Lucette with two of the policemen reclaimed everyone's attention. Lucette, having been the centre of attention for the better part of the day, flushed with wine and happiness, was all smiles and importance as she faced the constable.

'Well, Your Honour,' she said in her high-pitched voice, 'your men interrogated all my mistress's dresses and each one of them only owned up to wearing ribbons.' Hermione's cheeks dimpled as she fought to keep back laughter. The constable glared at Lucette and all about him.

'I have been wasting my time riding out here,' he snapped, making a stiff bow to Hermione. 'We have sadly been misinformed.'

As the constable and his men mounted up and departed, Hermione turned to Jacques.

'Thank you. I am much in your debt. Why does Claude Tilly make so much trouble for me?'

'Perhaps because you have what he wants. Come walk with me a little down the drive, for I must get back.' They walked across the courtyard to where Jacques had abandoned his horse. With his hand on its bridle, they crossed the bridge towards the drive leading to the road.

'Do you think he will stop?'

'Tilly? I doubt it. I think there is a streak of madness in the man. Some people thrive on destroying beautiful things. I will warn him off if you wish?'

Hermione felt hesitant; it had been a very long day, and suddenly she felt utterly tired. She looked to him for an answer. 'What would be best?'

At her sudden vulnerability, Jacques gave a little smile. The moment he had anticipated for so long had arrived. Before her lips could frame another word, his own closed on them.

'I have wanted to do that for a long time,' he murmured. Overwhelmed by her feelings, Hermione reached up and touched his cheek. He made fast her hand and kissed its palm. 'Come to see a carving I have done for the frigate. Come tomorrow.' Again their lips met and the kiss was long and deep, becoming so intense Hermione drew away.

'I do not want to leave you,' he murmured, crushing her to him and kissing her neck.

'It will be dark soon … you must start back.' Hermione broke away and walked towards his horse, which had wandered a few paces off. Taking hold of its bridle, she led it back.

'Till tomorrow … God speed,' she said as Jacques swung up onto the saddle. Their hands touched briefly, then he was away.

Hermione remained still, vaguely aware of a few early bats wheeling above her head and the sound of approaching laughter and chatter as the villagers headed back to their homes. Not wishing to meet anyone, she slipped into the trees. Her heart sang and raced and, oblivious of the dangers of darkness, she whirled around as in a dance. Then, lifting her skirts as if she were a child, she ran back to the château, feeling she would burst with happiness!

CHAPTER 20

here had been but little sleep for Claude Tilly. Throughout the entire night, his mind had been in a constant whirl, conjuring up fantastic images of Hermione Du Chesne being forced to hand over her dress. It was a great pity that he had not been able to witness her come-down, but it was wiser for people not to know his part in the affair. The real moment of triumph would come when she was brought to court to answer for her impudence. In the morning he rose early and dressed with exceptional care.

'Is it a special day for you, husband?' enquired Angélique Tilly, as he accepted his hat from a servant in the hall.

'It is indeed, madame! You might call it a day of reckoning. Make sure there is a plump bird in the pot, for I shall have quite an appetite!'

Angélique Tilly's curls bobbed as she nodded her head and dropped a little deferential curtsy, but though her expression was one of eagerness to please, her mind was in a whirl as she tried to grasp what might be the cause of his good humour. At least he was making time for her, for latterly it seemed he was always riding out early, and she very well knew where. From casual talk betwixt the stable lads out in the yard she had overheard it said he rode out to the village of Du Chesne. A thrill of jealousy passed through her as she thought of the beautiful châtelaine who had visited them at their new house at Rochefort. Dear Claude had influence. As a contractor for the Marine, he met many important people. Such men as her husband were attractive to women like Madame Du Chesne. Was she luring Claude to visit her?

Angélique glanced with anxiety at her reflection in the mirror which her husband had had delivered from Paris. It was important not to neglect her appearance. It was not only death that could carry off a husband! She had seen him taking a package into his bureau. Was it a gift the lady from Paris had given to him? Or was it indeed something which he had bought for the chatelaine? With a sense of indignation, her heavy breasts heaving with emotion, Angélique hurried along to her husband's bureau. As was usual, the room was in perfect order, and despite her excited state, she cautioned herself to take care not to disturb anything by a hair's breadth. Instinct told her to go straight to the carved wooden chest, and on raising up its lid she saw she was right, for on top of everything was the paper package. With utmost care, Angélique lifted it out and set it on the polished desk. The twine and the paper itself were coarse, which was puzzling, but as she loosened and slipped both away she gave a gasp of pleasure, for inside was one of the most beautiful collars she had ever seen. True, it was somewhat discoloured with age, but such was the workmanship that the edges of the floral motifs appeared to stand up. Angélique's experienced eye detected that this emphasis had been achieved by a padded stitch around the edges. It was the finest example of *Gros Pointe de Venise*.

'Oh, husband,' murmured Angélique, holding the exquisite lace up before her. 'This is certainly for a wife. How could I doubt you?'

It was not until past noon that Claude Tilly was able to gain admittance to the magistrate. His earlier euphoria was somewhat diminished, for the clerk's list for that day's proceedings had not had on it the name of Hermione Du Chesne.

'Ah, it is you, Tilly,' exclaimed the official brusquely when the timber contractor was ushered into his room. 'I wanted to see you.'

'And I you, Your Honour, for I had anticipated Madame Du Chesne would appear before you today.'

'Then you will be disappointed,' snapped the magistrate, 'just as the constable and his men were disappointed after making a futile journey into the countryside.'

'I don't understand.'

'They found *nothing* at Du Chesne ... not a scrap of illicit lace.'

Tilly's jaw dropped open in dismay.

'The dress the châteleine was wearing had no *point de Venise* on it. My men were sent out on a fruitless mission because of you.'

'But I saw it with my own eyes,' blustered Tilly. 'Other people saw it ... she must have changed.'

'Monsieur, I have had a busy morning. Through sickness at home, I am condemned to cold victuals. Even so, you are keeping me from them! The constable examined Madame Du Chesne's dresses. Furthermore, none amongst the villagers had seen the dress imagined by you. Let that be the end of the affair!'

Tilly's hand went out in a gesture of restraint as the magistrate rose from his seat. His small green eyes expressed his inner desperation and then they glinted as he thought of the solution.

'Your Honour, I have the proof! I have the proof at home. Allow me to bring it to you. No ... no, better still, come home with me for a good lunch. My wife Angélique is preparing *poule au pot* ... you will find she is a wonderful cook. And before we sit down to dine, I shall hand over the evidence which will condemn Madame Du Chesne.'

The magistrate viewed the odious little man before him with some uncertainty. Then the plump image of Angélique Tilly slid into his mind. Though he had never had the occasion to speak to the lady, she had always looked so fragrant. Those ample breasts, like twin mounds of proving dough awaiting the warmth of a man's touch! She looked like a woman who ate too much, who would be generous with her butter and cream ... generous in all things!

'Very well. I just have one small matter to complete with my clerk and I will join you, monsieur.'

Tilly inclined his head and withdrew from the chamber. Outside in the corridor he took a couple of *sous* from his purse and approached an errand boy lounging against the wall in the front entrance. 'You know my house … run there and tell Madame Tilly a most important guest will be joining our table. Everything must be perfection.'

On receipt of her husband's message, Angélique went into a spin. She pinched her cheeks for pinkness and flew up to her girls to urge them to change into their best dresses. Leaving the servants to hasten back and forth to see all was correct in the dining room, she rushed away to ease herself into her newest gown. To which she added her very own costly embellishment.

Claude Tilly ushered the magistrate into his bureau and directed him to a chair. With a sense of immense satisfaction, the merchant went towards the oak chest. All had turned out better than he could have envisaged. Having a magistrate break bread in his house, why, it would ease him into legal circles. For one bitter moment of disappointment earlier he had thought the Parisienne had wriggled free, but he still had her and inwardly he exulted. With a malicious chuckle he raised the wooden lid and reached for the package given to him by Raoul. It was not there! Tilly stood nonplussed, looking down into the chest. Behind him, the magistrate clicked his teeth with impatience. With a rising feeling of panic, Claude Tilly slammed down the wooden lid and rushed towards his cupboard. He pulled open the two doors … no package!

'Come, come!' snapped the magistrate with some irritation.

'I cannot understand it, Your Honour,' wailed Tilly, the expression on his face one of utter dismay. 'My good wife will perhaps enlighten us as to its whereabouts … so let us go to her without delay.'

With her two daughters on either side of her, Angélique waited within the dining room for her husband and his important guest.

Finally, the heavy oak door swung open. As though the magistrate were the King himself, Angélique made a low curtsy. Then she advanced, her lips slightly parted in a smile, but not so much as to reveal her broken tooth. Once more, in order that the full beauty of her gown should be seen, she dipped slightly from the knee and moved her right hand with elegance to draw attention to the collar, which she had patiently attached in place. Like that of a fish on a slab, Claude Tilly's jaw opened wide. His green eyes glazed over with shock.

'Aha! What have we here?' murmured the magistrate as his glance shifted from the plump hand and arm to the lace framing the ample breasts. The blood drained from the timber contractor's face. He turned to the man beside him with a sickly smile, clinging to the hope that his wife's stupidity had not been discovered.

'As you say, Monsieur Tilly,' purred the magistrate, hunger pangs screaming for retribution, 'I must not overlook my reponsibility under the King's law. Were it only a matter between us, but your servants ... standards must be set ... examples must be made! Even so, let it not spoil a good meal,' he added, accepting with alacrity the seat offered to him by his bewildered hostess. Claude Tilly turned murderous eyes on the buxom figure of his wife. His hand was impatient for the moment when he would be left alone with her.

*** *** ***

In other circumstances, the visit of the constable and his men might have cast a shadow over Lucette's day, but long afterwards everyone was still caught up with laughter, especially Lucette as she helped Hermione into her riding habit.

'Oh, I thought I'd choke at the expression on that constable's face ... sour as milk when he left. And I was so put out when Monsieur Maurellet snatched away my wedding bonnet and threw it on the fire.'

'It was a pity to take away your keepsake.'

'I have Georges,' responded Lucette, with a flick of her narrow hips as she went away to get Hermione's hat. 'I'll warrant that timber merchant put them up to it,' she went on, as she re-entered the room. 'Everyone saw him hanging about. He betrayed you, just as that bitch Agnès did. At least she had cause, with the old parents to see to, and no doubt with the Place de Grève promised to her by the police. He just wants to become cock of the farmyard here. He'll not give up till he has you out of here, madame.'

'Well, he won't,' replied Hermione, securing her hat with a pin. She was bubbling with happiness, and nothing else mattered.

'I would be obliged, madame, when you are at the shipyard, if you would thank Monsieur Maurellet for saving me from trouble.'

Hermione looked at the arch expression on Lucette's face enquiringly. 'What leads you to suppose I shall be at the Maurellet shipyard? As it happens, that is where I am riding,' she added casually, ignoring Lucette's sly little smile.

Angélique Tilly whimpered as she applied the sliver of raw meat to her cheekbone. It hurt terribly, but it was all her own fault. Claude had every right to be angry. She had got him into trouble, and the sum of money he was having to pay to the court was enormous. There would be no new dresses for the girls or her for a long time. In addition to the crippling fine, he had said it would be bad for business; even worse, it would make them objects of ridicule. His angry tirade had exploded into punishment as it usually did, but on this occasion, as he had punched her about the room, her heart had suddenly lifted with relief, and yes, joy. For the name he was screaming over and over again was that of Hermione Du Chesne. Even as the tears had run down her cheeks, Angélique had laughed inwardly to know he *hated*, not loved, the lady from Paris.

Within the silence of her grandfather's house, Perrette wandered from room to room taking stock of what would be hers when she was married to Jacques. Not that anything was unfamiliar to her, for she had played with her cousins in their house since childhood. Her fingers lingered on the dark polished wood of the cradle which had been carved by Henri. Not only had it been used by Jacques and André when babies, but it had been lent to her mother for herself as well. If she closed her eyes, she knew where each chair was placed in this room, and, in the salon, where Grandfather expected to find his pewter tankard and Jacques his cards. Although Annette still came in to clean and help, she herself had been acting mistress for years, and would continue to be, even if she and Jacques did not marry. Nothing would change, even if it broke her heart not to feel his arms steal around her waist and feel his lips brush her cheek. Her hand reached out again and pushed the wooden rail of the cradle. It swung gently back and forth on its rockers until at last all motion ceased and it was still: empty, and still. Perrette's chest heaved, and a desperate sob escaped from her lips ... never to have his children! How could she make such a choice? She sank down onto her knees, closed her eyes and prayed for the strength to stay firm, to let go of all that was precious, that had been her secret dream since being a little girl.

After a time, feeling her resolve renewed, Perrette rose, her lips pressed into a firm line as she made her way down to the kitchen. She picked up the basket of bread and cheese for Jacques and Henri, who, being so hard-pressed, did not want to lose time in coming up to the house. As she made her way through the orchard, she could not resist lifting her voice up in praise to God. It was such a heady feeling to know that she was communicating directly with him. Oh, why couldn't Jacques understand the power of it, the freedom of being close to God? Perrette smiled with the wonder of it, and she knew she must try even harder. If Jacques would only listen to a minister preaching, there must be a way forward for them. With a smile of determination to get her own way, Perrette opened the orchard gate and stepped out onto the lane. As she did so she heard the clip-clop of a horse, and glancing up the track she saw the horsewoman who had once called before. Perrette stiffened with displeasure. On the day she had pointed out the way into the shipyard, Henri had later explained the visitor was the owner of a large forest. Apparently, Jacques had bought timber from Madame Du Chesne's estate. Setting aside her extraordinary behaviour of visiting a shipyard unescorted, there was something about her which was disagreeable. Like now: she smiled too easily. The bodice of her riding habit was tight, which made it immodest. It was perhaps not her fault her hair had come loose and was hanging in black tangles about her shoulders, but why wasn't she wearing a hat?

'Do you have business here, madame?' asked Perrette, with a cold note of disapproval.

'Forgive my appearance,' Hermione laughed with an apologetic gesture. 'I lost my hat, and in truth, nearly my head! But on such a day, I wanted to see if my horse could outstrip the wind.'

Perrette's heart shrank with misgivings. She experienced a thrill of fear that she had never felt before. She did not want this stranger here … everything about her seemed threatening: her conversation, her full lips, the confident way she sat a horse.

'Are you here on business? Maître Henri and Maître Jacques are occupied on important work and can see no one!'

'Yes, I know.' Hermione nodded. 'I have come to see the model of the frigate before it goes to Versailles. Maître Jacques invited me,' she added, as an expression of surprise and doubt showed on the pretty heart-shaped face looking up at her. 'Forgive my informality … you will be Maître Jacques's cousin Perrette? I am Hermione Du Chesne.'

'Indeed,' Perrette said nodding, feeling such a rush of possessiveness that she could hardly speak. 'If my *fiancé* Jacques has invited you to see the model, madame, then so you must. But it would be a kindness and courtesy not only to Jacques, but to Grandfather, not to distract them when they are about the King's business.'

As the tiny woman's words impacted on Hermione, she stared down at the plainly dressed woman in dismay. She was utterly lost for words and swallowed hard to try to control the rush of emotions which began to overwhelm her. As if she had been winded, happiness was sucked out of her. With an inward surge of triumph, Perrette saw the shocked, distraught expression of pain in Hermione Du Chesne's brown eyes.

'Shall I say you called?'

'No … as you say, it is better not to disturb them. Best not to say I came.' Hermione drew on the reins, unable to put on a false face. Her mind was reeling as the horse wheeled around, and all she wanted was to get away!

The miniature cannons of brass faced outward through their open gun ports. Meanwhile, the complicated business of rigging masts and yardarms was underway. Jacques stood back and contemplated with pride what they had achieved. It was the most magnificent model he had ever seen, which in part was due to its dimensions. It gave a sense of reality which smaller-scale models did not … they were mere toys in comparison. This glorious ship painted in green and yellow looked ready to sail down the river and set off on a voyage manned by tiny folk.

'Has Jean-Baptiste completed the mainsail?' he asked, turning towards his grandfather who was adjusting the hang of the anchor at the cat's head.

'He finished some hour past. Your friend was too shy to come to look at her image.'

'She does not know about it. I wanted it to be a surprise,' said Jacques, his voice edged with disappointment.

'Well, it is too beautiful … figureheads should be jollier, with breasts like melons and pouted lips like plums.' Jacques smiled at Henri's words and walked around to the prow of the ship.

'It's a fine piece of work though I say it myself,' he murmured, running his hand along the curve of the slender neck and shoulders. The expression in his blue eyes was wistful as he stared at the figurehead's face. 'Perhaps she is ill,' he said anxiously. 'Maybe a message was delivered by her coachman to the house.'

'He was wily enough to bring your invitation for the wedding party here … it wouldn't do at the house if she who is your betrothed happened to be there,' remarked his grandfather dryly. Jacques glanced at him and the old man laughed in response. 'You might be fooling yourself, but not me. If Perrette should see the lady return here again, she might think it very strange. I was cross-examined last time. You have a certain reputation, my boy.'

'Those were different times, before I gave my pledge to Perrette.'

'My advice is to steer clear! We have enough trouble with a heretic in the family. Best concentrate your thoughts on those missing fashion pieces and compass timber which should be here weathering for the real thing.'

'The real thing! So, at last you believe we could build a man o' war?'

'I have never doubted our skill! And when our King sets eyes on the graceful lines of this hull, he will realize it is not only those conceited dogs at royal arsenals that can build his ships. There would be risks, of course, if a contract was offered … we'd have to take on more workers, and many a man has been ruined awaiting payment from the royal treasury. But I dare say both your father and your uncle would be cheering you on.'

His disappointment over Hermione part mollified by Henri's words, Jacques picked up his brush and began to apply gold leaf to the carved wooden image of the sun. At some point, he was aware of someone entering the mould loft, and he swung around in happy expectation, as had Henri, who instantly abandoned his ball of twine and stomped over to Perrette with her basket of victuals.

'I'm ready for this, my girl!'

Feeling a sense of guilt after her encounter in the lane, Perrette glanced anxiously towards Jacques. 'Will you not break off awhile, cousin?'

'I'll come to it soon ... thanks,' Jacques added. He smiled with appreciation, hiding his feeling of disappointment and emptiness. To try to make up for what she had done, but more to reassert her rightful position, Perrette walked over to take her place by Jacques's side. Her intention had been not to look at the model until it was entirely completed, but she saw that was not so far off.

'It is magnificent!' she murmured, as she took in the detail along the length of the frigate. 'How your sun will glitter!'

'Let us hope the one in the heavens will favour us on the day,' chortled Henri.

Perrette watched as Jacques transformed a final brown wooden ray to a radiant gold. He gave a sigh of satisfaction, and together they moved back to look at the whole. It was then that Perrette's eyes took in the face of the figurehead. At her gasp of protest, Jacques turned to her in concern, then back to the ship to see what might be amiss.

'I have not yet painted in the name,' he explained, thinking that was the fault she had found. Beneath her neat white cap, Perrette's face had become red with indignation. She turned to Jacques and spat out her words in fury.

'The name no doubt is to be Hermione!' With a gesture as if to push him away, Perrette turned on her heel and rushed away. Jacques shook his head and swore softly at his own stupidity. How could he have been so blind as not to see what offence and hurt the image of another woman would cause? He wondered whether to go after her, then gave a shrug. What was the point when within he was unrepentant? He had captured a wild beauty that expressed the spirit of his ship.

His eyes went back to the carved wooden figure, and they lingered on the face. The lips were slightly parted; he recalled their moist warmth when his own had caressed them beneath the trees of Du Chesne. He longed for more, much more. That she had not come today; should he take that as a sign that the mix between them would be too rich? And the complications of breaking with Perrette at a time when her deluded state of mind threatened to bring disaster on her ... it was not possible! He must somehow subdue the passion that was beginning to rule all his thoughts. As Henri had said a little while ago, he should confine himself to building ships ... here, carving this figurehead, he was in control and would not founder. The corners of Jacques' lips twisted into a bitter smile as his fingers touched against the swell of high breasts, then lifted away from the painted wood. Without pausing to eat anything, he walked purposefully past his grandfather.

'Are you finishing for the day?' the old man asked in astonishment.

'No, I am going to choose a fine length of oak for when I return from Versailles. I shall then begin to carve the full-scale figurehead of the *Hermione*!'

*** *** ***

A thunderstorm and heavy downpour on Hermione's ride back to Du Chesne had been scarce noticed by her. Its effects, however, took her to bed for several days, and when her cold had cleared, she had no will to get up.

'I've never seen you like this before, madame,' observed Lucette, as she collected a tray of untouched food. 'It is very lonely downstairs without you. Even Monsieur Olivier notices your absence.' Hermione could not help but smile at that. 'He says the curé would like to come tonight for chess, but how can it be if you are not there to look after them?'

'They managed when I was in Paris!' retorted Hermione, watching a spider's downward descent from the canopy overhead.

'They never stopped ringing the bell,' declared Lucette, snapping back all the bed-curtains. 'The curé brought a box of sweets for you this morning.'

'He probably wants to eat them himself without his housekeeper knowing.' Hermione sighed, irritated by the light. She pulled the linen cover completely over her head, hating herself for the spiteful thing she had said. All she wanted was to be left alone. How could they understand what it was like to be bewildered, so spellbound in a kiss that all else ceased to exist, to experience feelings of such intensity that even now her heart began to race as she recalled his arms holding her tight? The longing to be with him again; Hermione clasped her hand to her mouth to stifle a sob.

'Won't you get up?' Lucette's voice was gentle, so filled with concern that it nearly released the floodgates holding back Hermione's tears. 'It will all come right in the end, I'm sure.'

Hermione bit on her lip, knowing it couldn't. He had dallied with her like a wench in an inn. For him, that was all it had been, and if there were opportunity, no doubt he would try to seduce her and afterwards go back to his pretty *fiancée*. Why had he never said he was betrothed? A wave of angry humiliation swept over her and with a sudden, violent move she threw back the cover and got out of bed.

'Go and tell Monsieur Olivier he shall play chess. And I shall take my good teacher Olivier de Serres from the shelf, and while I am reading eat the entire box of sweets myself!'

As it turned out, the curé had toothache and the offer of a sweet brought a sad shake of his head.

'Why don't I ask Marie to bring you a clove? One pushed up by the tooth will ease the pain,' suggested Hermione, raising her head from her reading as he uttered a moan.

'This fine Normandy Calvados is helping,' he replied, his podgy hand taking up a black knight.

'I had thought,' continued Hermione, picking up on the Normandy theme, 'that we might use windfalls for cider, but de Serres says here that only the best of cider apples should be used ... I find that surprising, don't you?'

'You would not use rotten grapes for wine,' observed the curé, his concentration fixed on the board.

347

'I suppose not,' reflected Hermione, 'but I thought … '

'Please, Hermione! Silence! How can we concentrate with your constant prattle?' put in Olivier. Hermione pulled a face. On such evenings she wished she had a female companion, though for Olivier that would be even worse. She popped a sugared almond into her mouth and for a time was content to carry on absorbing advice from the *Théâtre D' Agriculture*. Then, in a mischievous mood, she casually addressed herself to the curé.

'Tell me, Father, have you persuaded Olivier to steer his experiments away from the discovery of the Elixir of Life to transmuting lead into gold?' The effect was as anticipated: both men immediately looked towards her and then to each other. The curé looked sheepish, and Olivier was definitely not pleased.

'They are different roads,' said Olivier.

'Quite so,' agreed the priest, his plump features smiling and eager. 'The substance that will prolong health would produce another form of gold. You would become a rich man.'

'It is not for that I am drawn to the journey.'

'Oh, my dear Monsieur Olivier, never once have I doubted your integrity. You cannot guess how happy I was to find I had a neighbour who knew names such as Kenelm, Digby, and Helvetius. I recall in some of my readings that there are those who are convinced the sun is melted gold at the centre of the universe. And as Hermione now reads about apples which are propagated by the seeds within, so others have claimed it is so with gold … a question of finding the seed within the gold.'

'I hold with neither of these theories,' declared Olivier vigorously. 'It is a question of fusion of metals through the three essential elements: mercury, sulphur, and salt. What we have recently set in motion will take months, but at the end we may shake the universe with our achievement.'

'And our obscurity will end!' breathed Father Grégoire, his face ablaze with his inner vision. 'Let us go and see that your fire is glowing under your crucible, Monsieur Olivier.'

With a smile, Hermione watched both men abandon their chess pieces and leave. Then, thinking to go and check on the stallion, she moved into the hall and picked up her cloak. As she came out into the courtyard, the sound of the men's voices floated back to her. She looked up at the moon, and the corners of her mouth puckered into a smile as it put her in mind of the fun of hanging out the lace. How ironic that Claude Tilly, according to the curé, had been ordered to court at Saintes for being in possession of *point de Venise*.

The door between the laboratory and the stables was ajar, and Hermione saw the curé and Olivier were fully occupied looking down at a manuscript. The outhouse, which had formerly been piled high with broken bits of furniture, had been cleared, and the stone walls bore newly erected shelves on which were all kinds of equipment. Set against one wall was the furnace whose fire had been continually fed for the last three weeks. Hermione left the door open to benefit from its glow and the candlelight and walked down to the last stall.

'Goodnight, my royal prince,' she murmured softly. In the near-darkness it was not possible to clearly see the black stallion, but its hooves stirred the straw. As it snuffled, her hand found its smooth warm neck. Behind her, Rouge sprang against her with a bark and nuzzled at her side. 'Are you jealous?' she asked, pulling affectionately at one of his ears.

'Is that you, madame?'

'Yes, Pierre. Monsieur Olivier is with the curé in the laboratory.'

'Then I'll lock up later,' answered the elderly retainer. 'I leave Rouge here at night now. Guillaume said someone tried to get in once, but the horses made such a din the thief must have run away.'

'Then be sure to lock the Keep every night,' urged Hermione in alarm. 'If anyone steals or hurts this royal colt, I dread to think what would happen to us all!'

CHAPTER 21

rom wanting to hide away in bed, Hermione moved to frenzied activity. She told herself everyone had their disappointments; she must learn acceptance and cast him out of her thoughts. Take Guillaume: never once had she heard him complain about losing the sight of his eye. He had learned to live without it. Then there was Father Grégoire; when she had first met him, he had been bitter about being sent to look after the souls of a small village. Yet on meeting Olivier, his manner had changed. Maybe within him ambition was still alive, but something else now held his interest. So must it be for herself! There was a forest, a house, and a garden to bring alive. One day, visitors in their coaches would come to admire everything. Till then, amongst other things, there was the battle against the rabbits to be won. The real protection for saplings against them and grazing deer would be one of those houses of glass which de Serres wrote about, but that, of course, was quite beyond her means. Still, there had been some progress: last year's pruning of the apple trees, and brushing their trunks and boughs with a wash of lime milk to remove moss, had had good effect. According to Marie, it had increased the yield.

Hermione passed into the cool fragrance of the storehouse, where Marie was hard at work.

'We shall have a good supply of cider,' she said, looking at the cider-press which Marie was wiping clean in readiness.

'Our cider was always cloudy.' The old lady nodded. 'Always cloudy, it was.'

'We shall make it clear this year, Marie!' Marie's sunken black eyes gleamed within the stiff cambric shade of her bonnet, but she appeared tired. With a surge of tenderness, Hermione pulled forward a stool and the elderly servant thankfully took a seat. 'You and Lucette have worked hard at preserving, Marie.'

'We did, madame, but that careless maid of yours did not fasten the baskets and the fish had the beans!'

'I did fasten them so!' shouted out Lucette, as she appeared round the door. 'It's likely goblins took them away.'

Hermione raised her hand to forstall the spat which was about to erupt. 'Do you remember, Marie, when we first arrived at Du Chesne, how you and Pierre threw things down on to our heads? Pierre, looked so fierce in his hunting cap. And when I heard Rouge bark, I thought he would rip out our throats. Those buckets of icy water …'

In her usual way, when someone told an amusing story, or a carter passed on exciting news from a neighbouring village, Marie began to nod, her body rocking gently back and forth at every word. Always eager for laughter, Lucette took up the teasing.

'My, that water was cold … soaked me through to the skin,' she contributed, making her teeth chatter as she gave a dramatic shiver. 'I said to madame, "Oh, let's get back to Paris!" Then I looks up, and swoosh, down comes another soaking.' The old servant tittered with delight. 'Icy cold!' shivered Lucette.

'Pierre wanted me to use the night pot!' Marie cackled. 'And I did, too!'

'Sounds ideal for that Devil's spawn Tilly,' put in Lucette, 'and I'll be the first to empty what's in it on to his ugly head. All the mischief that happens about here is of his making, I'll be bound. We should set a trap for him.'

'There are other ways than traps,' spat Marie. The harsh, hissing tone

352

of her voice sent a shiver through Hermione, and she laid a cautionary hand on one of the bony shoulders.

'It is best to hand him over to the police if we catch him making trouble.'

'My way is more certain,' said the old lady, rising from the stool and hobbling away.

'I've always thought it best not to get on the wrong side of her,' whispered Lucette. 'Like Master knows about rocks and things, she knows about herbs. There were always traders calling at La Voisin's villa, not only selling herbs but with frogs and bats, all done up pretty-like for spells.'

'La Voisin is no more,' said Hermione firmly, 'and so must be your memories. Just like my velvet hangings, with their silvery stars and moon, put away for ever.'

***

The collection of the model frigate had taken place. Each of its three sections had been carefully wrapped in wool and canvas, then lifted aboard a wagon and secured against jolting to prevent damage.

'The royal official was well pleased,' grunted Henri. 'And you'll be in Paris, my boy, to receive it.'

'You can count on it, Grandfather,' replied Jacques, pulling boot-liners over his silk stockings to protect them against the chafing of his boots. 'I have given Perrette strict instructions to see that you rest while I am away, to get your strength back. On my return, I am going to take you somewhere special. We shall go to see a section of Riquet's great canal.'

'I'll surely rest for that,' growled the master-shipwright, mopping his brow, for the day was hot, 'but not for some heretic telling me what to do! Her own mother says she will see her no more if she leaves the Church.'

'Poor Perrette,' murmured Jacques, buckling on his sword. 'It is a trial to be torn between the things one loves.'

'I've never known you to be torn by anything. You generally do just what you please and to the Devil with the rest.'

Jacques pulled on his riding gloves. 'Perhaps I now better understand conflict,' he commented with a wry smile.

'You certainly bear its scars from your travels.'

Jacques did not respond. Crossing steel with robbers and tavern brawlers was not what he was thinking of. He shook his head as if he would shake free the image of a face and, with a sigh, put on his hat. His spurs jingled as he advanced to bid Henri adieu. Deep emotion flowed between them as they faced each other, then simultaneously they embraced and held each other close.

The groom had saddled up his horse, and a second one was hitched alongside. It had been his intention to call in to say goodbye to his Aunt Marguerite and Perrette, but his cousin was hovering beside the horses.

'Mother is indisposed and wishes you God speed,' she explained. 'I have brought bread, sausage, and a cheese for your saddlebag. Do you have your court shoes and extra silk stockings? It will be difficult here with Grandfather,' she added. 'He barely speaks to me.'

Jacques gave a shrug of his shoulders. 'It would be easy enough for you to set matters right with him and your mother.' Mounting, he looked down at her and saw that her eyes were glistening with tears.

'It grieves me to make them unhappy, Jacques. But I cannot turn away from the path which leads direct to my Saviour.'

Jacques's expression was grave. 'So you mean to be baptised?'

'Please, come to hear our minister preach when you return! Dear cousin, it is only fair to hear before you condemn. I give you my word not to do anything whilst you are away. You and Grandfather have worked too hard for you to carry worries with you.' Perrette raised herself on tiptoe beside the horse and offered up her lips. Jacques leaned down and brushed her cheek lightly with a kiss.

'I thank you for that promise, Perrette,' he murmured, his mind now concentrated on the journey ahead.

With a mixture of sorrow and pity, Perrette gazed after him as he rode away; he was like a man who could not see. Martin, in comparison, might be plain of face, but when they pondered over the meaning of some biblical passage together, his features would light up with an inner joy whenever she helped to make it clear. Unlike her cousin and her grandfather, Martin treated her as an equal, and that made her feel special, even if he could not excite her in the way a smile from Jacques could.

***

It was Jacques's first visit to Versailles and, along with the other master-shipwrights who had constructed models, he was surprised to find there was special accommodation awaiting him. Indeed, a Master of Lodgings looked after all men of business visiting Versailles. Before the wagons arrived from the various arsenals, they were escorted in small groups to look at the gardens and the Park. Despite all that had been achieved, new excavations and alterations were still very much in progress. A larger orangery than Louis Le Vau's of 1663 was nearing completion, and Jules Hardouin-Mansart's design held all of them enthralled. The octagonal ornamental lake *Piece d'Eau des Suisses* which had been enlarged in 1678 had apparently further alterations planned to round off its extremities. At the centre of all this grand design was Andre Le Notre, whose imagination had been fired years before by his travels to the gardens of Italy. Within each of the intimate *bosquets,* the spectacular handling of water was sheer theatre. Against backdrops of clipped green box it sparkled like jewels, or thrust upwards in foaming white plumes from gilded mouths. No musicians were needed to delight the ear when water cascaded over rocks. The word on all their lips was *pressure.*

'How do they manage the supply of water?' murmured the master-shipwright from Toulon to Jacques. 'Thirty-nine hydraulic sculptures in the Labyrinthe alone! Even with the reservoirs and the pump drawing on the water of *Étang* de *Clagny*.'

'They don't leave the effects on all the time,' put in the court official showing them around. 'After the King passes on his walk, they turn them off. And just before he enters the next *bosquet*, the spigots are turned up and down to give him the full effect.'

'I wonder what will happen to all these ingenuities when the underground pipes rot away?' The master-shipwright chuckled with a wink to Jacques.

'There isn't wood to rot,' commented the official with a lofty expression, 'because the pipes are made of iron. John Wilkinson from England has set up a foundry on the Loire to turn them out. Feeding the fifty fountains requires twenty-two miles of pipes.'

'It is hard to take in,' exclaimed Jacques. 'It makes possible channelling water for miles without it leaking away. The whole of France will want them.'

Lost in their own reflections, the two men followed their guide towards the Grand Canal until a sculpture further along the alley on his right seized Jacques's interest. 'I'll catch up,' he assured the rest of their party as he broke away. Closing on the sculpture, he found to his delight it was indeed Pierre Puget's Milon de Crotone. In Toulon it had been the hands of the great master at work which had absorbed Jacques. Now the completed work set against the dark green backdrop of trimmed box seemed to have arrived from another land. Jacques shook his head in admiration as he took in the ferocity of the lion's attack, its claws sunk deep into the man's right thigh as its teeth savaged his wrist and hand, and the sheer agony depicted on the man's face as he sought to pull free the fingers of his left hand caught in the cleft of a tree trunk.

'Monsieur!' Monsieur!'

With reluctance, Jacques turned away from the sculpture as the agitated royal guide rushed towards him. As if some buzzing insect was at his side, Jacques closed his ears to the incessant scolding while he retraced his steps to catch up with the other shipwrights. Despite Puget's misgivings about being out of favour at Court, his piece was here.

'What drew you away?' asked the master-shipwright from Toulon, his expression filled with curiosity as Jacques fell back into step beside him.

'You should have come with me!' Jacques grinned. 'It was Pierre Puget's sculpture, which I saw him working on at Toulon. Tell me, why is such a great artist no longer in charge of decorative work at the shipyard?'

'I don't really know. Some say he could be very demanding. He has gone back to his home in Marseilles now. Of course, when Fouquet was in power, Puget chose to take on his commissions for Vau-le-Vicomte. After Fouquet's disgrace it was Colbert who became all-powerful ... a case of choosing the wrong patron.'

When they reached the head of the Grand Canal, and their guide was directing attention to a building which lodged two gondoliers who operated the four gondolas presented to the King by the Republic of Venice, Jacques began devising his own plan of action. No doubt royal servants would be directed to place the model ships along the water's edge, but he wanted to show the frigate off to its best possible advantage. Leaving the guide to answer the seemingly never-ending questions, he walked about, taking into consideration the waterway's length of two thirds of a mile. 'You look like an admiral planning where to anchor his fleet,' the master-shipwright from Toulon grinned, who had also broken away from the group.

'Something like that,' returned Jacques. 'There is a lot riding on it. If private contracts flow from this, it could be my family's first man of war.'

'We certainly need more of those. Our galleys and merchantmen trading with the Levant are continually being attacked by Barbary pirates. Will we see the King close up, do you think, Jacques?'

'More likely from a distance. It's the mighty Colbert I am hoping to see.'

Two weeks had passed when two wagons arrived from Brest and Le Havre. Two days later came one from Toulon, then his own, together with those from Rochefort. Like the other master-shipwrights, Jacques supervised the unloading. One swift inspection, as he parted the inner wool covers under their covering of canvas, reassured him that no harm had come to any of the gilded decorative work. It was late in the day, so, he left things as they were in readiness to reunite the three parts on the following day. That night, as they dined together, there was an excited camaraderie amongst the men, though Jacques purposely avoided Maître Joubert. As the wine flowed, the conversation touched upon the new schools of hydrography and the new opportunities in the Marine.

'My young brother was accepted as a cadet,' said Jacques in an aside to the man sitting alongside him at the trestle table. 'It surely will strengthen the Marine, taking in boys for their merit, rather than their family name.'

'Yes, you couldn't hope to become an officer in my day.' The man nodded, biting into a leg of chicken. 'There's more could be done to help us freshwater men, though the dredging of rivers has greatly improved things, as the dredging of harbours has done for seafarers.'

'Will it last?'

'Not with the army coming back from the Rhine and Holland. The King and his ministers will only busy themselves with thoughts of another campaign to send them on.'

'Meanwhile, they'll be rampaging over the countryside.'

'Then our visit here is timely lads, for if the King likes what he sees, we'll all have work to do before the army commandeers the royal coffers.'

'Let us drink to that!'

On the morrow, as they all marched down to the Grand Canal, the atmosphere was quiet and restrained. Certainly, the merry-making of the previous night had much to do with it, but no doubt, reflected Jacques, each man was running over the various technicalities of reassembling his model. The task was, of course, impossible to handle alone, but a good number of palace servants had been provided to lift up each of the heavy parts. For some moments, Jacques studied the sky and considered the weather conditions; there was a steady breeze. What he intended to do was against instructions, but as far as he was concerned, it was all or nothing. So, as soon as the three parts of the model had been eased into position, he walked around to the yardarm of the *Hermione* and prepared to unfurl the mainsail. The officious, braying tone of Joubert calling out to him made him pause.

'Monsieur Maurellet, what are you about?'

Jacques's black brows lifted in enquiry as the master-shipwright came hurrying towards him. 'As you can see, I am about to unfurl the mainsail,' he answered in a quiet voice.

'There is no need. Your frigate is to be put on to the water with sails furled.'

Jacques's gaze slid past Joubert to where the Royal Arsenal's model was already floating on the water with a wide spread of canvas.

'How so?'

'Because only one model is to fully display the rigging, and I have already arranged for that.'

'Then you must arrange again,' returned Jacques, going back to the task in hand, 'for it does not suit my purpose.'

'Your purpose!' gasped the master-shipwright, puffing out his cheeks in outraged surprise.

'As I understand it, Maître Joubert, we are here to provide interest for His Majesty. Is it not, therefore, appropriate to demonstrate the sailing qualities of our ships?'

'It is not necessary! Your model will conform to the rest. It will remain stationary in line with sails furled, or, I shall order it to be lifted out of the water.'

Jacques's eyes darkened with anger. 'Through your sly incompetence and spite, my grandfather was forced to work all the hours of the clock. This little ship shall fly down the canal towards our sovereign king and none shall try to stop it or they will go head first into the water!'

'Is that so, Monsieur Maurellet?'

Jacques swung about. It was the Admiral Duquesne himself who had spoken.

'It seems your style to make rash promises,' said the officer, with an amused glint in his eyes. 'So l shall expect no less than to see your frigate fly. But, be assured, if it so much as scratches another model, it will be you who will flounder in the Grand Canal, and your shipyard will continue building fishing boats.'

For answer, Jacques bowed low, his heart racing within his chest. He turned back to the *Hermione* and continued to unfurl, set sail, and secure. By mid-afternoon, the miniature fleet was bobbing up and down on the blue water. Amongst others awaiting the royal party was a ship of the First Rate with its gunports open as if waiting for the signal to fire. A Second Rate, painted black above the waterline, had its gunports closed, and on its quarterdeck had been placed the figures of officers perfectly attired in red jackets, white breeches, and large black hats. It was a nice touch, which Jacques wished he had thought of. No matter, however: with its exquisite carving of dolphins and garlands of roses, the *Hermione* held its own. His inner satisfaction brought a sigh to his lips. He would have so liked Hermione to see her image, here, at the very heart of the kingdom. God willing, if their frigate pleased, in a few years she would see a full-scale figurehead on a ship beating out to sea.

In anticipation of the royal party's arrival, Jacques went up to one of the liveried lackeys who had demonstrated some feel for what he was doing.

'Help me haul my model further down the canal. The Admiral Duquesne knows what I am about,' he added reassuringly. Whether the other master-shipwrights were taking notice, Jacques did not care. A swift glance over his shoulder told him most, including Joubert, were still fussing over their own small craft. As soon as he reached the point he was aiming for, he produced a spindle of thread. It was black and fine, barely to be seen with the eye, yet incredibly strong. The end of this he quickly fastened to the frigate's prow.

'Remember,' he said to the palace servant, 'after the King arrives, when you see me raise my left hand, let go your line and push the stern as hard as you can towards the middle of the water ... the wind will do the rest.'

'What if the direction of the wind changes, monsieur?'

'Then it will be the worse for me!' answered Jacques. With a wry smile, he started to pay out the twine.

On his return to the assembled master-shipwrights, Jacques positioned himself a little apart and at a point which he hoped would not lead to a collision. He was caught between excitement and impatience to have his part done. There was not long to wait before heightened tension suddenly changed into a flurry of excited expectation. Jacques glanced to his left and saw the imposing figure of Louis XIV. Everything about the regal figure was perfection. Beneath the brim of his large plumed hat, those compelling dark eyes would also expect perfection in others. Until this moment, he had not been nervous, but now Jacques's mouth was suddenly dry. If only there had been an opportunity to try out the manoeuvre on the Charente!

Amongst those accompanying the King was Duquesne, and near to him the man whom Jacques most admired: Colbert, Minister of Finance, Minister of Forests and Waterways. The Chevalier, who was in charge of proceedings, first led the King to the model of a First Rate, and Admiral Duquesne drew his sovereign's attention to the various features of the ship. At no point did they concern themselves with the master-shipwright who had constructed it and who, along with everyone else, stood apart from the water's edge. After the Brest offering, the group of courtiers advanced slowly to look at a galley which had been made at Toulon. Once again, the admiral gestured here and there and answered questions put to him by the King and Colbert. The royal party moved at a leisurely pace, so it would be some time before they reached Jacques. His stomach knotted with tension, and he was relieved that at least Duquesne knew what his intentions were. Finally, the King was near enough for Jacques to hear his voice asking questions as he pointed at things with his silver-topped cane. In two or three minutes they would be approaching him in the expectation of inspecting a frigate. Jacques looked anxiously down the shimmering water and, taking a deep breath, raised his left hand.

'Your majesty, we now come to a frigate constructed by a private shipyard.'

'If you recall, sire,' interposed the Minister of Forests and Waterways, 'your policy at Council was to increase the output of the new fleet by offering contracts to suitable yards.'

'I remember clearly, Monsieur Colbert. I always applaud entrepreneurs; their efforts in all spheres strengthen my kingdom. But I see no model here.'

Jacques heard Duquesne clear his throat.

'Our master-shipwright trusts Your Majesty will appreciate the sight of a model under sail.'

With a movement of his wrist, the admiral indicated Jacques, then motioned out along the Canal where could be seen the white sails of the *Hermione*. With a frown of irritation, Jacques realized the frigate was too centrally placed, as the miniature fleet at this end had slightly drifted, for which he should have made an allowance. Nevertheless, the frigate looked splendid: her sails were puffed out as they held the stiff breeze, and she was flying towards him like a swallow. A swift glance towards the royal party showed they were as enraptured as he himself. Steadily, Jacques wound in the line, which was not meant to aid the model's advance but only hopefully to pull it clear of trouble if necessary. She was going at such a rate that he could not help but gasp out loud with delight. Then, as if the Devil had heard, what he most dreaded happened. The breeze faded and the model slowed as the sails went limp; soon it would stop.

'So much for *theatricality*!'

The words were uttered in the pretence of a whisper, but Joubert's caustic comment was delivered for all to hear. Jacques scowled and tugged on the line as the King began to walk on. Then, as Jacques's hair lifted from his forehead, the pennant on the frigate stirred as the breeze revived. Louis XIV paused, took up an elegant attitude, and looked again towards the *Hermione*. Once more, the effect of the little ship was magical, as sunlight played on her yellow and dark green paintwork and set ablaze the gilded carvings. But her rate now, Jacques realized, was too fast. The frigate's line was bringing her directly towards the black and brown varnished ship from the Royal Arsenal at Brest. Smothering an oath, Jacques tugged on the line to try to modify the frigate's angle, but he realized it was hopeless. Nearby murmurs of concern broke out, yet it seemed no one dared to step forth from where they had been positioned. With rapid movements of his wrist, Jacques continued taking in the line while moving further to the right to lessen the impact between the two vessels. Suddenly, *Hermione's* sails flattened and drooped as again the breeze died away. Still she came on course, but slowing all the time, and with his pull on the line it was not her prow which struck the other ship, but her stern. There was a bang, followed by cries of outrage, but hardly hearing them, Jacques exerted all his strength to stop the little ship barely a foot away from the King.

'A fearsome attack, Admiral Duquesne!' Louis chuckled. 'Though methinks, had the Second Rate had her gunports open, your frigate would have been blown out of the water. That is, of course, had not all those little officers toppled over when she was struck!'

'A demonstration of what is in store for the English Navy, Sire.'

Jacques experienced a thrill of relief and wished with all his heart that Henri was present to hear the praise which was being lavished upon the quality of his carving. The King raised his silver-topped cane, and as he pointed to the bowsprit, he murmured something to Duquesne. The Admiral shook his head and looked towards Jacques.

'Monsieur Maurellet, please to step forward!'

As Jacques straightened from his deep bow, he found the imperious dark eyes of Louis XIV fixed upon him, sharp with curiosity. Once again, the King raised his cane and pointed at the figurehead on the *Hermione*.

'A face of some fascination ... perhaps a member of your family, monsieur?'

There was no denying the glint in the royal eyes, which took Jacques more off-balance than the question itself. He hesitated before answering, choosing his words as thoughts raced through his mind. This man had the power to forbid the sale of jonquils throughout France, to meet the needs of a royal fête; the power to send a *lettre de cachet*, to mobilize an army. Jacques inclined his head respectfully, to mask an eruption of jealous possessiveness within.

'It is of my imagination, sire.'

'Ah, a pity,' the King sighed, an air of boredom settling on his countenance. 'I am told by our Admiral Duquesne that you have strayed from our Council of Construction's Table of Dimensions.'

'I have lengthened the keel, which I believe will thrust a ship forward, sire.'

'Monsieur Colbert, I shall be obliged if you will carry on the discussion with this young man. For my part, I like the lines of the *Hermione*. If you think its sailing qualities answer to the Marine's expectations, then I should be content to see it bear a royal standard.'

The King walked on with his courtiers, leaving Jacques to face the man who even in illness drove France onward to glory.

'You are not unknown to me, Monsieur Maurellet,' began the Contrôleur Général, 'not so much for your skills with an adze, as for your information-gathering. Before he retired as Intendant at Rochefort, my cousin Terron de Colbert gave good account of your travels in the Baltic. Your report on our wine being watered down by some importers was of some concern.'

'It was my privilege to serve France, monseigneur. And after today, my grandfather's shipyard is eager to serve the Marine,' he added, not wishing to let the opportunity slip.

'My cousin's reports on timber for the Marine no doubt reflect your personal views on the forests of the north ... finer-grained timber than our own from Auvergne and the Pyrénées.'

'I believe it so, monseigneur.'

'But if our own timber serves adequately?'

'Adequate might serve on rivers, monseigneur, but not for a ship making way in wild seas.'

His reply, Jacques knew, was impertinent, but when sailors' lives were at risk it needed to be said.

Colbert scowled. 'I don't like what you say, monsieur, but I appreciate your frank view. However, like others, you do not appreciate the dangers which face France.' The minister was silent for a moment as he stared at the open gunports of the frigate. 'We are making great advances ... brass cannon are very fine, but think what it means now we are able to cast them in iron. Our Marine must dominate the trade routes. That is the way forward ... trade! But our country cannot exist without wood, and I'm not just thinking of men like you who turn out fine ships.

'There are the virgin forests across the Atlantic.'

'And when our ports are blockaded by the Dutch and English? We must be able to survive on what we have here. That is why the forest laws have been strengthened, and why a census of trees is being taken ... our forests must be guarded. For life as we know it is dependent on healthy forests. They are many and vast, and in consequence have been plundered at will with no thought of tomorrow. Tomorrow is a long time in the life of an acorn. Too long for Le Notre, who has had thousands of mature trees brought here on wagons. For a regular supply of wood from generation to generation we must not abandon silviculture to haphazard stewardship.'

Absorbing though the subject was, Jacques began to look for someone to rescue him, but the Admiral Duquesne had disappeared.

'Your tactics here today, monsieur, were audacious,' went on the Contrôleur Général, 'but they achieved their purpose: you captured the interest of the King. And for that, your journey to Versailles will change the course of your affairs.'

'I am much obliged, Monseigneur,' said Jacques, his heart soaring with excitement. 'The composition of our carving owes much to the inspiration of Pierre Puget, whose advice I sought at Toulon.'

Colbert's sole response to this was a frown, and without further delay, the most powerful minister in the realm hurried away.

Jacques looked towards the figurehead of the *Hermione,* a smile upon his lips. 'This day, Hermione Du Chesne,' he murmured under his breath, 'you have been admired by the King.' Reminded of his denial some moments earlier, he felt a twinge of guilt ... that kissable mouth, only a thing of his imagination! Yet it was near enough true ... mostly she had only existed in his mind. He had lain in bed month after month imagining every curve of her. If Perrette were baptized in the Reformed Church it would follow that he would be set free from his promise ... but how could he possibly wish for her to be condemned to perpetual damnation? With a pained, bitter smile, Jacques walked to the water's edge and stretched out his hand. His fingers curved around the supple span of the figurehead's waist. Only once had he held her in his arms.

Hermione knew what was at stake for him and Henri, yet she had not kept her promise to come and wish him God speed.

CHAPTER 22

ver since that wretched wedding, Claude Tilly had stayed well clear of Du Chesne. Eventually, festering injured pride changed into spiteful intent.

If only he did not have to rely on a slow wit like Raoul, who seemed to bungle everything. The timber auction had caused her serious injury, but everything else in comparison was mere annoyance. Surely, at some point his moment must come. Meanwhile, he would wear the Parisienne down with irritations like the persistent bites of flies on summer days. His hand in the affair of the lace had unfortunately been revealed by Angélique's blunder. The stupid woman would think twice before prying into his affairs again … as if a package of lace would be a present for her! No doubt those who envied his success had sniggered at him being hauled before the magistrate, and the excessive fine had caused them and those at Du Chesne much merriment. Tilly swore out loud as he stepped down from his coach, and the blacksmith, seeing who was entering the yard, looked uneasy.

'I've a lot of jobs on, Monsieur Tilly.'

'Send your lad out to my coachman. He is anxious about one of the traces.'

The blacksmith scowled and, with obvious reluctance, left off what he was doing to mumble a few words to the skinny youth who was working the bellows.

'You seem very nervous?' scoffed Tilly.

'Everyone knows, monsieur, you were the one to call the constable and his men to Du Chesne. You are not welcome here in the village.'

'I have the right of any traveller to visit you,' retorted Tilly airily. 'And you will continue to keep me informed of what is happening to Madame Du Chesne.'

'Nothing out of the ordinary.'

'Then *you* are not trying *hard* enough, Raoul! Get on friendlier terms with her coachman ... ply him with drink on market day.'

'But that is a busy day ... people would be put out,' mumbled the blacksmith.

Tilly's voice rose shrill. 'I don't care how you go about it! I expect to hear something next week, or everyone here will know *your* part in things. Here, for your trouble.'

Raoul's blackened hand snatched at the spinning coin and, with a furtive look cast towards the approaching sound of whistling, he dropped the coin into the pocket of his leather apron as the timber merchant returned to his coach.

'All is well, husband?' beamed Angélique Tilly as her husband stepped up into the coach. She pressed against her petticoats to provide more space, anxious to please and oblige for being included on such an important business venture.

Claude Tilly settled into his seat opposite her, his eyes unseeing as he considered the day ahead. He should not be neglecting the timber yard, but business acumen told him to make the most of propitious times. After all, he was an entrepreneur, one of the new men prepared to risk money in new ventures. This week's bit of business at Moulle was not high-risk. Not like sugar refineries, which now were unwanted. Snapping up the houses of Huguenots would bring in high returns. According to his contact at Niort, so nervous were the psalm singers, it took only one trooper to ride into a village and entire families would take to their heels, fearing dragoons would shortly be upon them. Tilly chuckled out loud. The priests might strive to persuade them to recant, but for himself, cheer them on their way out of Poitou! Hopefully, one day soon the booted missionaries would visit Saintonge.

'Might I share in your good humour, husband?' Angélique smiled, her curls bobbing around with the motion of the coach.

'I was just thinking,' quipped Claude Tilly, 'what a pity it is the châteleine of Du Chesne is a Catholic.'

Angélique frowned, not understanding, but not wishing to make Claude impatient, she let it pass with a nervous giggle. 'How am I to serve you today, husband?'

'By making up for that foolishness which cost me dear. You'll be looking at furniture, wife. The only skill you have. And if we can get what you think is of value for nothing from these wretched Huguenots, so much the better.'

*** *** ***

It was rare to come across Olivier sitting idle. He was either working in his room or in the laboratory. Hermione had come to think of the Painted Room as her own retreat, especially when she could not ride out to the glade and her three oaks. Most of this day had been spent in the High Forest with the contractor who was going to handle the exploitations in the autumn. As the man had been directed to her by Jacques, at some point in the morning he had mentioned that the Maurellet shipyard was in a ferment of excitement over the King's being much taken with their model frigate, the *Hermione*. The contractor had not made anything of the coincidence of the name, so why now, as she took a seat a little apart from Olivier, was the news still buzzing in her mind? Despite all her efforts not to read too much into it, deep within there was a bubbling of excitement and hope which would not go away, nor permit thoughts of painful obstacles to surface.

Olivier, sitting upon his stool, was clearly absorbed, gazing upwards at the painted central motif representing *Olympe*. As Hermione never tired of marking each change of season in her woodland glade, this room captivated her in a different way. Here, the painted medallions held fast trees in leaf, and garlands of flowers remained bright when all outside might be grey or covered in snow. In here were the gay colours of summer. It was the most amazing thing to have so many scenes to stare at during winter.

'It's like looking through windows at other worlds in here, Olivier,' she breathed, staring at the *Labours of Hercules*.

'They are fine, I grant you, but there are greater wonders,' replied Olivier, stirring from his reverie. He cast towards her a fond smile which warmed her heart. Such moments with him were rare. They lived under the same roof and yet were completely bound up in different hopes. Since she could remember, he ate whatever was set before him, and when at some critical stage in his work he had not bothered to appear, she had taken food to him. Then there were the times when he had gone away for months to Antwerp and Prague.

'Do you miss your travels?' she suddenly thought to ask. Olivier ran his stained and scarred fingers through his lank hair and gave a nod.

'I envy those great men I met in Oxford and London. Think what it would be like travelling towards the peaks of knowledge with such others. You strive to catch up with those ahead who have discovered a different route. If you get stuck ,there comes the push from behind, or a hand stretches out to encourage perseverance. Those men meet to discuss their experiments; their papers are printed. Think how I had to flee from Paris or risk being sent to prison, even executed, for my work.'

'You have the curé's interest.'

Olivier's thin lips twitched with something like a smile. 'He is surprisingly knowledgeable but cannot contribute like a man of natural philosophy. But I have always worked alone, except when I started on the path of knowledge. André I believe was his name. He would sleep in the laboratory for days to wait for transition.'

'André?' enquired Hermione, immediately alert to the name. 'You have not spoken of him before.'

Olivier looked vague. 'You were very young then. He came for a year or so. One day he came no more.'

'Weren't you anxious about him?'

'Anxious? Why should I be anxious?' Such was his glance of bewildered astonishment, Hermione raised her eyes to the heavens and shook her head. Olivier could be so selfish. She pondered for a while on what had been said. Then a fantastic thought took flight in her head.

'Tell me, Olivier,' she said, springing up from her stool and moving to the portrait over the fireplace, 'did your helper look like this gentleman? Like the Chevalier?'

'I do not recall,' faltered Olivier, rising from his seat. 'It is not how people look which interests me. Besides, many years have passed.'

'Look at the distance from the nose to the mouth, how far apart the eyes … their colour,' urged Hermione, trying to press him into that frame of mind he employed in his laboratory. Olivier's attention went to the painting, and to her satisfaction, Hermione noted he was alert.

'I suppose it could be he,' he murmured without conviction. Then, as if he had discovered something, he gave a little start. 'The ring … the A D and C are far too cramped. It is poor engraving … I recall thinking so at the time.'

'André Du Chesne!' gasped Hermione.

'Yes, that sounds right, André Du Chesne.'

'Olivier.' Hermione's eyes widened in disbelief. Slowly she held up her hand before his eyes. 'Like this ring?'

'Why yes. Just like that ring.'

'Not *like*, Olivier … it is the *same ring*! But why did you not say anything when I told you I had inherited Du Chesne?'

'Well, I suppose I didn't comprehend. I was unhappy you were leaving. Besides, I had forgotten all about him. He came and he went as people do.'

Hermione sank back onto the stool. Whilst accepting his explanation, she was barely able to believe such lack of perception. How could he not have made the connection? She looked up at him with a mixture of affection and impatience. Then laughter bubbled up within, until, overwhelmed, Hermione became helpless with it while Olivier went red with discomfort.

'Olivier, I cannot believe it! You are the cleverest person I know, and you are hopeless. How you found your way here I cannot say, but you must never leave, for you will never find your way back!'

As her guardian stalked away, unable to see what was so amusing, Hermione inwardly thanked God that he had not ended up in a dungeon at Vincennes. His stubborn nature would have made things far worse for him. Her attention went back to the portrait of André Du Chesne. So he had been to the rue de la Cocotte long before he had appeared that day asking for a reading of the crystal. What could it mean? Would Guillaume be able to shed more light? Outside in the courtyard, she found him chatting to Pierre.

As Rouge came bounding up to her, Hermione gave him a pat and approached the men. 'Did the pedlar bring any news?'

'He did that, madame,' responded Pierre, settling his hunting cap back onto his greasy grey hair. 'At Montpellier Huguenots have been sending petitions to the King to save their temple.'

'And you will not believe this, Madame Hermione,' roared Guillaume. 'Any of their ministers who abjure and come back to our church receive a *pension from the King*.'

'For all the trouble they cause it don't seem right,' grumbled Pierre. 'Our King should have every last temple pulled down. It might be many years back, but look what the heretics did to the church in Saintes; how they caused bloodshed and war with their heresies. Mark my words, there is trouble on its way.'

'I hope not,' murmured Hermione. With a troubled expression, she looked after the old man as he whistled up Rouge and headed off towards the stables.

'Tell me, Guillaume,' she asked, 'do you remember a gentleman named André who used to help Monsieur Olivier?'

The expression on Guillaume's broad face was blank. 'I can't say I do. The master had few callers. It must have been before my time.'

'I suppose it would be,' reflected Hermione, for Olivier had said she was very young at the time. 'It is nothing,' she added with a wave of her hand to let him go about his work.

On returning inside to the Painted Room, Hermione gazed at the portrait of the Chevalier with renewed curiosity. If he had come across her as a small child, then that was more likely to be the reason he had adopted her than her reading of the crystal. With a slight shake of her head, she sensed she would never really know. She flashed a smile at the handsome young cavalier.

'Whatever the truth, you will see you were right to entrust Du Chesne to a *parisienne* teller of fortunes.'

*** *** ***

Claude Tilly found the blacksmith waiting as he had instructed in the shadows near the entrance to Du Chesne.

'Well?' he demanded. 'What news of her coachman?'

'Your Honour, I did as you said. He was so drunk, his legs could hardly carry him downhill. Once he started talking, it was not easy to get him to stop. Except he kept wanting to talk about his time helping to build the King's palace at Versailles, and he knows a great deal about ...'

'Never mind about that,' snapped Tilly. 'The man living there – what is he up to?'

'He is Olivier Lefèvre, an engraver before his fingers started to shake. Then he turned to alchemy.'

'Alchemy,' Tilly breathed. In the ensuing silence, neither man was anxious to rush onward. The timber merchant's rapt delight shone in his green eyes as he toyed with the word in his mind. He had near guessed it himself when he had noticed the gentleman's burnished complexion as he stepped out of the coach on the day of the wedding.

Never had Raoul felt so important, and when he judged it was time, he swelled out his chest and followed up with the next offering.

'He had a large laboratory which he did not wish to leave.'

'So why did he?' pressed Tilly, with rising anticipation.

'There was someone called Nicolas La Reynie making trouble for him in Paris. So he ran away and came here. The coachman, Guillaume, used to work for him, not for Madame Du Chesne.'

'Is that so? Don't keep me guessing.'

'He began to clam up when I asked about her. Even with the drink, he was beginning to get suspicious. But he told me the alchemist will discover something soon which will fill chests with gold.'

'Gold,' gasped Tilly, a tight feeling pressing against his chest. He was excited, yet he voiced his doubts. 'Many people think alchemists are cheats and tricksters.'

'That may be so, Your Honour, but the curé is interested in his work.'

'He is? Good, very good! You've done well.'

'It took me from my work, sitting with him,' the blacksmith whined in a plaintive voice. Absently, Claude Tilly dipped into his pocket and pressed the promised payment into the rough hand.

'What else?'

'She has got a new contractor for her timber. And they are about to start picking the cider apples.'

'Ha,' laughed Tilly in exhilaration. 'I shall have to think more about this alchemist, but before I turn back home, let us have a little sport.'

'Where are we going?' faltered Raoul.

'Do you have a weapon about you?'

'A knife.'

'Excellent, and I my sword ... like the stinging wasps, we shall wear

376

this Parisienne down until the *coup de grâce*!'

***

Pierre led the way towards the first line of trees. Hermione could hardly believe her eyes. It looked as if some great wind had dragged fruit and leaves from the trees, and then a herd of cattle had crunched the apples underfoot to a pulp. Only a few days before, the russet golden globes had nestled beneath their green leaves, all swelling to perfection to make the cider. Hours of work had gone into scything the grass, pruning, and painting the trunks and boughs with lime milk. All for nothing ... total destruction.

'It is terrible ... monstrous,' murmured Hermione. 'Who would do such a thing?' She picked up an apple which had been sliced in half by something sharp.

'Are ... the rest?'

Pierre's expression as Hermione glanced round the orchard was grim. Without answering, he led her onward through the dappled sunlit scene of havoc.

'It is such a waste,' Hermione choked, her hands tightening into fists of angry frustration. 'A stupid waste.'

'It is the Devil's work,' exploded Pierre. 'It's the Huguenots.'

Hermione slowly shook her head. 'No, Pierre, I do not think so. This is the work of a man who hates me.'

'Then let me have his name, madame, and I shall run his gizzards through and slice off his ears!' Hermione gave a faint smile as the old man's hand went to the hilt of his hunting knife.

'You are too important to Marie and to me, Pierre. But never fear,' she said, as anger followed shock, 'I shall not let this pass!'

Throughout that day and the next, Hermione seethed with rage. The villagers went along to see the damage, and all talk was of how it might have happened. As Lucette helped Hermione out of her Sunday dress, she went back to the early days when goblins had beckoned to her from the orchard.

'If it were the little folk, they would have taken the apples unspoilt. Marie thinks so as well. This is the work of a human hand, and an evil one at that. I think, Madame Hermione, you have no further to look than that nasty Monsieur Tilly.'

To Hermione's relief, the gentle Angélique, for whom she had a liking, was not present when she was greeted by Claude Tilly at the smart new town house at Rochefort.

'My dear Madame Du Chesne,' fussed the merchant as he led her into his bureau, 'this is an exceptional honour. Do I take it you need my help again this autumn?'

'I have an *honest* contractor to handle the exploitations and to represent me at auction.'

'Good, good,' Tilly smirked as if he had not understood the slur, 'let us hope he proves not a *fool*. May I offer you refreshment … some cider, perhaps?'

Hermione's brown eyes flashed such dark fury that Tilly did not pursue his jibe. Even so, his inner excitement and malice blazed in his eyes. Hermione held the glittering green gaze, knowing now for certain it was he who had ruined the apple crop. It seemed likely that all the other petty mishaps had been inspired by him. He was demented, and there was no reasoning with such a man. With steady resolve, Hermione dipped inside her pocket and withdrew the gun given to her in Paris by Olivier. Claude Tilly stepped back, his face expressing total shock.

'Listen to me, you vile creature,' she hissed, holding the primed weapon steady while her free hand produced a battered and bruised apple, 'if *ever* you come onto my land again, I shall shoot you. Do you understand? Now eat this! *Eat it*!'

'It will give me gripe,' whined the timber merchant.

'That is what I am counting on; something to make you think about

378

your nasty, spiteful ways.' Hermione made a threatening movement with the gun. Claude Tilly stretched out, and taking up the battered fruit with an expression of reluctance, he stuffed the broken pieces into his mouth.

'Don't forget,' Hermione added when he had swallowed everything, 'I shall not report you to the police if you make more trouble. I and my people will deal with you!' She replaced the gun in her bag and, without another glance, walked to the door.

'Oh no, you'll not report me to the police, Madame Du Chesne,' gasped Claude Tilly, recovering from the shock of what had passed. 'That wouldn't help your Monsieur Lefèvre, would it?'

Hermione halted in the open doorway. 'What do you mean?' she asked, cold apprehension flooding over her.

'I dined with friends of mine recently, and they mentioned a name, Nicolas La Reynie ... does it mean anything to you? It did not mean anything to me when I heard it, because of course, I am but a provincial. You, being a Parisienne, would naturally know that he is the chief of police who has filled Paris with the smoke of witches and alchemists. I believe Monsieur Lefèvre is an alchemist.'

'He is a man of natural philosophy,' retorted Hermione, as calmly as she could.

'Whatever you wish to call it,' jeered Tilly, delighted to see her turn so pale. 'I thought I might take a trip to Paris and tell this chief of police all about the laboratory at your château ... *unless*!'

'Unless?'

'Unless you arrange for me to meet Monsieur Lefèvre. I would like to know whether transmutation is a fool's dream or whether lead can be changed into gold. Will you invite me, madame? Before the month is out!'

Hermione's brain raced as she gave a reluctant nod.

'Good. And now, if you will forgive me, I must take myself off to find an antidote for the little offering you brought. I assure you, madame, even one twinge of pain, and you shall receive it back tenfold!'

On the day after her visit to Rochefort, Hermione sought to convince Olivier of the danger he was in. He would have none of it as he moved about the laboratory.

'If there was danger, it is long past,' he snorted, taking a quantity of iron filings over to his scales.

'Even if the matter is now over in Paris,' cautioned Hermione, taking back for him the excess he did not need, 'you know what the police are like. Nicolas La Reynie will still have you hauled in.'

Olivier walked away from her without reply, and she watched him throw the filings into the crucible. She gave a sigh of impatience, wishing that he would listen. As he turned to move back to the workbench, she saw that his gaunt face was filled with misery.

'This has become my home,' he murmured. 'Where would I go?'

Hermione's heart contracted, and she wanted to put her arms around his shoulders, but she knew he would not like it. She bit her lip, searching for an answer.

'It is better we continue here without bringing attention to ourselves,' she murmured. 'If you meet him, could you somehow convince him that you are near to understanding how to change lead into gold?'

'It is not possible.'

'Not possible? But I thought it was another path of the work you do?'

'I do not say it is impossible. But it is not possible yet. Charlatans have tricked people in the past, which has led to ridicule. I am not a charlatan.'

Hermione strode up and down the makeshift laboratory wondering what was best to do.

'Then you will have to leave, Olivier. I could not bear to see you hauled off by the police.'

'It won't come to that … the man is only trying to frighten you. Du Chesne is my home, and I am staying.'

Hermione felt a rush of affection, and her mind was momentarily taken away from her anxieties. 'I'm so glad that you feel this is your home.' Then her expression clouded with anxiety, and she knew she must tell him about the past. 'But would you wish to lead Lucette to suffering in the torture chamber of Vincennes? For if this man contacts the police about you, it could come to that ... Lucette has seen things which could bring about her death.'

Olivier looked sharply at Hermione, for the first time giving her his complete attention. 'Do you wish me to leave? I will if it will keep you all safe.'

'I don't want you to go. But until I can think how to handle things, you have to disappear. Or, somehow, we have to keep him interested enough to stop him going to Paris.'

'If you want me to show him how to make gold, then I will,' said Olivier in a quiet voice. Hermione's eyes widened with astonishment.

'You can change lead into gold!'

Her former guardian gave a wry smile. 'Guillaume shall take me to Rochefort. Then, you shall see!'

CHAPTER 23

acques was in high spirits on his return home, eager to oblige everyone with his impression of Versailles. Aunt Marguerite and Perrette had arranged a grand meal for which family, friends, and their children all crowded around the table in the salon, eager to hear every detail of his adventure. Above all the splendid things he described, it was the *labyrinthe* designed by André Le Nostre which excited everyone. For whilst they nodded and smiled in wonder throughout what had passed between himself and the King, Jacques's impression was that something so overwhelming as one of their own to be talking to the Sun King was beyond belief. On the other hand, Aesop's statue at the entrance of the *labyrinthe* and all the animals from his familiar fables within were real! Once he had told them there were thirty-nine water features set at every intersection within the maze, where the sculptures were so lifelike you believed the creatures to be alive, there was a literal outpouring of questions.

'Did you see the ducks and the water spaniel, Maitre Maurellet?'

'Yes, they were the last fountain ... number thirty-nine.'

'What number were the cocks and partridge, Jacques?'

'They were the second water feature, but I can't remember all the numbers. I saw many of the animals ... the eagle and the fox ... the wolf and the heron. When the water spouts forth from their mouths, you think the animals are talking to each other.'

'No, they were spitting at each other,' piped up a small boy. Along with the rest, Jacques burst into laughter. Before he could think of a suitable response, the boy's smiling mother leaned forward in her seat.

'You said Charles Perrault thought it would help the little dauphin to learn about the fables. Did you see him walking in the *labyrinthe*?'

Jacques shook his head. 'I'm afraid not.'

'The statue of Cupid at the entrance holding a ball of twine should have been a warning, Jacques. You were lucky not to get lost amongst all those green hedges,' his Aunt Marguerite said in a tone to suggest she knew all about the subject. Suddenly, Perrette's clear voice cut through the chatter about carrying a ball of twine in a maze.

'Dear cousin, we are impatient to hear more about the frigate. Was the King as enamoured of the *Hermione's* figurehead as you?'

All the faces looked towards Jacques with smiling, naïve anticipation. As quick as himself to catch the ironic barb, his grandfather gave a snort of laughter. Like some callow youth, Jacques felt his face redden at the seemingly innocent enquiry.

'I'm glad you asked, Perrette,' he answered, regaining his composure, 'His Majesty King Louis not only admired the figurehead, but declared that if the design meets with the approval of the Council of Construction, he will be happy to see *Hermione* bear the royal standard!'

On the following day, since Henri was now recovered from the strain of building the model, they decided before they were caught up in other affairs to set forth to see the Canal Royal de Languedoc at Toulouse. This newly opened waterway, combined with the Canal de Garonne, completed the astonishing link between the Atlantic and the Mediterranean: the Canal of the Two Seas.

It was not often that both of them were away from the shipyard at the same time, but prior to his trip to Versailles, Jacques had arranged with an experienced engineer from Rochefort for a new slipway to be dug out during their absence, which would occupy most of the labourers. Perrette was all attention, offering to keep a discreet eye on things, as she put it. So eager did she seem to see them on their way, Jacques's suspicions were aroused, and after bidding farewell to Annette and his aunt, he sought her out.

'Walk with me to the stables,' he said, as she threw a final flurry of grain to the hens she was feeding. 'Does the promise you made when I set forth to Versailles still hold?'

'Not to do anything *foolish* while you are away?'

'Foolish and dangerous,' rebutted Jacques, trying not to rise to the mockery in her voice.

'I cannot make that promise again, Jacques.' Perrette's expression and tone of voice were now serious. 'I am to be baptised.'

'But Aunt Marguerite ... think how she will take it!'

'There is a pure and modest way to worship ... Mother is too old to understand.'

'Then I shall tell Grandfather we cannot go away.'

'You can't lock me away forever, Jacques. Besides, with the building of the new slipway, this is a convenient time.'

As they entered the stables and the groom led across the stallion saddled for the journey, Jacques clenched his teeth in a state of indecision. To let her go her own way in this would be like letting her throw herself over a precipice into a fire. How could he live with the guilt of knowing he had not stayed to stop it happening? As if reading his thoughts, Perrette stretched out her hand and touched his shoulder.

'God calls to me, and I answer only to him.'

'Then you will bring the storm upon us all,' snapped Jacques, brushing her hand aside. He placed the toe of his boot on the stirrup. Her small hand stayed him, her light blue eyes pleading for understanding. Jacques only felt overwhelmed with impatience. 'Nothing I say shall persuade you against it?'

'No.'

Jacques swung himself up onto the saddle and looked down, his expression grim. 'Then we shall all have to face the unfortunate consequences!' With a clatter of hooves, he rode across the yard to where his grandfather waited, and together they set off, walking their horses along the lane.

'You look grim for a man who is bent on amusing me,' growled Henri, as they turned up towards the road. For a while, Jacques remained silent until his frustration could not be contained.

'She is to be baptised this week!'

'The ingrate,' growled Henri. 'It will break Marguerite's heart. No Catholic will marry her ... has she thought of that?'

'I rather think she barely gives such matters a thought,' returned Jacques, his tone heavy with irony, though in truth he did not know whether he should be happy or sad. Personal considerations couldn't be thought of when violence towards Huguenots by dragoons was spreading like wildfire. Alongside him, his grandfather let out a curse.

'What is it?' he asked anxiously, as the old man wheeled about his horse.

'I've left something behind.'

'I'll go back ... what is it?'

'It's my pipe. I know where it is; you go on.'

Jacques did as bid. The old man hated being fussed over. Even so, Jacques would insist on the stages of their journey being short, and a good supper and early bed would ensure it was not too taxing for Henri. His thoughts were still in turmoil over Perrette. Would she turn back from the brink or bring disaster on herself? He recalled how put out he had felt when he had followed her to Martin's house and found she was consorting with fanatics. It was not just a question of bringing shame on the family and the consequent effect upon their business! What of her soul, cast forever into Purgatory? He often had doubts himself, but should he let her risk the terrible torments the curé warned of? Through the powerful de Rohan family, Soubise had always been a Huguenot refuge, but nowadays intolerance was sweeping across France. On the road back from Paris, a journeyman had told him how Huguenot houses were being deliberately chosen to billet soldiers. If after a time the family ran out of money to provide food and drink for their lodgers, the soldiers simply sold the family furniture at knock-down prices to anyone who would pay. Even worse were tales of Huguenot children being snatched away from their parents for religious re-education. At Versailles, it had been openly spoken of that Madame de Maintenon's influence had inspired the King to convert all the Huguenots in France.

As he loitered beneath the shade of an oak, Jacques contemplated its acorns. He fingered one shiny surface of the seed with a sense of sad regret. If only things had been different, more straightforward from the moment they had met, he could have enjoyed openly the thrill of courting Hermione Du Chesne. What now? Was he a free man? The image of Hermione's face in his mind banished complicated thoughts. All he could think of was his desire to see her and to feel his lips close over hers. A loud holler from behind broke into his delightful reverie.

'You were a long time,' he commented, curious to know why Henri looked so smug and pleased.

'My memory is not what it was,' joked the old man, avoiding his question. 'No need to look so suspicious, my boy. You'll see all will be well when we return. Now let me show you that I and the old horse can still set a pretty pace!'

As his grandfather's mount gathered speed, Jacques hesitated. Clearly, Henri had been up to something more than collecting his pipe. However, as the distance between them both was widening, he kicked on his stallion in pursuit.

***

The atmosphere within the laboratory was tense. Hermione found it hard to be civil to Claude Tilly, but it was important to humour him, to make him less alert to what was taking place, so her offerings of cognac were frequent and generous. Guillaume was present, but it had been thought best to keep this display a secret from Marie and Pierre. Unless all was explained, they would not understand, and for them to understand seemed unwise.

Hermione herself had been kept ignorant of what was to take place. It seemed to amuse Olivier to have her as a spectator. So, apart from ensuring everyone else was abed, calming down Rouge, and opening wide the laboratory windows, Hermione was watching the crucible just like Claude Tilly. Even with the windows wide open, the heat from the charcoal fire was intense. The timber merchant was not as close to the fire as Olivier, but Hermione saw that sweat was pouring down his face, as indeed it was on her own. Hermione took out her kerchief and dabbed at her forehead as Guillaume laid aside the bellows.

'Can I smell tar?' muttered Claude Tilly, mopping his brow.

'Came on the charcoal,' spat Guillaume. 'That Antoine who sells it is a clumsy fellow.'

'Now we have it,' murmured Olivier, as he gave a stir to the crucible. Along with Tilly, Hermione moved forward and peered down into the black pot. The lead had broken down and was now a swirling silvery molten mass.

'I see no gold!' scoffed Tilly.

'Nor will you yet!' snapped back Olivier.

With a show of ceremony, Guillaume handed over Olivier's leather gloves. With his hands protected, Olivier brought forth the crucible from the fire and carried it over to his bench. For a little while, he waited; then, as if to hurry along the cooling, he tipped the contents of the pot into a large shallow bowl of cold water, stepping back quickly from the ensuing spit and splutter. Once the cloud of steam had cleared, the heavy bowl was filled with a slithery, silvery mass of lead, but still no gold! Bit by bit, Olivier carefully transferred globules of lead from the watery mess into a large porcelain dish. Then he turned aside and opening up the strings of a red velvet bag withdrew a small glass phial. Within its red folds, Hermione glimpsed the glow of gold. As if reading her mind, Olivier partially withdrew a small bar of the precious metal and, having given a brief sighting of it, let it drop back into the bag. Retaining the glass phial, he removed its stopper and, with a light movement, sprinkled a little of the powder over the droplets of lead in the porcelain dish.

'The Powder of Projection,' he said in grave dramatic tones. Hermione saw Tilly's stare becoming more intense, while her own emotions were a mix of anxiety and excitement. Surely Olivier must fail, for if he really was able transform this molten lead into gold, the years of worrying about money and having to sit for long hours giving readings of the crystal to help buy food had been unnecessary. There had to be trickery at work. Hermione narrowed her eyes to concentrate as Olivier covered the lower part of his face with a thick rag, then took up a brown bottle.

'Both of you stand well back!'

As the bottle's stopper was pulled out, Hermione noticed a wisp of vapour-like mist escaping from its neck. Olivier immediately began to pour the clear liquid into the dish. It instantly started to fizz, and despite the flow of air coming from the open windows, Hermione gasped for breath, spluttering and coughing from the acrid fumes. Gradually, as her distress lessened, she realized that even Guillaume had been affected, for he was at the window taking in great gulps of air, whilst Tilly still had his hands covering his mouth and nose.

'So ... it is here!' cried Olivier, swirling the brown mixture in the dish around and every so often pouring some of it away. 'Step forward, Monsieur Tilly, and see the beauty of gold.'

With a bound, the timber merchant rushed towards the bench. Hermione followed.

'Incredible!' gasped Tilly, as Olivier poured away more of the noxious brown broth to reveal the grains of gold. 'Can it be true? You are a wizard!'

'No wizard,' replied Olivier sternly, as the little man tried to embrace him. 'It is the powder whose formula holds the power.'

Hardly able to believe what she was seeing, Hermione looked up into Olivier's blackened face. His eyes, she saw, were glinting with mockery.

'I will give you the gold which is here, monsieur, but only if you promise to keep my secret.'

'My dear Monsieur Lefèvre, nothing would induce me to speak to anyone about what I have seen here tonight. You have amazed me, and I shall see that you remain undisturbed here at Du Chesne. Of course, I would like to visit frequently, so that I might acquire your skill and learning. Will you consider that, Monsieur Lefèvre?'

Instant irritation creased Olivier's face, and his tone was abrupt. 'I have my own work, monsieur. I am not interested in gold. I seek the elixir which will prolong health and youth.'

'Of course, naturally,' agreed Tilly, receiving from Olivier's leathery fingers the grains of gold.

'And there is little skill for you to learn, for it is the powder which transmutes what is base to what is pure and beautiful. Now if you will forgive me, I am tired.'

'Of course, I will take my leave immediately. Goodnight dear sir, and goodnight Madame Du Chesne. I am most grateful, words cannot express.'

'Goodnight, monsieur. We can count on your discretion?'

'Madame, never fear, all is locked within me, and I have thrown away the key. But I really must insist on coming again to see such marvels!'

With a fawning bow, the timber merchant went on his way, with Guillaume as escort till he was beyond the Keep. By the time Guillaume returned, Hermione was still trying to persuade Olivier to explain everything.

'If it is not genuine, tell me how you did it, Olivier.'

'It truly is gold,' answered Olivier, sitting down on a stool.

'Oh, I believe that,' said Hermione, her eyes interrogating him.

'Except for those little bars in the bag; they are lead with a special coating which appears like gold. But the gold in the dish was real enough.'

'Then we shall be rich?'

Olivier laughed. 'I did not think you were such a *gull*, Hermione, especially after seeing all the tricks performed in Corneille's comedy in Paris. Just because I scorn trickery does not mean I do not know what the fraudsters get up to.'

'Does the Powder of Projection have the power?'

'My own little concoction for our visitor … as harmless as it is useless.'

'Then how?'

Olivier smiled. 'You shall help me when Monsieur Avarice returns.'

Whether Guillaume was party to Olivier's means of producing gold, Hermione did not ask, for his loyalties would always be to his old master. The week before Tilly's second visit was expected, as Hermione was inspecting the royal stallion, Olivier appeared through the laboratory door.

'When you've finished with that animal,' he called, 'I'll show you how to make gold.'

Hermione gave the black, glossy neck a final caress and, consumed with curiosity, lost no time in following Olivier.

In the laboratory, set out on the bench, was the old, blackened crucible and next to it was a pot of warm tar. Half forming an idea of where this might be leading, Hermione's cheeks dimpled with her wide smile as Olivier produced a pouch and shook out a handful of gold filings. These he dropped into the bottom of the crucible.

'Now, cover them over with the tar,' he directed. 'Spread it smoothly, but not too thick. Just sufficient to hide them should suspicious eyes look into the crucible.'

'So this is where the smell of tar came from.'

'That is why Guillaume put some on the charcoal … to mislead,' explained Olivier. When the gold was hidden, Hermione laughed with amusement.

'I don't care that we are not going to be rich … just as long as Tilly thinks he is.'

'It is not the answer,' rejoined Olivier with a frown. 'He will want more, and then more.'

'I know.' Hermione sighed. She cast her mind around for some way of dealing with the problem. 'What if we told him the Powder of Projection comes from China ... send him somewhere far away.'

'Maybe. Let us see what his reaction is when he comes here next week.'

Claude Tilly's expression, when he entered the laboratory, was of such excitement and greed that Hermione found it difficult not to laugh. On this second occasion his eyes were alert to Olivier's every move, and just as the older man was about to drop a quantity of lead into the crucible Tilly was bold enough to restrain his arm in order that he might first peer down into the black pot to ensure that it was empty.

Thanks to Guillaume's efforts with the bellows, the furnace was at a high temperature, and within the half hour the lead had broken down, as likewise, no doubt, had the tar lining of the crucible. The procedure Olivier followed was as before, with all of them coughing and gasping for air when he added the fuming Acqua Fortis from its brown bottle to dissolve the lead coating on the grains of gold. Once again, Olivier began to swirl about the basin and pour off the redundant, dangerous brew. The sparkle of gold at the bottom of the basin made Tilly squeal out in excitement.

'But you have the means to restore the château,' he exclaimed, turning on Hermione a puzzled look of sudden suspicion.

'That is not what the Powder of Projection is for,' thundered Olivier, his expression beneath his protective hat fierce as he glared at Tilly. 'A greedy man might misuse it to fill this room with gold ... but not I!'

'I am relieved to hear it, Monsieur Lefèvre,' put in Tilly swiftly. Then, his voice taking on a casual note, he flashed Olivier a conspiratorial smile. 'Pray, how came you by this powder?'

'Next time,' snapped Olivier, his feigned charm giving way.

'Yes, you will explain next time. Ah, these precious grains of gold!

Just think of the lead which could be changed ... but you are quite right,' added Tilly quickly, wishing to humour the alchemist. 'It is the discovery of the elixir which is important. I am impatient to hear about it, so do not leave me too long waiting to return.'

After Tilly had made his goodbye and left, Hermione turned with a laugh to Olivier.

'He believes he will become the richest man in France.'

'And I will be the poorest if he comes here too often,' remarked Olivier.

'What would be best to do?'

'I think,' replied Olivier, touching the red velvet bag, 'we ought to convince him a sack of powder would be worth the journey to ...'

'Kill him! That would be surer,' burst in Guillaume from the shadows. 'And I'm the man to do it!'

***

The outing to view Paul-Pierre Riquet's canal which began at Toulouse proved a great success. What a tragedy it was that the Marquis had died only months before his enormous enterprise had broken through into the Mediterranean. It seemed common knowledge that this native of Beziers had put his entire fortune into the undertaking and had died practically destitute. It had taken fifteen years, with something like twelve thousand workers wielding picks and shovels, and women carrying soil away in their aprons. The entire length was one hundred and fifty miles from Toulouse to the newly created port of Sete. In addition to the waterway, which many had begun to refer to as the Canal du Midi, the city of Toulouse itself was stunning. They had arrived in late afternoon when the sun was losing its power, though the red brick buildings still blazed a fiery scarlet against the cloudless sky. By the time they had rested on their beds for an hour, then changed for dinner, shadows outside were lengthening and the red facades of houses were darkening to purple. They had the good fortune to fall in with like-minded men, some of whom had sailed to Beziers. These men held everyone around the table spellbound as they described the engineering wonder of the staircase of eight locks at Fonserannes. Later on, another man related his visit to the *Bassin de Saint Ferreol*; the first dam ever built to supply water to a navigable canal.

'It is the greatest achievement in the world,' remarked his grandfather the next day as they walked along the towpath of the canal beneath the shade of the plane trees. 'Do you remember that fellow last night, the one whose dialect was so strong you couldn't recognise it as being French?'

'We are in Languedoc,' put in Jacques with a smile.

'Maybe so,' grunted Henri. 'He told me they have planted some forty-five thousand of these plane trees along the entire length of the canal, and not just to give shade along the towpath. Everything has been thought about: how the leaves will fall into the water and so line the bottom of the canal in order to stop the water seeping into the soil, and how the roots of the trees will guard against erosion of the banks.'

'Are you fit enough for more? I thought we could take a look at the Cathedral of St Etienne. Its rose window is supposed to be on a par with that of Notre Dame ... save you a trip to Paris. After that there is St Sernin's tomb.'

'Isn't that on the pilgrim's route to Santiago de Compostela? It will probably be very crowded.'

'Let's see how you feel after the cathedral.'

As they turned about to return the way they had come, Henri touched Jacques's arm, and in his eyes was the gleam of tears.

'Thanks, lad. Not only for bringing me here, but for opening up my life. When you get to my age, each day can seem very much like another, and you feel the sands of time are running out fast. Seeing all this, and knowing the great task we have ahead of us, if we have royal consent for the frigate, it makes me feel as young as you!'

'Does this mean you're going to buy my dinner?' Jacques laughed.

Toulouse shimmered pink in the early light of dawn as Jacques and Henri set forth for home. They were full of talk of one day returning to sail to the Mediterranean, but as the rose-pink city was left behind and every day brought them nearer home, their daydreams were overrun with nervous concern that they would find everything all right at the shipyard. When at last they handed over their weary horses to the stable lad, Jacques looked him straight in the eye.

'Any problems at the shipyard?'

'Not that I heard, Maitre Jacques. I think the men felt they could get on with things much quicker without interference.' Jacques gave him a playful cuff on the ears for his impudence and laughed.

'How was Toulouse, Maitre Henri?' asked the lad as he undid the girth of Jacques's stallion.

'What a city! Its pastel trade might have been taken over by indigo from India, but now it has one of the great wonders of the world.' Henri gave a groan as he supported himself on Jacques's arm as he tried to get his legs working again. 'Don't grin, lad. You'll come to this one day,' he gasped, waving the boy back to the horses.

'Come, a fire and a cognac will ease your old bones,' said Jacques, picking up both saddlebags and setting off to the house. As he opened the door to the kitchen, he was startled to find it dark within. 'What has happened here? It is not like Perrette to neglect a welcome,' he said, glancing about the cheerless room.

'We'll soon take care of it,' growled Henri, moving stiffly towards where the flint was kept. Jacques glanced at him in surprise, as he was never one to help. Nor did he seem at all surprised as he touched a flaming taper to the laid kindling. 'See, we'll have it cosy in here within a minute.'

'Something is wrong,' Jacques said, as his grandfather straightened up with a grunt. 'She knew we were returning today.'

'They know there is never any certainty when travelling.'

'Maybe, but there has not been anyone here for days. Look at all the dust! I'll go up to Aunt Marguerite's ... perhaps Perrette is ill? But why didn't Annette come and see to things?'

'I'm sure she is being taken care of.'

Jacques's hand fell away from the door latch.

'What do you mean,' he flashed back, his blue eyes narrowing with suspicion.

'I mean,' stammered his grandfather, 'taken care of by her mother.'

'No, you don't,' exclaimed Jacques. 'Something is going on here that you know about.'

'Well, I've an idea,' confessed the old man with an uneasy smile. 'She is safe.'

'Safe! Grandfather, what is this about ... what is going on here?'

Jacques waited, impatient for an answer, as his grandfather poured a cognac. His thoughts flashed back to the day they had left and how Henri had gone back to the house to get something. 'You didn't forget your pipe, did you?' he flung out. At his tone of accusation, his grandfather flopped down into his chair.

'I went to ask the curé to help Perrette. It was all I could think of,' he quavered as Jacques scowled. 'You told me she was going to be baptised. I thought he could persuade her from it.'

'Her mind was made up ... no one would stop her.'

'Father Francis promised he would save her soul.'

'How so?'

'She was to be taken off to a convent. Don't look at me like that, boy! It was for her own good! Once away from evil influences, Perrette will find her way back to God. And they will not let her go *until* she recovers her faith.'

Jacques picked up his hat and strode towards the door. 'Which convent have they taken her to?'

'I don't know,' admitted Henri, 'there wasn't time for many words.

Where are you going?'

'To bring her home.'

'No!' thundered Henri, staggering up. 'Would you help her on to disaster ... deny her salvation? I order you not to interfere.'

'We must each find our own salvation, Grandfather. Perrette shall make up her own mind. And if she needs to do that in Switzerland or Holland, then I shall help her get there.'

Without even going to look at what had been done during their absence at the shipyard, Jacques went to the stable to tell the lad to saddle him up a fresh horse. Then, he walked briskly to see his Aunt Marguerite, but though the door was open and there was a fire within, she was not at home. He lingered awhile, until, consumed with impatience, he returned to the stables and set forth at a fast pace to the curé's house. Although he was furious at the outrage committed against Perrette, an inner voice cautioned him to use guile, or the priest would soon sniff out what he was about.

'Good evening to you, Father,' he said with a grave smile as he came upon the priest walking in his garden. 'Maître Henri and I have just returned home. Grandfather has told me of your promise to save Perrette.'

'And that I have, my son,' rejoined the priest, flicking away a wasp.

'Did she cause you trouble?' asked Jacques tentatively. Like a blackbird, the priest inclined his head to one side and squinted upwards.

'You have not been firm enough with your cousin in the past, Jacques Maurellet. I seem to recall I was made unwelcome and treated harshly when I attempted to show Perrette the error of her ways.'

Jacques glanced away. 'Did you call upon Perrette again?' he asked casually.

A spiteful look came into the prelate's cunning eyes. 'Oh, I knew that would not please you, so it seemed best to take her off when she was walking to market.'

'Take her off? You mean abduct her?' gasped Jacques. 'That is

397

monstrous! Where have you taken her?' All good intentions fell away as his temper let fly.

'She has gone to one of the Houses for New Catholics, and she will not be allowed out until she shows repentance. And if it displeases *you*, her *mother* has wept with joy to know her daughter will be saved from mortal sin.'

'I *demand* her release!' thundered Jacques.

'As a Catholic I expect you to pray for your betrothed. It is to no avail asking me where she is,' Father Francis gave a dismissive wave of his bony hand, 'for I shall not tell you, no matter what!'

Jacques ground his teeth as the priest hurried towards the house, but he felt helpless. A year or so ago he would have applied to the courts, but with the Intendant Marillac's cruel excesses in Poitou the clergy were now in control, and they knew it. Jacques re-mounted his horse feeling impotent, a feeling new to him. It was no answer, but he decided to seek out the company of friends in an inn, not trusting himself to return to Henri in case he said something he would later regret.

CHAPTER 24

he night was dark save for the blacksmith's lantern, its swinging cast of yellowish light revealing nothing other than the dark mass of the burly man's body. Raoul knew the way well, so Claude Tilly was content to leave all to him as he indulged himself with thoughts of the chaos he was about to unleash.

'We had best stop here, Monsieur Tilly. Secure your horse to a tree or it may bolt with fright when the fire starts, and you will need a quick escape.'

Tilly acted upon the suggestion and thought also to tie his handkerchief to a lower branch to direct him to the spot later. Together with Raoul, he advanced on foot towards the tithe barn which, he now knew, held the full store from harvest.

'We are here, monsieur!'

The timber merchant's thin lips dragged back from the trap of his mouth into a wolfish smile. His fingers dug deep into the blacksmith's brawny arm as he whispered final instructions, followed up by a threat of retribution if they were not carried out.

There was no cover on the bridge over the Bruant, but Tilly was counting on panic. Besides, he felt invincible and reckless with excitement. The only sound reaching his ears was the gentle murmuring flow of the river below. Then an owl hooted and shortly afterwards came the distant double striking of the hour up at the church.

'Oh, you bitch,' he snarled out loud, 'you are in for a busy night!'

As his eyes strained into the darkness, he clicked his teeth with impatience and stamped his feet against the cold. Why was that fool taking so long? Suddenly, his nostrils pricked as a faint whiff of smoke was carried to him on the night air. So his dimwit of an accomplice had not fled back to his bed. Tilly cleared his throat; then, as a glow of light showed against the darkness, he laughed with fiendish glee. The fun had begun, and with every passing moment the fiery ball spread wider until, joy of joys, great tongues of orange flame shot upwards into the night sky. From the hovels near to the barn came an outburst of desperate cries of alarm, and running feet were heading his way. He shrank back against the wall of the Keep as feet clattered onto the timbers of the bridge. Whoever it was pulling on the bell opposite him did so but briefly, as answering voices within swiftly took up the alarm. Heavy bolts were drawn, the door swung inwards and dark figures dashed out. Though he could have touched any one of them as they ran past, so close was he, no one seemed aware of him. He slipped inside the Keep and headed towards the stables. There seemed to be no one about. Only the château's dog seemingly would try to bar his way, for its deep-throated barks became more frantic the closer he approached. The timber merchant's hand went to the pommel of his sword.

'If they think I am content with a few grains of gold, they don't know Claude Tilly,' he muttered, carrying on undeterred towards the stable door.

'Be quiet, you hound from hell!' he snarled as he unsheathed his sword. Behind the rough wooden planking, the hound's barks changed to deep, menacing growls. Tilly looked over his shoulder and listened to distant shouts and women's screams. Just as he had anticipated, everyone had rushed to put out the fire. The dog hurled itself at the closed door, its weight making the wooden planking rattle each time it crashed against it. Tilly's heart raced, and his eyes gleamed in anticipation. He lifted the wooden latch, pushed inward and lunged forward with the point of his sword, but he miscalculated and the brute rushed towards him from the right, sinking its teeth deep into his thigh. Tilly screamed in pain but managed somehow to make a sideways slash. As the blade made impact, the dog yelped and let him go, but relief was brief, as the full weight of the hairy body struck him. Somehow, Tilly managed to stay on his feet as the hound snapped for his throat. They were at such close quarters he could feel the brute's hot, stinking breath. As if he were using a dagger, he stabbed upwards, again and again. His own cries of pain mingled with those of the dog until with a supreme effort he lifted high his sword and drove it downward. The impact of steel against bone jarred his wrist, and he laughed with glee as the hound yowled. The heavy weight of the animal fell against one of his boots and, pulling back, Tilly let fly a vicious kick. Only now did he become aware of the din the horses were making in their stalls.

'You'll smell more blood,' he exulted tempted to carry on with his butchery, but the real purpose of his visit came first. With outstretched hand, he made his way in the dimness past the stalls to the door at the far end which led to the laboratory.

Conscious that he could be disturbed at any time, he made for the chest where he knew the Powder of Projection was kept. Sure enough, the velvet bag with its phial and the small bars of gold was there for his taking. In a jubilant mood, he secured the bag within his coat and returned to the stable to finish off his work. There was only one horse which required his special attention; the rest were not worth the bother. To his surprise, the dog was not dead, and but for its laboured breathing and whimpers he might have tripped over it, for it had dragged itself before the royal stallion's stall. Tilly let fly a vicious kick to boot it out of the way, and there came no more sound from it. With a jaunty whistle, he withdrew his sword. What a night! He had the gold, the magical powder was his! The dog was dead, or as good as, and now the royal stallion was about to feel his steel on its balls. By the time the Parisienne had recovered from the shock, his letter would be written and on its way to the chief of police in Paris. Certain torture and death awaited both her and the alchemist.

'Have I left anything out before I geld this royal ward?' Claude Tilly cautiously touched the edge of his sword ... razor sharp ... perfect for the task ahead.

In the darkness, the stallion screamed and crashed against the wooden panels as if sensing what was to come.

As daylight broke, the smouldering remnants of the barn were a desolate sight. All about, men and women sat and lay in exhaustion on the ground. Hermione lifted her head from her knees and turned to Guillaume, who was stretched out beside her.

'At least no one was badly hurt,' she said, trying to be cheerful. He did not reply, and she stared ahead, her expression dismal as she considered the catastrophe of facing winter without grain. With scant interest, she watched the boy Julien leading a horse along the drive. Upon reaching a group of men, the lad paused, and after some talk, they all came towards Hermione.

'Madame, our lad Julien found this horse tethered down the drive.'

Hermione stood up and looked at the horse with mild interest.

'I recognise it,' growled Guillaume, coming alongside. 'It belongs to the timber merchant.'

'Claude Tilly!' The colour drained from Hermione's face. 'This is him ... he began this fire. Will he never leave me alone?'

'If his horse is here, then so too must be he! Has he gone into the house?' thundered Guillaume, turning towards the château.

'The colt! The King's horse!' Hermione's terrified shout galvanised all those about her into action. The men and boys were fit and strong and quickly overtook her as she ran through the Keep.

'Tell them to be careful with the horse!' she gasped, as a man passed and raced ahead. With a pain in her side from the exertion and a sense of foreboding, Hermione arrived at the stable door. It was open and the men gathered outside were looking inward in silence. Guillaume, who had been gasping and cursing some distance behind, arrived at Hermione's side, and together they went forward. As the men parted to let them both through, early morning sunlight flooding into the dim interior revealed the worst: a floor darkened with dried blood. Filled with horror and fear at what she was about to find, Hermione crept forward. There was Rouge, his rough, brown coat matted and dark with blood. Hermione choked on her words and wept.

'Oh, what will Pierre say,' she managed at last, wiping her eyes with the back of her hand. Guillaume, who was squatting beside the dog, looked up and shook his head.

'He has been dead for hours … looks like he has been cut to pieces by a sword.'

His words so alarmed Hermione, she instantly looked up towards the colt's stall. Much of its planking was splintered and whole sections were sticking out, but the horse was still there, and alive! Yet as Hermione moved closer, she saw its eyes were wild and its mouth was covered in foam. It was standing silent, shaking violently as if with cold. Despite all this, a huge wave of relief swept over her that the colt had not suffered like Rouge.

'Quiet, boy, quiet,' she said softly. 'I can't get into the stall, Guillaume. The door seems stuck.'

Guillaume came over and gave the door a great shove. For a time, he soothed and calmed the frightened horse, then, putting a bridle over its head, he led it out of the stall. Hermione reached up, stroked the stallion's neck and led it outside into the sunlight. Her purpose was to take it over to the horsetrough, away from the horror and the smell of blood. Seeing Georges was amongst the men discussing what had happened, she was about to ask him to help bring out the rest of the horses when Guillaume appeared in the doorway, his expression grave.

'The door … Monsieur Tilly is behind it. He is dead!'

CHAPTER 25

ad Pierre come upon Claude Tilly before the stallion's hooves had done their worst, his hunting knife surely would have despatched him straight to hell. Guillaume had offered to bury Rouge, but with gentle hands Pierre had placed his dog in a sack and gone off alone. Some time later, Hermione caught sight of him emerging from the trees carrying only his spade. She felt his sadness; all of them would miss the rough old thing and his joyous gruff bark. Needless to say, Olivier seemed completely unmoved by events, only displaying interest when Guillaume returned the velvet bag, found beneath the straw in the stallion's stall.

'The secret of making gold stays safe,' he had quipped, as he threw the faux bars onto a heap of ore. As to the destruction of the barn, which had left everyone else in a desperate state of anxiety, he seemed oblivious. From an upstairs window, Hermione watched him set forth for his daily walk. His way took him past Pierre, who was drawing water at the well. To Hermione's surprise, Olivier walked over to him and laid a comforting hand on the old retainer's shoulder. Then he walked on, leaving Pierre cap in hand, staring after him. This of course, thought Hermione, was the inner man who chose not to reveal the kind heart that was within. If at times he seemed thoughtless or removed from the affairs of the day it was because his mind was always preoccupied with solving problems.

When Tilly's corpse had been carted away, Hermione had felt no pity. Indeed, she hoped he had suffered. Men, women, and children had toiled week on week in the fields, and all gone up in an hour! To vent her feelings, she kicked at the blackened earth as she walked with Lucette on the place where the barn had stood. A little way off, children yelled with excitement as they chased after one another.

'Life goes on for them,' she observed. 'Guillaume will have to buy in … it will be expensive, but there is nothing for it. At least this year at auction we should receive a fair price for our timber.'

'Well, there will be one lady who won't be shedding tears,' declared Lucette, as they set off back towards the house. Hermione turned on her a questioning look. 'The Widow Tilly … I bet she'll be glad to see the back of him! Speaking of tears, you'll hardly believe it, but I saw that blacksmith weep like a child when he saw what had happened to the barn. He said to my Georges that had the timber merchant lived he deserved to be broken on the wheel, and he will do anything he can to help!'

Hermione's dark eyebrows lifted with surprise. 'How kind. I always felt Raoul bore a grudge after that business with his mare. You can never really tell about people until there is trouble.'

With little to do on the land, the *veillées* began again and the little community came together each week to make all tools ready for the coming year. Once again, Hermione pored over her books on husbandry and a new one loaned to her by the curé.

'It was sent to me by the Marquis,' said Father Grégoire, hovering over her shoulder while he waited for Olivier to reset the chess board.

'Ah, we have not heard from him for some time,' teased Hermione, with a smile of invitation. 'What news of Paris?'

'The courtiers are drooping with boredom, for the King still continues to sit with his breviary and Madame Maintenon. She, of course, sets the example in saving souls! Do you know, she even had one of her relatives shut up in the Bastille until he promised to abjure. The House for New

Catholics has the regular honour not only of her visits, but also of the King himself.'

'I have never cared much whether people join the Reformed Religion,' commented Hermione, studying the design of a parterre.

'Toleration is little better than *indifference*!' said Father Grégoire in a stern voice. 'How I wish my parish had some Huguenots so that I might demonstrate my zeal. The Intendant Marillac and his dragoons have brought about thousands of conversions in Poitou.'

'Really, this incessant chatter is *too* much to bear,' exploded Olivier, springing up from his seat at the chess table.

'Oh, my dear Monsieur Olivier,' cried the curé, turning away from Hermione to bustle across the room. 'You should have spoken earlier! I will not keep you waiting a moment more! I shall even try to let you win this game!'

Hermione went back to her reading and the atmosphere took on a busy quietness with only the odd crack of the logs to disturb.

Although the military-style crusade to convert Huguenots was within a day's ride, the troubles did not really impinge upon Hermione until well after Christmas and into the New Year. As soon as the roads were no longer quagmires but firm again for travelling, with Lucette for company she set forth for Rochefort. Besides various essentials, there was a saddle to collect, though with fodder and grain to buy in for winter it now seemed a luxury. Lucette was in high spirits to have escaped from her duties. It seemed she had forgotten she had taken a husband, for her quick eyes immediately spotted a column of dragoons entering the road from a side street.

'Oh, see how their helmets gleam, madame. How tall they look in the saddle, such width of shoulders.'

'Those are their epaulettes!' said Hermione with a slight despairing shake of her head. 'Your husband's shoulders are far broader!'

Along with the other people out shopping, Hermione paused to watch the body of men pass by. Their sword hilts and spurs glinted in the sun, while the jingle of harnesses lent a festive note to the moment. They were a fearsome sight; no foreign soldiers would dare to attack France as long as she had such men, thought Hermione. A group of sailors who had paused to watch the troopers turn the corner suddenly began to jeer and laugh. As the last troopers bringing up the rear came into view, so appeared the cause of the merriment.

'Oh, look,' spluttered Lucette. 'Just see the bird legs on that old man!'

Hermione's feelings of pride changed to dismay as her eyes took in the three barefoot men. Except for their shirts they were naked; each neck wore a halter from which a long rope was tied to the tail of a trooper's horse. It was a sorry sight, and amidst the catcalls and laughter there were also hushed murmurs of sympathy. Hermione stared at the weeping women and children who were following on behind the tethered men. The spectacle aroused in her not only pity but a sense of anger. Why did they want to be *different* from everyone else in France? To make such trouble for themselves and their children?

'Where are they taking them?' she asked the saddler, who had stepped outside his shop.

'To prison ... the men probably will be sent to the galleys.'

As the dismal procession passed on, the craftsman returned into his shop and Hermione followed. While he was away collecting her order from the workshop in the back, she mulled over what he had said outside on the street. It seemed a terrible thing to send husbands and fathers to the galleys just for their belief. She was conscious from bitter remarks made by Pierre and Marie that the fighting between Huguenots and Catholics had once been ferocious in these parts. Thinking about it now, Hermione fell in with the view that if the King wanted everyone to be Catholic in France, then those who wanted to be different should leave before another dreadful war was started by the Huguenots.

'How's that, Madame Du Chesne?' asked the saddler, placing his completed work on the counter.

Hermione fingered the brown leather. 'It looks very fine.'

'I wish you had permitted more intricate work, Madame Du Chesne! Still, you'll find it much more comfortable ... the ancient one you were using was made for a shorter lady. It must have been very uncomfortable. Before I take it to your coach, I have taken the liberty of making a new bridle. I had hoped,' he added as he reached into a drawer beneath the counter, 'that I might bring my mare to be served by the royal stallion. Monsieur Maurellet across the river turned me away.' The name took Hermione unawares, and she lit up with gladness at its sound, but the saddler was awaiting her reply and her mind ranged over possible reasons why Jacques had refused his mare.

'If Monsieur Maurellet,' she began awkwardly, thinking she would now have to refuse the bridle, and that of course would also cause offence, 'does not think the breeding of your horse is suitable for the King's stallion, then I am afraid I also cannot ... '

'Oh, he was well satisfied with the mare,' the saddler assured her. 'It was the royal stallion that was out of sorts. Might I bring the mare to Du Chesne?'

Hermione nodded, for the horse was now four years old. 'Was his horse seriously ill?' she asked anxiously.

'Monsieur Maurellet looked very worried, but that could be because his *fiancée* has disappeared.'

'Disappeared!' gasped Hermione.

'She has been taken off to save her from the heretics. Old Maître Henri said it is best for her. If it were my daughter, I would feel the same ... wouldn't want her being dragged off to prison like the fools we have just seen.'

As she made the rest of her purchases, Hermione's mind was only half on what she was doing, for she was thinking about Jacques and his troubles. So distracted was she, she found herself at fault as she collided with a large lady in the doorway of a glove maker.

'Forgive me, madame. Madame Tilly! How ...' Hermione got no

411

further, for snatching hold of her two girls the widow gave a shriek, and as if escaping from the Devil the trio fled down the street. Hermione cast a rueful look towards Lucette who was carrying her parcels.

'It would appear she feels I am to blame for her husband's death. She never replied to my letter.'

'Well, you are in a way, Madame Hermione. After all, had you agreed to sell him the château, they would be living there now with him. While we might be living here, where there is more life.'

Hermione looked sharply at Lucette.

'Would you really prefer to live here ... surrounded by sickness and sailors with their bloody teeth hanging out?'

'But there are shops and people.' Lucette sighed.

'And your husband?'

Lucette's mouth turned downward into a pout.

'Exactly,' scolded Hermione. 'He loves the forest, and you had your share of excitement in Paris.'

On the morrow, she rose at first light, resolved to go to the Maurellets' shipyard to offer what help she could. She did not know whether she would be welcome at such a time, but Jacques had come to her aid on the day of Lucette's wedding, and had he not spent hours riding through the forest explaining how she might go about things, even to the extent of throwing off his jacket and joining her in pulling up weeds and cutting down brambles? How foolish he must have thought her little 'gardening' effort that day. Even now, the physical sense of him as they had worked together was vivid in her memory. Amidst the hanging vines and impenetrable undergrowth they had been shut away from the world, yet it had felt like possessing the whole world. He would never know how she had suffered thinking about him, but she was strong now. It was the time to offer help to a friend and to those he loved.

There was scarce a clear patch of water to be seen on the Charente at Soubise as large ships held at anchor waited to make their approach upstream to the arsenal. As Hermione rode through the Maurellet shipyard, the noise of saws and hammers made it necessary to shout at the top of her voice.

'Maître Jacques ... where will I find him?'

The two sawyers below Hermione paused and gestured towards the river. The tide was high, and what looked like a newly constructed fishing boat had just been floated off a slipway. Hermione hung back, waiting for Jacques to finish his conversation with the man at his side, but when he turned, he spotted her watching from her horse. Instantly, a welcoming smile lit up his face, and he began to make his way up from the river. His skin was brown from sun and wind, but she noticed there were shadows of fatigue under his eyes. Hermione swung her foot from the stirrup and accepted the help of his upraised arms to dismount. His hands for a moment retained their hold.

'I've missed you,' he murmured.

Hermione nodded, unable to prevent tears showing in her eyes; there was nothing she could say, nothing she should say. The unspoken feeling which flowed between them was fathomless.

'I heard you had trouble ... your *fiancée* has been carried off. Can it be true?'

Jacques's hands immediately lifted away from Hermione's shoulders, and his expression became grave.

'I don't believe Perrette to be under physical duress, not like the poor wretches who are being harassed by the dragoons. I have visited every convent hereabouts to seek her out, but the eyes that stare back at me through the grille are without pity; I get no answer. They will keep her on bread and water until she shows she will be a good Catholic. She will be suffering terribly, for her will is strong, and she will not give way to such tactics. I am at a complete loss to know what to do.' He gave Hermione a smile that was part ironic, part helpless. 'I had thought to seize our priest to shake it out of him ... he took advantage of my absence when Grandfather and I went to Toulouse. What makes it more difficult is that Grandfather and Aunt approve of what has been done!

But enough of my troubles ... how fares Du Chesne? You did not come to see the model before it went to Versailles ... and I had something so special for you to see. Why did you not come?'

Hermione glanced away so he should not see the expression in her eyes.

'I did set out ... then I realized it was not possible,' she answered quietly and could not help but glance up into the questioning blue eyes. Their expression was tender and reflected something of the pain she had suffered throughout the past months.

'Never mind. You shall see the real ship one day.' He smiled, breaking the moment.

'Have you heard whether you have the contract?'

Jacques shook his head and shrugged. 'They are wrangling over my dimensions ... but the model caught the eye of the king, so I am more than hopeful. In the meantime, we have a new slipway and more than enough work to occupy our men.'

'And the royal stallion? I was told ...'

'Monsieur Jacques!'

The shout from the river held a note of urgency. Jacques turned and gave an answering wave.

'Will you wait? There is no one in the house. You would be more comfortable there, and I will join you shortly.'

'No, you are needed. Let me help find Mademoiselle Maurellet. It is easier for a woman to ask questions ... truly! Which convent do you think it likely that she was taken to?'

'I am convinced Father Francis took her to the Abbaye aux Dames, but when I went there to find her they refused to admit me.'

'Then that is where I shall start,' announced Hermione firmly. She took up the reins of her horse and remounted before he could offer help. 'I will let you know the moment I have news,' she said, looking down at him with an encouraging smile.

Jacques gave a swift glance over his shoulder as further commotion sounded down at the water's edge. 'I should come with you!'

'That is the last thing you should do,' laughed Hermione. 'You look too threatening in every way for nuns!' With a cheery wave of her crop, she wheeled her horse around and rode off.

The brief contact with Jacques reawakened all the feelings Hermione had tried so hard to suppress. Foremost in her mind, however, must be the discovery of the kidnapped woman. On the day of her visit to Saintes, Hermione dressed with care and thought to have Marie put preserves, pots of cream and butter, and biscuits baked early that morning into a basket. A few subtle questions put to Father Grégoire had revealed the salt marshes on the shoreline of Saintonge brought significant wealth to the Abbaye aux Dames, but Hermione hoped the bearer of a few tempting delicacies would not be turned away.

The warm devotional sound of voices floated on the morning air as Hermione alighted from her coach. Was an unwilling, or by now compliant, Perrette amongst this community? Would her own visit be welcome news if Jacques's betrothed were to hear of it? Perhaps any means of gaining freedom would be acceptable if she was being held against her will.

Upon learning that Hermione had come to make a donation, the elderly guardian of the gate admitted her without further question. She was led across the yard into the abbey and into a small room complete with bench and small table. After some time had passed, which put Hermione into a state of impatience and anxiety, a nun with dark intelligent eyes glided in.

'What is the nature of your visit, mademoiselle?'

'I am Madame Du Chesne. I have here a humble donation for the sisters in their good work.' Hermione pushed across the table a bag filled with coins. 'It is not a great deal,' she confessed, 'so I brought too this basket which may also serve as a sign of my devotion.'

'We are always pleased to receive gifts,' nodded the nun. 'Is it your first visit to the abbaye?'

'It is, Sister. I have heard of your work from our curé, Father Grégoire. I also come to enquire after the whereabouts of a young woman whose family are known to me. They are devout Catholics and fear for her safety. If they knew she was here, they would not grieve so.'

'Her name?'

'Maurellet ... Perrette Maurellet. Has she found sanctuary here away from those who try to separate her from our church?'

Beneath the wimple, the black eyes of the nun fixed their gaze on Hermione's face, then moved downward to the crucifix about her neck.

'Are you a devout believer, Madame Du Chesne?'

'I try to be, Sister ... often I fall short.'

'Not so short as Perrette Maurellet,' pronounced the nun, with a grim note of displeasure. Hermione felt an instant leap of hope; she was here!

'So you know of Mademoiselle Maurellet ... ah, that will be such a relief to her family.'

'There is little relief, madame, for the young woman was as obstinate and intractable a sinner as I ever met. She refused to take Mass right up to the day she left the confines of our sanctuary.'

'She has returned home?'

'Who knows what has become of her,' retorted the nun, the deep lines either side of her mouth set in rigid disapproval. 'On the day we took in a delivery of flour, she disappeared.'

'Oh dear,' said Hermione, wondering whether this was true or whether the nun was deceiving her to conceal Perrette's presence.

'I speak the truth,' announced the nun in a shocked tone, which made Hermione flush with embarrassment.

'Of course,' she said. 'Monsieur Maurellet did make enquiry ...'

'I remember his visit well. Our guardian on the gate saw violence in his manner. Was it he who sent you here today, madame?'

Hermione shook her head. 'No, indeed not. Was Mademoiselle Maurellet in good health when she left?'

'For one who refused to eat, as well as could be expected. And now, madame,' added the nun in a brisk tone that indicated the conversation was ended, 'let me escort you back to the gate. Your donation is helpful, and I hope you will remember us in future times.'

Once confined within the privacy of her coach, Hermione wondered what she should do next. As she had been escorted back to the gate, the nun had revealed that it had been over two weeks since Jacques's betrothed had disappeared. It seemed unlikely she intended to go home, for had she wished to by now she would be there. For want of any other idea, she called to Guillaume to take the coach across the river. It was always a treat for the eyes to look at the painted glass and the mason's work at the cathedral of Saint Pierre. As usual there were many people milling around the great church, but the atmosphere seemed different ... excited, tense ... and on slipping between townspeople in the square, Hermione discovered the reason. Before the open doorway of the cathedral were crowded some thirty or forty Huguenots. The men looked obstinate and white with determination, as did many of the women. A few were openly weeping. Speaking in a gentle persuasive tone, a priest was urging them to enter, but his entreaties were in vain. Not a man or woman budged. As if losing patience, one of the encircling dragoons nudged his horse forward so that it collided with one of the men. The impact brought the Huguenot down and there was an outburst of laughter mixed with murmurs of sympathy.

'They should leave them poor souls be; there has always been peace till the soldiers arrived,' whispered a woman next to Hermione. The officer of the dragoons barked out an order, and then, as if they were herding cattle, the soldiers pushed the men and women into a line and marched them away.

'It is not as if they are thieves or murderers,' protested another voice. 'I say we show our sympathy by taking those good folk victuals tonight.'

Hermione had looked for Perrette Maurellet amongst the women, but she was not there. A trooper who was bringing up the rear of the unhappy column began to make sport of any lagging behind by pricking them with the point of his sabre. The cruel action made Hermione scowl. With such war-hardened troops ranging about the countryside, confinement in a convent had at least been safe for Perrette.

On the following day, Hermione decided to hold back from sending word to Jacques about her visit to the Abbaye aux Dames. What she had learned would only alarm him. Instead, she decided to ride out each day to the small villages around Saintes to try to find news of her. On one such day, hot and saddle-sore, she made her way home by way of her glade. The great oaks cast their shadows across the green sward and the stream, lively and sparkling, was irresistible. Hermione dismounted to take a drink and her horse followed suit. It was the perfect retreat from soldiers and worries, and the tumbled-down branch on which she was sitting had a swing about it. Now and again, Hermione encouraged it to sway. She watched a cascade of droplets caught by sunlight as the mare raised its head from the stream. It moved away and started to graze and Hermione was content to remain idle, watching the flash of dragonfly wings. With her back supported by the curve of the branch and legs outstretched along its length, she was so comfortable that soon she was lulled into sleep until what she thought was a dream of singing voices awoke her into the realisation that it was no dream but the sound of real people. Like a cat, Hermione bristled. How dare they invade what was most private with their psalms! She slid off the branch and crept forward, knowing exactly what she would find. And indeed, as she moved round a large boulder, the Huguenots were only feet away. On sight of her, the singing immediately ceased.

'Have no fear,' she said quickly, her irritation dissipating at the expressions of concern. 'I mean you no harm.' She glanced around the women to see if Perrette Maurellet was amongst them, but it seemed not until she noticed the petite size of a woman standing a little apart. Her clothes looked damp as if she had been caught out in the rain, though there had been none. Aware that she was being looked at, the woman drew back the tangled damp coils of her hair, and as she twisted it into a tidy plait, there was no mistaking the heart-shaped face.

'Mademoiselle Maurellet!' exclaimed Hermione. 'I have been riding out searching for you. Your family will be so relieved to know you are safe.'

The pale blue eyes widened with recognition but stared back without a glimmer of friendliness. In that moment of exchange, it felt to Hermione as if Perrette's eyes were piercing into her inner soul. She flushed with the guilt of loving this woman's betrothed. The rightful claimant to the man she held dear silently accused her. With a feeling of misery, Hermione looked to the Huguenot minister, who had begun to speak.

'Madame, you have come upon us at a moment of great joy, for our sister here was not so long ago baptised. Will you join with us in our final prayer?'

Hermione shook her head, horrified by the suggestion. 'I'll go to my horse and come back shortly. There are troops everywhere ... you are all in danger!'

'God will protect us,' returned the minister with a smile.

As Hermione sought out her mare, she wondered what help she could or should offer. Food at least, for apart from a few bags they appeared only to have what they stood up in. The three young children especially would welcome milk and the rest something from a pot. As soon as the sound of praying died away, Hermione returned and found the group gathered about the minister discussing where to go.

'Dragoons are visiting every town and village,' she told them. 'In Saintes they were taking people of your faith to prison. If you intend to spend the night in the forest, at least let me offer you a hot meal at Du Chesne first ... the children might be glad of milk.'

There followed further discussion, and then the minister put on his hat.

'We would be very glad to accept your kindness, madame. And if you have an empty barn, that also.'

With a non-committal smile, Hermione led her horse towards a mother with two small boys and a baby girl. The woman accepted her invitation and together they lifted the infants up onto the horse, then set forth with the group following on. Perrette Maurellet, Hermione noticed, had kept well back to the rear.

'We would not seek to stay more than one or two nights, Madame Du Chesne,' said the minister, as he came alongside and fell into step beside Hermione. 'If you have a safe place … we would not wish to make trouble for you.'

Hermione glanced sideways at the anxious man, trying to make up her mind. What would be the reaction of Marie, and especially Pierre, to Huguenots hiding away in the new barn?

'It may be safer to return into the forest after you have eaten,' she said with a note of regret. 'I'll let you have food to take you through the next few days, but I cannot count on the discretion of all my servants. And should our curé think to call, as he often does, there will only be determination on his part to persuade you and your companions to recant.'

'That we shall never do,' responded the man with a weary smile. 'Nor do we wish to cause you embarrassment. So it is best we do not come with you.'

He made to stop, but ignoring his words, Hermione kept walking and he kept up with her.

'I know my people well enough. They will not deny you all a meal,' she said, sensing how desperate he must be to fill his belly. 'And perhaps we shall find they will overlook your presence for one night, though I fear they would not be willing to hide you from the dragoons.'

'And we should not expect it, madame,' returned the minister cheerfully.

'How came Mademoiselle Maurellet with you, monsieur? At the

Abbaye aux Dames they told me she had escaped from their care on the day bags of flour were delivered.'

'And according to our dear sister, the miller's lad took more away than he knew. She came upon us by accident two days ago when we were in another part of the forest. The poor woman had not eaten for days.'

They lapsed into silence, only roused from their thoughts when the mother on the other side of the horse soothed and reassured the children. The distance between the ranks of tall trees began to widen, and they emerged into the open within sight of the roof of the Keep. One of the mother's shoes had caused a blister, and as she turned away to take her shoes off, her little girl, who had been holding her hand, started to cry.

'The bridge there takes you into the courtyard,' explained Hermione with a gesture for the minister and those following to carry on. 'Not far to go now, *ma petite*,' she soothed, stroking strands of fine hair away from the little girl's eyes. 'See, here comes Maman now, with her shoes in her hand.'

Hermione clicked her teeth, and the mare moved on. Now the erect dainty figure of Perrette was just in front, together with Matthieu the children's father, and the others who had been in the rearguard of the party. As the mare's hooves rattled the timbers of the bridge, Hermione saw that the building materials for work on refurbishing the chapel in the Keep had been delivered. Suddenly, the sound of coarse laughter and the neighing of horses from the courtyard beyond made her blood run cold. Only yards ahead soldiers were dismounting from their horses; twenty or so at least! It was too late for the men and women emerging from the shadow of the keep; they had been spotted!

Hermione grabbed the boys from the mare's back. 'Hush now,' she whispered. 'Mademoiselle Maurellet, *dragoons ... take them*!' She pushed the two small children towards Perrette and pointed to the door set into the stone wall. 'Take the stairs up to the chapel.' At the word chapel there was such hesitant distaste on the heart-shaped face that

Hermione felt like slapping it.

'Perrette, bring the boys!' The mother's whispered order was fraught with desperation as she plunged towards the doorway with her daughter in her arms. Perrette followed, grasping the two boys by the hands.

'Keep very quiet and I shall come when I can,' hissed Hermione to Matthieu and another man who were also seizing the chance of escape. She turned the key of the door within the wall of the Keep and dropped it into the top of her riding boot. Then, taking hold of the mare's bridle, she walked forward and emerged from the dark shadows into the courtyard. With a gasp of dismay, she realized the officer shouting at the minister was clearly taken with drink.

'Bonsoir, sergent,' she said as pleasantly as she could. 'I am Madame Du Chesne. Can I assist you and your men?'

'Why, madame, you have already done so by rounding up these Calvanist sheep. And my men have their shears ready.'

The minister cast towards Hermione a sorrowful look and she shook her head to express her denial of leading them into a trap.

'These poor people have not eaten for days. I have offered them a hot meal. You and your men are good Catholics; you surely will not deny them food and a fire?'

The officer laughed in an unpleasant way. 'They can have both ... just one if they agree to attend Mass, and the other if they do not recant.'

Hermione did not fully understand what he was getting at, but his tone made her feel uncomfortable. 'Then I shall take them inside to eat.'

'Only after each one of them recants. Get back on your horse,' he said lurching towards one of the troopers, 'and fetch the priest down here.'

'Surely it is a matter of ...' began Hermione, anticipating the stubborn refusal of the Huguenots.

'It is a matter of obeying the King!' roared the dragoon, thrusting his face right up against Hermione's. She shrank back from the reek of his breath and the fury in the red-rimmed eyes. With a mixture of terror and anger, she watched him swagger back towards the minister.

'You are their leader, so you shall go first to get your certificate. Down on your knees and swear you will go to Mass tomorrow.'

'I cannot do that, sir,' answered the minister in a mild but steadfast way.

'I order you to set an example to these heretics!' With a powerful cuff of his gloved hand, the soldier knocked the minister's hat flying. The poor man had turned deathly pale, but he merely shook his grey head with a resigned expression. Hermione glanced towards the house and saw Marie and Lucette watching from the doorway. Pierre, Georges, and Guillaume stood between the two horse troughs. With a discreet motion of a finger, Hermione beckoned to Guillaume, who immediately made his way across the courtyard. It was reassuring to have him near, though there was not a great deal that any of them could do against armed men. One of the women had courageously gone to pick up the black hat, and as if his patience had snapped, the officer shouted for her to leave it. He then dragged the kneeling man up from the ground.

'Madame here wants you to have some warmth. Two of you lads,' he barked, turning towards his men, 'come with me ... the rest of you make sure the sheep do not stray!'

Filled with consternation as to what was going to happen, Hermione reluctantly crossed the courtyard with the men. At the kitchen door the officer paused and looked down at Marie with a beaming smile.

'Have you a good fire lit, old woman, for this heretic to have a toasting?'

Though Marie always professed intense dislike of Huguenots, she did not respond.

'Oh, this is not a roasting fire,' complained the officer a moment later as he stood before the great fireplace. 'Let's have more firewood on, lads. And you, madame, where is your hospitality for us? Let's see what your cellar has to offer soldiers of the King.

'You do not behave like a soldier of the King,' snapped Hermione, beginning to lose her temper, a state of mind which overrode her fear.

'Oh, is that so, madame? And what would you know about soldiering, about *Antwerp* … about companions lying with their guts spread on the ground for the King? You get your cognac and be quick about it, or that pretty face of yours will bear the mark of my hand.'

Hermione stepped sideways to avoid the threat of his arm. She gave Guillaume a reassuring smile, for the last thing she wanted was for him to get involved in a brawl. As she hurried away with Marie, coarse laughter and lewd propositions followed after them.

'It does not look good,' murmured Hermione, as Lucette scampered after them. 'Of all the days for Olivier to travel to La Rochelle! He might have held them in check. Please God they are not going to do what I think they are.'

'He brought trouble on himself, madame,' declared Lucette. 'Do you think they are really going to roast him?'

'Please God not!' said Hermione, feeling sick with the horror of it. 'Marie, how can we stop them?'

'He only has to recant,' chirped Lucette. 'And it's best for the others.'

Marie again chose not to speak, but there was a kind of certainty about her as she chose the largest flagons to fill from the barrel of cognac.

'I begrudge wasting fine spirit on them,' commented Hermione.

'As much as they can drink, madame, if we are to have a quiet night,' hissed Marie, her black eyes intense with cunning.

Suddenly, from above, there sounded a great shout of terror changing to desperate screams of pain. Hermione and Lucette looked upwards with expressions of horror and fear.

'What can we do to stop them, Marie?' asked Hermione in desperation.

'He is a heretic,' retorted the old woman sourly. 'Make the soldiers pause to take a tankard. My valerian in this flagon, will keep the man safe till daybreak.'

Hermione nodded with relief, and taking up a flagon hurried upstairs with Lucette.

'After you've helped me, Lucette, go to Georges,' she ordered, 'or he'll be fearful for you. Oh, merciful Saints, they have started on him again.'

With her heart racing with terror as further screams rang out, Hermione entered the kitchen. It was bright with a great blaze from the fireplace. To her horror, the two troopers were holding the poor Huguenot before it with his breeches pulled down.

'In God's name,' she cried out, 'have you no pity?'

'There'll be pity the moment he renounces heresy!' shouted back the sergeant. 'Now let's have those tankards, and afterwards, have your wench look after my men outside.'

Mute with misery, Hermione watched them hold the struggling man even closer to the heat of the flames, so that he screamed and sobbed piteously for mercy. In haste to bring the cruelty to an end, Hermione sloshed the spirit into tankards and Lucette took them over to the soldiers standing in front of the fire. In an instant, they dropped their victim like a sack to the floor, but after quaffing the spirit they had him up again. The kitchen resounded to his desperate cries, and what with his wails, the singing of psalms outside and the reek of burning cloth and flesh, Hermione pressed her hands against her temples, thinking she would go mad if this was not brought to an end. The dark, squat figure of Marie entered, bringing another flagon. With a great shriek, the minister at last screamed out that he would abjure. With a whoop of glee, the men holding him let him drop to the floor once more. Hermione ran across to him and saw that his buttocks were one mass of black and bloody flesh.

'God forgive me,' the poor man wept, 'I was weak, but the pain, oh, such pain, I shall die from it.'

'Hush now,' she soothed, 'Marie will ease it away.'

Hermione looked over for her help, but Marie was plying the sergeant and the two troopers with more drink. But despite what Hermione had taken for lack of sympathy, as soon as she had served the soldiers, she came and stooped over the tormented man.

'Give him a little of what is left in the flagon … not too much, mind,' she hissed, her black eyes narrowing with a warning look. 'I'll go and mix some salve to ease his pain.'

The soldiers were now sprawled around the table and the sergeant had taken out a pack of cards. Moving quietly and keeping her head lowered to guard against any eye contact, Hermione took up the near-empty flagon.

'Good thinking, madame. We'll need a few more of those. And don't forget my men outside. Converting all these New Catholics is thirsty work.'

As if he had not spoken, Hermione ignored him, and as a consequence the sergeant flung out a booted leg on either side of her skirt and held her captive. Hermione took a quavering breath and dragged one foot upwards out of the grip of leather, steeling herself to bring the heavy pewter down on his head if he did not give way. With a coarse laugh, he relaxed his grip, and with exaggerated, care Hermione stepped over his right leg, which made him laugh again.

'Here, madame, give our hero his certificate. I'll sign it later … it's no use complaining, lads,' he barked as both troopers swore in protest as he took up one of the playing cards. 'I have run out of certificates.'

Hermione took the card and saw it was the ace of spades. She went across and moistened the minister's lips with Marie's brew, then assisted him to drink a little of it.

'I'm to give you this,' she murmured, handing down the playing card. 'Keep it by you, for it shows that you have recanted and they'll not hurt you any more.'

The suffering man stared at the ace of spades, and his expression filled with horror.

'It is the sign of the Beast,' he said, half choking from the effects of the spirit and his emotion. He hurled the playing card from him and, uttering a desperate cry, tried to rise. 'Dear Lord, I have failed the test, but I shall not do so again, even if I and my mortal flesh must die in the

426

flames. I renounce all things popish and …'

As erupted from the soldiers a great shout of fury, a figure appeared through the kitchen door. To Hermione's relief she saw it was the curé.

'What, you heretic!' roared the sergeant, trying to get to his feet. 'There is no need for that, good dame,' he shouted as Marie entered with a bowl and linen. 'We'll have the whole of his carcass before the flames to burn the Devil out of him.'

Hermione turned, expecting Father Grégoire to intercede. With a sense of shock, she saw, instead of compassion, an expression of excitement and curiosity; he was holding back.

'He is badly burnt, Father!' she cried.

'Take him up, lads,' roared the officer, struggling to rise. The two troopers also tried to stand, but then, as if they had been hit by some weight, they slithered forward and slumped across the wood of the table. Hermione looked over to Marie, and she saw the black eyes gleam with triumph.

'Too much cognac, Father,' explained Hermione. 'Marie can help the poor man now.'

The elderly housekeeper went to kneel by the injured Huguenot; Hermione laid an affectionate hand on her thin shoulder.

'Will they wake up?' she whispered. Marie slowly nodded.

'Not for a long time. *Too much* valerian … *not at all.*'

'So, did he abjure?'

The curé's question brought Hermione's attention back to him.

'He did, but only because of the torment of the fire. It was not from the heart.'

'Suffering is nothing if it leads to salvation,' rejoined the priest.

There was something so smug and comfortable about Father Grégoire, such lack of sympathy or of condemnation for the cruelty which had taken place that Hermione found herself beginning to dislike him.

'This is what you always wanted, Huguenots to convert!'

Though her words were said quietly, Hermione's tone was heavy with disdain. They were received by the priest with a bland smile.

'Nor shall I fail the flock outside. I shall have the soldiers escort them and their minister here to the church. My words will be more persuasive than flames. Bishop Bossuet and the King shall hear that in this small parish there is a priest with the power to convert the most stubborn of heretics!'

CHAPTER 26

t suited Hermione to be rid of the soldiers, but the curé's intention of having the Huguenots kneel outside the church throughout the night was cruel. From the open doorway of the kitchen, he issued his commands to a trooper standing outside.

'It is for our sergeant to give us our orders, curé!' replied the soldier in a raised voice as if calling for back-up within. When there came none, he shifted his position and peered inside beyond the cleric's corpulent body.

'What is this?' he growled, seeing the three men slumped over the table. With a feeling of acute anxiety, Hermione watched him stride towards his comrades and shake the shoulder of the nearest. Other than a loud snort, there was no response. He then lifted up the sergeant's head.

'They are heavy drinkers, but I have not seen them taken so hard before. The lads outside are sleepy with drink, but not like this.'

Hermione met his suspicious look. '*They* did not have a barrel of cognac at their disposal.'

'Did they get him to recant?' he asked, his gaze moving to the minister, who was lying on his stomach so as not to put weight on his burns.

'He did so out of suffering,' answered Hermione.

'Suffering is a means,' murmured Father Grégoire. 'A night on their knees will help the others reflect on how they have been misled.'

'We can't move off with prisoners,' put in the soldier hastily. 'Not till our sergeant says so when he wakes.'

431

The arrival of morning was not something Hermione relished, but she must take advantage of the moment. 'Your men must be exhausted. There is plenty of room in the new barn.'

'What about the psalm singers?'

'They can bed down in the hay loft. The outer door of the Keep can be locked for their protection,' she added as the trooper's face clouded with suspicion.

'*Zut*, but who holds the key?'

'I do.'

The soldier pondered awhile as he looked down on the senseless form of his sergeant. Then he gave a nod as if inspired. 'I shall leave two troopers to guard them and, if you do not mind, madame, I shall hold the key until morning. Are you content with that, curé?' he asked respectfully.

Father Grégoire nodded. 'A night's vigil for reflection would have served these misguided people, but so too will a stint on their knees in the sun.'

'What shall we do?' Hermione gestured towards the sleeping men. 'I expect your sergeant would want you to watch over them?'

'You're right, madame,' responded the soldier, seizing hold of her suggestion with an air of importance. 'I'll have some men carry them to your barn.'

Leaving Marie to watch over the suffering minister, Hermione led the curé to the *salon*.

'Monsieur Olivier is not here?'

'He is in La Rochelle.'

'A town which has promoted the Calvinist cause for decades,' commented Father Grégoire, as he wandered over to the games table. The chessboard showed an ongoing game. The priest lapsed into silence, his fingers hovering over the black rook as if to move it. Then his podgy hand lifted away, and his concentration returned to Hermione. 'In Cardinal Richelieu's day, his great dyke and chain stopped the English sailing into the harbour to offer aid to Huguenot rebels. If those people out there think to abandon France by way of La Rochelle, they are mistaken. Monsieur Olivier will tell you on his return that the port is heavily guarded, and quite right. Our duty is to save souls for God, not abandon them.'

With Father Grégoire gone away to his bed and the soldiers to the barn, the atmosphere lightened. They were all tired, and Marie, when Hermione urged her to go to bed, shuffled away without protest. Moments later, Pierre, who had been kept busy throughout seeing to the troopers' horses, could be heard shooting the bolts home on the kitchen door. For an hour or so, Hermione concentrated on her embroidery. Then, when she thought sleep had come to everyone, she crept along to the kitchen and began to pack a basket. By now, those she had hidden within the Keep must be desperate. Had the women managed to keep the children quiet? Thankfully, the stone walls were thick. With a black wool cloak flung around her shoulders, she stepped out into the courtyard. All was quiet save for the call of an owl and the restless stirring of the troopers' horses. There was no sound from the direction of the hayloft, where, no doubt, the two guards, knowing the Keep was locked, had also made themselves comfortable. Treading softly, Hermione made her way to the Keep, and taking the key from her riding boot she unlocked the small door set into the wall. Within was pitch black, but she knew the steps well enough. Certainly, her little party were still there, for a child was crying. So that she should not frighten them, she called out softly, 'Bonjour, mes amis, it is Hermione.'

There was utter silence, and then, as she entered the room, there broke out a rush of questions.

'We thought you would never come! What has happened?'

'Was there a man screaming? It was very faint ... we couldn't be sure.'

'Have the soldiers gone? We heard horses passing through the Keep.'

'I'm hungry, Mama. Has the lady brought food?'

Hermione moved cautiously in the darkness as the babble of voices interrogated her. She took from the basket two candles and lit them with the flint. The lighted wicks brought to life the inside of the chapel and the first thing she noticed was that the beautiful statue of the Virgin had been covered by a cloak. Hermione compressed her lips with anger, and, walking over to it, snatched the garment away. She threw back a challenging look towards the pale faces watching her, but no one spoke.

'There is milk when they wake,' she said, looking at the two boys curled up on a bed of cloaks. Each of them had a thumb pressed up into their cupid lips; such innocence. The mother's eyes caught Hermione's and they exchanged smiles at the ability of little ones to sleep through anything. 'It was the soldiers you heard,' she said, taking out sausage and cheese. 'They have gone to sleep in the barn.'

'Then we can get back to the forest,' put in Matthieu.

Hermione shook her head.

'The outer door of the Keep is locked, and they have the key. Your friends are under guard in the hayloft. I could take you into the house, where the minister is being cared for by my housekeeper. There is a way out from there, but it would be hard going in the dark, especially with children. Tomorrow the troopers are taking everyone up to the church where the curé is to receive each renunciation on oath.'

'*Never*,' declared Perrette Maurellet in a voice so strong it made strange contrast to her tiny body. Like a defiant queen, she stalked forward and caught up the cloak which Hermione had cast onto the floor. 'I shall walk with them and sing the psalm of David.'

'We shall all sing!' declared the sandy-haired man beside her, taking up her lead.

'What of these tiny ones?' asked Hermione.

'God will protect them,' answered the man with a grave smile.

'And their mother here will thank you when her children are taken away from her to be brought up as good Catholics.' At Hermione's words, the mother uttered a desperate cry and her arms tightened possessively around her little girl. 'I will leave you to discuss what it is you wish to do,' Hermione went on, handing out the rest of the food. 'I'll return in the morning to see what you have decided.'

'If we stay hidden, where shall we go afterwards?' quavered the mother, looking to Hermione and then to her husband. Hermione took up the basket and bade them goodnight, for she had no answer to give.

The dire consequences which might flow from Marie's sleeping potion had plagued Hermione throughout the night. To her relief, the sergeant was not angry, but subdued and embarrassed.

'It has never happened to me before, madame,' he said with an expression of bewilderment. 'I can drink most men under the table. That wretch of a minister got off lightly, and now I'm told the curé wants them all at the church.'

'That's right.'

'They really are the dullest people,' spat the sergeant, as his horse was led towards him.

The courtyard, since breakfast, had been all noise and bustle with the troopers saddling up and the Huguenots defiantly praying before they were marched away. Hermione glanced toward the Keep and was glad that she had relocked the door of its upper chamber, for so determined seemed Perrette Maurellet to join with those marching to the church, she no doubt would have done so had she been able. A hand touched Hermione's shoulder and, turning, she saw it was the minister.

'I have thanked your woman, Madame Du Chesne, for ministering unto me.'

'Are you still in very much pain?'

'Not so much as in my heart at my own weakness and at being treated so cruelly by fellow Frenchmen. Thank you for the good meal this morning. Remember to tell Mademoiselle Maurellet there are many ways to serve God.'

'I will.' Hermione nodded. 'You are a brave man. It is sad for the children that you set yourselves apart.'

'Ho, fellow, get back into line!' bellowed the sergeant, beginning to recover his bombast. Raising his hat to her, the minister went away to re-join his small flock. Then, without more ado, the whole of the assembly moved off under the Keep and out over the bridge.

As soon as everything had settled down to normal and there was no one to see her, Hermione slipped over to the Keep where she found the fugitives ready for departure.

'Did you have enough to eat?' she asked anxiously.

Perrette Maurellet gave an impatient gesture of her hand. 'Am I right in thinking they have gone?'

Hermione nodded.

'So that is why the door to this chamber was locked ... you never meant to let us go with them!' she exclaimed in anger.

'It seemed the sensible thing to do.'

'Sensible? How dare you presume to decide for us, Madame Du Chesne? I thought I made clear our intention to be united with our brothers and sisters, to share in their suffering and offer the weak support.'

'Your minister,' retorted Hermione calmly 'thought it best you remained to support this family.'

'Oh, we could have managed, madame,' blurted out the father. 'We do not wish to be a burden or to endanger anyone.'

'You are not a burden, Matthieu,' put in the sandy-haired man.

'There are different ways to serve God, your minister said,' Hermione told them in a grave voice. 'He suggested a life in a protestant country.'

'That is what I want,' Matthieu burst out, his expression alive with hope, 'freedom for my sons to enter a profession. You were a lawyer, Martin, now it is forbidden for you to practice. Our people cannot be doctors or midwives ... what has happened to justice in France?' The sudden energy of this mild man obviously took Perrette Maurellet by surprise. Her expression became uncertain, and she turned towards the sandy-haired man beside her and touched his hand.

'Is that how you feel, Martin? You also would go to a foreign land?' The slim, scholarly-looking man slowly nodded in reply. 'But why have

436

you not spoken before?'

As if unwilling to expose his feelings, the lawyer turned his hat around in his hands, but then he spoke in a firm voice.

'Because I feared you would not leave France, your mother, or your *fiancé*.'

'My mother has disowned me,' declared Perrette in a tight, bitter voice. 'And marriage to a man who believes in idolatry is not possible.'

'Would you come with us to England?' asked Matthieu.

'If the only way I can openly worship my God is there, then so be it. And I am sure,' added Perrette Maurellet in a voice edged with irony as she swung to face Hermione, 'Madame Du Chesne will be only too happy to arrange our passage!'

CHAPTER 27

rom what the curé had said, it seemed it would not be possible for the Huguenots to take passage on a ship at La Rochelle. This being so, it was more than likely that all other ports would be guarded also. As Hermione explained this to the fugitives, disappointment showed on every face.

'How keen they are to keep us, yet they forbid us to earn our bread,' commented Martin. Hermione held up a hand as they all began to voice their suggestions at the same time.

Perrette Maurellet's voice cut across the chatter. 'We shall go to my family's shipyard to ask my cousin Jacques for help. He will know how we might smuggle ourselves aboard a ship to take us away from France.'

'But my Louise can barely walk with her blisters, and the children … how shall we get there?' asked Matthieu, his face filled with concern as he turned to Hermione looking for help.

Within the hour, Hermione was sitting in her coach as if to go out for the day. As Guillaume put up the step and was about to shut the door, Hermione leaned forward towards him.

'You are really willing to take the risk?'

'Madame Hermione, if it were not for the little ones, the rest could walk to their salvation. You feel obliged to help them, so for this day my sword will be at the ready!'

'No violence, Guillaume,' said Hermione anxiously. 'A party

439

of dragoons is different from some wayside robber. If we do meet a patrol, leave the talking to me.' With a grunt and a shake of his head to show his disapproval of what she was about, Guillaume disappeared and hoisted himself up onto his seat. The horses moved forward across the courtyard; then, as it entered the shadows of the Keep, Guillaume reined in the horses and the party of Huguenots crammed themselves into the coach.

With so many packed inside, it quickly became stifling hot, but the leather curtains had to remain closed, for the Huguenots' sober dress would instantly give them away to anyone looking in from the road. After a time, Hermione could no longer bear the heat and being crushed up against the two men. She made her excuses and had Guillaume untether her horse, which had been brought along so that when it seemed safe she might ride on ahead to prepare Jacques. For a league or so she rode alongside the coach, ready to fob off any inquisitive soldiers with the mention of sick children and smallpox, and then, when they were within half a mile of the shipyard and all was clear, Hermione bid Guillaume stop the coach. As the Huguenots clambered out, grateful to stretch their legs, Hermione walked her mare towards Perrette.

'I am going ahead now to warn Maître Maurellet.'

The petite woman looked up at Hermione, her expression filled with anxiety. 'Be careful only to speak to Jacques. Grandfather Henri might betray us to the priest.'

'Why don't we go to my house? It is empty,' offered the lawyer.

'Best not to go into Soubise, Martin,' replied Perrette, touching his arm as if not to give offence for rejecting his offer. 'To one side of our orchard there is a storage shed. Tell Jacques we will go there.'

Hermione gave her a nod. Then, instructing Guillaume to wait for her on the Soubise road after he had dropped off the fugitives, she rode away.

The quiet of the shipyard revealed that the workforce had left for their midday meal, but Hermione found Jacques standing before the masting pond. On seeing her, his face lit up, but then his smile was immediately replaced by anxious enquiry.

'You are alone. You have not found her then?'

Hermione slid down from the saddle. 'She is safe, and on her way here.'

'Thank God. There have been terrible happenings. Men who have been to war are not the best to deal with differences of belief. You say she is on her way home?'

Hermione hesitated, wondering whether she should leave it to Perrette to explain her plans, but time was pressing. It was hardly likely that the group could hide for more than a day or so in an orchard.

'There are Huguenots with her.'

'I might have guessed!' exclaimed Jacques, raising his eyes skywards.

'Perrette said they are all known to you. All of them are determined not to abjure but to go to England. Our curé said it is now impossible for Huguenots to leave France?'

'It has become so ... too many skilled workers were leaving. Are you trying to tell me my cousin wishes to leave her family to go with these people?'

'I'm not sure ... I can't speak for her,' though I know she intends to ask for your help. Is it possible to smuggle them on a ship bound for England? Could one of your ships take them?' She looked around vaguely at the various boats in different stages of repair.

'And who is to sail such a ship?' asked Jacques, his tone ironic. 'Are you asking me to risk my own skin for Huguenots? Why should I?'

Hermione looked uncomfortable. 'To save them going to prison.'

'They can do that for themselves. It is easy – they only have to say they renounce their so-called reformed religion.'

'The dragoons tortured a poor man before my fire last night to make him say it. The nuns at the Abbaye aux Dames could not alter your cousin's mind. When I came upon her she had just been baptised. Today she wanted to join her companions when the dragoons marched them away. She is a very ...' Hermione struggled for a gentler word than obstinate.

'I know the strength of her will,' commented Jacques in a quiet voice. 'You are telling me she wishes to practise her religion in England.'

'I believe so.' Hermione watched with compassion as his arms lifted in a gesture of exasperation, then dropped as if accepting defeat. Tears came to her eyes.

'You are sad,' she murmured.

'*Naturallement*!' he answered, turning about and walking away. Not wanting him to bear his sadness alone, Hermione hastened after him. 'Perrette and I grew up together,' he said in a low voice as she fell into step beside him. 'She is like my sister ... when Uncle died it was meant to become more. I feel I have failed her.'

Together in silence they walked down towards the river. There came the singing of sailors aboard a great ship as it passed downstream. Beside her, Jacques made an angry gesture at it.

'Am I then to help her hide like a rat to reach a country I have no affection for ... to condemn my aunt to die without seeing her daughter again?'

'I don't know,' whispered Hermione. 'You must speak to Perrette. She will soon be waiting in the shed in your orchard. If you do not wish to become involved with those who are with her, I can take them away in my coach. I'll wait for your decision in the mould loft.' Filled with concern, she watched Jacques walk away with downcast head.

The mould loft seemed vast and desolate without the model warship on its lower level. Affected by Jacques's dark mood, Hermione wandered about disconsolate, idly looking at the various tools which all had a different purpose in turning trees into boats and ships. Outside came the chatter of voices, sounds of sawing and hammering as work resumed. With idle fingers she picked up three miniature trenails from the floor and tried to juggle as performers did with balls on the Pont Neuf. Time and time again she tried, until, with a laugh of exasperation, she flung them away as Jacques walked in.

'We have milk-faced Huguenots hiding in the orchard, and here you are laughing,' he commented, a wry smile lighting up his blue eyes.

'Has all gone well?'

'Perrette believes so,' he answered with an ironic expression. 'I am to take them to England! Perhaps as you brought them here, you will tell me how I am to reach the Atlantic without being seen?' Hermione pulled a face, and despite the gravity of the situation, or because of it, they both laughed.

'It sounds easy enough for a master-shipwright!'

'A pity my naval cadet brother André is not here to help. I shall have to tell Grandfather. It would be impossible to prepare and take a boat without his knowledge. He was the cause of Perrette's abduction, but her situation now is grave … he'll not wish his granddaughter to end up in prison. The *Crevette* out there on the river has just been refitted. For the right price, her owner might consider taking them to the open sea.'

'And then?'

'That depends on how I get on at La Rochelle,' he said with a sigh. 'Come with me to the stables. I'll explain while I'm saddling up. Afterwards, we'll talk to Grandfather. You might consider while I'm away whether you are willing to sign on as a deckhand … we'll be light-handed on the return trip, and the fewer people who know about this the better. Can I count on you?' Hermione nodded, barely able to take in what he was asking because it was so appalling.

The scene between Jacques and his grandfather was fiery, but it hardly made an impact on Hermione, as all she could think of was her terror of going out to sea. Once Jacques had ridden off, she did her best to soothe Maître Henri, then, she hurried to the stables and rode off to keep her rendezvous with Guillaume. Getting Perrette Maurellet and the others here had been one thing, but now everything was out of control. Hermione's stomach churned with fright, but if Jacques needed her, she could not run away. There was Du Chesne … how to explain her absence? One thing for certain: she could not tell Guillaume of the likelihood of her sailing down to the mouth of the Charente, for he would either take her back to Du Chesne by force or, more likely, betray the fugitives to keep her from harm. Finding him waiting in position aloft her coach all ready to set off, she suddenly thought to distract him with the offer of food.

'You'll be hungry, Guillaume. Why not have a pie and ale at the tavern before you set back? I am staying here.'

Guillaume's broad face creased with surprise. 'I like the thought of pie and ale, madame, but, begging your pardon, not your staying here.' With an unexpected movement, Guillaume stretched sideways and took a tight hold of the bridle of Hermione's horse. 'I know my place since we've come to live in these parts, but I speak now for Master Olivier. You've done your kindness bringing the heretics here. I'll not see you bring trouble on yourself, and, pardon me again, I shall take you back whether you say so or not!'

Such a rough, fierce expression of affection moved Hermione, and, hating to deceive him, she placed her hand reassuringly on his. 'Maître Henri's spirits are very low ... he is never likely to see his granddaughter again in this life ... she is leaving with the others in a day or so. By offering my company, I am trying to distract an old man from his dark thoughts. If, however, you and the others are not up to managing without me for a few days, I shall come back with you now.'

'Not up to managing!' gasped Guillaume, drawing himself erect and adjusting the patch over his blind eye. 'There is plenty to keep Marie and Lucette busy with picking fruits for preserving, and the master has always looked to me for help! As for the royal stallion, there isn't a groom at Versailles who looks after any horse better!' Hermione nodded her head vigorously in agreement as the big man's face reddened with emotion. 'Are those heretics under the same roof with you?'

Hermione shook her head. 'No, there are only Catholics in the house. Don't worry, Guillaume. You look after Monsieur Olivier; he

444

needs it more than I.'

Thus they parted; he set to go for a pie and ale as he burst into loud singing.

> *'Long live the King and good parishioners,*
> *Long live faithful Parisians*
> *And may it always come to pass,*
> *That every person goes to Mass*
> *One God, one Faith, one King!'*

Because of the old servant Annette, who since Perrette's abduction had begun once again to clean and prepare meals for Maître Henri, it was not possible for Perrette to enter his house, even had he so wished it. Perrette herself only wanted to stay with the others, so concerned was she about betrayal. Her anxiety was evident when Hermione entered the shed in the orchard.

'Grandfather will not tell Mother that I am here?'

Through the chinks between the shed's rough planking, the rays of daylight revealed the strain on the pale, delicate features. Hermione pressed into Perrette's hands a large jug of milk.

'Jacques persuaded him not to. The woman who came to prepare dinner believes I am here to sell Du Chesne's timber. Maître Henri told her to make up a bed for me in the chamber for guests.'

'Then you will be more comfortable than us,' commented Perrette with a brittle little laugh. 'My friend Louise's house is nearby. There are many things she would like for the children. Also, Martin has things which are precious to him.'

Hermione shook her head with reluctance, inwardly wanting to help but knowing it was too dangerous. 'I'll bring what I can to make you more comfortable here,' she murmured, 'but it is not possible to do anything more without arousing suspicion.'

In view of the Huguenots' discomfort, it seemed indecent to sleep soundly, but awakening at dawn the following day, Hermione realized she had. She shared a silent breakfast with Maître Henri, and as soon as the servant had gone she made porridge and took it down to the fugitives. They had had a miserable night, and Perrette had just led everyone out onto the grass to sit in the sun, believing it was safe as long as the children kept quiet. It was not until the afternoon that Jacques returned.

'The owner of the *Crevette* has agreed to take on the job,' he said, finding Hermione in the *salon*, where she was reading to distract herself. 'We'll leave before light tomorrow. No need to look so alarmed,' he added, flashing a grin as he set down a bulging saddlebag filled with food for the journey. 'I've found a captain of a merchantman willing to take them aboard off La Rochelle ... so you'll barely see the sea. Once the bell has sounded for my lads to go home we can take blankets down to the boat ... it will be cold for the children. We'll need to turn you into a fisherman,' he added, with another teasing look. Hermione tried to smile, but inside everything seemed to be churning. Her sense of dread was heightened later by the coarse fisherman's smock and woollen cap handed over to her by the owner of the *Crevette*, Antoine, who had come to make ready his boat. What would it be like to be surrounded by water with no land to set one's foot upon?

Before they left, Hermione prepared a hot soup to give heart to everyone. It would have been simpler to have brought the little party into the kitchen, but Maître Henri would not hear of it.

'They and their like are robbing me of my granddaughter. I'll not see them hungry, but they'll not eat under my roof, madame! You may tell Perrette I shall not go with her to make her goodbyes to her mother. It is too cruel a sight for me to bear after losing a dear wife and both my sons. Nor do I want her coming here to look for my benediction.'

There seemed little purpose in going up to bed, for Hermione knew she would never sleep. Instead, she snoozed in a chair, listening to the murmur of Jacques and Antoine's voices as they discussed the dangers ahead. Maître Henri had retired to his room, and Hermione supposed that he was not even going to say goodbye to Perrette, but then, when it came to the time of leaving, just as they were making their way in darkness to the river, Jacques spotted the swinging gleam of a lantern behind them.

'It's Grandfather! Quickly, Perrette, go and make your farewells to him,' whispered Jacques. Perrette Maurellet uttered a little sob and hurried away, and it was not until they had reached the water's edge that she returned, sobbing as if her heart would break. As Jacques helped her into the boat he could be heard doing his utmost to comfort her, but they all realized that she would never see her home or family again.

The approach from the mouth of the Charente to the royal arsenal was heavily guarded by military forts. Soubise lay downstream around a loop of the river from Rochefort, and whilst sentries were more likely to be wary of suspicious vessels coming upstream once daylight broke, Antoine and Jacques had stressed that everyone must be vigilant. It was evident that both men had known the river since childhood, for though all was darkness, there was a certainty about their movements as they made ready and cast off. Until the first light, there was no need for hiding. The children, who were wrapped in blankets, had incredibly remained sound asleep throughout being carried on board. Still deep in sleep, they lay on top of a heap of fishing nets, whilst the adults stood about on the deck leaning against the rail.

'Jacques says he is counting on invisibility,' announced Perrette to no one in particular.

'How can that be when daylight comes?'

'We will be invisible, Louise, because he believes that when sentries see the same thing every day, they no longer look at it. The *Crevette* goes out fishing regularly, so they will only think of fish.'

'And we shall smell of it after hiding under those fishing nets,' observed the lawyer, Martin, as he came to stand alongside Hermione. 'I haven't had a chance to thank you for everything, Madame Du Chesne.

It was kind of you to make soup.'

'It is a sad time for you all,' murmured Hermione. In companionable silence they watched for a while as the ghostly shapes of trees along the banks and the lights of a few vessels at anchor slid past. 'You must be sad to leave Soubise.'

'Oh, I was not there so long. My home was in Pons. The Countess de Marsan's persecution against members of our church there became intense. Petitions were sent to the King, but there came no reply, so I left. It was no hardship, for I could no longer practise law. I had some money put by, but I needed to work. Mademoiselle Maurellet took me on at the shipyard, but only as a labourer, because the rules of apprenticeship are strict. I wasn't very good with my hands, but I thought of our Lord, how he for a time was a carpenter. I thank him for guiding Perrette to your forest. Louise and Matthieu and I were overjoyed to see her. How I shall manage with a foreign tongue I cannot say, but I shall have Perrette to urge me on. She is a fine woman.'

'I am sure,' responded Hermione politely. She could conjure no real warmth towards Perrette, who had made her very uncomfortable about staying in the Maurellet house. Perhaps it would have been more seemly to have returned with Guillaume to Du Chesne and left Jacques to manage for himself. She bit her lip, overwhelmed by a multitude of different thoughts. Deep within, she acknowledged she was the last person who should help to take away from France the woman to whom Jacques had pledged himself.

For three hours the wind held good in their favour, and their silent progress was swift. With her head tipped back alongside that of the Huguenot lawyer, Hermione was enthralled as he stretched out his arm and pointed upwards to various stars.

'Do you think the English will be kind to you?' she asked, thinking he would soon see these very same stars in a foreign land.

'Yes. They have taken many of our people in, and some of their churches have raised collections to help us start a new life.'

'I'm glad for you,' murmured Hermione, still not really understanding why anyone would wish to live away from France.

Dawn broke as the *Crevette* gained the mouth of the river in time for the outgoing tide. Hermione called to Jacques with a gesture at the boats all about them.

'Are we invisible?'

He nodded, the wind catching back his black hair. 'So long as our passengers stay hidden under the nets. You look an odd sort of fisherman.' He grinned. 'But then most of them are ... isn't that so, Antoine!'

'I must be odd to be here.' The fisherman laughed, as he adjusted the dark brown sail, 'But it is more exciting than fishing, though I'll not return without a catch ... you're not paying me enough for that.'

'You owe me a fortune at cards,' protested Jacques. The laughter and raillery between the two men continued for a while, and seeing Jacques so reminded Hermione of the glimpse she had had of him in the tavern at La Rochelle. She liked to see him like this, sparkling and laughing, rather than the courteous restraint he sometimes showed when alone with her. Beneath the heaped-up fishing nets and tarpaulin, the children began to fret and cry.

'Can the little ones bear it for a little longer?' she asked, directing her voice down to those hidden away.

'Yes,' came back the stout response of their father, Matthieu.

'It won't be for much longer. Monsieur Maurellet says we need to be careful till we're out at sea ... there are boats nearby, and we can still be seen from the shore.'

The *Crevette* began to make her bid to leave the river and enter the sea, and both Antoine and Jacques became fully absorbed. Hermione found herself a spot on a coil of rope to get out of their way. Suddenly, as though there were a giant hand at work thrusting upwards against the planking she was sitting on, she was lifted high with terrible force.

'The current is running about four knots,' shouted Antoine who had placed Jacques at the tiller. Hermione scrambled onto her feet, and her horrified eyes saw they were surrounded by raging swells. The wind shrieked and slammed against the thin smock she was wearing, flattening it against her body. Another huge lift of the waters took her legs away, and she flopped back down onto the ropes. It seemed as if at any moment the boat would overturn or the timbers beneath her feet would suddenly burst apart. Then, gradually, as if they had escaped from a cauldron, the violent hurling about ceased and was replaced by strong pulls of a current, as Jacques shouted something about being at sea. Hermione got up onto her feet, so as not to miss seeing the entrance into the Charente from which they had emerged.

'I thought we would be turned over,' she cried, trying to make her voice heard above the screech of gulls.

Jacques nodded. 'It is the meeting of two waters, and the current and the wind are strong. Are you warm enough?'

Hermione laughed. 'I was shaking a moment ago, but not from cold. I am a coward.'

'Cowards are allowed,' flung out Antoine in passing. 'Just don't be sick on my deck!'

'Now I am beginning to enjoy it.' Hermione laughed, breathing in the air. 'It is so different from travelling on a river.'

'Then take the tiller and hold it steady.'

Jacques moved away to help Antoine trim the sails, returning every so often to adjust their course in order to keep seaward off the Ile d'Oléron, en route for the Ile de Ré. After about an hour had passed, Antoine took the tiller and told Hermione she could pull aside the canvas and nets and give everyone air.

'It's best to keep seated, our captain says,' she told them, amid the cries of relief, 'but when you do need to stand, be careful there is no vessel nearby.'

To offer some cheer, she gave out some of the small biscuits which she had made when preparing the evening meal the day before. It was sunny and, with the breeze, really quite pleasant to be at sea. Martin and Matthieu arranged the canvas to make a shelter from the sun, whilst the women spread the blankets beneath it to better effect and kept the children amused with stories.

Just as Hermione had never been out to sea, neither had any of the Huguenots, and the men, who had lost their reserve, were full of questions.

'How is it you can judge a current when you cannot see it?'

'Often by things on the surface,' answered the fisherman, Antoine. 'Watch those floats further in. Do you see how they are being pulled to the right even when the wind drops?'

'We seem to be making good progress,' declared sandy-haired Martin, who had removed his coat and opened up the neck of his shirt. Antoine laughed.

'In an hour the tide will turn, and if the wind weakens, we will find ourselves back where we started. That is why we are keeping so close to the Ile de Ré. There is a small cove there which I am familiar with. We can drop anchor while we wait for the tide to turn again.'

'And the merchantman to arrive at the rendezvous,' put in Jacques.

'This is more straightforward than I had supposed,' said the young father cheerfully, 'and the air is so ...'

'We are not out here for pleasure, monsieur,' cut in Antoine. 'If we are discovered, every man here will find himself chained to the oar of a galley for the rest of his life.'

His words were a stern reminder of the consequences for all of them if they were discovered.

'Forgive me, Antoine,' stammered Matthieu. 'You are putting your life at risk for us.'

'And not to mention *livres*,' murmured Jacques in an aside to Hermione. 'When Antoine takes us into the cove, it will be a good time for them to eat while we wait for sight of the ship.'

'Its captain won't change his mind?'

'No, I don't think so. I gave only half of what he was asking ... he'll get the rest when they are aboard.'

The food which Jacques had bought in La Rochelle made a good meal, though Antoine would not put the *Crevette* right in so they could eat ashore.

'It is too dangerous ... and we must be ready to sail to the merchantman.'

The sun was now in the west, and the more time passed, the harder everyone strained their eyes for sight of the ship. The tide was well on the turn, but though it pulled the *Crevette*, her anchor held steady. Then Antoine, who was standing in the bows, gave a shout. As they followed his gesture, Hermione saw a large ship making way from La Rochelle.

'She is under full sail,' observed Jacques, his voice tense with anxiety.

'What does that mean?' asked Perrette anxiously. In silence they all followed the progress of the vessel through the white-capped waves.

'It means,' replied Jacques with a bitter laugh, 'her captain is *cautious*, rather than *greedy*.'

'Shouldn't we show ourselves and try to catch it?' asked Matthieu.

Antoine shook his head. 'The bastard never intended to see us ... it is useless.'

'Then what are we to do, monsieur?'

'What shall we do?' his wife Louise echoed, her voice shrill as she gathered the small boys to her skirt. Hermione's heart lurched as the poor woman began to weep. Then Perrette turned away from watching the dark outline of the merchantman, which was steadily becoming smaller.

'We have to go on, Jacques. Please, Antoine,' she urged, looking towards the fisherman. 'Is it not possible to set a course away from France?'

'It is possible, Mademoiselle Maurellet ... safer than negotiating our rocky coastline, but we would need to be more than twelve miles out or the incoming tide would only push us back again, and the *Crevette's* anchor is too short for such deep waters. Our only course would be to work our way north towards Ushant and the English Channel, but the rocks and currents up there are more than I or my boat would choose to cope with.'

'I have money which might help overcome such difficulties.' Martin drew the fisherman aside. There followed an exchange between the two men which continued after Jacques had joined them. Then Jacques faced about and spoke.

'We sail at first light.'

The breeze was stiff and south-westerly, which was just what Antoine wanted. From Jacques, Hermione learned they were making four knots an hour. Later on, the wind slackened, and the full heat of the day was realised as the tar between the planking began to sweat. The brown sails were no longer a full-bellied curve, but flapped forlornly, then went still. Hermione looked towards the distant coastline, but no land was visible.

'A heat haze.' Antoine sighed. 'It's not unusual at this time of the year, but we could have done without it.'

Gradually, with visibility down to about five yards, they were curtained off and marooned in their own little world.

'Tide's on the turn.' Jacques's tone sounded anxious. He joined Antoine at the gunwale, and the fisherman threw out the lead.

'We're short,' he declared. 'We're going to lose some of the advantage we made this day, but it can't be helped … just as long as we don't end up on rocks.'

At regular intervals, the line with the lead was thrown out to take soundings until there came a shout of satisfaction followed by a splash as the anchor was dropped over the side of the *Crevette*. By night-time the haze had transformed into a seeping cold which chilled mind and body. Only the children held close to their parents within a blanket seemed impervious to it, for they uttered not a sound. The night seemed endless, but Hermione experienced no fear, only from the strong motion of the water, discomfort. Then the first grey purple streaks of the dawn sky appeared and the mist had cleared. The coastline seemed much closer, but with a gathering wind and full sail the *Crevette* was soon flying to regain the distance she had lost when coming to anchor. It was another blistering hot day, though the breeze didn't make it seem so.

'Your cheeks and nose are red,' remarked Jacques with a smile, as he passed Hermione to tighten a sheet. 'The others have some protection under the tarpaulin ... take Antoine's straw hat.'

'Then what will he do?'

Jacques chuckled. 'His skin is as tough as hide. He only wears it for style ... he claims it came up in his net. See,' he said, as the burly man approached and he snatched the hat from his head. 'You can make out on the ribbon the name of an English ship ... The *Mary Jane*.'

'Take it, mademoiselle. Just don't let any jack tars see it, or they may shoot you. What about more of those little oaten biscuits?'

Hermione pointed to the children who were playing beneath the shade of the tarpaulin and shook her head. With mock anguish as he took her meaning, the fisherman rolled his large mischievous eyes in despair.

'You shall have an extra ration of sausage,' she called after him.

The Ile d'Yeu, Noirmoutier, Belle Ile, all had stories to tell which Antoine and Jacques knew well, even though neither of them had visited the islands. Suddenly, bringing the interesting conversation about Fouquet and Belle Ile to a complete halt, a loud crack, something like a musket shot, sounded. Everyone looked around, just in time to see, towards the horizon, a downward strike of lightning. Gradually the air became increasingly heavy and tense, and as the storm moved closer, it began to rain. The waters, which had been lively with white-edged waves, now changed into a grey, boiling mass that seemed to rise higher and higher around the boat. Each time a large swell rolled towards the *Crevette* it seemed she would never rise high enough, and when she did, immediately afterwards she plunged downwards only to be lifted up high again. The screams of the children added to the terror of the storm which, with each passing hour, increased in violence. Jacques looked to where Hermione clung to the gunwale. Her face was deathly pale, for unlike the other two women, who were occupied comforting the little ones, she had no such distraction. Jacques called to her, his voice strong and firm.

'Give these canvas smocks to the men and put one on yourself.'

The boat lurched sideways, and as water swooshed onto the deck, Hermione lurched towards him.

'I am so afraid,' she gasped.

'Just concentrate on what Antoine and I tell you to do … don't be afraid. It will pass over.' The smile in his blue eyes calmed her, and with clumsy fingers, she pulled on one of the smocks. Then she clambered forward to pass the other two over to Martin and Matthieu. At that moment, a great spray and wall of water took away the tarpaulin shelter over the women and Hermione lost her footing. As she staggered onto her knees, she saw, in the midst of all this wild foaming terror, the baby girl suckling at her mother's breast. Hermione caught Perrette Maurellet's eye where she sat alongside the mother, and they exchanged smiles at the wonder of it. At least if we are to drown there now seems no ill-will between us, thought Hermione. As Jacques had predicted, the lightning and thunder had moved onwards, though the wind and rain continued to drive hard throughout the day. The crying of the children made everyone reach within themselves for strength to help them through the cold wet misery and the terror of being surrounded by heaving waters.

'At least the water has not reached the cheese.' Hermione laughed as she handed out small pieces to those who could eat. 'The canvas kept it dry.'

'More important, the drinking water has not been contaminated,' responded Jacques.

'How is it you and Antoine were not sick?'

Jacques flashed a sympathetic smile. 'We're used to the sea, though it doesn't always follow. It can happen to anyone.'

'Where are we?' asked Matthieu, who had taken the opportunity of the slackening wind to abandon his place in the stern of the boat.

'We are not sure,' confessed Jacques. 'It has not been possible to see the stars, and there is no land in sight, but the wind is weakening, and if the night is clear, it will help. Antoine believes we must be far west of the Ile de Sein.'

From their efforts during the storm, both Jacques and Antoine were exhausted. And so, together with Martin and Matthieu, Hermione took her share of the watch. Despite seeping cold, she must have dozed off, but with guilty alarm she suddenly woke at the shout of a voice. Across from her Antoine and Jacques were still stretched out in sleep. Again came the call and, looking upwards, she saw to her astonishment a burly sailor looking down from a huge ship. He was nodding and smiling in a friendly way, but she could not make out a jabbering word he was saying. Hermione shook her head as the chubby red-faced man made a gesture with his hand.

'I think that is meant to be a fish swimming,' said Jacques laughing, who had woken and come with Antoine to stand beside her.

'Is it an English ship?' she asked, as Jacques shouted up to the sailor in the same foreign tongue.'

'They fly the Jack,' answered the fisherman, 'and if they be homeward bound, they'll likely be hoping for fish.'

'Perhaps you had better tell him you are fishers of men,' smiled Martin, who with all the others was gathering to look up at the ship. With a smile, Jacques broke off his conversation.

'They are hopeful we might offer them our morning's catch as they are running short of fresh food.'

'Where are they heading?' asked Perrette, with a note of eagerness in her voice.

To England ... I've asked to speak to an officer,' answered Jacques.

There was not long to wait before a man wearing an officer's black hat appeared at the rail. With a gesture that took in the sorry group of women and young children, Jacques began to speak rapidly in persuasive tones.

'What is happening, Jacques?' questioned Perrette, as the officer disappeared.

'He has gone to ask his captain whether he will offer you passage. They are homeward bound for Portsmouth. Is that what you all want?'

Although Jacques's question was for them all, he was in reality speaking to Perrette alone. Hermione turned away from their intimacy as the small woman reached out to take Jacques's hands.

'Dearest cousin, it is what God intends for me. He brought us through the perils of the storm and now, in this great ocean, this English ship was guided to our side.'

Above the *Crevette*, the officer appeared at the rail accompanied by some burly sailors. After a further interchange between them and Jacques, a ladder was lowered down the side of the ship. As Antoine's manoeuvres closed the gap between the two vessels, three nimble seamen descended the ship's ladder at great speed and jumped aboard the *Crevette*. Taking up her mooring rope they swung it up to another of their party, who drew the *Crevette* even closer and held her steady.

'They are going to take the children first ... it would be too difficult for you to carry them,' Jacques reassured Louise. Though her expression was tense and anxious, she offered them up to the brawny arms of the seamen. Immediately there came howling protests, but in minutes the sailors had scaled the ladder and handed their burdens to the officer at the gunwale and two midshipmen, who each held a screaming child aloft. Down came the sailors again and motioned for Louise and Perrette to come to them. First went Louise, and then it was Perrette's turn. Hermione saw the pretty face was glistening with tears as she turned towards Jacques. They embraced and clung to each other, then kissed, and then Perrette, her face distorted with emotion, was reaching out for the ladder. It was an alarming sight as the wooden steps swayed with the motion of the ship, but above and below was a sailor to ensure her safety. Soon the two men had followed her up and very soon the ladder was drawn back up onto the ship's deck. There came the rhythmical sound of men's voices as they pushed on the capstan to raise the anchor. The pale faces of the fugitives looked downward upon the *Crevette*, and as they started to sing a psalm, the wind snatching away the words, the poignancy of the moment struck home.

Antoine loosened the fishing boat's brown sail. The wind claimed it, and the *Crevette* moved away, back towards France.

CHAPTER 28

he brown sails of the *Crevette* curved over the blue sea towards France. Since their departure from the English man o' war, Jacques's mood had been quiet, his manner reserved. Hermione did not try to distract him. He had lost a member of his family, and it must seem like a living death.

'He'll soon come round,' commented Antoine, as he accepted her offering of a slice of sausage. 'If he is like me, he'll be glad not to hear all that pious singing.'

'You are shocking, Antoine!'

'And so are you, Madame Du Chesne ... what would your servants make of you stinking of fish? At least when we enter the Charente our silvery haul here will make us welcome, and you'll see,' he said in a kindly way, 'your friend will be much cheered by the sight of its waters, as well as by your eyes if he permits himself to look into them.'

Just as it had been difficult to leave the river, re-entering was likewise fraught with hazard. Jacques needed constantly to swing out the lead, for in some parts there was but a mere metre of water.

'It's fortunate that the *Crevette's* draught is shallow,' shouted Jacques, as they surged forward through the boiling turmoil of the two waters.

'This is what she is good at,' yelled back Antoine, his bare feet moving with speed back to the tiller.

Up aloft and all about them, a noisy screeching of circling birds seemed hopeful of a share of Antoine's early morning haul. Hermione's gaze moved away from the silvery mass of mackerel and settled on Jacques, who had taken over the tiller.

'So, when will a Maurellet frigate cast its shadow on the Atlantic?' she teased.

The intense activity and danger in negotiating the mouth of the Charente had returned the sparkle to Jacques's eyes, absent since his farewell to Perrette. As he was about to respond to Hermione's question, Antoine interrupted them.

'Come, *mes enfants*, time to eat and drink to the success of our voyage. If the two bottles of wine I brought for this moment have not smashed, we shall arrive back at the shipyard in the best of spirits.'

Taking up oars, the men brought the *Crevette* to a sheltered spot beside some willows. On a grassy bank Antoine built a fire on the slab of lead which he kept for the purpose, while Hermione made a start on gutting fish and Jacques went to forage for dried twigs to boost Antoine's small supply of kindling. A feeling of gaiety had come upon them all as they busied themselves about their various tasks. How long had they been away? It seemed an age to Hermione, yet to sailors who were away for years, six or seven days was nothing. How those men must long to set their feet upon firm ground. For the first time, she truly understood the rolling gait of the sailors about Rochefort, and the thought made her laugh out loud.

'What is so amusing?' asked the fisherman. .

'I am wondering if the way I walk will give me away to everyone at Du Chesne?'

Antoine grinned, his large teeth a flash of white against his dark brown skin.

'We haven't been away long enough for that to happen.' He laughed, catching on to her meaning. 'It's one way of telling a freshwater man from a seafarer.'

Antoine's full red wine grasped the mouth, and though the grapes might have hoped for boar, it mattered not, for the fish had such a tang of smoke and the sea.

'I'm going to miss this,' commented Hermione, licking her fingers as she finished the last morsel.'

'You have fish in your river,' said Jacques, looking towards her with a happy smile as he crouched beside the fire and set the last skewer to cook for Antoine.

'Not with such companions, nor feeling such relief to be alive!'

Jacques sat back on his heels, his intent expression inviting Hermione to continue.

'Most of the time, I really believed the waves were about to swallow me up and take me with them right down to the bottom of the sea. Was there ever such a coward!'

Jacques reached out and pulled the rough cap from Hermione's head, releasing a mass of salty wet coils. 'I forgot who you were,' he murmured. 'But never did I think you anything but the bravest of hearts.'

'*Alors*! What about *my* courage,' complained Antoine, as Jacques leaned towards Hermione. 'Don't I deserve a kiss from you both?'

In such a light-hearted way they continued passage up river, until, sometime after noon, they sighted the masts at the shipyard. At this point, so his passengers might return unobserved, Antoine brought the crevette to the river bank. After bidding him goodbye, the two of them walked on, keeping to the shelter of the tall rushes lining the river.

'Will you stay the night? You must be tired.'

'It is best I return,' said Hermione, her polite tone reflecting the constraint which had come upon them as the stonework of the house showed through the trees. There was a little tightening around her heart for the loss of the carefree mood of their journey upstream. It was not just of his making; she herself felt self-conscious. Such had been her relief and happiness when Perrette had gone, it had left her with a sense of guilt. She could still recall Perrette's mocking expression and her words that day at Du Chesne: 'I'm sure Madame Du Chesne will only be too pleased to find us safe passage from France.' Now they were near the house it felt as if Perrette were watching her still, waiting for a gesture of intimacy towards Jacques. They hurried on in silence, and then, as Jacques's hand pushed open the wooden gate which led into the orchard, he swung towards Hermione, his expression intent and purposeful.

'Before you go, I want you to see something which is precious to me. I'll have your horse saddled while you change,' he added, as she hesitated.

In the salon they came upon Henri sound asleep in his chair beside the fire, the remains of his meal still on the table. With fingers to his lips, Jacques led Hermione through the room and upstairs.

'It is better we leave Grandfather to his dreams; otherwise he will delay you for hours. Is there anything I can get for you? Then I shall go and help myself to a shirt and breeches.'

After the door had closed behind him, Hermione withdrew her clothes from the carved beech chest. It was, of course, difficult to pull together the bodice of her riding habit without help. Close to defeat, for the exertions of the last few days were beginning to tell, she flopped down on to the bed, barely able to hold the heavy weight of the skirt. As soon as she had won the battle with the buttons, she thrust her feet into her riding boots and, picking up her hat, moved quietly towards the door.

Downstairs, the old man's breathing was still regular and gentle, and teasingly she blew him a silent kiss.

On the yard outside, Jacques was already waiting with her horse.

'You were quick!' she commented, taking in his change of clothes.

'I did not have to squeeze into a dress.' He smiled, running his eyes over her. 'What became of that young lad who helped haul in the sail … transformed into a chatelaine with a sunburnt face! The workers will be returning from their dinner soon, but there is just time to show you before Grandfather appears.'

Apart from some work on the bench, the vast area was empty except for templates cut on the floor above the customary chalk drawings. Jacques strode over to a corner and pulled the sackcloth covering from something large. Exposed to view was a carving in the early stages.

'You have already begun to carve the figurehead for your frigate! You are very confident.' Hermione laughed.

Jacques nodded. 'Yes, it is for the *Hermione*. Do you see any resemblance? It is still incomplete, which is why I so wanted you to see the model before it was taken to Versailles. King Louis wished to know if the face was taken from life.'

Hermione stared open-mouthed, suspended between surprise and pleasure; that her face as well as her name had been captured for a royal ship! Jacques's blue eyes blazed with pride and delight as she strove to find words.

'What answer made you to the King?' she faltered.

Jacques turned away. 'I told him you did not exist … that you were a figment of my imagination.'

'Do not exist? But, why?'

Jacques' sunburnt hand went to the creamy grain of the wood. With slow deliberation, his fingers traced along the lips, before moving downward to the curve of the neck and the rounded shoulder. His fingertips then lifted away, and the expression in his eyes as he turned about was intense and compelling.

'I said you did not exist because I could not bear the thought he might search for you!'

Hermione moved towards him, her lips parting to close on his.

***

On her arrival back at Du Chesne, it was not easy to distinguish who was the more upset, Guillaume because she had not sent for the coach or Lucette who, while helping her to undress, let out her pent-up feelings as if scolding a child.

'Where have you been? Your hair is stiff with salt! It can't have come from a stay at a shipyard on the river. You were perhaps at Brouage, though that is a place for broken-hearted sweethearts like Marie Mancini, while your eyes, Madame Hermione, if you don't mind my saying so, are wild with love.'

'How well you know the local tales, Lucette.' The King's boyhood love for Cardinal Mazarin's niece, who had been banished to Brouage, was as well known as its salt pans. Hundreds of ships left the port every day to take its salt to foreign lands. Perhaps the Huguenots might have been smuggled aboard one of those ships. No matter, for hopefully they would by now be safe in England. Hermione could not help it, but her heart sang that Perrette Maurellet was no longer in France! Nor could the days pass quickly enough before Jacques came to Du Chesne.

Lucette's nagging voice became louder and shrill. 'You have never done this before, Madame Hermione, gone off without telling me where you were going!'

'But I did tell you, Lucette,' soothed Hermione, glad to step up into the luxury of a warmed bed. 'I went to Maître Maurellet's house.'

'Very likely,' snapped Lucette with her familiar cheeky air, reminding Hermione of their days in Paris.

'It is better for you not to ask,' returned Hermione, her expression suddenly grave. 'When you told me you had worked for La Voisin, I kept it from everyone, to keep you safe and to keep them safe! So do not ask me any more where I have been.'

She could see that Lucette was bursting to pry further, but the young woman merely commented with a sly little smile, 'Well, you look very happy, whatever it is about.'

During her absence, all had passed as normal. The royal stallion was well, and only Olivier was full of complaints.

'It has been very dull without you,' he grumbled, when they found themselves together at breakfast.

'But when you shut yourself away with your manuscripts, we could all leave and you would not know it,' she teased, helping him to butter and honey.

'I always know,' he retorted solemnly. 'The rooms seem cold without you. When I am distracted, things go wrong ... remember the explosion when you had gone off to the bedside of the dying man.'

'So, *I* was to blame for setting back your work?' Hermione laughed, letting his words pass.

'You mock from ignorance, Hermione,' snapped Olivier. 'You have not witnessed the steps towards knowledge. How do you prove a glass sphere contains no air? In London I moved with men who watched a mouse die from lack of air within Boyle's sphere. Each step I take in search of an elixir is a small victory. Long ago, Paracelsus believed there could be found a way of prolonging human life. He wrote, "If metals can be preserved from rust, why not then can the human body be rejuvenated? If inanimate objects can be kept from destruction, why should it not be possible to preserve the life essence of animate forms?" He also said, "There is a force of virtue shut up within things, a spirit like the spirit of life, in medicine called Quintessence or the spirit of the thing." It is that which I seek, Hermione, to prolong life by holding disease at bay.'

Hermione nodded gravely, acknowledging his belief and his skill. 'Why, that would mean I would be able to see the acorns I sow grow into mature oaks!'

Olivier's clever eyes threw upon her a look of scorn. 'Such limited thoughts! Still,' he added in a gentler tone, seeing the hurt expression she could not conceal, 'it proved a fortunate thing for me the night I was moved to take you in and offer you a home! I also see that coming here has kept you safe from liaisons which in Paris would have taken you from me. Now, if you will forgive me, I must go and tell Guillaume to light the furnace ... there are more important things than eating.'

As the door closed upon him, Hermione burst out laughing, for he really was impossible. It would suit him for her to be shut away here for ever without a sweetheart ... but it was too late! She leaned forward to the vase on the table and breathed in the scent of a rose until its heady fragrance, like love, filled her whole being.

The intervening weeks might have dragged by had Hermione's mind only been occupied with waiting for Jacques's visit. However, approaches were made to her from Saintes, for the royal stallion to cover two mares. Then, sending her into a state of anxiety, an official came without warning to make a physical inspection of her royal charge. After this, he proceeded to examine the daily records of care and those listing mares brought to the stallion. Hardly had the dust settled after the satisfied official's departure than a pedlar selling his wares handed over a letter from Jacques.

Every aspect of the day was to be perfect, so, whilst Marie was preparing all kinds of special delicacies for their meal, Hermione and Jacques rode away from the chateau so they could be alone.

The lofty canopy of the high forest cast everything below into cold shadow, and this atmosphere of sombre quiet somehow affected their happy banter until it petered out altogether, leaving each of them to their own thoughts. Hermione began to question why she had chosen this way when they might have reached the glade in sunlight, but she had wanted the contrast. Jacques's first sighting of the glade was to be as if a curtain had suddenly lifted on a stage, the stream brilliant with the flash of dragonfly wings, the expanse of green sward busy with dancing butterflies, and her three oaks resounding with birdsong. Here the ranks of tall trees dwarfed and confined like the bars of a prison. And there was another reason why she had wanted to enter the woodland from this direction, For so long she had had to restrain the attraction she had felt for him; whenever their eyes had met and spoken, both of them had hastily looked away. Today, they were both breaking free of past constraints.

'You seem very sure of your way,' called out Jacques, who was following on behind.

'Not so easy when the seasons change. Everything looks different, especially when covered in snow. Did you get lost in the labyrinth at Versailles?'

'Not likely with royal servants chaperoning us all the time. Our attention centred on the water sculptures rather than on which path to take. Charles Perrault's advice to the King that Aesop's fables be featured within the maze was inspired – a brilliant concept. Do you always consider carefully before you take a new direction in life?'

Hermione laughed in response to the teasing note in his voice. 'I didn't think long about leaving Paris. It seemed a matter of life or death. But Tilly's offer to buy the chateau kept me awake for weeks. It seemed impossible to keep Du Chesne, and the only sensible course was to take his money and buy a town house in Rochefort. But the moment I learned from you that the forest could provide a source of income ... that was it! Oh, and let's not forget that wild decision I made to go to sea with you!' She laughed. 'What do you think of this area about us?'

'Your men have done some excellent pruning,' observed Jacques, riding alongside Hermione as the space between the trees began to widen.

'Georges took to heart your warnings about disease entering through dead branches. Now you are going to see the place I love most, and here we are!' she breathed, as they approached the dense screen of thorn and holly. Suddenly, the brown speckled body of a mistle thrush flashed across their way, its harsh call making her mare rear up in fright. Hermione's hand went to calm her, and she glanced uneasily towards Jacques to see what his reaction was to this ill omen. His expression was as if nothing had happened, so she firmly cast the warning from her mind.

'I'm going to bind your eyes so that you shall not see until I say so,' she laughingly ordered, as they dismounted.

'Today I am your slave,' Jacques teased, walking over to her. In mock obedience, he lowered his head so that she could knot her kerchief into position, but as she stepped backwards his hands seized her waist and pulled her close.

'Now nothing in the whole world shall keep us apart,' he murmured, breathing in the scent of her skin.

'No, you must wait,' she protested, trying to stifle his kisses. Part laughing, part responding to his urgency, she moved backward, pulling him in the direction which would give the most dramatic view of the glade. It was not easy, as her prisoner's desire was solely directed upon herself, and his persuasive kisses, complicit with the intensity of her own yearnings, were weakening her resolve. Hermione clung to the hard lines of his body, feeling that soon nothing beyond love would exist, yet she made one last effort to hold off.

'Tell me what you think,' she gasped as she pulled away the kerchief. 'Aren't they magnificent?'

Jacques's lips pressed a fervent kiss against her neck, but at her insistent tone his glance flicked upwards over her shoulder. There was silence, and then a shocked gasp escaped his lips. For there, towering above him, was the largest stag-horned oak he had ever seen. The master-shipwright remained mesmerized as his hands fell away from Hermione's waist. The tree must be well over ninety feet to the top of its crown. He took a step forward, barely able to believe his eyes as they took in a second giant, and a third, slightly smaller, but whose trunk, through its screen of green leaves, he estimated must have a girth of over twenty feet. Jacques's heart surged with excitement; oh, that Henri were here to see!

'Well, what do you think?' repeated Hermione, slightly piqued by the cooling of his passion, yet pleased that the dramatic effect she had planned had clearly moved him. Jacques turned back to her, his expression a mixture of jubilation and disbelief.

'They are indeed magnificent ... you have found what we have not, in months of searching; a wing transom and the sternpost for the

Hermione.' With a whoop of delight, Jacques flung his arms around her, and, lifting her off the ground, whirled her around as if she were a child. By the time her feet touched the ground again, Hermione's senses were reeling. As she gradually steadied herself, she stared at him in confused disbelief. Surely he could not mean …

'What is it, *cherie*?'

As if a cold hand had grasped her heart, Hermione stepped away, filled with a sense of dread.

'You cannot think that I would cut down such trees,' she said, not wanting to believe him to be serious. The smile slid away from Jacques's eyes and lips.

'You cut down trees all the time,' he replied, his dark eyebrows lifting in puzzled enquiry.

'In the high forest yes, here it is different. The Druids visited this woodland long ago … see the sacred mistletoe up there, hanging about the oak's bough? This is where the Chevalier's lady was killed … many believe the tree spirits claimed her as a sacrifice.'

'What nonsense, Hermione,' declared Jacques with a dismissive laugh. 'These trees are compass timber of the first quality! It can take years to find such pieces. Never fear … I shall pay you handsomely for it.'

Hermione went rigid from head to toe as the joy of the day fled.

'You will pay not one *sou*,' she said, her voice expressing her bitter sense of disappointment. 'The oaks are not for sale, and as long as the forest belongs to me, they will stay rooted in the earth where God put them.'

'I fear you are mistaken,' replied Jacques quietly, as he debated within as to what to do. He took another keen look at the grotesque, misshapen trees, each one of which offered to a shipwright what money could not demand. Into his mind flashed an image of the model frigate speeding down the Grand Canal in full sail. He had to have them! Hermione would quickly adjust to their absence. 'Colbert's forest law,' he continued with a grave expression, 'states that trees within fifteen leagues of the sea, or ten leagues of a navigable river, can be conscripted into the King's Marine.'

'This is private land,' she flashed back.

'It matters not,' rejoined Jacques in a kindly tone. 'When the manteau impresses the Fleur de Lys into the bark of the oaks, they will no longer belong to you, but to the King!'

CHAPTER 29

 week had barely passed when Julien and other boys rushed into the courtyard with the news that Maître Maurellet and important-looking men were riding towards Du Chesne's wood.

'You've kept sharp eyes, Julien,' said Hermione, patting the breathless, black-haired boy on his shoulder.

'Shall we stay on guard, madame?'

Hermione shook her head.

'No ... just let us know when you next see strangers heading towards the wood.'

With Guillaume riding one of the carriage horses, Hermione set off to defend the oaks. Despite being held back by the lack of pace of Guillaume's mount compared to that of her own, Hermione was certain of arriving before Jacques and his party, as the way from the château was more direct.

'Should you be armed, madame?' asked Guillaume, casting an anxious look at the pistol thrust through her waistband. Hermione's hand went to the pistol, and the feel of it made her feel secure, just as it had throughout the journey when they had fled from Paris. For this confrontation she wanted the intruders to realize she was in earnest.

'Just because they see it does not mean I will use it, Guillaume, but they won't know that!'

The day being hot, even before Hermione had a glimpse of the flash and sparkle of the stream through the trees her mare had quickened her pace in anticipation of drinking water. The trespass of the Huguenots, whom she had come upon praying near here, had been unwelcome, but this day's imminent intrusion was far worse and made her heart pound with anger. Guillaume's unhappy expression, as he entered the glade and looked about and up at the great stag-horned tree, indicated he had reservations about what she was doing.

'There must be other oaks as big as these three, madame,' he said.

'It's their shapes, Guillaume ... see how the two main branches fork. I never gave it a thought before.'

'Well, the felling won't be so bad. After all, it's not as if you're short of trees ... it will give the rabbits more space!' Guillaume guffawed with laughter and slapped his great thigh at his joke. Hermione managed to swallow down her vexation; she realized that for most people it was not normal to sit looking at trees. How could anyone understand why she was so protective of the trees here when barges laden with her timber had been sent down the Charente last year and would be again, come autumn? Only Marie was different; she was bound up in the magical power of the oaks and in their past.

The heavy oppressive heat was bringing about an ominous feel in the glade, and buzzing flies were a constant irritation. Guillaume had picked a stem of ferns for Hermione to use as a switch, and it put her in mind of that first year when Jacques had come upon her lying flat on her back with a great clutch of them in her hands. She could recall his laughter, and then off had come his jacket and he had worked alongside her for hours. That cleared patch of earth now showed small shoots where she had planted acorns.

The mare beneath Hermione shifted restlessly as the jingle of metal and murmur of voices began to impinge on the customary sounds of the woodland. Laying a finger across her lips, Hermione indicated to Guillaume the need for caution. With her gaze directed to where the sounds were coming from, she glimpsed the movement of riders.

Jacques closed his ears to the voices of the officials droning on about the improved sanitary conditions at Rochefort. His thoughts were concentrated on what Hermione would do, for no doubt she would have been warned of their approach. From somewhere to his left, he heard the whinnying of a horse, and an ironic smile touched his lips. She was waiting for them!

'Why make it so difficult for everyone, *chérie*?' he murmured under his breath. With a signal to his stallion, he put some distance between himself and the keepers of the *manteau*, thinking it would be best for Hermione if he confronted her on his own. He guided his horse between a thicket of brambles, and as he emerged into open ground, there she was, looking every inch the haughty châteleine. Her face beneath her large hat was set in a grim, defiant expression, and, worse, his glance took in the pistol at her waistband.

'Are you going to shoot me?' he asked in a mocking voice. Her brown eyes stared back non-committal and hostile.

'I am here to make one last appeal,' she said proudly.

'It is too late.'

Close at hand, the sound of hooves scuffing through last year's leaves conveyed a sense of urgency. Hermione rode forward and laid her hand upon Jacques's arm, her voice and expression changing to desperate appeal.

'Please send them away, Jacques! There must be compass timber in other forests ... Angoulême, perhaps.'

'You would think so,' he returned, with a smile of regret. 'Ships can rot for months unfinished on the blocks, even years, waiting for the right pieces. Men's jobs depend upon this contract, Hermione.'

'I don't care about your yard!' she hissed, as a party of men entered the glade. She looked them over and saw the metal box strapped across the back of one of the saddles. Ignoring Jacques's attempt to seize her bridle, she rode forward.

'I am Hermione Du Chesne,' she called out in her strongest voice.

'You are trespassing on my land. The trees you are here to mark are not for sale ... they belong to me!' Her left hand hovered near the pistol and with some satisfaction she saw the nervous look of surprise on two of the three faces. The custodian of the box, however, merely doffed his hat and made a polite acknowledgement of her presence.

'It is an honour to meet you, Madame Du Chesne. We are officers of the state about the King's business. The Contrôleur Général's regulations must be enforced. Should we meet with any hindrance, the penalties will be severe. I am sure you would not wish your serving man yonder to be flogged or sent to prison.'

Hermione paled, and her courage began to dissipate, part by a feeling of being outnumbered, and more out of concern for Guillaume. With another polite flourish, the official replaced his hat, and as if she were no longer present, the group of riders dismounted and gathered in pompous dignity around the box. Each of the men produced a key, then in turn they unlocked one of the three locks which made secure the content of the box. Its lid was raised, and the *manteau* was lifted out and handed to Jacques. Hermione bit on her pride, and sliding down from her horse she hurried after him as he moved towards the tree she knew as La Reine.

'My dear friend,' she pleaded softly, seeking to stay his hand. Jacques cast a sideways glance at her, and as ever, a deep chord vibrated between them.

'If there were some other way,' he responded softly, 'but I really need them. They will become something beautiful, a ship for the world to see that bears your name, the *Hermione*. It will bring glory to France. It will help to keep France safe.'

'And likely will be blown sky high into thousands of splinters by English gunners. The oak belongs here, to the insects and creatures that depend on it.'

Jacques gave a slight shake of his head as if at a loss as to how to answer her childlike view of things. His expression appealed for understanding

478

but was answered by steel in her beautiful brown eyes, and his resolve hardened. Decisively, he broke away, and with an upward motion swung the *manteau*. As though she were transfixed, Hermione stared as the iron head pressed its imprint onto the bark of the tree. Then the *manteau* lifted away, leaving for all to see the fleur de lys of Louis XIV.

CHAPTER 30

he display of a pistol in Hermione's waistband had been a sort of desperate bravado on her part, Jacques concluded. Nevertheless, he did not underestimate the strength of her feelings, which in his opinion were sentimental and blinding her to all reason. Autumn was the optimum time for felling, before wet weather made forest tracks impassable. To delay until spring was not an option, as then of course, the sap was rising. With the point of his chisel, Jacques tapped to define the delicate curve of an earlobe and silently considered what Hermione would most likely do next ... slow down the navvies? Is that what you are going to do, my angry one, delay the making of a road to the river? Then, my love, we shall have to stop you before there is bloodshed.

Jacques's fingertips flicked away tissue-thin slivers of wood, and he stepped back with a critical eye. The grain of the wood took him from the curve of her hips upwards through the slender span of waist to the swell of her breasts. He uttered a sigh. 'We were so close; why do you have to make us so unhappy?'

Some feet away, working upon a religious study intended as a peace offering for Father Francis, Henri Maurellet broke his absorbed concentration of hours. He set down his tools on the bench and shuffled over to take a closer look at Jacques's work.

'It is the most splendid piece of carving you have ever done,' growled the old man. 'Though the eyes ... their expression has more challenge than I recall on the model. Am I right?'

Jacques gave a wry smile and put his arm around Henri's shoulders. 'Come, let's go for a drink and forget about ships and defiant women. You can tell me about old times when everything was better in Mazarin's day.'

'Laugh, my boy, but in those days you didn't have daughters forsaking their church and breaking their mothers' hearts to go and live in a land of heretics.'

'How is Aunt Marguerite bearing up?'

'You've seen her yourself. She'll only find peace in the grave.'

'Perhaps when we have news Perette is safe and content, we'll all find peace of mind,' commented Jacques, storing the figurehead away and covering it over with care.

Hermione knew if she could delay things long enough, the moment for felling would be lost and the trees would at least be safe until the following year. Together with Pierre, Georges, and Guillaume she walked the woodland, calculating the most likely line of approach any contractor would make to get at the oaks.

Pierre, who seemed to have found fresh vigour since the interference from officialdom, fingered his hunting knife and glared in the direction of the road.

'They've no business coming onto Du Chesne land,' he rasped. 'The Chevalier would have put them to flight with cold steel. You leave it to us, madame; we'll have no townspeople interfering in our lives.' Recalling Pierre's vigorous attack on her arrival at the château, Hermione turned to Guillaume with a wry smile, but his good-natured face only mirrored the elderly retainer's hostility. It was as if he had been born and raised in these woods, so indignant was his expression.

'We don't have to hurt anyone, just make it difficult for them to do their job,' she stressed, realizing how things might get out of hand.

And so two weeks of intense activity began; rope ladders were made,

482

aerial walkways created from which older children could drop down stones or fishing nets to hinder intruders.

'Get one of those rocks on your pate and you'll have a headache for a week,' observed Georges, watching his brother hauling a sack of stones up to a rough platform in a tree.

'It won't keep them out forever,' said Hermione, beginning to feel anxious about what she had set in motion. 'If only bad weather would come to keep them away.'

Very soon news came that a team of oxen pulling a wagon of navvies was heading towards Du Chesne. Pierre blew on his hunting horn to signal everyone to make their way to their positions. For this encounter, Georges, his brother, and Julien's father stood behind Hermione armed with pitchforks and axes. Guillaume stood to her right, his great sword at his side. This time, if she needed to exert her authority, Hermione intended to use Olivier's pistol. With every passing minute, her nervousness increased, but then, as a wagon filled with workmen rumbled into sight on her land, the thought of the reason for their coming here ignited her fury. Purposefully, she stirred her mare forward to meet them head on. A skinny youth who was riding alongside the wagon, seeing her advance, reined in his horse and made a gesture for the driver to stop.

'Why have you come here?' Hermione called out.

'To clear trees and make a road!' answered the rider with an air of importance.

'I do not need a road on my land,' retorted Hermione, her voice cold and firm. 'Begone! Do not set foot on my land again!'

The youth looked taken aback, until, reaching into his leather jerkin, he drew forth a paper and waved it with a triumphant smile

'My father has been contracted to deal with the exploitation of three.'

'I am not interested in contracts. Take your men off my land, or it will be the worse for you.'

The youth gave a nervous laugh, and, clearly at a loss as to what to do, he looked to the navvies seated in the wagon for help. Their response to his dilemma were hoots of laughter. His thin, pimpled face flamed red, and in a shrill, almost strangulated voice, he ordered the driver to proceed. Hermione pulled out her pistol, and, holding it out before her, pointed it at the youth.

'Turn back, I say!'

The contractor's son took no notice, so, with lips pressed tight and eyes narrowed, Hermione pulled back the trigger and fired. Her aim was directed above the rider's head, but the loud report of the pistol made his horse rear, as did her own. As if to cover her, Guillaume unsheathed his sword and took up his stance, daring every one of them to come on. At the same time, an arrow from Pierre's bow slammed into the wood of the wagon. The navvies sitting within it were open-mouthed with shock. Some sprang up, letting fly a string of oaths as they snatched up spades and axes, until a second arrow, finding the wooden handle of one of the spades, made them all duck down for cover.

'Get out of here, you devils!' roared Guillaume, making feinting movements with his sword, 'or I'll have one of your livers to fry with mushrooms!' With his great shaggy head and black eye-patch, he was a frightening sight. With a reloaded pistol, Hermione rode back to his side and took aim with a steady hand.

'I beg of you not to, madame,' shrieked the youth, his eyes wide with terror. Without further ado, he dragged at the bridle of his horse and, pumping away at its sides with the heels of his boots, raced away at speed. The bewildered driver gawped at Hermione with a plaintive expression as he sought to turn around the team of oxen. It was a long job, but at last the wagon was on its way, and only when it reached the road did its driver look back.

'Keep your poxy trees,' he yelled.

'They'll be back,' commented Georges, who had come forward to stand beside Hermione.

'I'm sure so,' she nodded, 'but we have delayed them by a day ... that is all we need to do … delay, delay, until it is too late to fell. Thank you all for standing by me.'

'It was not hard, madame.' Julien's father smiled. His expression, usually closed, now was sharp with curiosity. 'Were you really going to shoot him, madame?'

'Not today.' Hermione laughed, carried away by a great surge of joy that things had gone so well.

Later on that day, from the window of her chamber in the tower, she had a partial glimpse of Guillaume walking the royal stallion about the courtyard. The sight was irresistible, and she hurried downstairs.

'How splendid you are!' she said, patting the horse's silky, muscular neck. 'And how brave is your groom! This morning he held off twenty brigands – no, a *hundred armed brigands* - coming to steal my trees.'

Guillaume gave a great snort of laughter and beamed from ear to ear with pleasure. 'You are making a clown of me, Madame Hermione.'

'No, truth to say, I am not, Guillaume. You are brave and loyal … even though I know your heart is not in this matter. Like the others, you are angry about townspeople coming to tell us what we must do, but as for saving the oaks, I do not think you care.'

Perhaps to avoid answering, the big man crouched down and took up one of the stallion's hooves into his big hands. Then, as if satisfied about something, with the palm of a hand he gave the hoof a brush and straightened up. For a moment, he adjusted the patch over his blind eye, and then in a casual way began to speak.

'Have you ever considered how fair a ship is, Madame Hermione? How life is changing for the better with all the things they carry to us: spices, and the chocolate which ladies like to drink?'

'I'm not against ships, Guillaume,' she answered, walking on with him and the stallion. 'I just want to protect what is mine, and I must think of a way, for we cannot hold them off forever.'

'You know my sword is always at the ready,' he returned cheerfully. 'Though you are right. I would rather protect you than trees.'

Hermione watched the big bluff man lead the stallion towards the horse trough, his leather boots creaking with the weight of him. At times, he was absurd, more often irritating, but she did not want anything to happen to him.

On the following day, the contractor's wagon returned, but this time leading its advance was a man who was presumably the contractor, in company with the youth who never stopped looking about over his shoulders. As soon as the wagon had negotiated the turn from the road and was facing towards the woodland, the navvies aboard sprang out, clutching spades and axes as if they were weapons. From behind a protective screen of trees, Hermione could see that yesterday's tactics would not scare the men away today.

'You were right, Georges,' she murmured to the woodsman who had roused the alarm. 'If this is the father, he looks much tougher than his cowardly son. I don't want the children to get hurt.'

'They won't. I've told them to run if we get the worst of it.'

Hermione put the toe of her boot into the woodsman's proffered hand as he stooped to give her a leg up onto the saddle. As soon as she was settled, she glanced at Pierre.

'On the sound of your horn, we start the attack. Please don't kill anyone,' she added anxiously. The old man nodded, his grey, watery eyes alive with excitement. Then he strutted away, his bow slung over his bony shoulders and his hunting horn in his hand.

'Pity Rouge isn't with us,' commented Guillaume. 'Plenty of flesh to keep his teeth busy. Don't fret, madame, Pierre will only wing them, and so will I. We have to make them think there are easier ways of earning their bread and that there are more of us here than in fact there are.'

Hermione rode off a little to the right from where she could track the contractor's advance. The two riders had now reached the boulders which, like door posts, led through to a flat and narrow stretch of land bordered on either side by trees. It was not certain they would take this way, but more than likely, for elsewhere the ground was uneven and made treacherous by networks of twisted roots. Sure enough, the contactor turned around and waved on the wagon driver to follow through to the even ground. Hermione held her breath, praying that Pierre would correctly judge the moment when the navvies were clear of the boulders and surrounded by the trees. The workers came forward cautiously, and suddenly there sounded the strident note of a horn. The group of men paused and looked defiantly about them. The two riders reined in their horses, whereupon, as if a herd of screaming piglets had been set loose above in the greenery, the air resounded with high-pitched screams while a hail of stones pelted down onto the heads of the intruders. Many of the missiles found their mark, but the contractor roared for the labourers to move on. Hermione spurred her horse forward to drive back a group who were breaking out from the aerial assault.

'Get back!' she shouted, firing off the pistol. Its ball brought down a branch over their heads, and they turned and ran. Hermione followed them and spotted Guillaume driving back others who were entangled beneath one of the fishing nets. Their shouts rang out as with great swings from the flat of his sword he let them have it as they cursed and struggled to get free. Nor was there escape from the stones, for as the remaining navvies moved onwards, so did the boys overhead. It was impossible to see their rude walkways or where they were, and the beleaguered men had no means of getting up to them. Then, as a large rock caught the contractor's son on the temple, he lost balance and fell from the saddle. His horse lurched round, and seemingly not able to free his foot from the stirrup, the screaming youth was dragged along the forest floor. With an angry flourish of his fist to the trees above, the contractor wheeled his mount and set off in pursuit of the bolting horse. Left without their leader, the navvies turned round and took flight. After firing off her pistol to encourage them, Hermione followed. One man, she saw, had an arrow embedded in his thigh, and another a broken shaft protruding from his buttocks. Confident that none would think of returning this day, she set off in search of the contractor. When she found him, he was kneeling beside his son who, head in hands, was sitting on the ground crying. Hermione rode her mare around them in circles, for her blood was up, and she wanted to make sure they would never come back.

'Tell Jacques Maurellet he had best find his oaks elsewhere.'

The contractor scrambled to his feet and ran towards her, his face livid with fury.

'It is not Maître Maurellet who will hear of this lawless behaviour, madame, but the Intendant at Rochefort !'

With a laugh of defiance, Hermione raced back to join the others. Beyond the boulders she could hear sounds of laughter, and, indeed, there were the boys letting down their ladders and descending like squirrels.

'They couldn't reach us, Madame Hermione,' screamed Julien, his black hair standing up in tufts and his grimy face covered with scratches, yet all smiles. Filled with concern, Hermione touched one of the bloody gashes on his face, but in the way of boys, he roughly pushed her hand aside. 'This is the best game we have ever played, madame!'

'Julien, did you see old Pierre let fly his arrows?' burst in another boy.

'Will you show me how to shoot, Pierre?' chortled an older lad, as the wiry, green and brown clad figure of the elderly retainer emerged from behind a bush.

'Well, madame, they were no match for us,' he said with a swagger, as he slung his bow over his back. 'And your man Guillaume here has a mighty strong arm. Anyone would take him for a local man!'

'Another day delayed,' cried Hermione, her eyes shining with pride. 'And I think they will not want to return to work at Du Chesne!'

CHAPTER 31

 summons from the Intendant of Marine had arrived, and Jacques was on his way to Rochefort. He sat apart from the lads who were handling the boat, preoccupied by thoughts of the disagreement between himself and Hermione. His unhappy gaze took in the immense forest which stretched onward towards the arsenal. In that mass of greenery, could he find compass timber to equal that at Du Chesne? He swore under his breath, knowing it was hopeless. Local shipwrights had been wandering there for years taking their pick. There would be nothing to match Hermione's three oaks. Nowhere on his travels, or when training as an apprentice to his father, had he come across such immense girth, nor such vitality in trees of such great age! All three had been made to serve and delight a shipwright. If they were not taken now, eventually they would weaken and decay, instead of which they could be transformed into a magnificent ship of war! No longer rooted in obscurity, they could feel the force and life of the ocean: skim over the grey Atlantic, the milky green of the Caribbean, the blue of the Indian and the Pacific. With the shipwrights' skill, the courage of their hearts could withstand the onslaught of forces where oceans meet. Jacques's eyes gleamed as his imagination was fired, and he returned a wave to a local pilot who was escorting a First Rater downstream. Beneath the warship's lantern was the royal crown and under it an image of the sun. All the decorative work was newly gilded,

and cupids and sunrays were a blaze of molten gold. Jacques's admiring gaze took in the curve of the freshly painted hull as his own craft moved slowly upstream past the great ship of war.

'I saw her on the way up to the arsenal, Monsieur Jacques,' sang out one of lads, coming to stand near him. 'They've made her look like new … no prettier sight 'cept for a maid, is there?'

Jacques smiled agreement, and then his smile faded as a recollection slid into his mind. He uttered a groan. One moment her lips had been responding to his with hot urgency. All had been excitement and happiness. All within his grasp, only to be thrown away by his high-handed manner. Jacques clenched his teeth, hardly able to bear the memory of her cold dismissal. Why hadn't he been patient enough to talk about the sale of the oaks at a later time? With hindsight he could see that now, but when the blindfold had dropped away and he had seen those great trees he had been overcome with shock and joy. Might she by now have forgiven his clumsiness? Perhaps It would smooth things over if Henri rode over to explain what each compass piece would mean to a royal frigate. Hermione then would understand that ships were of more use to France than an idyllic spot, no matter how charming.

The Intendant looked up with a faint smile as Jacques entered the chamber.

'Thank you for answering my summons so promptly, Maître Maurellet. Once again, you have my congratulations.'

'Thank you, monseigneur. We are relieved the Council of Construction accepted our dimensions,' rejoined Jacques, immediately lifted out of his black mood.

The Intendant made a gesture with his ringed hands and smiled sympathetically.

'With some slight modifications, of course, but your innovation has not been quashed completely,' he said diplomatically. 'Remind me how long your family has owned the yard?'

Jacques's eyes blazed with pride as he thought of his father Nicolas.

'We Maurellets have always been there, monseigneur. The only member to go elsewhere is my brother André, who has joined the Marine as a cadet officer ... perhaps one day he will sail on the *Hermione*.'

'Ah yes, your choice of name was approved by the King, who has taken a personal interest in the frigate. Even more reason for things to go swiftly and smoothly! You gave assurances that your yard can handle such tonnage, and that your workforce will be increased.' With swift, thick fingers the Intendant rifled amongst the stack of papers on his desk and ran his fingers down listed columns. 'The clerk of the arsenal who inspected your yard reported you were missing vital compass timber ... what is the position now?'

The question sucked the joy straight out of Jacques, and his expression became troubled.

'There could be some delay.'

'Delay! There can be no delay, monsieur!' snapped the official, envisaging the effect of such news on the Minister of Marine and, in particular, on the Minister's exacting uncle, the Contrôleur Général. Still agonizing within, Jacques's glance took in Pierre Puget's drawing of the *Poupe de la Dauphin-Royal*; the carved figures on its upper works were glorious! So would be those on the *Hermione* too ... bringing glory to France wherever she sailed. The official's fingers drummed with impatience, but Jacques remained hesitant, a state of mind, he reflected, which seemed prevalent in him these days.

'I wondered about the forest here,' he started, and was immediately rewarded with an icy stare. 'Perhaps Louis Le Froideur's inventory missed some compass timber.'

'His thoroughness has never been in dispute!'

Jacques bowed his head, only too aware of the Inquisitor-Commissioner's distinguished reputation.

'I have seen what I need ... but it is a question of the felling.'

'Ah, a recalcitrant owner who wants to keep the oaks along his drive ... a Huguenot, no doubt?'

'No, not a Huguenot, but the trees are greatly prized by the lady.'

'A woman ... then dazzle her with a few pretty gems. She'll soon forget the trees. Her reluctance is probably designed to inflate the price.'

'I do not think so,' replied Jacques, his tone reserved. 'The lady is not like that.'

'Well, you decide on your own approach, Monsieur Maurellet,' carried on the Intendant with a note of impatience. 'If you meet with any resistance, have the contractors escorted by soldiers ... there are plenty of dragoons, and it will offer them a change from chasing Huguenots. I'll write an order for an escort now for you to hand to the commander of the garrisont.'

'There really is no need,' protested Jacques in alarm.

'Monsieur, you are already in a race against time if you are not to build with green wood.'

'We would not do that,' countered Jacques, with such *hauteur* that the Intendant half-rose in his chair in apology.

'I did not mean to offend; I just do not wish you to meet any obstacles as you did with the building of the model.'

Jacques' expression hardened as he thought of the injury to his grandfather's health and the strain of racing to get the frigate completed. The Intendant, fearing an angry outburst, stood up and, moving around his desk, led Jacques towards the window which gave a view to where a ship of the Second Rate was being refurbished.

'Let the sight of a great ship rising on your side of the Charente be your answer to the jealous eyes on this side of the river. Some here would like to see you fail, but we need private shipyards like yours to bring glory to His Majesty's Marine.'

***

It was one of the busiest times of the year, but Hermione could not give her mind to anything. The euphoria of driving away the contractor and

494

his navvies had diminished, leaving the remembrance of his threat to make complaint to the Intendant at Rochefort. Even though there had been no return of the oxen team and wagon, Hermione felt the need to constantly check on the trees.

As Pierre had predicted, the mast would be heavy, each green crown likely to shed more than a hundred and fifty thousand acorns ... pannage for the greediest of pigs. On reaching the glade, Hermione left her horse to graze and strolled over to the smallest of the oaks. She stooped under the Dauphin's green branches to get away from the heat of the sun. Within the barricade it was cool, damp, and dark. Trying not to think about the hateful imprint of the *manteau*, Hermione leaned back against the trunk, her thoughts gradually going back to the night she had been lost in the storm. These trees she had taken for huge witches. It seemed ridiculous now, but then, when lightning had transformed black branches into outstretched arms and skeletal fingers to bar her way, it had been a place of terror. Now she knew the wood and the High Forest better. Even so, it would be folly to tarry at the approach of darkness when the spirits of evil roamed free. The day also held dangers, for a boar could gore a man to death, and even a horse. Hermione pressed her fingertips deep into the crevices of the bark and, with a deep sigh, released all her tension. It was unthinkable that all this weight behind her could come crashing down to the ground. She turned inward and protectively stretched out her arms around the tree's trunk. Her fingers strained to reach further, but they stopped far short of halfway round its total girth. Remaining so, with her cheek pressed against the rough bark, she murmured her pledge.

'I will not let anyone destroy you ... not even a King!'

There followed a need to embrace the other two of her giants, as if, somehow, it might protect them from the force of the *manteau* and give them, as well as herself, strength for what lay ahead. So after her fingers had pressed and released La Reine, she ascended the incline to the great monarch of the glade. Straight away, the wren, as if in waiting, flew out from its branches.

'*Bonjour, poulette au bon Dieu,*' she said, trying to search out a crumb, for she had come without. 'They want me to sell the spiders' home and your perch; what think you to that?'

The tiny bird darted away, leaving only the leaves to rustle an answer. Hermione's fingertips touched a cluster of acorns; nothing, nothing was worth this living entity's destruction. Jacques and his grandfather must find other trees, and she would pray each night for their success. It would be truly splendid to see them lay out the keel of a great ship on blocks, but not if it meant the destruction of all this. Pursing her lips, Hermione whistled to a blackbird and at will strolled like the deer beneath the trees. Eventually, she made her way to the stream and stretched out on the turf, drowsily letting her fingers trail in the cool water as she pondered on whether her reflection was carried away by the water till it reached the river. How long she slept, she couldn't say, but the sound of voices awoke her. Hermione sat up in alarm, and through the trees she glimpsed the hindquarters of two horses. Intent on not being seen, she made her way from the stream and headed towards the smallest of the oaks. From the other side of the Dauphin's trunk sounded a compelling voice.

'Have you ever seen such dimensions, Grandfather? And you'll see the next one offers the perfect stempost in width and length. But come and see the real monster of the three.'

With her emotions whirling, Hermione remained rooted to the ground as the men moved away up the rocky incline. Her breathing quickened with anger until she was almost breathless. How dare they! How dare he come without her consent to speak about her trees as if they were some choice cuts of mutton!

'And this, Grandfather ... is it not the most magnificent knee wing transom you're ever likely to work on?' Jacques Maurellet's laugh rang out with boyish glee. 'This tree must be near two hundred and fifty years old, yet listen to its sound heart, for I know it will ring true!'

There was quiet, and then, resounding around the glade, came the sound of iron testing wood. As if someone had wielded a weapon against a child, Hermione ran out into the open.

'Stop it! Stop it at once! How dare you touch that tree? What are you doing here?'

The two men swung round and stared in surprise as Hermione raced up the bank towards them. Jacques Maurellet let the handle of the hammer slide through his fingers till it hung loose by his side.

'What are you doing here?' Hermione demanded, a trifle more calmly. 'You know these trees are not for sale!'

'Oh, but my dear Hermione,' responded Henri Maurellet, sweeping off his hat with a flourish. 'Forgive us coming here direct, but we decided not to disturb you. Jacques did say you were hesitant about selling these fine trees. Perhaps he did not explain the importance of such oaks. Why, each of them will render compass timber that will serve a ship of our tonnage to perfection.'

'That may be, Maître Maurellet,' Hermione returned with polite restraint, 'but while I am châteleine of Du Chesne, they will not be felled.'

'Not for all the gold in the kingdom?'

'No!' responded Hermione, not allowing herself to be affected by the elderly man's jovial but mocking tone.

'Have you considered the honour?' persisted the elderly shipwright persuasively. 'A ship bearing your name, an image of your lovely face admired by hundreds of onlookers as the King's ship passes down the Charente. A glorious frigate for His Majesty! It could even be the flagship for the royal fleet. Perhaps you don't understand. Look, my dear ... see here.' Henri Maurellet swung about to face the vast trunk of the tree. 'It is quite rare to find a trunk that divides so ... and with such dimensions! It will provide the transom which will bear the greatest weight in the ship, holding up – '

'Maître Maurellet,' cut in Hermione, trying to control her trembling voice, 'nothing you or Jacques can say will change my mind. You were kind and generous to buy timber from the High Forest when I arrived here, and for that I shall always be grateful. And you, Jacques,' she said, turning to include him, for he had wandered away as his grandfather spoke, 'you spent hours advising and showing the men what they should do. I would like to help you more than you could suppose, but I cannot and will not in this!'

The two men glanced towards each other, and Hermione could tell that Henri was clearly uncomfortable. Jacques swung the heavy hammer to and fro between his fingers, until, with an upward movement, he held its metal head in his left hand as if weighing it and his thoughts.

'You will always have our friendship and support, Hermione,' he said softly, 'but can we count on yours?'

Hermione stared at him, and paled with disappointment as she took his meaning. She shook her head in silent answer, hardly able to understand why he should be so persistent over something so important to her.

'It's time I returned,' growled Henri Maurellet. 'Best you two sort out this matter between yourselves.'

Making a stiff bow of farewell, he stomped away. Hermione watched in silence as the old man picked his way through ferns towards the two horses. She heard his sudden grunt of pain as he heaved his heavy body up onto the saddle. Then, with a gesture of a hand, he shouted across the expanse of sward, 'Gather acorns at the mast, dear lady, and the trees won't be lost to you!'

Such was Hermione's sense of outrage at his unwelcome suggestion, she turned away from the elderly shipwright's wave of goodbye. The moment he was out of earshot, she whirled around to face Jacques.

'Do you intend to come like a thief at night to cut them down?'

Jacques's thick black eyebrows drew together, and his blue eyes held an expression of regret.

'It will be after the mast, of course. Today I shall only make a note of

498

their dimensions.' In utter bewilderment, Hermione watched as he set down the hammer and, from the canvas bag on the ground, took out a metal caliper. With angry, disbelieving eyes, she watched him place the caliper against the bark where earlier her arms had held fast. As he began to move round to measure its girth, in a rush she made up the ground between them and snatched away the instrument.

'All you tell me is the law of the land,' she gasped, her eyes flashing with fury. 'This tree, this earth upon which you stand, belonged to the Chevalier Du Chesne. By his will, it is now rightfully mine.'

'You will receive top price for the timber,' responded Jacques, not looking at her as he bent to retrieve the caliper. His calm indifference was more than Hermione could bear, and with full force she lashed out wildly. The heavy gold ring on her finger struck his cheekbone, slightly splitting the skin. His shocked look of surprise was momentary, then he had her wrists in a grip which made her cry out.

'I hate you!' she screamed, kicking out to try to break loose. Their bodies collided in a conflict of wills until emotions abruptly veered, and he was no longer holding her wrists, but crushing her body to his. The whole of her cried out for him as kisses and hands urged her on to where she had not been.

'Promise,' she gasped, 'promise you will not take my trees.'

'I promise,' moaned Jacques, his lips pressing against her throat and the swell of her breasts. They sank to their knees, caught between urgency and exquisite delay. Thoughts were slipping away, but some distant part of Hermione's mind called alarm. She reached forward and clasped hold of Jacques's face, her fingers threading deep into his black hair.

'Swear to me,' she breathed in a rush, 'on your word of honour, that you will not take the oaks.'

It was as if she had doused him in cold water. The fiery ardour in his dark blue eyes died, replaced by cold disdain.

'You are asking me to strike some bargain?' he flung out with contempt. He jumped to his feet and, moving off, began to gather up his equipment.

With shaking fingers, Hermione tried to put her dress back into order. She could hardly think and had no control over the tears which gushed from her eyes as she ran towards him.

'I never want to see you again!' she cried as he whistled up his stallion. 'Don't ever come back onto my land or you will regret it!'

Jacques swung himself up onto the saddle and cast on Hermione a look of cold detachment. 'It will be best for you not to delay things. You have put one contractor to flight, but if you care for your people, you had better not encourage them to break the law, lest there be bloodshed. These trees bear the lilies of France. And you are not above the King!'

CHAPTER 32

he first glimpse of dragoons riding escort to a wagon of navvies filled Hermione with dismay. The hardened expressions beneath the metal helmets instantly revived unbearable memories of the Huguenot minister's screams for mercy as he was held before the kitchen fire. It could well be that this company of soldiers would not be brutal to Catholics, but any physical resistance would be put down with force. A further consideration was the new barn with its precious store. It would be a catastrophe if it were set alight, and if a Claude Tilly could do it, so might angry soldiers. It was no longer sport for children to throw stones at armed men. Through Georges, Hermione sent word to Julien to keep his friends away from the soldiers and navvies and not to climb up into the trees. Pierre and Guillaume she bade go about their usual work.

'I can't have bloodshed,' she explained to Guillaume, as he handed up her riding crop.

'Let me come with you, Madame Hermione.'

'No, you have much to do here for Monsieur Olivier. I am only going for a ride, and I shall stay well clear of the soldiers, but I need to think.'

Hermione's state of mind as she rode out was not the customary one of happy anticipation before visiting the glade, but of dread and foreboding. Adding to the sense of menace came the deep bellowing of a stag announcing the start of the rut.

All seemed normal within the glade as Hermione dismounted, until, walking around the green spread of the Dauphin, she spied through its branches the imprint of the *manteau* branding the tree like a criminal. Stony-faced, she walked along to La Reine, whose outstretched branches stirred at her approach. Hermione's hand went to the disfigured trunk; such a small mark in comparison to the width and height of the tree, yet the Fleur de Lys signified its doom! She moved away up the incline and with unhappy eyes scanned the great wall of bark of Le Roi's mighty trunk. Like a proclamation of execution was the mark of the *manteau*. Her fingers tentatively touched the bark as gently as touching a wound. She turned and took in the entire scene below. How would this place look without the two oaks below, and the king of them all here on the ridge? The question was so terrible she was unable to grasp it as a possibility. Someone had to help her! She hesitated, then sank down onto her knees between the proud sharp ridges of roots and tried to order her thoughts ... to calm herself, so that she might ask Mother Mary for help. As her hands clasped together, another force flowered within her and in her mind's eye the lovely face of Aglaé de Saintyon appeared.

'Help me to save them, madame,' she prayed out loud. 'Show me a way to keep them safe.'

Who could say whether her prayers had been heard, but on the following day, strong winds made the woodland hail down thousands of acorns. With a heavy heart, she asked Georges to take sacks and fill them with acorns from her three precious oaks. When she arrived there an hour later she found he had paused in his gathering to watch two stags fighting. The great beasts, with antlers interlocked, were moving backwards then forwards as if in some macabre dance. The huge clashing impacts as they came at each other made a dreadful grinding noise. Just one thrust of their points could inflict a deep wound or even death. Gradually, the younger challenger's neck was being forced sideways till it was almost touching the ground. Somehow with a twist of his head he managed to disengage, and then he was off.

'Hasn't the experience, madame,' declared Georges with a grin, as Hermione joined him. For a moment longer, she kept her gaze on the victor as he stalked majestically back to his hinds. Peace had descended and, after drinking at the stream, the herd moved off in a leisurely way up the stony bank. Pausing at the top, the great stag lifted back his head and bellowed a warning to any other would- be contenders, but no challenge was returned. With an imperious turn of his great head, he looked back down upon the glade, the spread of his huge antlers dominating the ground where Aglaé de Saintyon had died beneath the mighty stag-horned oak.

'Two kings,' murmured Hermione. 'If only one of these could make the soldiers of another king go away.'

Working from dawn to dusk, sleeping under rough shelter at night, within a week the contractor's men had made a road to the river. Hermione felt utterly powerless as they made camp at the edge of the glade and began to cut away the lower branches of the Dauphin. What could a few poorly armed peasants do against workmen who were protected by soldiers? Unable to bear watching any more, she relied on Pierre each day for news. He reported that the oak had been surrounded by a bed of logs in order to cushion its fall. The axe would do its work on the morrow. Just after daybreak, Hermione fled to Saintes.

'It would have been more distracting for you at Rochefort,' commented Lucette, as the coach rattled along the road.

Overwhelmed by a sense of defeat, Hermione's response was glum.

'At least at Saintes I won't have to see officers from the royal arsenal.'

'Oh, but they are what make it fun,' trilled Lucette, pulling free a strand of blonde hair from beneath the cuff of her bonnet. 'Three trees are so very few to lose, Madame Hermione, when you own so many. And it was rather strange, if you will pardon me for saying so, to while away hours on your own in a wood. I mean, people don't unless they are out hunting … better to make a garden as you planned.'

Lucette chattered on about the interfering ways of George's mother and Marie's forgetfulness. Hermione offered a nod here and there, whilst inwardly preoccupied with how to save the other two oaks. It *had* to be possible! There had to be a way, but without some vast army, how could she stand against the King?

On arrival at Saintes, leaving Lucette to drift around the stalls on the market square, Hermione entered the cathedral and knelt for a long time in prayer, but nothing came to soothe the turmoil of her thoughts. Before leaving, as was her custom, she lit a candle for the parents whom she had never known. With her purse still in her hand, she decided to go and buy *bonbons* to cheer herself. The grey skies of the morning had obviously just been pierced by the sun, for a glorious, golden shaft of light streamed through the painted glass of the window high above. Hermione paused; what a divine gift were colours, and how fortunate she had been as a child to see the panels of glass at Notre Dame and the church of Saint Denis. Like the spark of a flint firing a wick, the name of the Benedictine abbey aroused within her a glimmering of hope … though she could not quite grasp why. During the entire journey back to Du Chesne, she turned over in her mind remembered images of soaring stone arches and statues of saints, but to no avail. Yet whatever was hovering at the back of her mind, she sensed it was important. Eventually, near demented with the whirl of her thoughts and Lucette's prattle, she pressed her fingers to her pounding temples. Surely after a night's sleep the answer would come.

The dreadful deed had been done. The changed appearance of the glade made Hermione cry out in shock. The particular section of the tree which the Maurellets wanted had been cut off intact and hauled away to the barge on the river. What remained lay like a headless corpse across the sward. Men and women armed with hooks were stripping away the bark to take to the tannery. Hermione hung back like one afraid of death, her nostrils filled with the smell of resin. Like blood, it faintly stained the white wood of the stripped trunk. She could not stop, nor even bother to wipe away the tears which streamed down her cheeks. Nothing, nothing could put it right; the Dauphin was now just so many cubic feet of timber, with only the rings on its stump to speak for its past. With a heavy spirit, she made her way over to La Reine. Like a choppy sea underneath its boughs, faggots waited to embrace their next victim. Workmen were already beginning to lay leafy branches from the felled oak on top of the faggots, so as to cushion its fall. Hermione went over to them, trying to look dispassionate and calm.

'When do you intend to cut it down?' she enquired in a casual way.

'In a day or so, but we need to take away the rest of yonder tree first to make room for it. We had quite a struggle to get the special piece which the master-shipwrights wanted along to the river; even with eight oxen it was heavy work.'

Hermione nodded thoughtfully. She trailed back to the felled Dauphin and placed her hand in farewell on its naked trunk. It was then she noticed a knot-hole from which protruded a slender twig bearing a small green leaf, and Hermione's heart squeezed with hurt at such a tiny symbol of defiance. As her fingertips touched the leaf, like a blinding flash her inner eye came alive with what she had been straining to recall: a man from whose flesh a tree was sprouting! It was a window depicting the tree of Jesse at Saint Denis. Hermione sank to her knees, covering her tears of relief and laughter from the workmen. She had the answer! She had been given the answer! There might not be time to save La Reine, but there was hope for the king straddling the ridge!

In the morning, Hermione went to see Olivier in the laboratory, to ask for his help with the plan she had conceived during the night.

'Would you tell me how I might make something burn really bright and hold its shape in the dark?'

The alchemist looked at her as if she had lost her senses. 'Is it important?'

'It is a matter of life and death.'

'Then sit down, Hermione, and tell me exactly what you are planning to do.'

Time was of the essence, and much depended on whether Georges and Victor could scatter the contractors' oxen at night. Hermione told Guillaume to offer the men wine and dice, anything without bringing trouble on himself, to divert and slow them down.

For her own part in what she was planning, Hermione spent several hours sitting in the hall gazing up at the trophies of ancient hunts. Lucette, who had already passed through twice, on the third occasion did more than cast her mistress an odd look but stood stock still and followed her gaze to the head of a stag with a wide spread of antlers.

'Do you want me to get him down, madame, for Marie to put in the pot?' she enquired in her pert way.

'That will not be necessary,' murmured Hermione, wishing she had been more careful, for the last thing she wanted was for Lucette to guess what she was planning.

'I was just wondering whether to have all these old things taken away. Perhaps when there is money to buy paintings.'

'The fire's the best place for them, especially that snarling wolf … though you could always sell his teeth, madame. Many old crones would like to have those gnashing away in their mouths.'

Hermione laughed as the young woman bustled on her way. Her words, however, had revived the memory of the toothless old woman who had come up to beg money from Robert outside the theatre on the night preceding La Voisin's execution. *Papier-mache*: *that* was the way to make the head and face of the stag! As for the antlers, it suddenly occurred to Hermione they could well be awaiting her in the forest, where she had seen a stag rubbing his head against a tree to remove his velvet. She leapt up from her seat and went to ask Guillaume to saddle up her mare. It took two hours to find the actual spot where she had seen the stag, but there were the discarded antlers lying on the ground. Into her sack they went, and at speed Hermione returned to the château, fully fired up to set to work.

For her workroom, Hermione decided on the tower overlooking the *pigeonnaire*. Olivier and Guillaume alone were to know what she was doing, and only because their help was vital. Each morning, Guillaume reported on the progress the contractor was making, and as he gave the agreed knock on the door of the room in the tower two days later, Hermione could see by his expression it was not good news.

'They have not approached the big one up on the bank, but they're felling the second oak down below today. The lads did their best to drive the oxen off further, but they are slow creatures. I'm sorry, Madame Hermione, I knew you would be upset. But there is some good news,' he offered with a sloppy grin which put Hermione in mind of Rouge. 'It being so peaceful like, the dragoons have gone back to Rochefort. And the villagers will support you because Marie has told them if the tree bearing the mistletoe is cut down, blood will flow.'

'Thanks, Guillaume,' said Hermione, giving the glue which Olivier had provided for the *papier-mâché* a stir. 'I have to accept there is nothing I can do today, but if we can at least save the last one …'

Though he had prepared her about the felling, the sound of the axe carrying to the château was dreadful to hear. Later on, when she steeled herself to ride out to see what they had done, came the shock of seeing La Reine toppled. The sight near took Hermione's breath away. The tree was suspended on the great mound of branches, its trunk taking up the whole length of the glade like a great long bone. She burst into tears. All that life! All the creatures which had lived in it, had used it for shelter from sun and rain. Hermione hit her clenched fist on to the palm of her hand to release some of her fury: *'Mon Dieu*, you shall feel some pain for this, Jacques Maurellet!' she gasped. The foreman of the workers marched up to her with a look of concern.

'Are you feeling ill, Madame Du Chesne?'

'It is nothing,' she muttered.

'It was kind of you to send us a barrel of wine,' he went on awkwardly, 'though we had heavy heads the next day. That is why we are a little behind in our work. Maître Maurellet will be here tomorrow. He wants to cut the compass timber himself and, later on, the one on the ridge.'

'Would that be Henri Maurellet or his grandson Jacques?' asked Hermione, nearly spitting out the names.

'They are both coming.'

'Good! I am delighted,' said Hermione. 'Offer them some wine with my compliments.'

'I would gladly if there were any left,' declared the foreman sheepishly.

'You shall have more. We cannot have you facing nights in the darkness without some cheer,' responded Hermione, her feigned bravado masking the churning of fury within.

On the morrow she ordered out the coach again, which put Guillaume into a miserable state.

'Merciful heavens,' he moaned, tugging at his coachman's uniform which was much too tight. 'All this travelling is going to kill the horses, madame.'

'Nonsense! They have too little work, and that is why they are so fat,' she replied unsympathetically.

'Where today?'

'Soubise.'

'Oh? I heard Maître Maurellet was coming today to supervise the cutting of the fashion piece.'

'Quite so, Guillaume,' agreed Hermione with a steely glint in her eye. 'And should we see him and his grandson, Monsieur Jacques, do not stop, but ply your whip! I have no wish to speak to them.'

'Then why are we going to Soubise?'

'You ask too many questions. There are other things to see besides the Maurellet family.'

Throughout the journey they did not encounter any riders, so Hermione supposed the master-shipwrights had cut across country. As soon as they were near the approach to the shipyard, she called up orders

510

to Guillaume. The coach immediately turned off the road to move along the lane which led to the shipyard, with Guillaume grumbling loudly about women never making up their minds. Hermione ignored him, and as they entered the shipyard, she put her head out of the window and smiled as a workman approached.

'Maître Henri and Maître Jacques are not here, madame.'

'Yes, I am aware of that,' rejoined Hermione with another smile, 'but I have brought something for them. I shall leave it at the mould loft.'

'Shall I come with you, madame?' asked the man respectfully.

'Oh, there really is no need,' responded Hermione. 'What I have to do will take but minutes.'

CHAPTER 33

here could be no return to violent resistance or the contractor would simply send for the dragoons and there would be bloodshed. With the influence of Marie, Hermione hoped the villagers would keep a vigil before the contractors set faggots and branches in place to cushion the fall of Le Roi. If Father Grégoire would also attend, if only for a short time, it might inspire more people to visit from further afield in the parish. So, filled with hopeful expectation, Hermione rode up to the presbytery.

'I will not detain you long, Father Grégoire,' she said, remaining standing as he gestured for her to take a seat in his bureau. 'Your housekeeper tells me you are expecting a visitor.'

'No one so important that I do not have time for you, dear Hermione.' The curé beamed, his chubby cheeks dimpling as he hurried her to a carved oak chair. Hermione's heart lifted with encouragement.

'Feelings are growing very strong about the Druids' oak.'

'Yes indeed, my dear. Marie seems very upset. But it is the law of the land, and we should not interfere with the Marine, for that is to interfere with the King.'

'Surely, praying for the oak is harmless enough?' coaxed Hermione. 'If you could come and lead the prayers, it would mean a great deal! And not only to our people, but it might soften the hearts of the workmen.' She paused and looked expectantly at the priest, hoping her words had swayed him a little, but his expression only conveyed discomfort as his eyes slid away from hers. He shifted impatiently in his chair.

'I'd like to help, but it might not be looked upon as appropriate behaviour by my bishop.'

'Surely, God's will is greater than the King's law?'

'But is it God's will, child, to save a tree whose only distinction is the pagan mistletoe hanging on its bough and a poor soul who died beneath it? We could debate such matters all day, but, alack, I need to prepare for my visitor. So, till tomorrow at Du Chesne. I am looking forward with great relish to my dinner with you and my friend Monsieur Olivier.'

'Of course,' responded Hermione, unable to hide her disappointment.

The priest stretched out his chubby hand and patted her arm. 'It will all come right, I'm sure.'

Hermione returned to Du Chesne by way of the forge, and she was barely past its entrance when the blacksmith came running out after her.

'I shall come tonight to pray at the oak, madame,' he said eagerly. 'I've wanted to help you for a long time, Madame Du Chesne. It is good to see the new barn full, after the wrong Claude Tilly did you. This tree is different from the others. It has magical powers, like the old dame Marie's warning: *It took a life. If it is felled, blood will be spilt!*'

Hermione gave a nod. 'Remember to bring your lantern, Raoul. There will be reed lights for any without.'

Father Grégoire's refusal to attend the vigil was a disappointment. In fact, there was much about him lately that had troubled Hermione. For whilst it had been only right for him to try to bring the Huguenots back to God, there had been cruelty in his look when he had directed the soldiers to march them off to the church. Indeed, according to Lucette, he had had the minister and his followers kneel in the full blaze of the sun for hours outside Saint Hilaire. What had come as a surprise to her this morning was Raoul's eagerness to help, which had, albeit in a small way, made up for the curé's rebuff. Everything hinged upon what came of this night!

Roused from her thoughts by the whinny of her mare, Hermione saw she had been brought to the top of the drive, where a cluster of women were standing around Pierre outside the shacks. Their skirts were hitched up into their waistbands, their muscular legs fully on display, and she did not need to guess what they had been about, for their flesh was stained dark red from treading the grapes. Du Chesne did not have many vines, but enough to provide its own wine. Pierre was very much in charge, and he had evidently walked back with the women. To Hermione's delight, she saw he was trying to hold on to a wriggling puppy.

'I'm glad to see you have changed your mind!' Hermione laughed, as she reined in her horse. 'You've missed having Rouge.'

From beneath the peak of his worn hunting cap, Pierre squinted upwards at Hermione. 'There'll not be another dog like Rouge,' he declared firmly, 'but we're overrun with rats.'

'Two more like this in the litter, madame,' put in one of the women eagerly.

Hermione smiled. 'You will have to persuade Pierre. It sounds as if we need all three of them. How is Michel?'

'He is no better, but would be, for a sight of you for a few minutes, madame.'

Hermione dismounted and waved aside the woman's anxiety to see all was in order within the wooden shack. What with the lack of light and the smoke from the fire, it took a while for her eyes to adjust, but at last she made out the white face of the child and his shy smile as he looked towards her from the family bed in the corner.

'Bonjour, madame. Maman is not here.'

'I have just been with her. She is talking to Pierre outside. He is going to take one of your puppies, possibly more.' Hermione's gaze went to the broken box behind the door, and the small bodies tumbling around the bitch made her laugh.

'I wish we had puppies here all the time,' murmured the child. Hermione moved towards the bed and sat down on a stool.

'How are you today?'

'Better, madame. The pain is not as bad as in the night. I am sorry they are going to cut down the great oak. Pierre told my mother you are very unhappy.'

The young face was filled with such concern that a sense of shame swept over Hermione. What was the felling of a tree, compared to the trouble before her!

'I would gladly see it go if it would make you better, Michel.'

'But it has given me something to think about, Madame Hermione,' smiled the boy. 'When it rained this morning, Maman put my tree outside. I will show you if you will bring it to me.'

Hermione strode back to the door, and pulling it wide she saw beside the entrance a small pot of earth.

'Georges told me how you planted acorns when you first came here,' Michel explained, his eyes filled with excitement as he took the pot from Hermione. 'So I asked him to get me an acorn dropped from the Druids' tree. Let me show you.'

'No, you must leave it asleep in its bed,' laughed Hermione, 'until you see the baby shoot peeping through.'

'If they cut down your great oak, I shall give this to you, madame.'

'In spring, Michel, you and I will go on my horse to plant it in the glade.'

'Shall I still be alive?'

The question was asked without fear. Somehow holding on to her emotions, Hermione took a small hand in hers and, leaning closer, kissed the boy's hollow cheek.

'Not a day goes by without everyone telling Mother Mary how precious you are to us. So look after this acorn, for I depend on you to have its green shoot ready to plant out in the sunshine next year.'

The only contents of the room which Hermione had put to secret use at the top of the tower was a heap of broken furniture which, when she and Lucette had been searching for Aglaé's diamonds, had barely warranted a second glance. Part of the stone floor was now covered with lengths of black material which Hermione had obtained by cutting up old cloaks. On the table was a pot of black paint and, beside it, a cylinder which she had made by passing a long slender stick through a hole she had bored in the base of a large pewter jug. It was a poor copy of one of the props she had seen backstage after the performance of *The False Enchantments*, but as long as it was effective, that was all that mattered. What a pity Robert and the other actors were so far away. Their master of props would have made all the effects she needed so easily; she was hard put to remember how they went about making their masks, which Robert had once explained were inspired by the Italian Commedia dell' Arte.

From outside the door sounded the ring of footsteps, and, as the door opened and swung inward, Olivier entered.

'I have brought the solution,' he said, staring down at the black material strewn on the floor. 'Are you making curtains?' he enquired, with a look of astonishment.

Hermione took up her cylinder. With an expression of mystery, she held up the metal container before Olivier's face, then pushed home the wooden stick until its small handle lay flat against the entry hole, whereupon out from the other end appeared a large piece of white flimsy material which was attached to the end of the stick. Making a theatrical flourish, Hermione waved the material about for a few moments, then, when she gave a swift tug on the handle, the cloth shot out of sight back up into the metal tube. She laughed with delight, but the effect on Olivier was as if he had seen a dozen devils. His nostrils flared with indignation, and his expression was cold and filled with distaste.

'I don't know what you are about, Hermione, but I have no intention of becoming involved in cheap trickery. I am a man of learning! Please do not ask me to waste time in my laboratory again!'

Stung by his words, yet jubilant about the progress she was making, and needing to know what to do with his solution, Hermione rushed after him to the door.

'What is the solution?'

'Different glue,' snapped Olivier, his impatient voice and footsteps floating upwards as he hurried away down the stone steps. As Hermione was wondering how this particular glue might serve, his voice filled with derision, rang out. 'Sprinkle gunpowder from the bag I left on to it, and the shape you spoke of will burn into the eyes of the credulous for months! Be sparing with the gunpowder, though, or you'll set us all on fire!'

As she returned into the circular chamber, Hermione smiled. She had possibly found a way to bring even the King to his knees!

A *papier-mâché* cross proved easy enough to make, and as soon as it was dry she would coat its upper surface with the glue and sprinkle on the gunpowder. Hermione considered the metal canister and decided to make its effect more dramatic. Setting out the things she needed on the floor, she spread out the flimsy white material and applied a little of the glue, then carefully sprinkled just a pinch of gunpowder over the sticky surface. It needed to dry somewhere before she withdrew the material back up into the canister, so she set it down on a broken stool with the white material hanging free over its wooden edge. She had taken but two steps away when the metal tube rolled off the stool and landed with a noisy clatter on the floor. As Hermione bent over to retrieve it, she glimpsed something sparkling through the clutter of broken furniture. She crouched down lower to get a better look, and there was indeed something further back in the shadows which glittered and shone. Filled with curiosity and mounting excitement, she threaded her hand and arm between and through a barricade of wooden obstacles until her fingertips made contact with something silky and rough. Pushing further inward, she grasped hold of whatever it was and, in giving a great yank, caused the unstable pile to collapse. Another fierce tug and she managed to drag out a narrow length of wood onto which was secured a piece of cloth. What she saw made her cry out in disbelief. Stupid with amazement, she stared at the black velvet and, absent-mindedly, her fingertips began to stroke the silky pile which prompted a childhood memory of thinking it felt like a black kitten. As she fingered a sparkling moon and half of a star worked in silver, her thoughts were taken up with a variety of possibilties, but one above all else. Could it really be the same ... but how? Hermione's thoughts returned to the Rue Cocotte; how the firelight and candles used to make the stars shine in the little room where she gave her readings. What could this mean ... was it some strange coincidence? Marie must know what this once had been a part of, and where it had come from, but best not to bring her here or she would see the work in hand. Hermione picked up the splintered length of wood with its attached material and hurried from the tower down to the kitchen.

The elderly housekeeper was on her own kneading dough. Without saying anything, Hermione showed her the embroidered velvet and beckoned for her to follow. Other than to wipe her hands on a cloth, Marie showed no reaction as she shuffled after Hermione. Once they were in her own bedchamber, Hermione went to the trunk which held the crystal and unlocked it. She pulled forth the black velvet hanging with its costly spangles of moons and stars, her fingers seeking for the ragged end. Once she had found it, she took up the length of wood and brought the two halves of the embroidered star together, holding it fast as she turned towards Marie. No longer was the expression on the housekeeper's wrinkled face guarded; she had become deathly pale with shock. One work-roughened hand went to her heart, and as if her legs had given way, she sank down onto the edge of Hermione's bed, something she would normally never do.

'What is it?' cried Hermione, dropping the velvet to take up some bedside water for her. The old lady waved it away with a motion of her head. Still she stared, looking from the velvet on the floor to Hermione and then back to the velvet again. 'How can this be, Marie? How can it be that I was wrapped in this as a baby and left for Monsieur Olivier to find? How came the velvet from here?'

The elderly housekeeper seemed unable to speak, and her fingers kept fidgeting at her skirt. At length, she made a gesture towards the glow of the stars.

'You had this in Paris?'

'Yes. Did it once belong to the Chevalier?'

Marie shook her head and looked at Hermione with an expression of wonderment. 'Travelling players brought it here.'

'So,' exclaimed Hermione, seizing eagerly upon an immediate assumption, 'my parents were travelling players! But why did they abandon me in Paris?'

Marie's deep-set black eyes looked up at Hermione and slowly she shook her head. Hermione sat down beside her, barely able to contain her excitement. 'Tell me about my mother, Marie. Can you remember her? Do you think they were in some kind of trouble? I have never told you that Monsieur Olivier came upon me abandoned outside his house in Paris?'

'It was the master told the man and woman to take you to Paris. They were to go to the house he kept there.'

Hermione's mouth fell open, and she waited expectantly, but Marie's face closed over.

'That's all I can tell you, madame. I swore never to tell a living soul.'

'But you have to, Marie! You cannot leave me not knowing.'

'The master, it seems, left you not knowing before he died!'

'Knowing what? Marie, don't cast me back into darkness, be merciful! "*Honour thy father and thy mother*" ... how can I, when I do not know who they are, or if they are alive? Whatever it is you know, I swear before all the Saints that I shall never betray it to another living soul. I shall take it to my grave. Have pity.'

Once again, the black eyes pierced into Hermione and, as if satisfied, the old lady nodded.

'The wife of one of the players had a baby boy and much milk. She and her husband were given money to keep silent, to take the baby girl to Paris. The Chevalier left days later. He came back only once and locked himself away with her portrait for two days. But he never spoke of the baby girl, save to say she had not been brought to his house in the quarter named the Marais ... the baby was no doubt dead, and he was glad not to be reminded of the love he had lost. His heart was broken.'

'So the Chevalier is truly my father,' murmured Hermione tentatively, astounded by the possibility. Marie nodded. 'Then ... my *mother*?' Hermione breathed, her thoughts racing to consider possibilities. 'Could my mother be Aglaé de Saintyon? But you said she was killed when she was thrown from her horse before they were married.'

'There were wedding plans. Mademoiselle Aglaé, in company with her brother and sister-in-law, were here on a visit. The Chevalier and she were keen riders and had slipped out early to ride in the forest on their own. It was as they reached the wood her pains began, well before her time. The Chevalier raced back here for my help.'

'He left her in the wood giving birth on her own?' gasped Hermione.

'The poor master could hardly think. Nor could I believe what was happening ... she was so slender, it had not shown at all. In a moment, he had me sitting behind him on his horse and we were racing back ... every moment I feared I would fall off. When we reached the Druids' oak, I could see Madame was not long for this world, for she had not stopped bleeding.'

'The riding habit,' murmured Hermione, remembering the blood-stained skirt she had found in the attic. Marie nodded absently, her mind now caught up by those events of sorrow.

'Even after Madame had died, Master wanted to stay clasping her to him. But I was firm and called him to his daughter. She was the tiniest newborn I have ever seen. As the Chevalier touched her small hands, his eyes were streaming with tears. But his mind was more with the dead, and it seemed in his grief he did not care whether the baby lived or died. All that mattered was Madame's name should not be dishonoured. Pierre made it seem Madame's neck had broken when the horse threw her, and that it had crushed her under its hooves. We brought her back to the château, and I laid her out myself and placed her in the coffin so that no one of her family would know. Her maid was a silly young thing and grateful to leave it to me.'

'And the baby?' whispered Hermione, hardly able to believe it was herself she was asking after.

'I hid her up in the tower where you came upon this,' replied Marie, pointing to the splintered frame. 'It was furnished as a bedchamber then. The wife of the actor tore the velvet away from a piece of scenery … she thought it would keep the baby warm in the trunk. With the tragedy, it was not thought odd that the players were sent away. There was a terrible dark feeling at the château, and Mademoiselle Aglaé's brother was impatient to be gone. He and his wife and their personal servants left with the coffin, which was to be interred in their family vault. Within hours, our Chevalier set off for Paris.'

Hermione stared down at the ring which André Du Chesne had entrusted to her keeping. At that time, there had been so much she had wanted to know. 'When I asked the Chevalier why he had adopted me, he answered, "Who else?" I took his meaning to be that he had no one else in his lonely world.'

'Don't you understand,' hissed the old woman. 'To acknowledge you as his daughter would bring dishonour on his lady!'

Hermione fingered the heavy gold band on her finger, her mind caught up in a whirl of emotion and considerations. She was no waif, but of known parentage, and if Aglaé had a brother then, if he were still alive, she had an uncle, and possibly cousins! With a twist of the gold band, the engraved letters of the ring came into view: *Honorem est silentium*. Hermione repeated the words out loud. 'Honour is silence, and so it must stay.' Tears welled in her eyes as she thought of the life she and her parents might have had. Filled with a desperate need to be with her own flesh and blood, she rushed from the room.

The portraits in the Painted Room were all she had of them. As never before, she yearned to be able to step through the frame to embrace André Du Chesne, but to no avail. She could only find release in speaking out as if he were with her.

'I have forced Marie to break her word … but I needed to know. My life took the life of your dearest love. Did you forgive me at the end?'

The dark, smiling eyes gave their benediction, and Hermione gave a sigh. Her glance took in the ring on his finger, and she was suddenly struck by the thought that those hands had clasped her as she took her first breath, whilst her hands had held his at the very end of his life. The intense sense of loss was countered by the joy of finding what had been missing all her life and a deep sense of belonging. The light filtering into the room struck against the frosty glitter of the diamond necklace around Aglaé de Saintyon's neck, but Hermione's eyes skimmed upwards, seeking the face of her mother.

'Maman.' she said, taking delight in being able for the first time to claim the sacred word. Behind her came the sound of a shuffling step. It was Marie. A stirring of respect and affection flowed from Hermione towards her, but she knew there was no way of expressing it without embarrassing the older woman.

'I always felt, deep inside, you were their blood,' pronounced Marie gruffly. 'That is why you brought Madame's portrait to hang here. The master had engaged an artist to capture his darling's likeness, and it was planned that after the wedding it would hang here, opposite the one of our master.'

'Instead, he was to lock himself away with it in the tower,' murmured Hermione, remembering the moment she had pulled apart the curtains around the bed. To find a portrait within them had been a mystery then, although she had rightly guessed the depression left on the pillow had been made by someone who had lain staring at the beautiful young woman in the silvery dress. How he must have wept, she thought.

'Just as you sensed they should be together, Madame Hermione, so the oak called to you, and it is why you are now trying to protect the sacred place where your mother died in giving you life.'

The navvies' reaction, when the small procession arrived at the glade that evening, was one of bemusement, and they seemed content to let the women and children kneel and look upwards at the oak.

The great trunk of La Reine, which had stretched across the whole open expanse of sward, was now gone. No doubt its great compass piece was on its way downriver to the Maurellet shipyard. Hermione thought of her visit there and wondered grimly if Jacques had yet come upon her handiwork. Part of her was pained and ashamed by what she had done, yet she only had to cast her eyes towards the two huge stumps, whose rings showed they both had been rooted into the soil over two hundred and fifty years ago, to feel savage gratification that she had caused Jacques pain.

As the light began to fade, the blacksmith arrived, together with Georges, who went to kneel beside his mother and Lucette. After a time, the woodsman produced his pipes and started to play softly. Bats began to take flight, and, once the candles were lit from Raoul's lantern, the scene took on a different feel. An owl hooted, and, as another replied, there began the intense murmuring of prayers. Hermione bowed her own head as she reflected on the astounding change in her life. Above her was the great oak to which she had been led during the storm, which from the very first she had sensed held great meaning for her. Yet, even so, she had never envisaged what destiny had had in store.

'I would have thought Guillaume should be here,' whispered Lucette, interrupting her thoughts. 'If I had to come, so should he.' Hermione did not answer, for while she might have counted on Lucette's help, the girl was often loose-tongued. What was about to take place not only needed to be convincing, but had to be kept secret for ever. So, increasingly on tenterhooks, Hermione waited for Guillaume to make his appearance. The navvies, seemingly bored, had disappeared back into their hut, leaving one outside smoking his pipe. It was growing rather cold, and women had begun to wrap shawls around their children and huddle close. Hermione kept her eyes expectantly on the ridge above, and suddenly there it was. Georges must have spotted it also, for he had stopped playing and was rousing Lucette, who seemed to have drifted off to sleep.

'Oh, see,' called out Hermione, in a loud voice. Her cry of wonder was immediately taken up all around as something like a white cloud drifted about in the dark at the top of the ridge. The thought of Guillaume striding around in his black outfit might have set off laughter in Hermione, but the shame she felt at deceiving those about her, and what might happen to Guillaume if he were discovered, kept her subdued and increasingly anxious. He seemed to be getting carried away, making wide sweeps with the floating white cloud. Then, as he obviously remembered to pull the material back up the canister, the cloud disappeared. There came a loud, collective sigh from all around. Hermione bit nervously on her lip, hoping he would be able to light the flint as he turned his back on the watchers below. But he had, for a great cry went up from all the women and children as the white apparition reappeared, only to be consumed in a bright burst of flame. Then all was black. The burning vision had disappeared. Amid the cries of wonder and excitement, Hermione breathed a sigh of relief.

'Oh, madame, is this not a sign?' croaked Marie.

Hermione felt ashamed. 'You are cold,' she murmured, as the old woman's hand brushed by hers. 'Let me help you onto my horse and lead you back.'

'If I die of cold,' retorted Marie Paultre, 'I shall die happy after what I have seen. The spirit of the Holy Ghost! Du Chesne has been blessed. If only the Chevalier were here to see how Mademoiselle Aglaé has been honoured.'

The news of the vision spread rapidly from parish to parish, until, on the third night, there came near on a hundred people to kneel in prayer. It was beyond what Hermione had hoped for.

***

Since accompanying his grandfather to supervise the felling of the second oak at Du Chesne, Jacques had been fully occupied with shipyard matters. In addition to everything else, there was the problem of an overcrowded yard ... where best to place the great compass timbers for weathering.

'There won't be much sun now,' he reflected, as he talked things over with Henri, 'but come late spring, it will be striking fierce. As we lie this side of the river, shrinkage will be on this side of the piece. It may help to accentuate its curve.'

'I agree,' growled his grandfather. 'The knee wing transom hasn't arrived yet ... is there some delay in felling?'

Jacques gave a scowl and nodded. 'The contractor rode over this morning. It seems a holy vision has been seen near the tree, and hundreds of people are flocking there to pray. They can't get near it. He wants the dragoons brought back, but I told him to hold off. I'm going to ride over this evening to see what is going on.'

After further words about where to put what, for the yard was crammed tight with more than three thousand oaks for the hull of the frigate alone, as well as timber for other uses, Jacques entered the mould loft to pick up his favourite knife. The first thing he spotted as he approached his bench was a package tied with red ribbon. Intrigued and filled with sudden hope, he smiled as he noted his initials written upon it in a clear strong hand. The handle end of an axe had been laid across the package, presumably to secure it as the contents were quite light. With care, Jacques pulled on the bow of the ribbon, and, as the paper fell away, he saw inside a sprig of oak leaves. They were somewhat dry, which indicated they had been left a day or so ago ... perhaps the day when he and Henri had gone to Du Chesne? As Jacques fingered the lone acorn which was still attached, his smile faded as an uneasy feeling crept over him. This must have come from Hermione, but why come all the way here to deliver a few leaves? Jacques glanced about him, and, in doing so, noticed that the figurehead was no longer propped up against the wall, but was lying flat on the floor. It was unlikely it had slipped there, for he always took great care over his pride and joy. With a feeling of great disquiet, he strode across to it and pulled away the protective linen cover which had been thrown across it. What met his eyes made him gasp. As if receiving the thrust of a knife, he reeled backwards. The intriguing face had been mutilated! Like a wound opening up the bridge of the nose and down across the lips were deep hacking cuts into the wood.

'No, no, it cannot be!' he cried, shaking his head in disbelief. He stared, realising someone had attempted to chop the head of the figurehead in two but clearly had lacked the strength. 'Why, why?' he asked, running his hand through his hair, as he tried to comprehend who would vandalise something so beautiful. He returned to the bench, feeling as though his heart would break as he touched the bright red ribbon and the sprig of oak leaves.

'How could you do this to me?' he choked, his eyes filling with tears at the hurt. 'We had something precious. Now it is finished ... *finished!*'

As Jacques roared out the word, he snatched up the axe and in a few strides was standing over the figurehead. With one great blow of the axe, he finished what Hermione had begun.

CHAPTER 34

hat a faithful heart Guillaume had proved to be, Hermione reflected, as she waited for him in the upper chamber of the tower. A younger, more athletic man would have served better for the job, but discretion was everything. With this in mind, she wondered whether it was prudent to trust Raoul. It was taking a great risk involving him, yet without his help it would be difficult for Guillaume to set light to the cross. Georges would have been ideal; he had demonstrated his loyalty time after time, but in this matter he would be scandalized by what she had in mind. The one thing which had reassured her about Raoul had been his refusal to talk about payment. When asked if he would do something dangerous for her for which she would reward him well, his answer had been 'I only want you to think well of me, madame, so that I can sleep at night.'

Even when she had warned that discovery might lead to the fire or the wheel, he had declared that his life was hers to do with as she pleased. What had induced this fervour towards her she could not say, but his manner seemed genuine enough. If she had got it wrong, Hermione shivered at the thought of what would happen to them all. However, the way things were going on here, they would all be safe because nothing would be happening tonight. She gave a sigh of frustration as she looked at her pathetic attempt at the head of a stag. It had been easy enough to make the cross, pasting together strips of paper, but how to create a stag's head? Even if she knew, there was no time left for the *papier-mache* to dry and harden. As someone knocked on the door, she snatched up an old dust cover and flung it over the various effects. She gave permission to enter, and Guillaume lumbered in.

'I had hoped to have everything ready,' she said with an apologetic smile. 'You did very well the other night. I didn't mention it at the time, but I had been worried you would not be able to fire the white cloth. It made a terrific blaze! It will be more difficult tonight. Remember to take up position right in front of the tree; if you stray too far away, your silhouette might show if there is moonlight. Are you certain the blacksmith can be trusted?'

Guillaume shifted his feet. 'He was angry when you sent his old nag packing, but since the barn went up in flames, he hasn't stopped asking how he can be of service to you. I'd offer him some money, though, just to make certain.'

'I did, but he refused.'

Guillaume's good eye narrowed.

'Perhaps he is counting on his new mare being covered by the royal stallion. Besides, with all these people coming to pray at the tree, it's bringing him more work. And when all is said, I will be glad to have his company. It's grim work on my own.'

There was anxiety in Guillaume's tone, and it brought Hermione up sharp. All her thoughts had been on saving the trees, and here was a man's life at stake.

'I can't let you do this!' she announced abruptly. 'If you are discovered, you might be tortured and burned!'

'I won't get caught,' Guillaume reassured her, recovering his bravado. 'Luck is always with me. See how it saved me a good eye! Besides, three of the women in the village are setting up a stall to sell pasties to the people coming to pray. I don't want them disappointed after all their baking.'

Hermione's gaze went from him to the dust sheet covering the effects on the floor. The oak was so much more than so many cubic feet of timber. 'I would do it myself,' she murmured distractedly, 'but I must be seen with everyone.'

'Then leave things to Raoul and me,' broke in Guillaume, interrupting her thoughts. 'We'll not let you down. Shall I wear the black robe and hood again?'

Hermione's heart swelled with gratitude, and she gave a nod of agreement.

'The cross is ready, but, I still have the head to make.'

'A head! What kind of head?' gasped Guillaume, looking dumbfounded.

Hermione burst into laughter.

'Tomorrow is the twentieth of September ... you surely have not forgotten the saint's day?' Guillaume shifted uneasily, and to put him out of his misery, Hermione pulled away the cover hiding her efforts. She picked up the antlers she had found in the forest and handed them to him.

'Saint Eustace ... patron saint of hunting.'

'*Mon Dieu!*' the big man gasped. 'You didn't say anything about wearing great big antlers. How shall I see? Shouldn't they be attached to a head?'

'Yes, that was the idea, but that mess down there is all that I could manage. What can I do? Even if I knew how to go about it, it's too late now for the materials to dry.'

'If it's a big stag's head you need, leave it to me. There are several below in the guards' room.'

'I had thought to take one from the hall, except it would be missed.'

'Well, no one goes down below, Madame Hermione. I'll fix it on to a pole and that will save me from playing the fool,' remarked Guillaume with a pleased expression.

'Oh, you are marvellous,' said Hermione. 'At least let me see how these would have looked on you!' Before Guillaume could protest, she darted forward and put the antlers on top of his wild bush of hair. 'Hold them tight while I take a look at you. Ah, yes,' she gasped, shaking with laughter, 'a perfect fit! No challenger in the forest would dare take you on!'

'*Zut!*' grumbled Guillaume as he took up a mock pose. 'If Lucette could see, she'd split her sides!'

'Well she will only see what everyone sees … and you must never tell her … never! It must always remain a secret between us, Guillaume.'

With all their laughter, they had not heard the approaching footsteps, and before either of them had time to move, the door opened and Father Grégoire entered, gasping for breath.

'Lucette forgot to tell me there were so many steps to climb to find you,' he said, mopping his brow with a handkerchief as the door swung shut behind him. 'Why, what have we here?' Hermione's heart sank as his gaze took in the *papier- mache* cross and the ridiculous spectacle of Guillaume struggling to free himself of the antlers, some of whose points had got caught up in his hair.

'It was for …' she faltered.

'I came to tell you,' cut in the curé swiftly, not permitting her to proceed, 'that the bishop is coming to pray at the shrine tonight.'

'The *shrine*?'

'Yes, my dear Hermione, our little parish is finally making a stir. I shall lead the procession, of course, with the bishop … so much to do! My housekeeper is practically dropping with exhaustion after getting the house ready for our illustrious visitor, who of course, will be staying the night. Well, I mustn't keep you,' he went on as if he were blind to everything. 'I just wished to let you know how important the oak has become to every believer.'

'Thank you so much, Father Grégoire,' murmured Hermione, as the curé turned to take his leave.

The priest's plump hand stayed momentarily on the latch of the door and his expression, as he glanced over his shoulder, was conspiratorial.

'God works in mysterious ways, my children. Let us keep the *means* secret, or we may all find ourselves disappointed.'

The procession setting forth from the church that evening was so long, that an hour after Hermione had entered the glade in company with the bishop and the curé, people were still arriving to join the kneeling congregation. Conversation was whispered, but even so its muted buzz sounded like a vast swarm of bees. Hermione felt tense and nervous as if she were about to step on to a stage, though it was poor Guillaume who had the principal role and was running the risk of discovery. It was too dreadful to think what could happen to him, and also to Raoul for helping him. If the worst happened, she would tell the bishop she had ordered both of them to do it.

Taking advantage of the opportunity to slip away whilst the two priests were deep in whispered conversation, Hermione positioned herself at the edge of the crowd, ready to help if there was trouble. Though how would she be able to prevent Guillaume from being set upon in such an event? At least the blacksmith would be safe, for as soon as the cross burned out and he had helped Guillaume to turn about, he was to slip back into the crowd. If only she could have confined the task to Guillaume alone; Raoul only had to speak out and that would be the end of everything. It would not just be the oak that was brought down, but her own life and possibly Guillaume's too. She looked around to see where the contractor and his men had stationed themselves, but despite the candles it was too dark to see. She knew there was a rider near to the great holly bush, because the light of a lantern showed there at the height of a horse. Time dragged on, and it seemed as if dawn would soon be on its way. What was delaying Guillaume. At least the stag's head he had found was a splendid specimen, and by the time she had painted the face and the antlers white and the back parts black, her confidence in the plan was restored. Out here, though, all she could think was … would it work? Would it look real, or would the bishop guess, and then what would Father Grégoire do? He knew everything, of course, and if things went badly she realized he would put ambition before her and Guillaume. Hermione took a deep breath to steady her nerves and stared intently up towards the ridge. The next moment she exclaimed out loud in surprise, for though she knew what to expect, the effect above her was more dramatic than she could possibly have hoped. There was the white head of a huge stag, whose span of antlers looked like great white branches against the blackness of the night. Even more startling within the points of the antlers was a blazing cross.

A great cry went up! 'Saint Eustace!'

'It is Saint Eustace,' repeated a man nearby in a tone of awe.

Hermione's heart pounded. The gunpowder sprinkled on the glue coating the *papier-mâché* had created such intense brightness that even when she momentarily glanced away, the fiery image was still bright in her eyes. Then, as the flaming cross started to fade, under her breath Hermione urged Raoul to action. 'You're leaving it too late ... help turn Guillaume around ... go ... allez vite!' To her relief, as the cross disappeared, the white face of the stag and its spread of white antlers was replaced by the darkness. Hermione glanced to right and left to see if anyone was voicing doubts, but all faces in the candlelight seemed enraptured. Suddenly, out of the corner of her eye, she again glimpsed the flicker of light from the direction of the holly. The rider was on the move ... and in the direction of the incline! Then, masked from view amongst the trees, the dancing light disappeared. Seized by a rush of alarm, Hermione sprang to her feet, only to find one danger replaced by another as a dark, squat figure ran in front of the kneeling ranks.

'Listen to me!'

Hermione held her breath in alarm, for it was Raoul's voice. He had come to betray them!

'Do you think you have seen a miracle?' the blacksmith cried. 'We have been blessed by Saint Eustace!'

Relief flooded over Hermione; then, remembering disaster was still likely, she slipped away. Once beyond the worshippers, she ran as fast as she could over the rough ground. Suddenly, ahead, she glimpsed the dancing light. Guillaume was to put the pole which had held up the flaming cross, together with the painted stag's head, into a sack the moment he was out of sight of the worshippers. Then he was to carry it back to the château and throw it into the lake, weighted down by a boulder. His progress would be slow, slower than whoever was ahead of her. Hermione gasped with pain as she ricked her weak ankle on the root of a tree, but there was no time to stop. For the first time that night the moon sailed out from the dark covering of clouds, and a man's cry of alarm sounded nearby. Then she saw that the lantern's light was now directed upwards, as from the ground. Closing in on it, she came upon the abandoned stag's head and nearby the outline of two men. At the unmistakable sound of a sword being drawn from its sheath, Hermione's heart skipped a beat as Jacques' voice rang out.

'I don't want to hurt you! Be still and let me see who you are! So, Guillaume, it is you playing the patron saint of hunting. Did your mistress put you up to this?'

Hermione stepped forward into the dim light. 'Leave him be. I ordered him to do it.'

'You risked Guillaume's life for a tree? Have you any idea what they will do to him if I throw Saint Eustace's head down into the congregation? He will be burned alive.'

Hermione shuddered, her mind's eye thrusting her back to the Place de Grève and the crowds cheering as horses wrenched a man's body apart, the air bright with sparks and the horrifying stench of burning flesh.

'*Mon Dieu* ... what have I done? I know you will not give up Guillaume to them. He did it all for me. I wanted to save the oak, and I will take what comes. I shall say I slipped away to hold up the stag's head. No one will say anything different ... they will be too angry.'

'We can't have that, Madame Hermione,' said Guillaume stoutly.

Jacques sheathed his sword. 'Get back to the house before you are discovered, Guillaume,' he ordered roughly, 'and destroy that silly head before it is seen!'

Hermione stood mute, her thoughts in a turmoil as Guillaume dropped the painted head back into the sack, and he lurched away with all speed. 'So, it would seem your ingenious travesty has transformed your tree into a shrine,' remarked Jacques, his tone harsh and sarcastic. 'And you left your special gift for me in the Mould Loft.' There was silence as he lifted the lantern and held it before her face. Hermione tried to maintain a defiant stare, but the shame of destroying his work made her cast down her eyes.

'Now you know how I felt,' she murmured, 'having to hear the sound of the axe cutting into wood ... the terrible quacking noise of that heart-shaped steel that pulls away bark as if it were tearing away flesh. You claimed to love me, but the moment you set eyes on the oaks you were determined to have them at any cost. And now, this precious oak, where I was ... Hermione bit back the words and fingered her father's ring so as not to break faith. It was not possible for her to explain the true depth of her feeling, so instead she flung at him just any angry words. 'You are a cruel, unfeeling, avaricious brute!'

The intensity of her fury robbed Jacques of speech. For some reason, the powerful image of Pierre Puget's lion attacking the captive athlete flashed into his mind. Here she was, a veritable lioness, sinking her claws yet deeper into him.

'How painful do you think it was to see oaks that had survived for hundreds of years destroyed for some ship which in a trice could be blown sky high out of the sea or eaten away by worm? Through them I came to Du Chesne ... they gave me my life here! But you wouldn't understand that. Only the Chevalier would understand.' Hermione's voice broke. For the first time, Jacques acknowledged that her strength of feeling matched his own. They had done each other grievous hurt. With a brief movement of his lips, he blew out the lantern, leaving between them only moonlight. He moved away and, hoisting himself on to his horse, sat motionless, drained with disappointment. Love between them had seemed so certain, yet somehow they had lost their way. Was all 'twixt him and this woman come to an end? From deep within came the familiar call which was beyond understanding. He wheeled his stallion about and returned to Hermione.

Out of the pocket of his coat, Jacques withdrew the sprig of oak leaves which Hermione had left on the day she had mutilated his carving. He looked down and considered that which had brought them together and that which had driven them apart. With a rueful smile, he gave the stem a twirl. Then, plucking away the lone acorn with gentle care, he eased the creamy seed out from its cup.

'Hold out your hand,' he commanded. Hermione hesitated, then offered up her hand. On to its palm, Jacques dropped the cup of the acorn and drew her fingers safely over it. He held up the seed for Hermione to see. Then, closing his hand tight about it, he rode away.

THE END

MY THANKS TO:

Jacques and Marie-Jeanne Badois, for their hospitality when visiting their beautiful château La Roche Courbon.

Prof Elisabetta Brusa, for generously taking time away from composing her Second Symphony, to read, discuss, and spot errors.

Clair Fullerton for her valued help – her boundless encouragement.

Robin Cannon for reading and offering valuable feed-back.

Gilbert Edwards, for his tips on the work of a farrier.

Peter Goodwin, for checking the passages on ship construction.

The late Andrew Phelan, for his tips on sailing.

The late, Paul de La Grange Sury, for translating seventeenth century, French forestry law.

Tom Hyland – Nottingham teacher for unveiling the mysteries of chemistry.

Readers: Nottingham painter, Jane Mary Judge for her encouragement and Linda Jayasekera.

Cheering me on to publish after Nick's death: My stepson Tony Medawar, Nicola, Guy and Lara. Nephew Gareth Collins, Amanda, Rhys and Finlay. Nephews: Tom and Benjamin Collins.

My brother, Norman Collins – physiotherapist, who has run his Nottingham practice for 58 years. An inspiration – never to give up.

Friends: Eva Ratz, Aleksandra Marsh, Louise Smyth. Prof. Jerry and Dr Peggy Kirk. Sue and Chris Gale, Jane Dean, John and Eve Byrt, Susan and Robin Metzner, Marie Henderson, Barbara Dixon, and Cousin Ena Jones. Mary Cunnah – the acclaimed welsh landscape artist, Janet Richardson and Professor Anne Williams.

Marie Robertson in Vancouver.

Companions on research trip – nephew Hadyn Collins, Ann de La Grange Sury and my dear friend, Samantha Collins in Albunuelas, whose sense of fun and laughter has been such a support.

The London Library and its gifted staff.

Nancy Webber: Copy Editor, for her sensitive, handling of the manuscript.

Irving Dworetzsky for revision of the blurb.